The Small Blue

HANNAH SHELBOURNE

ISBN: 9798262085675

For Audrey, who loved the butterflies

Prologue

At some point I started running. All I could hear was my breath and the pounding of feet on hard, ploughed ground, my chest shaking with each heavy thud. The air had turned bitter – there was ice and wood smoke in it – but I was clammy with sweat. My skin burned with panic. I kept thinking he was following me, but I knew I was just being stupid, and I wasn't going to stop again to prove it.

When I reached the woods around the lake, the ground was a dark blur; I snagged my feet on wiry brambles and stumbled. My lungs heaved. There were cracks and rustles in the hidden undergrowth but my pulse beat louder than them all. Through the trees, the silent water gleamed.

Something was there, I could feel it in the pit of my stomach. It terrified me, but I wasn't shocked: I'd known it long before I'd heard its menacing whisper or dreamed its nightmares. I'd known ever since that day I cheated death. I shut my eyes and saw the mottled light of the surface again, my arms through the murky water, floating like reeds. I felt it pulling the life from me. Fear shook up from inside and I willed it to disappear, but suddenly there were tears in my eyes, and my path was just black shapes and the taunt of the water.

The next moment I was falling, screaming. My cry echoed out over the lake, so chilling it winded me. I bent, almost retching for breath, my hands digging into the dirt and thorns. I scrambled to my feet, but the fall had taken all my energy. I tasted blood again, but I didn't care. The ghost was at my back. It was too late to turn around now.

Despising my weakness, I limped on. My head whirled with memories, my whole body shaking with pangs of fresh grief. I saw his face again in my mind and reached out to him with my will, calling him back to me from wherever he'd gone. Just for a second, I imagined the relief of falling into each other's arms again, but it was too much.

My breath wouldn't steady. I had to keep going now, though sobs still shook me. I heaved myself on like a wounded animal, one foot in front of the other.

Some twigs snapped behind me and I froze. There *was* something there. Something real. A body moved in the darkness, coming closer. I'd been found. But I couldn't place the noise – where had it come from? I was caught between relief and terror. Was I being rescued, or had he been following me after all?

PART ONE

HANNAH SHELBOURNE

Chapter 1

July 1939 (six and a half years earlier)

Afterwards, Cliff said I'd pretended to get into trouble because I just wanted him to save me. If he really believed that then he obviously hadn't seen the fear in my eyes. But he'd always been full of himself. In truth, before that shelteringly hot July day, I'd never thought of him as anything more than just Cliff, the boy we'd grown up with. Not quite a brother, but a cousin, perhaps. A wild boy with dirt beneath his nails, who, at fourteen, already had the beginnings of a beard. A boy who worked long days at the farm while Alec and I still tramped the two mile walk to school and back every day.

We'd slept out in the woods the night before, blankets strewn on the beaten down earth. By the time we reached the lake, the sweat and dust had run into every crack in my hands; I could feel it sticking around my eyes, behind my ears and neck. We threw off our clothes and lunged into the water, the cold shock of it like heaven. Alec and Cliff weren't afraid to be naked, but I'd been self-conscious for years, so kept my knickers and camisole on, pushing it down as it floated up around my armpits. Cliff kept looking at my breasts but it didn't shock me: he had a reputation with girls. He and Irene Dursley had been caught doing it in the telephone box one dark night in February – the gall of him! – and Irene had been sent to live with her grandmother in Somerset a week later. The landlords in Finton always guessed he was old enough to drink in their pubs, so the girls who frequented them guessed he was old enough to kiss them. But I was not one of those fast girls, or Irene Dursley. In fact, I was so painfully naïve then that it never occurred to me that anyone would ever desire me in that way.

If Cliff really knew what I'd been feeling as the boys started scrapping in the water, he'd have laughed at me. My jealousy sat inside me like an old bruise, perpetually prodded, never allowed to heal. I'd never minded Cliff until he and Alec began sneaking off together, laughing at jokes they wouldn't share with me. I was a girl, so apparently I wouldn't understand. But Alec was my twin and we'd always understood each other. We were meant to be together, but in recent years I'd felt like an intruder. Naturally, I blamed Cliff. My brother was fickle, but he would never betray me.

A splash of water filled my nose and I jerked to see Alec beside me, his red hair wild and spiky where he'd run his hand through it, a mischievous grin on his freckled face. 'What are you waiting for?' he goaded, the tense of his jaw indicating he was either about to duck-dive away or lunge at me. Behind him, Cliff coughed gracelessly, and Alec's eyes darted away, so I seized my moment and lurched forward, lifting my arms and showering us with water. In one swift movement I slammed my palms on his head and heard him suck in breath before I plunged him under, laughing as he wriggled and kicked me. After a moment I let go and his face appeared through a dome of water, his mouth wide open and eyes tightly shut. He held his hands up in surrender. 'All right! All right!'

I kicked away from him, anticipating his retaliation, but Cliff was too quick. Suddenly Alec was underwater again, and I watched Cliff's wide grin as he pressed down with his brawny arms, counting the long seconds in my head and wondering if he would ever think to do the same. When Alec reappeared, he was bubbling with laughter, and the two resumed their bare-chested scramble.

'I'm going for a swim.'

'Don't let the ghost get you!' Alec called after me, and I stuck out my tongue. Last night he'd told us his favourite story as the fire died down: the local legend of Beatrice Whitman, wife of the mad captain who lived at the Manor. The Whitmans were still considered 'new' to Barnfield, having only been at the Manor since just before the Great War. They were rich beyond my comprehension, one of those families who'd made their fortune in manufacturing a few generations ago. A hard-working grandfather had once sweated and bled for the money that ran in their veins. Dad said that the Manor estate had once encompassed the whole village and much more of the surrounding countryside than it did now, but when Mr Whitman bought it for his new bride in 1912, there was only Manor Farm left, and the land between the Manor and the village, plus a handful of houses and cottages, including ours. A Finton man named Bridges managed the estate and collected the rents: he knocked on our door every quarter and inspected the house once a year to make sure we were looking after it and the roof wasn't about to cave in. Dad said there'd been much talk of improvements, but most of the plans had come to nothing:

when Captain Whitman lost his mind in the war, he was locked up in a mental asylum for years, and his young wife Beatrice, a city girl who'd always hated Barnfield, shut up the Manor and fled to London with their son.

Years later, when the captain was finally allowed home, Mrs Whitman dutifully returned to the Manor, but his life as a recluse was too much for her, and rumour had it she kept a lover in London. The story went that the captain – in his jealousy and madness – killed his wife, and now she haunted the Manor, calling out for retribution. Alec told it with great gusto, mimicking her melancholy cries and, if the mood took him, her shapely figure and turned up nose. Sometimes he made the old captain go at her with a bloody knife, or strangle her with his bare hands. Cliff and I egged him on.

It was just a story, although we'd believed it once, partly because we were children, and partly because the adults never liked to talk about it. She'd really died from pneumonia, that's what Mrs B said. It's what the doctor had said in the pub after he left the Manor, but no one had known the Whitmans well enough to verify it, and that's why the rumours began. Mrs Whitman wasn't buried in Barnfield, which added to the mystery, and Captain Whitman hadn't been seen for years, although his madness was legendary. Their son, Wilfred, was all grown up now, but like his mother was too good for Barnfield, despite the fact they still owned a substantial part of it.

With Mrs Whitman's story on my mind, I turned my back on the boys, swimming out towards the little island at the far end of the lake. It was a destination for cooler days, a good few minutes to get the blood pumping. The island was more like an overgrown tuft of earth, about twenty feet long, with a few meagre trees and shrubs and plenty of brambles. It was difficult to clamber up to it from the water without shredding one's feet in the process. As I drifted towards it, I started to notice what looked like leaves falling through the air, quickly realising they were butterflies, sweeping and spinning. It brought to mind a picture I'd once seen in a storybook, faeries dancing in mid-flight. It was such a pretty spot; the young Mr Whitman had to be very rich and stupid to own a place like this and never even visit it.

The water was silk around my fingertips. Cool air rose to kiss my cheeks. I lay back and let the cold numb my skin, spreading my arms out like the branches of the trees around me. Their leaves whispered their secrets above the noise of the boys at play. An invisible breeze stroked my toes, wriggling just above the surface. I sensed the vast lake stretching out around me. My brother let out a triumphant hoot, and the whoosh and crash of water told me he'd momentarily got the upper hand over Cliff.

'If there's going to be a war, then I'm going to fight,' Alec had said the night before, after he'd pissed on the fire and we were huddled up under our blankets.

I'd laughed. 'How will you manage that, baby-face?'

'I'll find a way.' He sounded so resolute that I half pitied him. He nodded to Cliff, asleep against a tree. '*He* won't have any problem.'

I thought of Cliff's drinking, his man's jaw and arms. Irene Dursley and the Finton women who coloured him with their lipstick. 'No, I suppose not. There'll be papers, though, won't there? They'll check.'

Alec grunted. 'He won't let that stop him.'

'Is that what he said?'

'He didn't say anything. He didn't need to.'

I sighed. 'Well, let's hope it comes to nothing.'

But Alec had just glared at me then, his eyes black in the half-light. 'Don't be a child, Gracie. It's too late for that.'

I pushed myself upright in the water, feeling a sudden shiver of cold. I didn't really think my brother and Clifford Archer would be able to blag themselves into the Army at the age of fourteen. I didn't even think there'd be a war. What bothered me was how glibly Alec spoke of knowing Cliff's mind, as if it were Cliff who'd been born two minutes earlier, not me. I suspected Alec wished that was true, owing to the amount of time he spent living in Cliff's pocket. Cliff tolerated him – I'm being unfair – I knew he appreciated my brother's friendship, but I could see too how Alec wound him up. Cliff preferred to be alone: he'd take himself off fishing without mentioning it to Alec; he'd sleep out some nights and watch the sunrise, catch us a rabbit for tea. That was just his way, but Alec despised being neglected. Cliff always came back to us in the end, and Alec always hid his hurt, but the reality was, Cliff was a closed book. I doubted anyone would ever be able to find out what was going on in that head of his.

My legs were tiring from treading water, so I started to head back towards the boys and our clothes strewn on the dirt-shore beyond. Shadows from the pretty boathouse stretched out across the water. It was then that a sudden wave of pain hit me, a twisting cramp in my head and stomach: too much sun. I floundered, almost slipping under before remembering to kick again. The boys' shouts were growing fainter, and I fought the urge to be sick. I paddled on, feeling the shiver of the vast depths, the water beneath me going down and down, darker and darker with no end. My vision started to spin, and in desperation I gulped a mouthful of water, pursing my lips at its filthy taste. It seemed to help – my dizziness subsided – but my face and fingers tingled and my head ached fiercely. I needed to get to shore.

I swam on, feeling weak and foolish, wondering if I could find the humility to call out to Alec, but I was suddenly distracted by a shape on the shore. There was something in the shadows of the boathouse, a figure that I couldn't blink away. For a childish second I thought it was Mrs Whitman's ghost. I pushed the idea out of my head, but my teeth started to chatter nonetheless. This figure was real: a ghost made flesh. I squinted, just able to make out a man's lined face, drooping shoulders.

I pushed on, my whole body trembling, my brain pressing behind my eyes. It felt like a trick, yet the strange man still stared back at me, his dark hair streaked with grey, his cheekbones sharp. I was almost at the boathouse now, the boys to the right of me, oblivious to everything. I wanted to catch their attention but I was in a dream, forcing my weak body onwards, captivated by the man, thin creases threaded over his skin like cobwebs. He wasn't staring at me, I realised now. His colourless eyes looked past me at nothing, and finally I realised who it was standing before me. *So, this is you, Mad Old Captain Whitman.*

Panicked, I whipped round to wave at the boys, but my body was suddenly not my own. In a flash I was under the water, then heaving myself up in mortification, trying to catch my breath. The water blurred my vision, but I saw the captain was still there, watching. My pulse rose and I cursed my legs for failing me. Hadn't I swum here a hundred times before? But there was a menace in these waters today; I could feel it clawing at me, trying to pull me under. In that second I knew I wouldn't make it to the shore, so I tried scrabbling towards the boathouse, but the water felt as thick as treacle. Suddenly my nose was full of it, and I snorted and coughed, the rasp of my lungs terrifying me. Where were Alec and Cliff?

The next moment I was under the surface again. My lips gaped but there was no air. There was no up nor down, no surface to seek nor floor to find. Nothing, except the quietness of my terror, the disbelief of it.

Then, a glimpse of skin. The blur of arm or leg. Suddenly, hands firm on my waist, pulling me upwards, carrying me forwards. Water rushed over my face and crisp air burned my throat, forcing me to choke as I lurched to find my footing on the lake floor.

'My God! What happened?'

The silence was now noise: the ring of air in my ears, the crash of the water and my grating, urgent breaths. I swayed on wobbly knees, falling into Cliff's naked chest. His hands were still on my waist.

Alec grabbed my shoulders, pulling me from Cliff's grip. 'Gracie?' Through dripping eyelashes, I watched him look me up and down. 'You alright?'

I could only nod, dazed and humiliated. My feet sunk into the mud but the water was still up to my shoulders. I remembered it in my lungs and eyes just seconds ago and spluttered again.

'What happened?' Cliff asked again, his hazel eyes so full of concern. I had never seen him look that way at anyone. I tried to explain that I'd felt ill suddenly, but I hated how feeble I sounded. I turned to the boathouse, but the captain was gone.

'Didn't you see him?' I asked when I'd finally got my breath back, but the boys looked blank. 'The old captain!'

Alec squinted. 'The lunatic?'

'He was there, just standing there.'

The boys exchanged glances and smirked.

'He was!' I insisted.

'Was he holding the knife?' Alec said with mock horror, then patted my shoulder. 'You've had too much sun.'

'I saw him.'

Alec smiled and started wading back to the shore. Cliff sighed and hoisted my arm over his shoulder. I wanted to tell him I didn't need his help, but my legs were still weak and my head burned like hell. Maybe I had imagined it all. I leant into Cliff's side as he carried me forward.

'What did he look like, then?' he said, but I knew he was humouring me.

'Forget it.' My foot caught on a jagged stone and I lurched forward with a yelp. Cliff caught me quickly, his breath in my ear.

'I've got you.'

I ignored the searing pain in my foot and wondered at how easy it felt to be held like this, half naked and drenched. Cliff's mouth twitched in a smile, and he relaxed his hold a little. I lifted my foot and saw ribbons of blood colouring the water. 'Damn!'

'Better get that bound up.'

I grabbed his shoulder again, hopping now and feeling utterly defeated.

Alec chuckled as I reached the shore, my hair streaming, foot dripping blood on the hard, dry ground. But he gathered my clothes and helped me dress, then ripped the arm off his shirt to bind my foot. 'Lucky it's an old one, or you'd have bled to death,' he said. 'It's not like you to lose your nerve.'

'Well, Gracie's a woman now,' Cliff teased, but it sounded strangely like a compliment. 'Women faint.'

Alec laughed. 'The sight of old Captain Whitman made you swoon!'

I whacked his shoulder and he grinned. The sun had turned his brow and nose pink, and scattered pale new freckles across his face. It was only a few years ago that the two of us had strayed up the path to the Manor and peeked through the garden gate at the house. There hadn't seemed to be anyone around, but we'd crouched down nonetheless and spoken in whispers as we watched the windows for a glimpse of the captain. It had been a hot day then too, and Alec had itched at his shirt while we waited.

'Come on, let's go back,' he'd said eventually.

'Just a few more minutes.'

He whined an objection.

'What's the matter? Scared?'

He pressed his lips together and narrowed his eyes in determination, then stood up and waved his arms above his head, shouting: 'Hello! Captain Whitman! Come out, come out wherever you are!'

In a burst of hushing and giggles I pulled him down to the ground again, and he collapsed into laughter and hiccups. 'You're the scaredy cat,' he'd declared, but just then a pheasant launched out of the long grass with a clumsy shriek, and Alec almost jumped out of his skin. We'd laughed all the way home.

The memory brought some calm with it, and I let Alec tease me as Cliff tied a knot in the makeshift bandage. He took my arm and we left the lake and woods behind us, heading back to the village across the golden wheat field.

Cliff lit a cigarette. 'Good job I was there to save you.' He cast me a sideways glance and winked, then passed the cigarette to Alec, who sucked on it then started to whistle.

Ignoring Cliff's suggestive smirk, I pulled on my brother's arm. 'Don't tell Dad.'

Alec snorted. 'Course I won't! I'm sure I'd wind up getting the blame somehow if I did.' Our father's life was monotonously neat and uneventful. To the rest of the world he seemed steady and unremarkable, but I always had the sense that his pressed clothes, passive conversations and fastidious routines were like a cage holding him together, and any disruption might cause untold damage. What kind of damage, I couldn't imagine.

Suddenly Cliff slapped Alec's back and leapt forward into a sprint. 'Race you!'

Alec swiftly dropped my arm and hurried after him, laughing. I watched as they disappeared into the woods ahead, hobbling pathetically to catch up with them. Blasted foot! And blasted body too, for giving up on me. I cursed myself for being so stupid.

When I reached the brow of the hill I stopped and turned back towards the lake. It glittered through the trees, a golden scar in the landscape. Beyond it to the right, the Manor stood in the hazy distance, a thin path drawn into the field that bordered its verdant garden. And along the path something moved: a small figure, blurred by the heat rising off the land. I watched him until he reached the Manor's gate and melted into the horizon. When he was gone, I heard the scuttle of the wheat in the breeze, and my breaths, sharp and shallow. I pictured Captain Whitman again on the shore, remembering the cold water against my neck, the grimy taste of it in my mouth. I shivered, and turned towards home.

CHAPTER 2

June 1941 (two years later)

We squashed together on the low narrow beds, Jean and I on one side, Alec on the other, knees pressing knees. The shelter was as black and damp as the coal shed, but outside the bright moon glared down on us like a treacherous searchlight. Alec scratched a match and the brief flame glimmered in his eyes and teeth, clamping down on his cigarette.

'Favourite cake?' said Jean.

Alec groaned.

'Come on!' she pleaded. 'It keeps my mind off things.'

The siren wailed.

'Oh… fruitcake.'

'Not true!' I said, as the orange glow was passed my way. 'It's a Chelsea bun.'

'That's a *bun*,' said Alec.

'It still counts,' said Jean.

'It's been so long since I had one I forgot they existed. Pass it back, Gracie.'

Jean nudged me. 'Hey, me first!'

Alec sighed loudly as our cousin took a long drag. She'd been with us since January, when Portsmouth was blitzed. 'Hurry up!'

Jean chuckled as she handed the cigarette to him.

'You better not have got lipstick on it.'

We laughed at him. It was hard to match this Alec with the one who left for Finton each morning in a pressed shirt and polished shoes, gas mask slung over his shoulder.

'It's the middle of the night,' Jean told him. 'Anyway, you can't see a thing so it won't hurt you.'

The siren groaned and I felt Jean shivering next to me. I pulled the damp blanket from the foot of the bed and wrapped it around us. She leant her head against mine. 'How can Uncle Leslie bear to stay inside?'

'He doesn't like small spaces,' Alec said flatly, the orange tip still burning.

'Nor do I, but I don't want to be bombed to pieces either.'

'It's because of the war, you know, the Great War,' I said, in a tone that made me sound like I knew what I was talking about. Alec and I had deduced this from the fact that Dad had never directly referred to his claustrophobia, and since he never spoke about the war either, we guessed the two were connected. We'd just noticed over the years how Dad avoided going inside the coal shed, how he always got jittery if the bus was crowded, and even left the privy door open a crack, despite his otherwise infallible decorum. I imagined him lying alone in his bed as we heard the first tremor of distant planes and wished I was there too, pressed up against him. Did he shut his eyes? Did he think of us, squashed like sardines in a pigsty, hiding from death? My stomach churned, and I swallowed loudly.

'Oh, Alec, hand it over!' Jean said tersely. The cigarette died on her lips.

The drone was growing louder. I pulled my legs as close to my chest as they would go, wrapping my palms over my kneecaps, exhaling warm breath onto the back of my hands.

'You don't need to worry,' Alec said, almost shouting now. 'They're only interested in the cities.'

'Well I bloody know that, don't I!' Jean snapped.

I put my shaking arm in hers as the planes whined high over our heads. It was true, Barnfield wasn't a target. But later, when they returned from London, we'd hold our breath, in case they had any bombs left to drop on us. A couple of nearby fields already had craters, and Finton's church had had half its windows blown out; the local boys collected and traded the shrapnel like conkers. Wasn't it only a matter of time before we too heard the scream of a bomb over our heads and prayed to God that this thin corrugated metal shell wouldn't become our coffin?

The dirge began to subside, the engines replaced once more with the siren's steady cry. Jean sniffed and I kicked Alec gently. I heard him scramble beneath his bed and the slosh of liquid against glass. 'Here,' he said, handing the bottle to Jean. She took a swig and passed it to me. The brandy burned my throat and I coughed clumsily.

'You should really learn to handle your drink,' said Alec. 'You know, Cliff says those new land girls can drink any man under the table.'

'Bully for them. Good job I'm not a land girl then.'

'Not a chance!'

It was a moot point, since Dad had forbidden me from ever joining a service. I'd read in the paper how the WAAF flew planes between airbases, ordinary girls just like me. The idea seemed so fantastical that I'd quite set my heart upon it for a few days, but I must have laboured the point too far with Dad. It wasn't like him to snap, but he'd held me in a long, firm glare and said, 'I pray to God the thing is finished with before you both come of age. It'll be a dark day if Alec ever gets called up, but I sure as hell won't see *you* in a uniform as well.' He'd been standing by the fire, and resting his clenched fists upon the mantelpiece, pressing them so hard I thought they might bleed. In stunned silence, I watched with a watery sensation in my stomach as he struggled to regain his composure. He folded his lips in, his shoulders hunched. He looked like a man about to crumble with despair or explode with fury – both terrified me – and when he finally turned back to me and gave a steady, minute little nod of understanding, I realised I'd been holding my breath, and all thoughts of the WAAF withered away.

Since then, I'd known better than to even raise the subject of service. I never mentioned it to Alec, but I saw how Dad stiffened when my brother talked about joining up, or turned up the wireless to listen to the newsreader, or read the paper aloud with enthusiasm.

'I think you'd make a fine land girl, Gracie,' said Jean.

'Well, I suppose we'll never know.' Jean seemed far more disappointed than I'd ever felt, so I reassured her: 'It doesn't matter. I don't really want to leave.' The WAAF fantasy had turned out to be a nine-day wonder. I certainly didn't hanker after action like Alec did. I was quite content to stay in Barnfield. Why would I want to leave the tranquil beauty and comfort of a place I'd loved all my life? Although I did wonder if that made me exceptionally dull, or worse, a coward too frightened to take even the smallest risk. 'Anyway, Mrs B says I'm a shoo-in to take over from Alfie when he gets called up.'

'Take over what?'

'At the Post Office, ninny. She can't manage on her own.'

Alec tittered. 'Imagine Mrs B on a bicycle! She'd buckle the wheels.'

'Fine words for the woman who practically raised us,' I said curtly.

'Give Dad some credit,' he retorted drily, and I smarted a little because usually I was the first to leap to Dad's defence if anyone ever insinuated that we'd suffered for lack of a mother.

'What on earth would you do at the Post Office?' said Jean disparagingly, ignoring us.

'You know, sorting and doing rounds and such. And Mrs B says she could use my head for figures when it comes to the accounts.'

Alec made loud snoring noises.

'It's war work!' I protested.

'You're too young for war work,' Jean pointed out.

I told her Mrs B said I had a good head on my shoulders, and she needed someone who knew the place already. I'd suggested Alec, but Dad had bigger plans for him.

'Well, it doesn't sound very exciting, but I suppose it's noble enough. But would Uncle Leslie allow it?'

I hadn't had a straight answer from Dad yet, but I answered with complete confidence: 'Well yes, I wouldn't even have to leave home.'

'She could still cook our breakfast, go to work, and be back in time for dinner!' said Alec cheerily. 'The best of both worlds!'

Jean tutted. 'And if you don't get work at the Post Office, Gracie, what'll you do when school's over?'

If Mrs B set her mind to something, then it usually happened, so I was certain there'd be no problem. Mrs B had a way of bending Dad's thinking in her direction when needed. 'I suppose there's always a typing course…' I yawned before I could finish my sentence, such was my enthusiasm.

'Typing?' Jean scoffed.

'The typing pool girls at the bank are vicious,' Alec interjected. 'I wouldn't sacrifice you to them, and neither would Dad, I should guess. He'd rather have you wrapped up at home, doing nothing.'

'He's only trying to protect me. But I'll have to do *something*. Something useful.'

'Disguise yourself as a boy and join up with me,' said Alec.

'I'd pass for a better man than you.'

He kicked my ankle. He and Cliff had both tried to enlist already, but Cliff had been recognised. They talked about travelling to Chichester next time, but Cliff wasn't as bloody-minded as Alec, and my brother was never going to fool anyone that he was old enough.

'Well, Uncle Leslie can't stop you when you get called up,' Jean said to me.

'Oh, he's hoping Gracie'll be married by then,' Alec said with a smile in his voice.

'I've more chance of joining the Army with you!'

'Oh?' Jean sounded surprised. 'You don't think Cliff will ever ask you?'

Alec tittered.

'I thought you two were, you know…' She nudged my shoulder.

'Yes, well, I'm very fond of Cliff…'

'Very, *very* fond sometimes,' Alec added.

'You certainly looked so the other night.'

It was true, Cliff and I had grown closer recently, and there were times when our friendship leant towards more, when we shared kisses in the shadows, and I felt the warmth of those strong arms that had wrenched me from the water nearly two years ago. It was only natural – what sixteen-year-old girl wouldn't enjoy the attention of a handsome young man like Cliff? But that was as far as it went, for indeed many other girls *did* enjoy his attention, and the tales Alec told sometimes after their jaunts to Finton were enough to make me blush scarlet.

'Cliff's a terrible flirt,' I told Jean.

'An *expert* flirt,' corrected Alec.

'That doesn't upset you?' pressed Jean.

Perhaps it should have. 'It's just Cliff,' I said honestly. 'It wouldn't suit him to be soppy. I'm not sure it would suit me either.' I imagined him buying me flowers or reeling off compliments and shivered involuntarily. 'Ugh, no, it would make my skin crawl! I think I prefer him how he is.'

'Doesn't Uncle Leslie mind about you two carrying on together?'

I hesitated. Dad never said much about anything, so I didn't really know. He seemed to like Cliff well enough, but he'd been a fixture in our lives for so long it was hard to tell. Cliff was always welcome at our table, more often than not now his old mother had died and he lived alone in one of the rooms over the Manor Farm's stables. He might be a bit rough around the edges, but he added a bit of colour to the house and even he knew better than to flirt with me in front of my father.

Jean took my silence as my answer and said, 'Well, I have to admit, I'm a little relieved about you and Cliff.'

'You don't like him?'

'No… Only…' She leant into me and whispered: 'The first night I met him, he pinched my bottom.'

I burst out laughing.

'Gracie!' She nudged me. 'You must love him really, just a little bit.'

'Oh, probably. Just a little bit.'

The siren continued to ring. Alec took another swig from the bottle. He drummed his feet on the dirt floor, his knees knocking against mine. I pulled the blanket up around my neck and rubbed my arms.

Jean gave a short sigh. 'Come on, Gracie, your go.'

'Mmm?'

'Cake!'

'Oh, chocolate.' My tongue tingled with the memory.

Alec groaned. 'Enough! If I can't eat it, I don't want to talk about it!'

'I'll save my sugar for your birthday,' Jean promised.

'All I want for my birthday is to get out there and kick Jerry's arse!'

'Well, when I'm in the Wrens, I'll write and tell you about all the adventures I'm having,' she boasted. 'I'll make you green with envy.' I imagined the sour look on Alec's face and smiled. Jean was a year older than us and her father had no qualms about her joining a service. Even if he had, she would have defied him anyway.

'I won't be jealous of washing sailor's hats or mending rope.'

'Shut up, Alec.'

'What if they don't take you?'

'They better had! They have the best uniforms!'

Alec laughed. 'Ah-ha! Now we have it!'

'If I'm going to be serving my country I might as well look good doing it. Heaven knows I won't get a chance with rationing.' She pulled her arm tighter around me. 'Oh, poor Gracie, the postal uniforms are so dreary and heavy. Still, they're not as bad as those awful boxy monstrosities the land girls have to wear.'

I'd always thought the post girls in Finton looked so smart and efficient. Ever since Mrs B had hinted at the opportunity I'd been looking forward to donning my own little hat and jacket. 'Well, I don't really know about clothes…'

Alec snorted. 'There's an understatement. Have you seen how she darns my shirts?'

'Darn them yourself, then!'

'You need the practice.'

Jean shushed us and tried to change the subject, but I was too busy thinking about zooming along the lanes on my bike with a postbag slung over my shoulder. I was itching for it to begin. I had a few months left of school and no other prospects other than interminable housework and helping Doris Howard with the Women's Voluntary Service. According to Dad, this was something to be grateful for. Alec had already left school to work as a junior clerk at the bank in Finton. I, on the other hand, would have the privilege of being mistress of my own home without the burden of a husband. I was not required to go to work – surely everything a young girl could wish for? It was the future my parents had always dreamed of and worked so hard for, which made my lack of appreciation for it all the more bitter. It bored into me like a parasite, sapping me of energy and filling me with dread as I sat out my last days in the schoolroom. I was the eldest there; most of the farmers' children moved about or left earlier. Bright boys had gone to the grammar school, and wealthy girls, like Doris, to Finton Girl's. Only a handful of us came from middling families, with parents desperate to see us educated to the utmost. Mrs B showed me how to cook and sew and run the house, and Dad brought me books from Finton library whenever I showed an interest in something. But what was learning for, if only to scrub floors and beat carpets and cook meals and wring laundry and wait for a husband? 'When the war's over, we could get some help in,' Dad had said one night, perhaps noticing my water-wrinkled hands. And then what? A life of gentle leisure, tea and social climbing with Doris Howard? Was that really what my mother had wished for me?

The siren's whine mutated briefly as we picked up the first low hum of the returning planes.

'Shit,' said Alec under his breath, and I grabbed his and Jean's hands and felt our pulses surging. If only Dad could stomach the shelter. For all its dank gloom, surely it was better than being alone in his bed. We could have done with his staid, calming presence. He could have placed his palm on my shoulder and told me to be brave.

Jean let out a little squeak, as if she'd screwed herself up so small there was no breath left in her. She squeezed my hand, the pain in my fingers a blessed distraction from the swelling drone and the images hammering in my head: front page headlines; blazing fires; razed buildings; lists of dead.

The shelter began to vibrate. They were flying lower now. Was that a good sign? I pressed my forehead to my knees and Alec pulled my hand to his chest as if he had the power to protect us from any of it. My skin froze and prickled beneath my sweat. The whine pierced like a knife twisting in my ears. The engines were impossibly loud, shrieking and whirring as if they were flying just feet above us. What if a target hung over our heads tonight?

Then suddenly the image of old Captain Whitman flickered in my thoughts; not the ghostly figure near the boathouse, but an old man crouched in a shelter, all alone. My heart swelled with unexpected compassion, my eyes filled with tears, and in my terror I prayed feverishly and silently for mercy, for our lives to be spared: Alec, Jean, Dad, and old Captain Whitman too.

Alec let go of my hand and I whimpered. My head was tucked down, my eyes squished shut. I groped for him again, shouting his name desperately.

'They're going!' he cried above the noise.

My ears rang so fiercely I could barely hear him.

He shook my shoulders. 'Listen! They've passed us!'

I lifted my head fearfully, my whole chest throbbing. He was right. The engine noise was beginning to fade away. I steadied my breathing and gritted my teeth to stop them from chattering. There was something defeatist about admitting relief.

Alec was already up, pulling the curtain from the shelter's mouth. He stooped to peer outside, then lit another cigarette as the engine noise grew softer. I pushed the brandy bottle far back under the bed; Dad never came in here but it was better to be safe than sorry. The moonlight caught Jean's face as she folded the blanket; her cheeks shone from tears just wiped away. She tucked her wavy hair behind her ears and avoided my eyes.

The planes were gone but the siren still blared. Alec shuffled his feet, sucked hard on his cigarette and passed it back to us. 'That's that then. Time for some kip.' He hesitated as if to ask if we were coming.

I glanced at Jean and gave him a knowing look. 'I'll wait for the all-clear.'

Jean smiled unconvincingly, her white hands sprawled tight over her knees. 'Oh, yes… me too.'

Alec shrugged and ducked outside. After a few seconds we heard the outhouse door slam.

I stretched my arms out. My back was aching from sitting so crouched, and without the blanket, the chill of the night made me shiver. Jean was staring down at her feet as if the old wellington boots had a story to tell. My head was dog-tired and thronging and empty of small talk. All I could think of was the planes still flying out into the night, and the day we heard about Portsmouth on the wireless, and how Jean arrived the following week wearing odd, ill-fitting clothes, because none of her own had survived.

At last the siren simmered to the all-clear and Jean let out a short breath. She grinned at me, patted my knee and kissed me on the cheek; in the daytime it would have left a bright red mark. We stooped to stand, emerging from the shelter blinking like newborns. The night's shadows made the garden look like a scene from a film, monochrome and eerie with the all-clear's drawn-out cry. The house's blacked out windows yawned into the night. I glanced up at Dad's bedroom and thought I saw his curtain twitch.

Alec flushed the toilet and burst out of the privy, pulling his dressing gown tighter. 'Look lively!' he said as Jean and I stretched, his grin obscured by clouded breath. I hurried to reach him before he got to the back door, flinging my arm across his shoulder and ruffling his hair. He whistled back to Jean, Alec's coat draped over her slender frame like a cape, still hovering round the shelter and gazing up at the sky, nervous and awed, as if she'd never seen it before.

'They're gone, Jean.' I sounded so calm, as if I hadn't been cowering from death minutes earlier.

'I know… I know.' We waited for her to cross the grass. Her boots made footprints in the dew. 'I'm still thinking about cake,' she said as we went inside, her voice faltering. The kitchen smelled of last night's fish pie.

I shut the door behind her as Alec called goodnight from the hallway.

'What's your favourite then?'

'Anything. Walnut, Victoria Sponge… anything.' She shrugged off the coat and hung it up. 'I'll find some marge in Finton and we'll make a carrot cake,' she said decisively. 'But you'll have to help me. I always burn everything.'

We bustled up the stairs, eager to be back in our beds.

'I'll help.'

'It'll use up my rations but I don't care. It'll be worth it.'

*

The rain pelted down for my first ever post round that September. I threw a mackintosh over my new uniform but I could smell the fusty, damp wool after ten minutes, and by the time I was peddling out into the lanes I was a few pounds heavier and my face was washed raw and shiny. I had to blink the rain from my eyes as I turned a corner and saw a familiar figure sitting on a sheltered stile.

'Cliff!' I slowed to a stop, smiling. 'What are you doing here?'

'Slacking off,' he said with a grin, then jumped down and grabbed my waist, almost pulling me off my bicycle.

'Hey!'

He lowered his chin and looked up at me with false bashfulness. 'I just wanted to kiss the new post girl. I've been here for nearly half an hour, you know, waiting for you.'

'Go on then.' There was no one about but I looked around anyway before kissing him. 'You'll get soaked.'

He shrugged nonchalantly. He was the only other person I knew who didn't mind getting wet, who seemed to quite enjoy it really. We'd often ventured out into the fields or woods on a stuffy wet Sunday afternoon together.

He tugged at me, and my stomach tingled. 'Come on, hop down a minute.' He nodded to the large oak behind him, and for a moment I imagined nestling into its roots with him, resting my head on his solid shoulder, listening to the rain pattering the leaves. It would be easy and peaceful, no prattle, no interruptions. That was the best side of Cliff, the *real* him, I thought. We'd spent more than one evening together like that recently. But there was no time for idling today.

'I've got work to do, young man.'

'So you have.' He ran his tongue over his bottom lip as he smiled. 'I'd say the uniform suits you, if I could see it under all that.'

'If you're lucky, I'll give you a twirl later.'

'I'm always lucky.' He took another kiss, then nodded to the bag. 'Anything interesting?'

'None of your business. You might be a German spy for all I know.' He pulled a face and did his best goose-step, and I shoved his shoulder. 'Don't!' There'd been too much talk about invasion in the papers recently, and it felt like tempting fate.

He circled me in his arms again. 'Oh, don't worry, I'll keep you safe.'

I believed him, in a way, even though I knew he couldn't. I believed he'd try. He was honourable, and strong, and I felt safer then with him than I had for months. I was so tempted to hop down and take shelter with him, but it wouldn't do to skive off on my first day. I turned away from his handsome eyes and rallied myself somehow. 'Now get back to work or Goffman will give you the sack.'

He shrugged, kissed me again and let go of my waist. 'Your loss, Miss Wells.'

I trilled my bell as I sped away, feeling a lightness in my chest and not caring about the rain one bit.

CHAPTER 3

July 1943 (two years later)

'Cliff not joining us tonight?' asked Dad as we sat down to supper. It was a hot day; I'd been in the kitchen for over an hour and could feel sweat running down my back.

'He's busy,' Alec mumbled.

'He's in trouble,' I said, serving up the corned beef fritters.

Dad raised an eyebrow and looked from me to Alec. 'With whom?'

That was indeed the question, but Alec's sour expression seemed to answer it.

'He signed up yesterday,' I said, feeling the gravity of it afresh.

Dad unfolded his napkin and carefully laid it on his lap. 'I see.'

I sat down between them and we all began eating in silence. The clock on the mantelpiece ticked, and through the open window we heard one of next door's chickens announcing a late egg.

We'd all known Cliff would sign up now he was eighteen. Despite being in a reserved occupation, he wasn't the type to avoid active service. He might not be as gung-ho as Alec, but for a boy like Cliff, the idea of working out the war in the fields of Barnfield was as good as cowardice. Mr Goffman, his employer and in recent years a father-figure of sorts, had practically begged on bended knees for him to reconsider. Cliff was Goffman's protégé and 'godsend' – reliable, strong, and he had a magic touch with the tractor. The 'bloody land girls' could never match up to the Herculean Cliff. He'd been living in the farmhouse for over a year and it was common knowledge that he'd take on the Manor Farm when Goffman retired.

'I don't know why you're so po-faced about it,' Dad told Alec. 'I daresay Gracie has more of a right to be miserable. Cliff is her beau, after all.'

Alec snorted and sprayed chewed food onto the tablecloth. I kicked him under the table.

'Gracie doesn't have time for courting,' Alec said, parroting me. It was technically true, although Cliff and I still managed to meet up alone every now and then, and always had plenty of kisses for each other, not that Dad needed to know about that. Perhaps he already did; perhaps Alec had let it slip or Mrs B had warned him about it. In any case, it wasn't a crime, and I wasn't being indiscreet. Cliff had been faithful in his attentions to me, at least, although I had heard he'd broken one of the land girl's hearts somehow or another. I wasn't sure I wanted to know all the details.

Dad knew nothing of Cliff's exploits, he saw only the steady, hardworking boy we'd grown up with. 'Clifford Archer is a decent boy,' he went on, his solemn eyes fixed on me, 'with improving prospects. I'm sure you could do a lot worse.'

I smiled at Dad's pragmatism, but Alec, with mock-serious eyes, reached his hand across the table and took mine. 'Think of the beautiful children you'd have,' he teased.

Dad shot him a disappointed look to wipe the smile off his face. 'And what's the meaning behind your sulking?'

Alec shrugged sullenly.

'Jealousy, I suppose.' Dad's disapproval swelled in the silence. 'Well, your papers will arrive soon enough.' He cast his grave eyes back to his plate and another long silence stretched out, the kind that always followed any mention of the war. I glared at Alec and hated that I had to try hard not to smile when he pouted back at me and fluttered his eyelashes.

Later, Alec came and leaned against the back door while I ironed in the kitchen. Occasionally a drop of sweat dripped from my brow onto the clean shirts. 'You shouldn't tease Dad. It's not good for his nerves.'

'You mean *I'm* not good for his nerves. He can't wait to get rid of me. And I can't wait to be gone.'

I threw a balled-up sock at his head. 'Oh, hush! Stop sulking.' Alec had always loved stirring up trouble, especially recently, now Cliff would reach the promised land of combat before him. 'What's got into you?'

'I'm bloody bored,' he said through clenched teeth, kicking his heel against the doorjamb.

'Then give me a hand.'

I'd been serious, but he sneered a laugh and mumbled, 'You know what I mean.' He whipped a packet of cigarettes from his pocket and bit one to light it, his shoulders arched. He couldn't stand still for a moment. He'd always had too much energy, never able to sit and pay attention in school; he'd felt the sharp bite of Mr Prevett's cane more than anyone. Dad had made him try for the grammar school once, but he'd always struggled with his writing; it was another reason he hated his job now and why he seemed positively possessed by restlessness. Even in the small hours he'd wake me by pacing around his bedroom next to mine or thundering up and down the stairs to use the outhouse or fetch a glass of water. He'd yawn and squirm over breakfast, and grunt as he left for Finton with Dad, donning his hat as if it weighed a ton and carried a curse on it.

'Well, Dad's right. Your papers will come through soon. Only a few weeks to go.' It was hard to sound encouraging about an event that I'd been dreading for so long, however much Alec was looking forward to it. But his frustration was palpable. He was not cut out to work in a bank, however much Dad or Mum might have wished for it. He was made for Cliff's life and that was the truth of it. He'd have given anything to be outside in all weathers, for long days on the farm and a pint of beer at the end of them.

He exhaled a long, smoky breath. 'Promise me you'll bring them to Finton as soon as they arrive.'

'They won't come yet. And I can't just drop everything for you, you know.'

He screwed up his nose and shook his head, as if to say I was taking myself too seriously, that my job was nothing compared to the service he'd give.

'Promise *me* you'll come back when it ends.'

His eyes twinkled and he shrugged. 'I'll do my best. It might never end.' He sounded unnervingly wistful.

I wiped my brow with my wrist. 'Talking of letters, I heard from Jean this morning.'

'How's that boyfriend of hers?'

'Fiancé, now.'

'Well, they didn't waste any time. So that's the end of her naval career, then.'

'They're going to wait till it's over.'

He smiled slyly. 'We'll see.'

Jean had sent me a photograph of her standing tall in her uniform. I kept it on the mantelpiece in my bedroom and every time I saw it, I thought of the months she'd stayed with us. The house was dull without her. I'd fancifully hoped that she'd developed a taste for the country and would come back to live with us one day; she had no home in Portsmouth anymore. But her marriage would take her all the way to Lincolnshire, and I was beginning to wonder whether I'd ever see her again. But nothing was set in stone, and at least she was happy. 'You know she loves the Wrens,' I distractedly told Alec. 'She's in it for the duration. Wouldn't give it up that easily.'

He raised his eyebrows and flicked his cigarette away outside. 'And what about you?' He smiled impishly. 'Would you give up working for Cliff?'

I chuckled. 'I'd give up as much for him as he would for me.'

'From what I've heard, you're not giving up much at all.'

'Don't be crude,' I snarled.

'He likes you, you know, but you've been knocking about with him for years now and can't blame him for looking for his fun elsewhere.'

'I don't.' I kept my voice steady, refusing to take the bait. Alec could be insufferable when he was miserable. 'I think you're imagining that I'm in love with him.'

'Aren't you?' His incredulity betrayed him; he'd hero-worshipped Cliff for years.

He laughed to himself. 'Well, I bet he'll want a sweetheart to write to when he leaves.'

'Cliff doesn't write, and he'll never be short of sweethearts.'

'He'll keep your picture in his pocket…' he mocked.

'And hide it every time he meets a pretty girl!' We laughed. I folded an ironed shirt and pulled another from the basket. 'I will miss him though.'

'Don't you think you'd make a good farmer's wife? You must have thought about it.'

I pulled a face. Of course I'd thought about it, in a girlish, whimsical sort of way. But no more than I'd imagined what it might be like to fly in an aeroplane or join the Wrens with Jean. I'd never dreamed of being a bride or having children in the way that some girls seemed to. Witnessing Doris Howard's wedding preparations these past few months, it had all seemed an exorbitant waste of time, energy and rations. Jean gushed about her fiancé in her letters and pressed me for gossip about Cliff, but I never had much to tell her. I liked the evenings we spent together – he, Alec and me – when the sky was bright till late and we took the long route round the farmland after supper. I liked the way he'd swing my hand, and kiss me goodbye when Alec's back was turned; or when I happened upon him on a walk, and it seemed like he was as much a part of the place as the trees or the stream or the hedgerows. It would be strange when he was gone, like a part of Barnfield had been uprooted. I would miss him, and life would be greyer for it, but in a few weeks' time Alec would be gone too, and the thought of that made my chest ache so fiercely that all thoughts of Cliff evaporated.

'At least you know Dad would approve,' Alec went on. 'Now that Cliff's going up in the world.' His voice had turned bitter again.

'That's not what he meant.'

Alec looked unconvinced. I'd never really understood the animosity between him and Dad. I knew Alec found Dad's silence on all matters war-related infuriating, but that was to be understood. And it was true that Alec hadn't exactly lived up to Dad's expectations as far as his burgeoning career at the bank was concerned, but Dad was too kind to let something like that stew and sully his relationship with his only son. Besides, it had been festering for much longer than that.

I had no memories of Mum but there was a picture of her in a frame in the dining room, and the older Alec got the more he grew to look like her. He had her wide smile, her almond eyes. The photo was grainy and grey but Mrs B said that Alec had Mum's blood red hair and freckled face. She said our mother had loved to laugh and tease too. Dad never talked about her (of course) but we knew he'd adored her. We knew he'd nearly fallen apart after her death, and if it hadn't been for Mrs B taking Alec and I under her wing, we might have ended up with Aunt Lois in Portsmouth, sleeping in the box room that was ultimately obliterated by a bomb.

It was hard to imagine Dad in such throes of grief now. We'd never known him to shed a tear or raise a hand in anger or even guffaw at something in the newspaper. Alec and I were only three when Mum died. We'd grown up with a placid, straight-edged man who'd taught us manners and shown he cared for us in quiet, unassuming ways. And for all those years, Mum's photograph had watched on, silent and unmentioned. Did Dad see her face when he looked at Alec? Perhaps Alec reminded him of her tragic death. Perhaps he couldn't help comparing them, and Alec would always fall short of an angel.

Alec was picking at his fingernails and whistling an irritating ditty, so I nodded to the dirty dishes in the sink and told him to make himself useful. He cut himself on a knife and swore loudly, sucking the finger and making such a clatter that Dad came in from the living room with alarm in his eyes, paper under his arm. 'I thought a cat had got in here,' he said without any hint of humour. Alec hid his bloody finger in the water and shrugged in explanation, while Dad glared at the single plate dripping on the draining board. 'Make a thorough job of it, boy, or Gracie will have to wash them again.' He smiled at the pile of neatly pressed shirts on the table and kissed my head.

Alec rolled his eyes and brooded. He waited till Dad was gone before looking me up and down. I could see the hurt in his eyes that he was trying to disguise as contempt, and wondered what jibe he'd come out with. 'You see? Already the image of a perfect wife.'

'Heaven forbid!'

'A shilling says Cliff proposes before he leaves.'

I laughed, but he glowered back at me, so I lifted my chin and said, 'You're on.'

CHAPTER 4

In an ideal, peacetime world, Doris Howard would have married in a cathedral and had her wedding reception in a grand hotel, with a three-tiered wedding cake and well-dressed guests composed of the cream of local society. I doubt I would have been invited. As it was, her mother had to settle for good old Reverend Dearling at good old St Barnabas, and a modest tea in the village hall. Nevertheless, Doris looked radiant in her white silk gown with her bouquet in one hand and her decorated pilot, Ron, in the other. The Howards had hired an obsequious photographer, but Doris's 'village friends' weren't allowed in the photographs, so we hung back as the oiled, portly gentleman positioned the family around the church door.

The weather had held, against the odds, but it felt more like a curse than a blessing, and I could sense the impending storm in the air pushing down like a pillow, impatient to suffocate. Throughout the ceremony, Alec had gazed with aching envy at Ron Fielding's rigid posture and striped shoulders. I'd spent the second half of the service picturing him in a similar uniform; with Ron in front of us, it had been easy to imagine every detail of thread and brass and braid, yet Alec's face didn't look right with it, like a child dressing up in adult's clothes. I pictured Cliff too, envisaged him with a moustache, and stern, indecipherable eyes. In the church Cliff had looked comically uncomfortable in one of Dad's old stiff-collared shirts, fidgeting every few seconds and appearing to take no interest in the wedding whatsoever. I imagined him flying over Barnfield in a Hampton or Wellington and almost laughed out loud at the absurdity of it all.

By six o'clock the heat was cloying and unbearable. Ladies fanned themselves and men did constant battle with their collars and ties. I hadn't had the coupons or time to make a new dress, and the one I was wearing was too tight around my chest. Sweat was spreading out under my arms, and I sat beneath an open window in the village hall in a futile attempt to keep cool.

Alec and Cliff were either side of me, watching the happy couple tour the room. Alec had always had a soft spot for Doris and was doing a poor job of hiding his jealousy. She was an absolute knockout, but she was older than us and had only ever had eyes for distinguished men with expansive prospects and bank accounts. We'd never met her fiancé before. Even if he hadn't been busy with Fighter Command, we didn't really move in the same circles as the Howards. Doris had gone to the local school until she was about ten and we'd all spent quite a lot of time together back then, but when her mother plucked her out and deposited her at Finton Girl's, we saw her less and less. Mrs Howard seemed to tolerate her daughter's friendship with us as long as it remained within the confines of Barnfield and the Women's Voluntary Service. According to Mrs B, Mrs Howard and Mum had been friends, which always led me to question my mother's judgement of character, for Mrs Howard was the biggest snob in the village.

'She must be boiling in that dress,' said Alec, nodding at Doris.

'I bet she's looking forward to taking it off.' Cliff raised his eyebrows and smirked when I rolled my eyes, then put his hand round my shoulder. His thumb brushed the skin of my collarbone.

Someone had taken up residence at the piano in the corner of the hall and was hammering out a jolly tune, much to Mrs Howard's chagrin, if her pinched expression was anything to go by. A handful of children were jumping and dancing in the centre of the parquet floor, but it was too hot for anyone else to consider it. 'Cliff's got two left feet anyway, Gracie,' Alec consoled me, tapping his toe absentmindedly to the tune. I glanced over to Dad, standing near the far wall watching Reg Howard's moustache wiggle beneath his bulbous nose. He caught my eye and almost imperceptibly raised an eyebrow, then moved his focus back to the bride's father and his doubtlessly tedious story.

Nearing our corner, Doris broke away from her husband and glided to greet us. She glanced at Cliff's arm on my shoulder: 'You two look cosy!'

'Congratulations, Doris.'

Her eyes flickered over my too-tight dress. 'Wasn't it a beautiful service?'

'Delightful,' said Alec with sarcasm that Doris ignored.

'I hear you'll be leaving us soon, Cliff.'

He nodded. 'Next week.'

Doris brought a hand to her chest. 'I expect you'll miss him dreadfully, Gracie! I can't bear to be separated from Ron!'

'Well, Cliff and I aren't married, Doris.'

Her upper lip twitched. 'No, indeed.'

Cliff grinned at me. 'But you will miss me, won't you *darling*?'

I shoved him playfully and Doris gave us a perplexed little frown. 'I hope we'll be seeing you at the meeting on Tuesday, Gracie?'

'I'll do my best to get there,' I lied, for by the time I'd got in from work and prepared the supper, I'd never have time to cycle into Finton for the WVS meeting. Doris had a housekeeper, so she didn't understand. In any case, Dad wasn't keen on me being out late without the boys, as if they carried some kind of godlike power to protect me from a German bomb should one fall unexpectedly.

I was suddenly aware of a lull in the room. The piano stopped and conversations hushed. All eyes seemed focused on the doorway. I followed the sheepish gazes to a young man hesitating just inside the entrance to the hall, well-dressed in a dark grey suit, his hair deep brown and short. I couldn't see his face, but I instantly knew who he was from the very prominent dark red scar on the back of his neck: the illusive and now notorious Wilfred Whitman.

I'd known of Mr Whitman's return – or Flight Lieutenant Whitman, as he now was –for about a week. Working at the Post Office meant Mrs B and I were privy to certain news before others, but for the last couple of days he'd been the talk of the whole village: the wealthy, seldom seen son of a madman, returning in wartime with (according to gossip) horrific injuries. The rumours were rife and varied. Some said he'd been in a dogfight and crashed. But why come back here, after so many years away? Didn't he have a home in London? Lips whispered. He'd jilted a lover and needed to lie low, or had his lover jilted him because of the accident? Tongues tutted. No, no, he'd lost his marbles like his old man. He was a deserter. He was a lunatic. Most seemed to agree that he was a mystery at least, an outsider who should be approached with caution. I hadn't a clue what to make of him, all I could think of was the eerie, distant look in the old captain's eyes that day at the lake, and a sense of threat began to wrap itself around my shoulders. Memories of the murky water and Mrs Whitman's ghost story. I forced myself not to shudder and leant into Cliff for comfort.

'What's *he* doing here?' Cliff muttered with a flare of irritation in his voice.

Flight Lieutenant Whitman's hands were in his pockets, and he looked stiff and awkward, as if he'd rather be anywhere else. The pianist warily struck up again but all conversations around us had fizzled, the unexpected visitor still the focus of the room. We were all waiting to see what he'd do next.

Doris, tied between wanting to gossip and needing to welcome him, whispered to us, 'Mother issued an invitation to the Manor, although I have to say we didn't expect a response.'

Only Mrs Howard would dare invite the old captain to an event, I thought. Everyone else was too frightened or awed by the Whitmans.

With shoes creaking on the floor, Flight Lieutenant Whitman walked swiftly over to Mr Howard, shook his hand and nodded. There were quiet words exchanged, and within a few seconds the men were talking easily and ripples of conversation were rising around us again.

'He'll be here to pass on the captain's respects, of course,' said Doris. 'He and Daddy fought together in the Great War.'

Alec rolled his eyes at me. *All* our fathers had fought under the captain in the war, and Mr Howard wasn't the only one to have moved up the ranks beneath him. He'd started as a Tommy, just like Dad and Mr Bainbridge and everyone in Barnfield, but finished as a lieutenant, which was what mattered, apparently. What mattered to me was that Dad had got through it at all.

Doris straightened herself up and began to walk over to the new arrival. As an afterthought, she whispered back, 'He's *dreadfully* disfigured. You mustn't stare!'

I watched them intently, curious to see the wounded face

that, as far as I knew, no one in Barnfield had actually seen before today. I certainly couldn't recall seeing him in the past. He was a good ten years older than us, possibly more. He'd grown up at a boarding school and in one of the family's other houses somewhere, so I had no memory of him at all, despite the fact he was technically our landlord. The men didn't talk long, and as the visitor turned to leave, I drew breath and braced myself to be faced with something truly horrific.

That face! It was enough to make my throat tighten and my mouth go dry. But it was not at all what I'd feared. The crimson mark on his neck curved up over his chin and onto his lower lip, and his right cheek was pitted with smaller scars and burns. It was indeed a terrible disfigurement. His skin seemed at war with itself, scarlet in places and a sandy-puce in others, angry and deathly all at once. But it was his eyes that shocked me: they were breath-taking – almost unreal – an astonishing spiral of brilliant blue, azure hiding indigo.

I knew it was rude to stare, but I couldn't take my eyes off the mysterious Wilfred Whitman. There was a youthfulness about him, in his glossy dark hair and eyebrows, and the unbroken parts of his skin. Yet the way he held himself made him seem much older, and there was something familiar in the tilt of his shoulders. Even amidst the chaos of his skin, the likeness was unmistakable: he had his father's nose and brow, but where the captain's eyes had been grey and vacant, Wilfred's were large and heavy, as if they couldn't contain all he'd seen in the world. As he made a beeline for the door, he cast his eyes down, away from the wall of faces craning to stare at his scarred features. Not wanting to be a part of them any longer, feeling suddenly ashamed, I wrenched my gaze away.

Cliff was just as curious as me, it seemed; he watched with hard eyes as Flight Lieutenant Whitman left. But Alec was smiling at the blush on my cheeks, for he seemed to have the ability to see through me, especially in moments of weakness. I felt like I'd been caught out, even though I'd done nothing wrong. Even if Alec could read my mind (as he often pretended he could), what was wrong with being a little overawed by a stranger? Hadn't everyone in the room been struck by him? By his scars, most definitely, perhaps not the handsome eyes, although surely I wasn't the only one who'd noticed them? Nevertheless, I threw Alec a warning look. He grinned, folded his arms and surveyed the room, voices raised and gabbling now that the unexpected visitor had departed.

However strange and eccentric, the Whitmans were still a wealthy, respected family, and Mrs Howard wore Wilfred's visit like a crown, her face transformed with smug pride. 'Oh yes! *Dear* Captain Whitman!' she simpered to our neighbours. Mrs B winked at me, for I'd lost count of how many times she'd referred to him as *mad old* Captain Whitman in the Post Office. But we were all guilty of that. It had taken a good couple of months for me to get used to delivering post to the Manor when I'd first started on my rounds, for fear of encountering the old man again. Two years on and I hadn't even caught a glimpse of him. I sometimes wondered if he was real. Perhaps I had imagined him on the shore that day, but then, Wilfred's face had borne such a likeness…

Cliff nudged me. 'Here we go...'

Doris had been making her way around pockets of people, and was now hurrying over to us, gushing what was by now a much-repeated report. 'Flight Lieutenant Whitman was *so* delighted to have had the opportunity to stop by and pass on his good wishes! I daresay Captain Whitman himself would have come had his health allowed it, but his son assured us his father is in good spirits.'

Alec and Cliff looked highly dubious and unimpressed.

'But what happened to him?' Alec asked, flicking his gaze

back to where Wilfred had been. 'How did his face get all mashed up like that?'

'Alec!' I hadn't meant to say it so loudly, but the words smarted like a graze. Some people stared and I flushed and shrank back under Cliff's amused gaze. 'That's no way to speak of the injured,' I mumbled half-heartedly.

'Flight Lieutenant Whitman is on medical leave,' Doris explained, as if she'd been aware of this all along. 'He's been recovering in hospital and has come to the country for some much-needed convalescence.' Quietly and hastily she added, 'I expect.'

'But was he in a crash?' Alec pressed, like a schoolboy hungry for a grisly story.

Doris frowned. 'Really! It's none of our business.'

Cliff swept his arm around at the clusters of chattering folk around us. 'It seems to be everyone's business.'

Doris's lips tightened and she looked sharply around her for others to relay the news to.

Alec breathed a low whistle, glancing furtively back at the door. 'I bet he wishes he'd died.' I glared at him again, ashamed of his tactlessness, knowing he was really just trying to make a show of bravado in front of Cliff. But Alec only shrugged back at me, adding, 'Well I'd rather die than look like that.'

'Alec!' I hissed.

Cliff shifted next to me. 'Oh, keep your knickers on!' He was now scowling too.

'Am I the only one who thinks he's actually quite good-looking?' I said pointedly, just to shut them up more than anything else, but I immediately regretted it, for though Alec laughed, Cliff turned his glower on me.

He looked like he was about to snap at me, but as he turned away he muttered, 'Well, I don't like him.'

'Why not?' My tone was dangerously prickly. I didn't really

want to provoke an argument. I wanted to forget it all now and go back to celebrating. But the boys' behaviour had bothered me and the heat had made me irritable.

'He owns half the village,' said Cliff, 'and the farm, and never once stepped foot in it, I bet. And what has he done to deserve it? Never done an honest day's work in his life.'

'You don't know that. We don't know anything about him.'

Cliff looked aghast, incredulous that I was defending Wilfred. 'He was born into it, Grace. People like that barely know how to wipe their own arses.'

Alec sniggered.

Cliff shook his head. 'It's not right. I work that farm, and live on it…'

'It's Goffman's, Cliff.'

'Now maybe, but one day it'll be mine.' He hesitated, his eyes alight with a sudden optimism. But it died when he said, 'Even then, it won't *really* be mine. It'll always be Whitman's. Even though he probably couldn't care less about it.'

'Isn't that just the way of things?'

'Well, I'd rather he wasn't my master,' he grumbled. 'Something off about him.'

'The Whitmans are all toffs,' Alec said coolly.

Cliff wrinkled his nose in disgust, and said under his breath, 'Or fucking mad.'

I desperately wanted to leap to Wilfred's defence, but I knew as little as everyone else, and I didn't want Alec insinuating anything. The Whitmans were nothing to me; why should it bother me so? It was probably just the memory of the old Captain and the heat making me feel unsettled. But hadn't Alec and Cliff seen the sadness in Wilfred's eyes too, the rawness of his horrible scars? They were so desperate to go and fight themselves, yet here was someone who'd already put his life on the line and paid such an ugly price for it. We didn't know Wilfred, but he'd never done us any harm. To pick him apart so maliciously seemed in such poor taste.

Doris had moved on to another group and Alec slunk outside for a cigarette, moaning about the heat. Cliff leaned towards me, the scent of sweat and soap rising from his now collarless shirt. 'What's the matter with you?'

'That was uncalled for.'

'What?'

I sighed. 'What you said about Wilfred Whitman. There was no need to be so cruel. Or crass, for that matter.'

He chuckled. 'You sound like Doris.' He stroked the side of my mouth to make me smile, but I wouldn't. 'Oh, come on, Gracie. So what? The Whitmans *are* mad. Everyone knows that.' His eyes twinkled with mischief and he pressed his lips together as if trying to keep in a secret. 'Anyway, never mind about that.' He puffed out his chest and nodded to the room. 'What do you make of all this?'

'What? The wedding?'

He nodded.

It was all charming, as it only ever could have been with Doris and her mother at the helm, but I wasn't in the mood to make small talk so I said something benign about the flowers.

'But you wouldn't want a big wedding, would you?'

I shrugged.

'Would you?'

I stared at him, unable to read his eyes. I'd never heard Cliff talk about weddings in his life. I thought of Alec's shilling bet and shrunk away a little. 'What a stupid question,' I laughed.

'Well?' he pressed, with sudden urgency and anxiety in his tone, as if he really wanted an answer.

I was sure Alec had put him up to it, but even so, I couldn't find a suitable quip to respond with. His gaze was starting to unnerve me, but Mrs B saved me, falling into Alec's seat, fanning her face with her hands. 'I do love a wedding, even if it is as hot as the fires of hell.' She nodded to Mrs Howard. 'I've just spent the last fifteen minutes hearing all about Ron Fielding's houses. *Houses*, dear, for there are two of them, don't you know?' We'd heard all about the blasted two houses ever since Doris first got engaged. Mrs Howard loved to linger in the Post Office and discuss the minutiae of the bathrooms and finery of the furniture. 'You'd think she was marrying the houses, not the man!'

'Well, she is, isn't she?' said Cliff cynically.

'You're as bad tempered as Alec,' I told him.

He sighed and stood up. 'I need a drink.'

Later, having helped to tidy the chairs and sweep the floor, I left the hall and its scent of sweat and warm margarine behind me. Cliff found me in the neighbouring churchyard, staring at Mum's gravestone. His own parents were buried a few strides away, with wooden crosses marking their dates. We stood with the earth and my mother's bones beneath our feet, as well as the child's, whom Alec and I had secretly called Annie, because Mrs B had told us she'd been a girl. 'And Child' was no way to mark someone's existence, however fleeting. I'd called my doll Annie too, and for a while Dad had let me set a space for her at the table and pretend to feed her food. I must have forgotten to do it one day, then stopped altogether. I still had the doll in a box in the loft.

When we were children, Mrs B would take us to visit Mum's grave occasionally, or we went with Aunt Lois if she was visiting. Dad never took us and never went himself as far as I was aware. Even so, I liked to imagine he snuck off sometimes to stand by her stone in the murky light of dawn or dusk, and remember her, his heart swollen with secrets. If I remembered

Mum I'd do that, however proud. I would probably still cry too, but I didn't anymore, because at around the age of ten I realised I only wept because I felt sorry for myself: I had no memories to recall and I didn't really feel Mum's loss at all. I felt her absence, and, standing beside Cliff then, a deep anger and sadness for the lives wasted. I would have liked to have had a little sister. I would have liked to have a mother too, and a father whose mind wasn't always elsewhere. But essentially it was a selfish kind of sadness, and the guilt it left me with meant I visited rarely.

Cliff pulled my arm gently and we began walking back to the hall. I had lost track of time and dusk was beginning to settle. The warm evening air felt like velvet on my skin. It was the kind of night to sleep out under the stars, if it weren't for the war and the fact that I was apparently too old for that sort of thing now. Still, I liked to think Cliff would say yes if I suggested it, and imagined us lying together in the old spot, sharing one of his cigarettes and spotting glow worms in the darkness.

When we were out of the graveyard Cliff broke the silence and started talking about something that had happened at the farm yesterday, but I wasn't really listening. The heat from earlier had caught up with me. I quickly abandoned my dream of sleeping beneath the stars. All I could think was how delicious it would be to plunge my aching feet into a bowl of cold water when I got home. But Cliff kept on, chattier than I'd ever known him. He seemed distracted or rattled by something and I wondered if he was still thinking about Wilfred Whitman's surprise appearance and the ghoulish tales of the captain and his dead wife.

I saw Doris and Ron beneath the tree by the hall, and Alec smoking with a handful of people over by the gate, but Cliff squeezed my hand and led me in the opposite direction, along the wall of the building. There was chatter from inside, and thick, languid chords still being played above it. We slunk into the shadows, and he turned his body so I had to stop with my back against the wall. He leant his arm just above my head in the way he usually did when he was about to kiss me, but I wasn't really in the mood.

'I've just got to say it,' he said on a sigh, looking back to where we'd come from. He ran his fingers through his hair and stared back at me with agitated eyes. He let his arms fall, only to bring them to his head again.

Perhaps I was foolish to stand there clueless and disinterested, with my hands on my hips, waiting for him to speak. It shouldn't have come as a shock, Alec told me later. But apparently, I was an idiot.

'I want you to marry me.'

I spluttered out a short laugh. 'What?'

Cliff laughed too as if I were playing a little game with him, but I was thinking the same thing. 'Come on, Gracie. I'm trying to be serious here.'

'I can see that. Did Alec put you up to this?'

He scowled. 'No.'

'You know he bet me a shilling you'd ask me.'

Cliff laughed cynically. 'Well it was a safe bet, you shouldn't have taken it. Alec knows all about it. And your dad. I asked his permission, you know.'

Quickly the smile fell from my lips and my stomach dropped with the weight of my ignorance. I had a sudden urge to run away from him, but he was planted in front of me, his sturdy frame and now stern expression keeping me captive. How could I have been so naive? All Alec's teasing and Dad's little talk over dinner, Cliff asking me what kind of wedding I'd like. It was all so blindingly obvious, and yet, I couldn't believe it was true. I knew Cliff and liked to think he knew me. I felt like I'd stepped into a trap.

He huffed at my silence. 'You can't be that surprised.'

'Of course I'm surprised!' He drew back a little and I realised I was shouting, so I went on in a whisper, 'Cliff, in all the years we've known each other – all our *lives* – you have never been serious with me!'

'Well, there's a first time for everything. Look, I know I'm not perfect, but I'm doing well for myself, and I'm going to need a wife when I get back.'

I couldn't help laughing. 'Then ask one of your other girls.'

He waved a hand as if swatting a fly. 'Someone who isn't afraid to get their hands dirty. Those girls are nothing, Gracie, you know that.'

At least he didn't deny their existence. Despite myself, I felt a little flutter of foolish pride in my chest. 'You're not saying you love me, are you?' There was a queer mixture of hope and dismay in my tone, and I had the sense that whatever his answer, I'd feel unsatisfied.

He screwed up his mouth a little. 'Don't go all lovey-dovey on me. I care about you. You know that. And I know you care about me.'

'Yes, but we never talked about getting married before. It's just a bit unexpected.' He looked miffed and disappointed, and I felt a flicker of guilt. It wasn't entirely unexpected, it just felt odd hearing him say it, like he was trying to trick me. 'Look,' I softened my tone and rubbed his arms in a conciliatory way, 'you're just saying this because you're nervous about leaving.'

'I'm not nervous,' he said flatly.

I gave a short sigh. 'Well, I'm not marrying you, Cliff.'

'I'd gathered that.'

'Did you really think I'd say yes?'

He shrugged. 'I don't see why not. I always thought you would. Your dad thought you would. And Alec says it's all you talk about.'

I pictured my brother's grin and said, 'I'm going to kill him.'

Cliff placed his hands on my shoulders and looked me squarely in the eyes. There was no hint of romance, or even lust in his gaze then, but he was entirely earnest when he said, 'I know we fight and mess around but… I think we're all right together, don't you?'

'*You* mess around. With half the girls in Finton if Alec is to be believed.'

'Well he's not, and you know it.'

'Even so…'

'You've never said it bothered you before.'

'Well you weren't proposing then, and I can't quite believe you're doing it now. You know I'd drive you mad.'

'Yes, you probably would.' He pressed his lips together to fight a smile. 'I'm already starting to regret it.'

'Good.'

'But I think, when it comes down to it, we could make a good go of it. You love this place as much as I do. And I'll be back as soon as… if I'm still around.'

'Oh, Cliff, don't talk like that!'

'Think about the farm, Gracie – it'd be ours! We'd be set for life.' He glanced away and bit his lip, then looked back and kissed me hard on the lips, his stubble pricking my chin. He ran his hands down my arms until he was holding my hands, his palms rough and sweaty. When he pulled away he looked shy and sweet and I felt the pull of guilt in my chest.

'Oh, Cliff! Why did you have to say anything? Now you've spoiled it, you great oaf!'

He grinned. 'Think about it, won't you?'

'Wouldn't you rather forget it? Put it down to a moment of madness?'

He gave me a long, steady look, a twinkle of humour in his

eyes, but resolute nonetheless.

'All right, I promise I'll think about it.'

'Good girl. Can't have anyone else snapping you up while I'm away.' He let go of my hands. For a moment I thought he was going to burst out laughing and Alec would appear from around the corner, declaring it all a big joke, but he just winked and began to stroll back, stopping at the corner and turning back to me. 'Aren't you coming?' He sounded so chipper, as if I'd already given him the answer he wanted.

'No. I'll see you in a minute.'

He smiled and left me in the shadow of the hall. I fell back against the wall and sighed out slowly. I couldn't believe he'd asked Dad's permission, that Alec knew about this before I did. It felt like they'd been plotting behind my back. And didn't they know me at all? I didn't want to marry Cliff. I didn't want to marry anyone; I wasn't yet eighteen. Did that make me foolish and ungrateful? I pictured Doris and Ron standing at the altar and tried to put Cliff and me in their place, but it just didn't look right, like two photographs glued together, pretending to be one. I imagined going home and telling Dad that I hadn't accepted Cliff's offer. I didn't want to disappoint him. I gritted my teeth and groaned, then covered my face with my hands. I needed a cigarette.

I was just about to leave my shady little solitude when I heard a rustle from behind the other corner of the hall. It was too soft to be a bird or even leaves, and though my mind was elsewhere, something about it made me freeze and prick up my ears. There it was again, unmistakable: the shift of fabric, the presence of another person. The shuffling sound had fallen silent but I turned towards the far corner of the hall where I was certain it had come from.

'Hello?'

There was no reply as such, except for the very definite

confirmation of my suspicions: the scratch of a match, closely followed by a thin swirl of cigarette smoke. Now they'd been discovered, this person was no longer trying to hide their presence. But why hide at all? Why not answer me? And how long had they been listening? Long enough to have heard my conversation with Cliff, surely. I cringed at the thought.

'Hello?' My voice was girlish and petulant now. I walked to peer around the corner, and stopped, stunned, faced unexpectedly with Wilfred Whitman leaning against the back wall, and the orange glow of his cigarette as he held it to his lips. That extraordinary face, painted with violence. I gaped at him like a fish, so surprised to find him there, and humiliated at the thought of everything he'd heard. 'Oh,' I managed eventually, my cheeks burning. 'I didn't know there was anyone here.' Why did I sound so apologetic, when he was the one lurking in the shadows, alone?

He stood up straight. Up close, he was much taller than he'd seemed in the hall. 'I'm sorry, I should have said something, but…' His voice was low and smooth, and there was an awkwardness about the way he stood and smoked, with one shoulder slightly higher than the other.

'I…' The word hung in the air between us and I looked away. My mind was racing too fast to think of anything else to say, remembering his shoes squeaking in the hall, and everyone whispering, the blueness of his eyes. I looked back at them quickly, but they were dark holes in the shadows, and I blinked, feeling utterly exposed.

His silence unnerved me. He should have stepped forward by now. He should have been holding me in polite conversation, easing my embarrassment. Wasn't that how people like him were supposed to act? Yet he only watched me, as his father had done years before from the lakeshore, while I kicked and choked in the water. My feet might have been on dry ground now, but my head was still swimming, my pulse floundering, as Wilfred stood and smoked. Our lack of words had drawn a circle around us, and now I felt trapped in it. Somehow the world was different in this tiny corner of Barnfield. It was a place where Cliff proposed to me and Wilfred Whitman was hiding away like a nervous animal. It was a place I didn't want to be.

I could hear laughter and chatter as people left the hall. I wanted to run and join them but Wilfred had me spellbound, pinned to the spot. He took another drag on his cigarette, so slow it was as if time stood still, then dropped it to the ground. He moved his foot over it without breaking eye contact with me. I felt a bead of sweat run down my back and disappear into the fabric of my dress. I felt something else too, something terrible and dark inside me, as if the ground had cracked beneath my feet and I'd slipped into some awful oblivion.

The sound of Alec's voice jolted me: 'Hurry up, Gracie!'

Alarmed at the intensity of my relief, I heard myself say, 'I have to go,' as if I had no right to. But Wilfred didn't answer and after I turned away I couldn't bear to look back at him and his horrific scars again. I fled like a frightened child, my chest thumping as if he were still right in front of me.

I took Alec's arm on the walk home and he laughed and teased me for being flushed and overly sentimental about the wedding. But my head was giddy, blood throbbing hot and fast in my temples. I could sense the promise of exhaustion in my body, and felt somehow detached from reality, as if a part of me was still standing in the shadows with Wilfred Whitman, waiting and wishing for him to speak.

Sometime before dawn I dreamt of the lake, not knowing that it would be the first of countless restless nights waking from the same nightmare. I was swimming, and Alec and Cliff were nowhere to be seen, but Captain Whitman was there on the shore, looking through me, oblivious to the fact that I felt frightened. Then I began to sink, but I wasn't flagging, I was being *pulled*. I felt fingers scratching my ankles and looked down into the cloudy depths, and there beneath me were grabbing hands and a horrific dead, grey face with closed eyes. It was a face I was sure I knew, but the harder I looked, the more distorted it became. I tried to wriggle out of its grip, screaming to the captain for help, but I was mute. My mouth filled with water and I could no longer breathe, and I knew then that no one would come and save me.

CHAPTER 5

With Flight Lieutenant Whitman back at the Manor and letters arriving for him almost daily, I guessed it was only a matter of time before I'd see him again. I'd half expected him to turn up to church the day after the wedding, but the glares and whispers of the previous day must have put him off showing his face in public. Even so, I thought of him as we knelt for prayers, and how he'd looked in the shadows of the hall: broken yet somehow defiant. How the smoke had slowly coiled like a snake from his mouth, around his scarred neck. His smooth voice with his clipped vowels. Each time I visited the Manor on my rounds, I found myself searching the windows for his face in vain.

I didn't tell anyone that I'd seen him behind the hall. Cliff and Alec would make fun of me, just as they had when I saw the captain by the lake, and I knew they'd make more scathing remarks about Wilfred's poor face and supposed madness. The rumours had been further embroidered since his unexpected appearance at the wedding; by Tuesday morning Mrs B and I had heard everyone's thoughts on Flight Lieutenant Whitman. Each time the tinkling bell over the Post Office door announced another customer, I braced myself for the inevitable mention of his name. Safe and ordinary subjects were skirted first: the weather, Doris's radiant bridal beauty, the news from the papers. Then a sharp intake of breath before: 'And what about young Wilfred Whitman? What a surprise! Did you see his face? Such a good-looking man, such a waste!'

When I was in the Post Office I kept my head down and let Mrs B do the talking. Neither of us appreciated gossip much but even so, I could tell she was suspicious of my reticence. A couple of days after Cliff left for training, I returned after the morning round to find Mrs B trapped in conversation with Doris's mother. Mrs Howard's slender hand rested by her ration book on the counter as she cooed and tutted over her new son-in-law's bravery. Mrs B gave me a brief, weary look of relief as I opened the door and went to hang my cap and jacket on the hook by the telegraph machine.

'At least I still have my Dorry with me for the time being. They'll move to Finton when it's all over, God willing.'

Mrs B, whose only son had been gone for two years said, 'The sooner the better.'

'And how about you, Grace?' Mrs Howard simpered disingenuously, the force of her perfume almost overpowering her words. 'You must be missing your Cliff terribly.'

I almost laughed at her. *Your Cliff*, as if I'd tamed him. People had generally come to think of us as a couple, despite his antics with the land girls. I thought of our kiss goodbye at Finton station, and the woolly scent of his uniform. I'd expected him to bring up the proposal again but he hadn't mentioned it since the night of the wedding. I hadn't even told Dad. It was like I'd imagined it. In the end, Cliff just grinned, said 'chin up' and told me to practise my cooking for when he came back on leave.

Mrs Howard patted my shoulder in a show of tentative sympathy. 'Clifford's a strong lad, and you must be strong too. I'm quite sure he'll do very well.' She withdrew her hand and I got the impression she was holding off the urge to wipe it on her skirt.

I nodded, smiling as kindly as I could, wishing she'd change the subject. She was fishing for some shred of gossip, no doubt. She was a beautiful woman, her skin remarkably healthy for her age, her hair as glossy and dark as her daughter's. She was always immaculately turned out, as if she were perpetually on her way to lunch with the mayor. But her beauty soured every time she opened her mouth, and her censorious looks and expressions gave the impression that, like a promisingly rosy windfall lying in the grass, her core was brown and rotten.

I was saved by the bell, jingling as the door opened and two elderly sisters, Hannah and Edna Smythe, shuffled in. The Misses Smythe were overdressed for both the weather and the occasion; they leaned on their twin ornate canes and smiled at Mrs B and Mrs Howard over the rims of their glasses. The conversation changed quickly to the weather and the war.

The Post Office was dark and cramped, in the front two rooms of Mrs B's pokey half-timbered home, with low-beamed ceilings and a polished oak counter and shelving. Five people within was certainly enough to make it feel crowded. Before the war, the shelves had been jammed too, with everything from paper and envelopes to brass polish, rope and jars of rainbow-bright boiled sweets. Now the stock was significantly depleted, but it was the nearest thing to a general store without getting the bus or cycling into Finton.

'Of course, Doris is doing wonders with the WVS,' Mrs Howard gushed.

'Dear Doris!' the old ladies trilled.

'They're ever so lucky to have her.' With this Mrs Howard threw me a shrewd little look, undoubtedly insinuating that I should spend more time volunteering for the war effort. But working brought in money, which was always a good thing in my book, and it just so happened it was more engaging than folding blankets, making tea, and filling out government forms. 'Doris is so relieved that she doesn't have to work anymore, now that she's married. You should consider that, Gracie, when Clifford comes home on leave.'

I wondered for a minute if the rumour mill had caught wind of Cliff's proposal, but guessed from Mrs Howard's serene smile that she was just getting carried away with herself, as usual.

'I'm only seventeen, Mrs Howard.'

'Tush! I married when I was eighteen. Besides, dear, you're practically a housewife already. Your poor father…'

'Well, yes you're right, I really ought to give marriage some thought,' I said a little too enthusiastically, exchanging glances with Mrs B, who was trying to keep a straight face. I made my retreat into the back room. 'I'd better be getting on.'

'Not so fast, young lady!' said Mrs B, handing me a telegram.

Thank God, an escape! I checked the addressee and without thinking said, 'For the Manor?'

I could *feel* the Smythe sisters' and Mrs Howard's antennae buzzing, almost hear their hearts beating faster. Mrs B shot me a withering glare and I closed my eyes, feeling utterly stupid as Edna Smythe cooed, 'Well fancy that!'

'For whom? The captain or his son?' said Hannah in what was probably meant to be a whisper.

'I'll thank you not to divulge everyone's business, Gracie,' Mrs B scolded gently. 'Careless talk costs lives...'

'Oh Kathy!' Mrs Howard hooted. 'We're not spies!' Perhaps not German spies, but by the end of the day most of the village would know that Wilfred had received a telegram and they'd be wondering what it was about. Why had I put my foot in it? For it was *his* name, after all – Flight Lieutenant W Whitman – and seeing it brought the memory of

Doris's wedding back to me, that feeling of vulnerability in his presence, the sense of mortification. How many times since had his infinitely blue eyes found their unwelcome way into my thoughts when I should have been working or thinking about Cliff? I grabbed my jacket and cap. So much for an escape.

'To see him at the wedding…' Hannah Smythe muttered. 'It was all I could do not to cry out in shock. Such a shame!'

'He's obviously lived through some horrors,' Edna mused.

'But you know what they're saying don't you?' asked Mrs Howard. 'That he's taken after his father. That he's not quite right in the head.'

'The same could have been said about his mother…' Edna interjected knowingly. 'There was always something odd about her.'

I saw Mrs B flinch slightly and wanted to shout at them to stop. It was all my fault that we'd got onto the subject of Wilfred, and I hated to think that I was responsible for yet more fuel to this fire of gossip that seemed to surround him.

Edna sucked her teeth in disapproval.

'Who's to say there's any truth in it?' offered Hannah.

Mrs B opened her mouth to interrupt, but Mrs Howard was too quick: 'I can't say I'm too surprised about Flight Lieutenant Whitman, not when you think of *poor* Captain Whitman. All those years in an asylum. And Mrs Whitman too…'

'Such a strange lady.'

'Rude and immoral, if you ask me.'

'But she died so young! Tragic!'

Mrs Howard whispered, 'I always thought there was something fishy about it. We only found out when we read about it in the paper, and by then she was already buried. Just a couple of lines, if I remember rightly, not even a proper obituary.'

Mrs B said firmly, 'Well, Flight Lieutenant Whitman would have had to organise it, and he probably didn't know what was what. A young man suffers for want of a father's instruction.' Her face hardened and I guessed she was thinking of Alfie.

'Well,' Mrs Howard carried on, inhaling deeply, 'I doubt *he* ever lacked a father's instruction.'

'You mean Mrs Whitman's fancy man?' Edna jumped in.

Hannah Smythe blushed scarlet. 'Really! I thought that was just hearsay!'

'Hearsay, indeed! It's common knowledge. I saw him myself once, I'm sure.'

'Certainly no reason to feel sorry for the late Mrs Whitman, then,' Mrs Howard decreed.

Mrs B rolled her eyes and said, 'As you say, it's probably all just hearsay.' She gave me a stiff, reproachful glare and I made a quick exit.

Within minutes I was peddling away from the village along the lane that led to the Manor, cursing myself again for my loose tongue, and smarting at the thought of Mrs B's disapproving eyes. After days of silence on the matter, to then blurt out and flush as red as a beetroot as I had would only make her suspicious. She would quiz me later. She'd ask why Flight Lieutenant Whitman was giving me the jitters and I'd make up an excuse about his scars or something, which would make me sound heartless and shallow. But it would be easier than explaining what had happened at the hall, and having to go into the whole business of Cliff's proposal too.

A storm had swept through a couple of nights previously and taken the close heat with it. The roads were dry again, the air mild and fresh. As I sped along the deserted lane a trio of Cabbage White butterflies soared on the capricious breeze, dancing over the hedgerow and disappearing out of view.

I soon reached the two large brick gateposts that flanked the driveway to the Manor; the iron gates and railings had been stripped away to be melted down for weapons, and the once grand entrance looked naked and shamed because of it. Still, it was by far the most distinguished address for miles. Its early lords and ladies must have seemed like royalty to the ordinary folk of Barnfield. Even now, with its senile master and extremely thin staff, there was still a local reverence for the estate and its inhabitants.

There was a strange little gatehouse or lodge at the head of the drive, a square building that looked almost like an oversized pigeon loft, with crumbling tiles and peeling window frames. Its once-white door was dusted grey and green from mildew and mould, and slug trails zig-zagged across the cracked paint. A servant would have made his home here in grander times, but the raised room that looked down on the road was dark and deserted; it was obvious no one had stepped inside for years. As far as I knew, the Whitmans only employed the captain's nurse, a general housemaid and a gardener now, and none of them from Barnfield, which was the cause of much disapproval in the village.

I peddled on, through the short avenue of oaks, my tyres crackling on the mossy gravel driveway. To the left, fields stretched back towards the village. On my right was a narrow, ill-kept lawn and a long yew hedge (if they did have a gardener, he wasn't doing a brilliant job). Ahead was the Manor itself: leaded windows glinting like buried treasure amongst fading red brickwork; a green front door framed by a neat porch and a scrappy trailing rose.

When Alec and I had snuck up to the back garden gate as children, we'd seen wide windows and a classic stone façade, but the front was the original part of the house that dated back hundreds of years, and didn't appear to have been cared for much since then. The roof tiles were laced with lichen and there were streaks of green damp beneath the gutters. The image of mad old Captain Whitman hiding within sprang readily into my thoughts as I slowed into the turning circle.

Leaning my bicycle against the little porch, I took a deep breath and rang the bell, then rapped on the door – my confident, post girl knock that hid my nerves admirably. I hoped the housemaid or nurse would answer. We were meant to give the telegram directly to its addressee, but this one wasn't marked priority, so would it really hurt if I gave it to a servant?

I heard footsteps behind the door and braced myself, for it was Wilfred; I could sense his intense gaze on me even before he opened the door, and suddenly all the unsettling feelings from Doris's wedding returned.

'Oh, hello again,' he said immediately, kindly, and smiled, his skin jagged and taut where his lip had healed.

I forgot to breathe for a moment. He obviously recognised me, which made me wonder if he too was recalling all the awkwardness of our previous meeting. But he seemed like an entirely different creature today, standing there with slippers on his feet, light tweed trousers draping his legs, black braces pressed against a colourless shirt. He looked so at ease, and I felt a weight lifting from my shoulders, sensing there would be no repeat of the strange silence from before. 'Good afternoon, sir. I have a telegram for you.'

'Thank you.' He glanced at it briefly before slipping it into his pocket without opening it. His perfectly blue eyes had lost all the darkness they'd held in the twilit shadows of the hall. In the bright light of day, he seemed gentle and unthreatening, and despite his scarring, his face was quite beautiful, with a strong, slender nose, fine cheekbones and full lips.

I stepped back toward my bike. 'Good day.'

'Wait! I'm sorry, I should have introduced myself the other

night, but you took me a little by surprise.' He reached out his hand. 'Wilfred Whitman. How do you do?'

'And you surprised me,' I said, shaking his hand briefly. 'Grace Wells.'

'Pleased to meet you. Apologies again about giving you a shock the other night.'

'That's quite all right.' I was glad everything had been put right, but still blushed furiously at the thought of all he must have heard, not that it mattered now. 'Well, I ought to be getting back.'

'Yes, yes, of course.' He nervously lifted his hand up to his scarred cheek and then brought it down to his side again, as if it were a habit he was trying hard to break. What had really happened to him? It was difficult to imagine the chaotic disaster that had caused those scars; it seemed almost impossible on a beautiful morning like this. 'It was good to meet you, Grace.'

I winced at the familiarity. 'And you too, Flight Lieutenant Whitman.'

He frowned irritably. 'Wilfred, please.'

'If you insist.'

'I do insist,' he said, more confidently than before. 'Goodbye, then.' He raised his hand.

'Goodbye.' I mounted my bicycle, and felt his eyes on me as I peddled away, but when I looked over my shoulder a minute later he was gone, and I wondered if I'd just imagined him watching me.

That evening, as I drained the potatoes for supper, Alec announced, 'I'm having a drink with one of the land girls on Friday night.'

'Oh? Which one?'

'Linda.'

I recalled a broad-shouldered girl with auburn hair and pretty green eyes. 'Doesn't she have a boyfriend?'

He threw me a petulant look as he sat down at the table. 'They all say they have boyfriends. Most of the girls in Finton have boyfriends as long as it suits them.'

I smiled. I'd used that line myself once or twice in the past.

Alec bit at a fingernail. 'It's not serious anyway. Just passing the time till my papers come through.'

'Charming. Does Linda know that?'

'If she doesn't then she's simple. Besides, no girl's ever going to take *me* seriously.' He yawned and sighed. 'What a godforsaken backwater we live in! I'm not even that keen on her.'

'Then why are you—?' I asked without thinking, feeling foolish when he gave me a disparaging glare. 'Ugh, you boys are all the same!'

'You girls aren't much better.' He caught my eye with a laugh but then looked away, serious.

'What do you mean?'

'You know how to play the field as much as we do.'

I frowned at him. 'I do?'

'Not *you*,' he squirmed, shrugging off the comment, but I felt my skin prickle with doubt. It probably meant nothing – Alec said a hundred silly things a day – but I felt in the silence that followed that he was holding something back. His eyes flicked to mine again and he looked surly, annoyed. Was he angry with me for some reason, or was I just being paranoid? The encounter with Wilfred earlier on had thrown me off balance; the thought of his face, those eyes, his awkward yet overly familiar manner. I'd never met anyone so strange. I felt a shiver crawl up my back and shook it off, and Alec looked at me again. 'What?' he said lazily, as if he didn't really care if I answered.

'Nothing. Someone just walked over my grave.'

He raised an eyebrow and pressed his fingernails into the soft wood of the table top. I leant over and kissed him on the head. His hair smelled of sweat and hay dust.

'Get off!'

'You put on a good act but I know you're a big softie at heart. You'll find a girl who loves you one day.' He snorted derisively but didn't argue. I nudged his shoulder. 'Move. I need to lay the table.'

He hopped up from his chair obligingly and watched as I draped a cloth on the table: the faded one that Mum had embroidered.

'It's alright for you,' he said, picking his fingernails again. 'You're lucky.'

I smiled as I got the cutlery out of the drawer. 'Oh yes? Why's that?'

'You've got Cliff.'

'I haven't got Cliff and he hasn't got me, whatever you and everyone else seem to think.'

'I know he proposed.'

'Then you know I turned him down.'

'You owe me a shilling.'

'Bugger off.'

He laughed and ducked when I tried to grab his ear. 'But you'll marry him eventually, won't you?' He didn't wait for a response. 'You know what I mean. You don't have to think about it anymore. No more chatting up or making a fool out of yourself.'

I remembered the Finton dances I'd gone to with Jean. It was always Doris who'd invited the most attention. We used to laugh ourselves giddy at some of the lines she heard; I'm sure Alec tried to steal some of them. Cliff had never needed clever words. Cliff had charmed them all, it seemed, all those pretty girls who'd held out their cigarettes and touched their chests absentmindedly as he spoke. I'd never fallen for him like that. Was that why he liked me best? Was I more genuine, or was I just safe and dependable? But Cliff didn't seem like the kind of man who wanted a safe life. He was a child of the woods. He followed his own path.

Alec was still engrossed in his nails. He didn't notice me lost in thought. I looked down at the little table set for three and sighed.

CHAPTER 6

The following day I was on my own in the back room, sorting through the second post, when I saw Wilfred's name again upon an ordinary little envelope. I stared at it for a minute or so, his face so clear in my mind – that tangle of beauty and scars – and I felt ridiculous and overwhelmingly guilty. All I'd said to Cliff was that I'd think about his proposal, but it seemed he and practically everyone else had taken my answer as read. Alec's certainty that I would marry Cliff eventually made me wonder if it was inevitable anyway. Now I'd had more time to consider it, it didn't seem such a mad idea. But I still felt too young to be getting married. It was the blasted war's fault, putting everyone on the spot. If Cliff hadn't needed to leave suddenly we might have naturally got to this juncture in a couple of years, but now it just seemed forced.

I filled up my bag, placing Wilfred's letter at the bottom, knowing it would be the last I'd deliver that day. I thought of Cliff as I did my rounds, tried to imagine where he was billeted for training and what he was doing, if he'd write and tell me about it or leave me guessing. I couldn't picture him anywhere. At least I didn't worry for him. He would be in his element with those other men, competing to be the strongest with the least amount of effort. It was Alec I ached for; just the thought of him leaving made me queasy. I wished there was something I could do to keep him here, but I was powerless. It was our eighteenth birthday on Saturday, and his papers would follow swiftly. He would leave, just like Cliff, and Jean, and I'd be left behind to worry about them all.

When I reached the Manor's gateposts I tried to distract my sombre thoughts and began planning what I should say if I saw Wilfred again. Just an amiable 'good afternoon, Flight Lieutenant Whitman' would be fine, and certainly no 'Wilfred', however much he insisted. My cheeks burned as I conjured the image of his face so perfectly in my memory, as if I'd only just turned away from him. Perhaps I should avoid eye contact, and therefore any further embarrassment. But most likely I wouldn't see him at all. I'd just pop his letter through the door and then trundle back to the Post Office. The thought of that filled the pit of my stomach with such heavy disappointment that I almost felt sick.

I slowed as I approached the Manor. There was a car parked in front of the porch and as I coasted into the turning circle a middle-aged man in smart Air Force blues walked out of the house and got into it. He was very handsome, with pale brown hair and a neat moustache, and he caught my eye and smiled benignly as he shut his door. Behind, Wilfred was standing in the open doorway, watching. His gaze followed the car as it turned back down the driveway, and after a few seconds he looked at me and pushed back his shoulders, his eyes glistening as if I'd woken him from a dream and he'd only just realised I was there.

I stayed on my bicycle and opened my bag. I didn't want to stop; his presence was so unnerving and to my shame I couldn't deny how attractive I found him. He looked pale and anxious, obviously preoccupied by the man's visit. I wondered why he'd been there and if it had anything to do with the fact Wilfred was standing in his own home in civvies while his peers were out in active service. Mrs Howard's words raced through my head again. What if it was true, what people said about him? What if he was as crazy as his father? I tried to shake the thought from my head as I held out the envelope to him, thinking of Mrs Howard and the Smythe sisters and how I was just as bad as them.

'Thank you,' he said, taking the letter and putting it straight in his pocket again. He glanced back to the empty driveway, then ran his hand over the back of his head, turning back to me with a nervous smile. He covered his face with his hands and breathed a heavy sigh of relief or exhaustion.

Still on my bicycle, I watched, frozen, as he pulled his fingers down his face and rested them in a steeple shape below his nose. I felt compelled to ask him if he was all right.

'Yes. Yes, sorry, I…' He seemed flustered and embarrassed and I sensed the spark of panic in his eyes as he endeavoured to focus on anything other than me. He nodded towards where the car had been. 'It's been a difficult afternoon.' He left a long pause, inviting me to ask him who the man was and why he'd been there, but I wouldn't. It wasn't my place. 'I could do with a drink.' I took this as my cue to leave but he called out – 'You wouldn't join me, would you?' – only looking at me on the last word. His eyes were wide with what seemed like fear or desperation. He touched his injured cheek again and held his hand there, waiting for my answer.

The very idea of entering this man's house – the *Manor* house – and joining him for a drink seemed bizarre, and the fact that he didn't appear to understand that made him even more perplexing to me. *He's not quite right in the head.* 'I can't,' I said quickly.

His eyes flickered with disappointment briefly. 'Please,

Grace.'

How could he say my name with such ease? 'I'm still on duty,' I explained, my voice wavering. His gaze was intensifying, his blue eyes burning holes through me.

'A cup of tea then?'

I looked down, pretended to glance at my watch. The time was irrelevant, I was at the end of my round and had nothing to get back for that couldn't wait twenty minutes. Was that why I'd left his letter till last? Hadn't I secretly wished to see him again?

Wilfred was still just standing there, his right arm trembling very slightly by his side, waiting on my answer as if it meant more to him than anything else in the world. Now was the time to tell him that it wouldn't be proper, something that was true in any case even if Cliff wasn't in the picture.

'I really shouldn't.' I was horrified to hear the insincerity of my tone.

'Shouldn't?'

'Mustn't.'

He seemed to smile and there was a long pause. The open door behind him teased me with a dingy view of the Manor's hall. 'I don't think a cup of tea ever hurt anyone, Grace.' His voice was like warm velvet and made the suggestion all the more inviting. His eyes glimmered and I hated them for a moment, for I knew I would give in.

'All right then,' I relented, dismounting, 'but I can't stay long.' Guilt engulfed me instantly. I was in the wrong, but curiosity had got the better of me.

A wide, grateful smile broke across Wilfred's face and he touched the back of his neck again. I had never seen a man so jittery, and couldn't banish the rumours of his madness from my head as I leaned my bicycle against the porch. My pulse beat a little faster as I glanced back to the empty driveway and followed him through the front door. I felt as if I was about to enter Buckingham Palace and meet the King himself.

The Manor's cool, dark hallway was probably the size of our entire downstairs put together. A narrow, carpeted staircase snaked its way up from the left of the room, and I caught a glimpse of closed doors on the mezzanine landing above. There was wood panelling on all the walls, dark as treacle. A little light shone in from an open door in front of us to the right, showing up the unpolished brass stair rods and a few cobwebs strung from the high coving. The place smelled large, of rooms that hadn't been lived in for years, of furniture gathering dust and damp corridors. Perhaps there was no maid after all; it didn't seem like the place got much attention. What would Mrs Howard think if she knew how shabby it was? There were three other doors off the hallway – all shut too – and I wondered if Captain Whitman or his wife's ghost were hiding behind any of them.

Wilfred shut the front door behind him and I felt ludicrously out of place, enclosed in an unknown hallway with an unknown man.

'Can I take your hat and jacket?'

I caught his scent as I passed him my cap – expensive and masculine and everything unfamiliar. Why had he invited me inside? I was suddenly terrified. Did he wish to take advantage of me? Force himself upon me? I wouldn't be strong enough to push him away, and was there anyone else here to hear my cries? I eyed the door – had he bolted it? I shouldn't have agreed to come inside. I'd changed my mind but it was too late.

I tried to calm myself. I was letting my imagination run wild. He was probably harmless, however peculiar. Nevertheless, I still had to endure tea with him, and all for a stupid moment of pity. I should just tell him I'd made a mistake and it didn't feel right, then I could leave immediately. He'd understand. He'd apologise and I'd apologise and it would be embarrassing but no harm would be done.

But I said nothing.

He reached for my jacket and I slipped it off my shoulders, feeling instantly light and cold without the heavy wool on my arms. He hung it on the hat stand beside us, then held out his hand and gestured for me to walk towards the open door. I led the way, feeling like a trespasser. We walked into a large room so flooded with light that my eyes stung briefly. Dust motes rode the air, swirling and golden in the sunshine. Tall French windows revealed the enormous garden outside, a canvas of green with smudges of floral colour.

'I'll go and see about some tea.' He left me suddenly through another door at the far end of the room, his footsteps trailing behind him. I heard the creak of stairs and the murmur of distant voices.

What would Cliff do if he knew I was here? Would he tease and laugh at me, remind me of my scrape at the lake? I imagined what I looked like, standing there hesitantly in the Manor's grand living room, and couldn't help thinking he'd find it funny. But if he knew my heart, if he knew the guilt I felt, would he still be laughing? If he knew how Wilfred's face shook me, wouldn't he be furious?

Steadying my breath, I turned to face the rest of the room. Despite its size it was modestly furnished, with two comfortable looking mustard yellow sofas facing each other and a low table between them. There were two empty cups there, one with a splash of tea in its saucer. I imagined Wilfred and the mysterious airman finishing them just moments before I'd arrived and made myself look away.

A worn leather armchair sat beside the hearth to my left, a tartan blanket slung across its back. Was that the old captain's chair? The rest of the dark wood furniture was functional and unpolished; a bureau nestled below one of the windows, cluttered with papers, and an equally messy sideboard pressed against the wall to my right. The floor was carpeted with a couple of fine-looking Turkish rugs, but they were in need of a good beating, speckled with dirt and dust. It was a lived-in room, a home, and I felt like the intruder I was.

I didn't know what to do with myself so I searched for distraction in the paintings on the walls: a few oils of pretty vistas and a couple of dainty silhouettes. Some cases of butterflies caught my eye and I moved closer to them. Their wings were remarkable: gaudy violets and acid yellows; shots of burning red and umber; flecks of bright blue and jet black. Some were enormous and some as tiny as a ha'penny. A large Peacock stood out for its familiarity, its wings splayed, its colours dim. Alec had caught one once and pinned it to a card. He'd put it on the mantelpiece in our bedroom, but the wings had lost their lustre without the quiver of the evening breeze or the frenzied, startled fluttering that seemed to make them glow even brighter, and when they fell to pieces months later, it was almost as if it had died all over again.

I heard Wilfred approaching and hastily stepped back from the frames. He looked up and smiled faintly as he entered the room. 'Won't be long.'

I froze. I couldn't think of a single appropriate thing to say.

'Do sit down,' he offered.

I chose the sofa furthest from him and sat primly as he moved to the sideboard and poured himself a large whisky from a glittering crystal decanter. 'You don't mind, do you?'

I shook my head.

Just then a young maid entered which made me jump, although I tried to hide it. She was carrying a silver tray with a dainty, steaming teapot, a tiny jug, and cup and saucer on it. She looked about my age, though thinner and dark-haired, and she avoided my eye as she placed the tray down on the little table and gathered up the empty cups. Thank God I didn't recognise her; I didn't want anyone else finding out I'd been here. I half expected Wilfred to introduce us but then realised that one wasn't supposed to acknowledge servants, which made me feel pretentious and more out of place than ever. I couldn't stop thanking her anyway, to which she bobbed, although refused to look at me.

'Will that be all, sir?'

Wilfred nodded and the girl left, shutting the door behind her. I watched dumbfounded as he came over and delicately poured me some tea. 'Milk?'

'Just a dash.'

His mouth twitched with a smile and he handed me the cup, then sat down on the sofa opposite me. 'You must be wondering who that man was.'

'It's none of my business.'

'His name is Wing Commander Merrell. He is my godfather.' He paused as if I should answer or ask something else. 'He is also my commanding officer, and we were discussing my return to service.' He stared at his glass. 'I've been on leave for quite a while.' He made a breezy little gesture towards his scars as if that explained everything. 'But it's time for me to go back.'

'Will it be soon?' I hadn't meant to say it but somehow the peculiar intimacy of the situation we now found ourselves in authorised my prying.

Wilfred didn't look up from his glass.

I shifted awkwardly in my seat, sensing I'd overstepped the mark. My mouth was dry, and I took a sip of the hot tea. I felt the burn on my tongue like a blessed penance. 'I shouldn't have…'

Wilfred shook his head. 'No, no, please, there's no reason to apologise.' He looked up at me and I smiled back thinly but every bone in my body wanted to leave. He turned his focus to his drink, and I realised in the sunlit silence that followed that my question was still unanswered.

The room ticked and waited for words, and I found my eyes resting on his scars again. But then he looked up and caught me staring, and I turned hastily towards the grand marble mantelpiece, away from his candid gaze. There was a tarnished silver photograph frame there, a young woman's face trapped behind the glass; a soft-focus studio portrait, making her look almost like a Hollywood actress. Dark hair and smoky eyes. Skin like porcelain. Her heavy diamond earrings gleamed like clusters of stars.

'My mother,' Wilfred said, following my gaze.

It was the first image I'd seen of her. I hadn't imagined she'd been so beautiful. The captain had always been an old man to me and Mrs Whitman's reputation as a disdainful snob had painted her as a drawn, ugly woman in my mind. This was the star of Alec's ghost stories, the woman who supposedly met her end at the hands of her husband and now haunted the Manor and its grounds. That horrible day at the lake flashed in my memory again, the foggy water and the withered old captain on the shore. Was he really a murderer? I wished my tea would cool so I could drink it faster.

'How long have you been working at the Post Office?' Wilfred asked.

'A couple of years. Since Mrs B's – that is, since Mrs Bainbridge's son was called up.'

He nodded. 'Do you enjoy it?'

'Very much.'

'Why?'

I hesitated, surprised by the question and unsure why he'd

asked it. 'Because it's active, and useful.' I could feel my cheeks flushing.

'You could join a service.'

'I can't leave my father and brother.' I said it so quickly it sounded like an excuse. But it was true, wasn't it?

He nodded, whipped a silver cigarette case from his pocket and offered me one.

'Thank you.'

He lit my cigarette and handed it to me. It tasted like expensive chocolate. 'And how old is your brother?' he asked, as if he was completely unaware of the effect he was having on me.

I tore my thoughts away from his beautiful eyes, back to Alec, and my insides turned with that familiar dread. 'He'll be eighteen next week. We're twins.'

He nodded slowly, touched his scars and smiled apprehensively before adding, 'And your *friend*,' he hesitated, clearing his throat awkwardly, 'the one you were with at the wedding?'

In a hot second every detail of those moments with Cliff behind the church hall came rushing back to me, and I fought the urge to bury my face in my hands and scream. There was no escaping the truth now. 'Cliff left for his training last week.'

Wilfred exhaled slowly and the room was filled with a shifting haze of smoke. 'And you two are engaged?' He wasn't even going to pretend he hadn't heard.

'No, we're not engaged.'

'Oh?'

'No.' I couldn't bring myself to look at him. 'Not yet, anyway.' Why did I say that?

Suddenly Wilfred got up and opened the French windows, allowing the crisp air to rush inside. 'Seems like too nice an afternoon to be cooped up indoors. Come and see the garden.'

There was nothing I could do but put down my tea and follow him outside onto the great terrace, into the dazzling sunshine. In front of us, the Manor's huge lawn stretched down past informal, burgeoning flowerbeds and vegetable plots to a green painted fence and the wheat field beyond. And there, in the distance, was the twinkle of water through trees: the lake.

Behind me, the Manor's friendlier face gazed up at the flat blue sky. I felt like I'd fallen down a rabbit hole into another world. I pictured Mrs B waiting back at the Post Office, the pile of ironing at home, the places I belonged. But here I was on the Manor's terrace, alone with Wilfred Whitman. What did he want from me? I couldn't stop thinking about Cliff and how disappointed he'd be in me. My head was reeling with him, and Wilfred and Alec; they were all getting jumbled up in my mind and I couldn't work out who I was aching for the most. I felt wrung out and disorientated.

Wilfred turned to me. He still had his drink in his hand and he took another sip. The sunlight glared critically onto his face, ignoring his fine features and exhibiting his scars in all their unsightly anger. There seemed to be such an overwhelming sadness emanating from him, but perhaps it was just the pity I felt. The longer we spent together the less I felt I could bear it. There was a great grief waking in me, a bitter sense of loss, probably owing to Alec's imminent departure, but I sensed the tide of tears within me, rising to break free. 'I should go.' As soon as I said it I wished I hadn't. Despite all the unease, despite knowing I shouldn't be there, I realised then that I wanted to stay.

Wilfred avoided my eye, nodded to himself. 'Of course. But before you do, can I ask you something, Grace?'

I stiffened, sensing this was the real reason he'd invited me in. There was something ominous in his tone. I almost shuddered in trepidation.

'I'm interested to know, what do people say about me?'

I felt the weight of his words and swallowed loudly. I could think of a hundred things people said about him – and his parents – but wished to tell him none of them. Why should he care anyway, an intelligent, wealthy man like him? He was separate from us. He barely even lived here.

Wilf refused my reticence. 'Tell me, please.'

'Does it matter?' But he wouldn't let me off the hook. He wanted an answer and he would wait for one. My heart thudded hard and heavy in my chest. 'Some people say you've got shell shock.' I thought I saw him smile for a brief moment, but I must have been mistaken.

'So, they think I'm mad?' His tone was almost light.

I looked away, ashamed.

'Is that what you think?'

My opinion was surely irrelevant. I was just the post girl and we'd barely spoken before today. But on daring to look at him again, his eyes seemed so large, as if his heart was trying to escape through them, and I found myself saying truthfully, 'I don't know what to think.'

He looked to the heavens as if he couldn't bring himself to say anything further. It seemed he was angry with me. Perhaps I should have lied. I certainly didn't want to believe any of the rumours about him but I couldn't read him now, and nothing he'd said or done so far could be described as normal.

He finished his cigarette and stabbed it into an ashtray on the wrought iron table behind him. I wished I could put mine in it too but didn't want to stretch past him and get even closer, so I held on to it.

He squared his shoulders. 'It's not true.'

I forced the smallest of smiles, frightened by the hint of aggression in his tone, frightened of him entirely. 'I'm glad.'

'You are?'

'Of course.'

'Why?'

He asked too many questions. 'Because it's a horrible thing.'

He finished his drink and put the empty glass on the table. Without anything in his hands he seemed vulnerable again. He shoved them in his pockets and looked down at his shoes. 'This war is a horrible thing,' he said softly, and cleared his throat. His eyes looked glassy.

I couldn't stand this any longer. 'I must go, Wilfred.' His name felt so odd on my lips.

He nodded. 'Yes.'

When I went to stub out my cigarette, I caught his warm, exotic fragrance again, and moving away from him felt like breaking a promise.

Back inside, the room still smelled of hot fabric and dust. He led me to the hallway and handed me my jacket and cap. 'Good afternoon, Grace. And thank you.' His gaze was raw and earnest, his face momentarily in shadow, his sapphire eyes almost black.

I nodded politely, stepping quickly into the familiarity of the front porch and driveway, the gateway to normality. My relief was tangible; my hands shook as I mounted my bicycle. He kept his eyes on me, his stare indecipherable, and I felt the nearness of him as pressure in my bones, desperate to be free of him so I could breathe again.

'Goodbye, Grace.'

'Goodbye, Wilfred.' There was nothing left to be said, so I peddled away, half hoping that would be the end of it, but somehow feeling that this was only the beginning, that Wilfred Whitman and I would surely cross paths again.

CHAPTER 7

On Wednesday morning I was mid-round when I noticed a sleek, black car parked outside the church gate, and knew it instantly as the Whitman's, since no one else in the village could have afforded one like it. There was no sign of Wilfred, but as I carried on with my deliveries I could feel the presence of him nearby like a ghost, and the predictability of our meeting again held me in such unbearable suspense that I passed the church several times just to try and get it out of the way. Though we were apparently on first name terms I wasn't sure if he'd even want to acknowledge me. We'd only ever spoken in private, away from prying eyes. What would people say if they saw me passing the time of day with Wilfred Whitman in the village?

Mrs B had already questioned me about it. After my sojourn at the Manor she'd been full of questions about my tardiness. It was on the tip of my tongue to tell her about Wilfred and his extraordinary behaviour. I was so tempted to share the odd things he'd said to me and describe the Manor's interior and gardens. But in the end my conscience persuaded me to protect my secret, so I lied about stopping for a rest and feeling tired, and Mrs B felt my forehead and frowned.

Since then, I hadn't been able to stop thinking about him,

playing the afternoon over and over in my imagination until I was no longer sure how it had happened. Every time I shut my eyes I saw his face so clearly, I felt I could reach out and touch the point where his scar met his lip. It distracted me from worrying about Alec, at least, but I found it no less unsettling.

I carried on with my round, expecting Wilfred around every corner, and feeling a queer mixture of relief and disappointment when he wasn't there. I found I was dawdling, eking out the delivery for as long as possible. With each second I grew more impatient and more anxious, so by the time I stopped to chat with a neighbour about the previous night's raid, I was practically shaking with nerves. I crossed near the church one last time before returning to the Post Office. The car was still there, but the churchyard was deserted, the great wooden door shut, and I guessed Wilfred was inside talking to Reverend Dearling. Perhaps we weren't destined to meet again today after all.

The Post Office bell tinkled above me as I went inside, yawning.

'Ah, here she is,' said Mrs B in a rather controlled voice, and I looked up and stopped dead in my tracks. 'Flight Lieutenant Whitman's been waiting for you.'

Wilfred was standing by the counter, in shirtsleeves with his hat in his hand. Behind him, Mrs B glared at me with narrow eyes that demanded answers, and I knew that I wouldn't be able to get away with any fibbing later.

'I hope you don't mind,' Wilfred said. 'I was in the village and just wanted to…' he stopped and looked at Mrs B, whose sudden, unnatural smile looked more like a grimace. 'Actually, Mrs Bainbridge, I was wondering if you could spare Grace for a few minutes?' He turned to me again. 'I was wondering if we could take a quick walk together?'

My pulse was drumming so hard I was sure he could hear

it. I'd been preparing myself to see him again, but not like this. My thoughts were all panic. 'A walk?' I said it like he'd suggested we swim the Channel.

'I suppose so,' said Mrs B with more than a little suspicion. 'Just for a few minutes, mind.'

'Yes, of course, thank you.'

Wilfred started towards me. I was so alarmed I could have run from him. I felt the blush burn my face but couldn't break his gaze. He seemed much taller in the cramped familiarity of the Post Office. I caught the scent of his aftershave again, noticed his broad shoulders beneath his thin shirt and thought how strong, how masculine he seemed today, far from the nervous man I'd taken tea with.

He opened the door for me and the bell jingled. I stepped outside and we stood in silence for a moment.

'You're surprised to see me,' he said.

I didn't need to answer. Of course I was surprised to find him waiting for *me*. I wanted to ask him what he was really doing here but couldn't find a single word.

'I had an appointment with the reverend and I wanted to see you before I left.'

I hesitated, confused but secretly thrilled. I'd told myself I'd been dreading seeing him again, but standing beside him now I knew that wasn't true. I'd missed him, strange as that seemed, but the realisation was both a revelation and damnation, and my joy quickly turned to guilt.

Wilfred gestured towards the church. 'Shall we walk?'

There were a few people outside their houses who looked up in curiosity as Wilfred and I walked past slowly, side by side. I wished them all gone. I would have to explain myself now; Mrs B, Dad, Alec and even Doris would all hear about this. And Cliff, eventually. They'd all ask what I'd been doing with Wilfred Whitman, and what would I say? I didn't even know the answer to that myself.

'I'm rather used to it now,' Wilfred said. 'The staring.' He was referring to his scars. I remembered people's reactions to him at Doris's wedding.

'I don't think they're staring at you. I think they're staring at *us*.'

He put his hat on and cleared his throat. 'Perhaps you're ashamed to be seen with me.'

'No! No, but I think people are surprised to see us together.' I didn't blame them; I could hardly believe it myself.

He looked down at me and smiled a warm, easy smile. His scars were almost hidden from view and the skin on the left side of his face was extraordinarily smooth. 'I just wanted to apologise for the other day,' he said, looking ahead. 'It's becoming a bit of a habit isn't it, apologising every time I see you?'

'I arrived at a bad time.'

He nodded. 'Yes, but it doesn't excuse my behaviour. I shouldn't have invited you in. You didn't want to talk and I shouldn't have asked you all those questions.'

He was wrong, I had wanted to come in and talk to him, though I might not have realised it at the time. Perhaps he shouldn't have pressed me to tell him what people thought of him, but I didn't want him to think I disliked him; the very idea that he might made me panic. 'Please don't feel bad,' I said as we reached his car. 'Mrs B says that a post girl sees and hears everything but knows nothing.' She would always tap her nose and wink when she told me that.

'You're very gracious, Grace.' He laughed at himself.

The sound of that laugh and the sight of his jagged smile moved me, and I heard myself saying, 'You can call me Gracie.' Only the people who knew me well enough called me that.

He nodded, and I thought I saw him smile again, though he

brought his hand up to his scars as he did it. 'Well, most people seem to call me Whitman nowadays, but it was always Wilf before that.'

We filled the little silence that followed with light, nervous laughs, and I sensed we'd crossed an indefinable line.

'But I don't know many people around here,' he went on. 'I only remember fragments of my childhood before we left.' He cleared his throat. 'And by the time Father moved back I'd finished university and was doing business in London.' He made it all sound so ordinary, as if everyone's father 'moved back' from a decade away in a madhouse and all young people went to university and then on to London. He could almost convince me that he was as rational as they come, but I couldn't forget everything he'd said at the Manor, his edginess, and his very being here with me in broad daylight on a sunny August morning. Our company, our friendship – if that's what it was – was incompatible, and I felt like we were both being too polite to mention it. But at some point we'd have to admit it, turn around, and head back to our very different homes and very different lives.

'I never really got an opportunity to make connections,' he was saying.

I didn't imagine that Barnfield was the kind of place people like him made 'connections'. Nor did I point out that none of the Whitmans had ever tried to integrate with the village, that they were notoriously detached and reclusive and didn't even employ servants from Barnfield, much to the locals' chagrin. Mrs B had told me that even the socialite Mrs Whitman, before she died, had shunned local life, earning her reputation as a snob. Instead, I asked, 'And will you move back to the Manor?'

'It's my base for the moment. Our Kensington house was damaged by a bomb last month.'

'Oh, I'm sorry.'

He shook his head. 'It wasn't a direct hit. I hope to be able to patch it up, one day. And I ought to pay some attention to the Manor.' He leaned forward and said, almost conspiratorially, 'It's fallen into a bit of a state over the years, I'm afraid. The whole estate's been neglected – all the books need seeing to, the cottages, the farm – but it's a little more than my father can manage at the moment.' He held my gaze, a knowing look.

'And you can manage it?' I hadn't meant to sound so uncertain, but his little smile immediately relieved my humiliation.

'I think I already told you – I'm not mad, Gracie.' He was so close now I could feel the heat of him on my face. He was smiling and I tried to as well, but I was caught in his blue gaze and my pulse was thrumming and it took all my strength not to step away. I knew people were watching us. I didn't want to give them anything to talk about, anything more than they already had.

In a moment Wilfred stood tall again. 'I hope I'll have a chance to get to know the village better in the future, when all of this is over.' I sensed there was something behind his words, something he was hiding. I didn't know him at all, but he seemed to be a man of secrets. 'But it'll have to wait. I'm leaving first thing on Monday morning.'

I felt my heart sink and hoped it didn't show. I wanted to ask what position he held but I couldn't get past my nerves. No one had ever had such an effect on me. It was natural to be shy around strangers and people I wouldn't normally mix with, but it was more than that with Wilfred. With *Wilf.* I knew what it was, but I didn't want to believe it. I felt my insides twisting and breaking and hated myself for being so stupid.

We walked to the driver's door and Wilf put his hand on the

polished handle. 'I should probably leave her at home and cycle like you, what with the petrol rationing,' he said, his tone a little more confident. 'But I've always enjoyed driving. One of life's pleasures. And I don't have much cause to do it.'

I looked down at the gleaming paintwork, glass and chrome, lost for words.

'Have you ever ridden in one?' he asked me.

'A car?'

'A Bentley.'

'Oh! No!' The idea of it made me laugh. I'd ridden in a car a couple of times and found it claustrophobic compared to the bus to Finton.

'Well I'd be glad to take you out for a spin,' he offered casually, opening the door, the scent of sunlight on leather and motor oil rushing out.

I hesitated, dumbstruck, trying to find an answer in the car's shiny mirrors or Wilf's open face. Was he really inviting me out with him? 'I don't think that would be a good idea,' I said evenly – miraculously – bearing in mind the hammering of my heart.

Wilf's mouth twitched in a smile. 'You're right.' He looked back at the church, squinted. 'Well, perhaps we'll bump into each other again before I go.'

'Perhaps.'

'And I promise I'll be the perfect gentleman if we do,' he said with newfound buoyancy as he climbed into the driver's seat. 'No short fuses or hiding round corners.'

I couldn't help smiling, captivated by his vulnerable charm. Every moment with him was extraordinary. I'd found it disconcerting at first, but now, on the point of him leaving, it seemed strangely thrilling, and worth every risk that came with it.

He started the engine and held his hand up in a wave, shut the door and wound down the window. 'Bye, Gracie.' The car purred as he drove away.

'Goodbye, Wilf,' I replied, but was certain he hadn't heard me.

I returned to the Post Office with a falsely casual air that dissolved as soon as I saw Mrs B leaning against the counter with her arms folded. 'What on earth did he want?' she said sharply.

It was impossible to pretend it was nothing, but in truth, I didn't really know what he'd wanted. He'd come to find me, ostensibly to apologise, but it seemed he'd wanted to talk more than anything.

Mrs B rolled her eyes at my silence. 'Gracie, that man has not once stepped foot in here, and today he waited for ten minutes just for *you*. How does he even know your name?'

'He asked.'

'When?'

I wondered if I'd have to tell her everything, or get away with keeping some of it to myself. 'When I delivered the telegram the other day.'

She sucked her teeth. 'I see.'

'He just wanted to apologise.'

'For what?'

'He was a little short with me then.'

A look of concern passed across Mrs B's face, the kind she'd always adopted when Alec and I had got ourselves into trouble. I was reminded of a hundred scraped knees, of quivering bottom lips and coming home from school with a note and my tail between my legs. 'Did he threaten you?'

I laughed. 'Of course not!'

She frowned, unsure – of him or my reaction, I couldn't tell. 'What did he say?'

'I'm not sure I can remember.'

Her nostrils flared and my cheeks burned. 'It seems a bit excessive to come all the way out here just to apologise for being short with you.'

I couldn't argue with that. But then I remembered, 'He was seeing the Reverend.'

She raised her eyebrows. 'Was he now?'

'He just told me.'

Mrs B huffed. 'Someone ought to tell *him* you're engaged.'

I felt the blood rush to my cheeks again. I wasn't going to tell her that he already knew, and I hadn't the strength to argue that in fact, it wasn't even true. Instead, I pretended to be affronted. 'What are you suggesting?' But it didn't wash with Mrs B.

'You know very well, Gracie.' She waved a finger at me. 'Don't act as if you don't know what men are like, and women too for that matter.'

'I really don't think there was anything untoward about it,' I carried on, lying through my teeth, thinking of how my pulse had leapt on seeing him and how he'd asked me to go for a drive. Was that why he'd really been waiting for me?

'Be that as it may, you'll have set tongues wagging, no doubt.'

I glanced at the window. The road was empty where Wilf's car had been moments before.

'I've never seen your face that colour.'

I felt a shiver of cold guilt. Was she teasing, or could she see right through me?

'Flight Lieutenant Whitman's a handsome man,' she went on.

I had to clear my throat before saying, weakly, 'Yes, he is.'

'But so is Cliff.'

I tried to laugh. 'I'm sure half the girls in Finton would agree with that.'

She let her stern look fall away. 'Is that what this is

about? Cliff may have done his fair share of gallivanting about in the past, but, let me tell you, he's soft on you. I should know. I've watched you all grow up and I know what you're like. I know you like to play it down, but you love Cliff, Gracie, and he loves you. You do realise that, don't you?'

I couldn't answer. She'd always been able to read me, but she was wrong this time. I wasn't playing it down. Yes, I loved Cliff, he was as much a part of my life as Barnfield, and I couldn't imagine being without him. But I didn't love him enough to be his wife, to give up my independence and devote myself to him for the rest of my life. It was the truth, and I'd taken it for granted that she and Cliff and Alec and everyone would understand that because they understood me. But they didn't. I suddenly felt so alone.

Mrs B must have thought I was being contrite. She added, 'The Whitmans are a queer bunch. You ought to keep your distance.'

'But what happens if another letter arrives for the Manor before he leaves?'

'Before he leaves?'

I'd put my foot in it again. 'On Monday.'

She nodded slowly. 'You talked about that then, did you? What else did you chat about?' Her glare was too accusing.

'I was just being polite.'

Mrs B walked into the back room, calling out behind her, 'If another letter arrives for the Manor, I'll deliver it. Better to be safe than sorry.'

CHAPTER 8

On the morning of our eighteenth birthday, I rose early to cook the bacon I'd saved for our breakfast, only to find Dad up already, scraping some scrambled eggs onto a couple of plates by the stove. 'I thought you deserved a rest. Happy birthday, my dear.' I kissed him on the cheek, then said I'd go and wake Alec, but he told me not to, placing the plates on the table and taking a seat. 'Let him sleep. I'll make his later.'

The sun was already streaming in through the window, and the day held the promise of warmth: the perfect summer's day, ripe and lazy, the kind to be carefree with friends. I wondered what Cliff and Jean were doing today, if the sun shone on them too. I thought of Alec snoring in his bed, and the excitement he'd feel on waking, not for any birthday presents or celebrations, but for the papers due to arrive in a matter of days. I was glad I had to go to work; I didn't think I could bear his joy. Perhaps that's why Dad let him sleep. But I couldn't help hoping, as we ate our eggs side by side, that maybe he was building up to say something to me, something suitably auspicious for the occasion. Some nugget of wisdom that would relieve my anxieties and carry me through to brighter days.

In the end, he pushed his knife and fork together, squeezed

my hand, and told me he'd wash up. He said Mrs B would pop round in the evening with a cake, and we'd celebrate our transfer into adulthood with a sip of the good sherry.

I left my sleeping brother with a kiss on his forehead and smiled fondly at the clothes strewn across his bedroom floor, the half-drunk cup of tea on his bedside table. But my throat tightened at the old collection of conkers lying cracked and dull on his mantelpiece, and the pencil marks on the doorjamb where Mrs B had measured us as children. How could a day make so much difference? How could this boy now be a man, ready to leave the country with a gun in his hand? That I was now a woman never even crossed my mind.

My spirits were buoyed later when I found a letter from Cliff in the postbag. I held on to it like a promise, keeping it unopened in my pocket all morning while I did my rounds. Mrs B had knitted me a cardigan for when the weather turned cooler, and she sang *Happy Birthday* to me over a cup of tea, pretending the tears in her eyes were from the steam. Our discussion about Wilfred was forgotten, and when I told her about Cliff's letter I was pleased at how genuinely excited and relieved I felt about it.

After we'd shut up the Post Office I sauntered towards the church, turning the letter over in my fingers, noticing the smudge on the address, my name underlined. It was the first letter I'd ever received from a man and the only token Cliff had ever given me. I thought about taking it home, but didn't want Alec looking over my shoulder the whole time. He'd been waiting for a letter as much as I had – probably more so – but I felt like I needed to open it alone.

I jumped the stile and headed out towards the Manor Woods and our old camping spot: a worn clearing watched over by trees that encircled it like guardian angels. I settled down on the ground, leaning my back against a tree, smiling as I remembered one particular night, when Cliff had fallen asleep before Alec and me, and we'd watched a huge beetle crawl up onto his face. Cliff had woken with a start and a cry, and Alec had nearly passed out from hysterics. I pictured Cliff's heavy-eyed, grouchy face, and how he'd been in a foul mood afterwards. It seemed an age ago now. I shut my eyes and wished he was back here with us and nothing had changed, that any moment now I'd hear his footsteps crackling through the undergrowth and see him walking towards us with a string of fish flung over his shoulder.

I tore open the envelope. His letter was short, as expected, just one side, beginning with birthday wishes for Alec and me. Cliff didn't ask a lot of questions. The busyness of life's minutiae didn't interest him and I doubted it occurred to him that I might want to know what he did all day, if he'd made friends, if he ever got nervous or excited or homesick. He gave me no details about his training. Was he allowed to tell me things like that? Doris had shown me some of Ron's letters, with big blacked out lines halfway through paragraphs. But Cliff just wrote that they were being fed well and he didn't miss my cooking one bit. He would have short leave once training was over and would write ahead to warn me. He asked how we were all doing and if I was getting lonely without him.

There was no mention of his proposal or renewal of his feelings but I sensed them hiding behind each word. It seemed a very carefully worded letter for a man like Cliff to write to his sweetheart, unless he'd anticipated I'd share it with Dad and Alec. Even so, he didn't even sign it 'Yours', only stopped writing and scribbled his name. I reread it a few times and wondered if I was imagining things; I doubted Cliff had put that much thought into it. Most likely he'd just written it in a hurry.

I folded the paper and popped it in my breast pocket. It was just the kind of letter Cliff should write – admittedly I wouldn't have known how to react if he'd told me he loved me or how thoughts of me kept him going or any of the usual sap. There was nothing to move me except the letter itself, an alien thing from someone who'd never had cause to write to me before. I was pleased he was doing well, but my sadness stirred again, and I stayed in the woods for over an hour. I couldn't bring myself to stand up. I was worn-out after a morning's work in the rising August heat, and the letter only served to remind me that Cliff was gone and Alec was soon to follow.

What if I hadn't stayed there? What if I'd gone straight home with the letter? I certainly didn't plan what happened next.

When I finally got up, legs weary, the pang of hunger in my stomach, I just turned and began walking on through the trees towards the hill brow, towards the lake, as we'd always done on hot days like this. I wasn't thinking of swimming. I wasn't thinking of Wilf or even crazy Captain Whitman and that day when Cliff had rescued me. Perhaps it was fate's hand guiding my footsteps, or maybe I knew on some level what would happen. But in all honesty, I was just hot and tired. I was half thinking of Cliff's letter, half planning what to piece together for our birthday supper from the larder's dregs.

The field leading down to the lake was thick with wheat; in a few weeks Goffman and the land girls would be harvesting it. Harvest was Cliff's favourite time of year – every dusk brought drink and a satisfying sense of exhaustion. I thought of him as I stepped cautiously through a thin track left by the tractor, trying not to trample too many stalks. The heat had thickened, and the few wispy clouds seemed motionless in the pale blue sky. A milky haze covered the trees beyond the lake like a drape of voile. The crickets sang as spiky ears scratched my elbows; I'd left my jacket at the Post Office and had rolled my sleeves up, but I was still overdressed for the heat. I dabbed my sweaty brow as I strolled on towards the trees and the shining lake. Only then did I think of swimming in the cool water and tried to shrug off the irritable flash of fear that followed. I was cross with myself for letting it bother me still, but I couldn't shake the sense of the water falling away beneath me. Captain Whitman's stern, erratic face. The intense relief when Cliff pulled me up.

Reaching the cool shade of the trees felt like entering another world, the water sparkling and burning my eyes as I cracked and snapped my way through the undergrowth. I'd made up my mind not to swim but perhaps just have a little paddle in the shallows. On this side of the lake the trees and shrubs thickened at the banks, so I planned to head further round towards the little shore and the boathouse. But I stopped before I'd even turned towards it.

The boat was out on the water, and Wilf was in it. He'd seen me already and was looking my way, although he was too far away for me to make out his expression. The boat bobbed up and down a little and he sat there with the oars in his hands and his sleeves rolled up as far as they would go. He looked relaxed, the complete opposite of how I felt. As he started rowing easily towards me I thought about running back out into the shimmering heat of the field, but my legs were planted amidst the weeds and exposed roots, and instead I just watched him come closer. I sensed the draw of blood from my head to my chest with each shallow breath.

Just a few days ago we'd walked together in the village and he'd casually said goodbye. But would I have been content never to see him again, even after the warning Mrs B had given me, even with Cliff's letter in my pocket now? Whatever had begun between us felt unfinished. There were questions I longed to ask him, about his face, his family, his war. I felt a great, physical craving to know and understand him better, and all of a sudden – with the sun on his back as he glided towards me – anything seemed possible.

I felt I ought to apologise for trespassing, but Wilf's expression was anything but angry. He smiled gently and kept his eyes on me. I thought he might call out something like 'hello again' or 'what a surprise', but he stayed silent. He looked so content and tranquil, as if we were old friends and he'd been waiting for me to arrive. But he couldn't have anticipated my being here, I hadn't known it myself until my feet had found their way to this spot; yet there did seem to me to be a kind of inevitability about it. It felt almost as if I'd been waiting for this moment since the first time I'd seen him at Doris's wedding. It suddenly made perfect sense to be standing on the bank of the lake with this strange man as he threw a rope over a tree stump and pulled his boat towards me.

'A beautiful afternoon,' he said easily as he stood and held out his hand.

There was no invitation. There was no question that I wouldn't be joining him.

A smile crept to my lips. His grip was firm and reassuring as I teetered off the bank and into the little dingy. I found a seat amongst a net and some empty jam jars.

Wilf nodded to my uniform. 'Are you finished for the day?'

'Yes.'

'You're not in a hurry, are you?'

I wasn't annoyed with him for being presumptuous, or even surprised. There was something boyish and delightful in his tone, and I smiled at his informality; it warmed me and united us somehow. The whole situation was absurd but we'd both embraced it and were acting as if it was perfectly normal, although my heartbeat soared. There was no doubt now of the attraction between us. I tried to block out Mrs B's voice in my head and convince myself I was in control, but truthfully every second that passed seemed to draw me closer to him and I wasn't sure how long I could resist him. I must have known, the moment I stepped off that bank, that I had already surrendered to him.

'No, I'm not in a hurry.'

'Good,' he said with a secretive grin, casting off, and I felt a dull pull in my stomach, like pain, only sweeter.

The oars cut through the bronzed water effortlessly. As we left the bank behind, I sensed the murky depth beneath us and found my hands gripping the little seat. I felt dizzy all of a sudden, remembering the taste of the lake in my mouth, the stories of his mother's death, the intensity of my nightmares. I cast my eyes down to the net and the jars. 'Are you fishing?'

There was a glimmer of mischief in his eyes. 'No, wait and see.' A slight breeze rippled his thin shirt. His tanned arms flexed with each pull on the oars and I held the seat tighter to save myself from reaching out to them. How ludicrous to feel so attracted to a man I knew to be odd and secretive, a man I didn't even trust. Was this how I was meant to see Cliff? But I doubted anyone could feel such thrills for a boy they'd grown up with, and surely Wilf was more attractive because he was unfamiliar? Perhaps it was just pure lust, but I'd never wanted anyone with such a tangible ache as I felt for him in that moment.

He was rowing us towards the island at the far end of the lake. As we got closer, I saw a cluster of large buddleias there, past their best but still a riot of colour, heavy lilac and white blooms absolutely teeming with butterflies. I'd never seen so many. They filled the sky like confetti. Wilf hadn't even turned to look at them; he was watching me.

'Amazing, aren't they? I used to come here when I was a child,' he said quickly, reaching for the rope again and drawing us up to the lush bank. 'It seems to be a good year for them. I used to enjoy catching them but haven't done it for ages.'

I looked again at the jars and the net and realised the point of the excursion. Wilf gathered them up in his arms and threw them one by one onto the island; there was no danger of them shattering in the dense undergrowth. He stood and leapt quickly from the boat, finding a footing and holding out those golden-brown arms for me, like a hero from a storybook. As he helped me up I felt he held on to me a little longer than necessary, but I didn't care. I caught his eyes briefly; they were bluer than ever.

He trampled down some of the greenery so we had a small area to stand in. He picked up the net and handed it to me. 'Why don't you have a go?'

I hadn't tried catching butterflies since I was a small child. I aimed near the buddleias, but despite the abundance of insects my attempt was embarrassingly fruitless.

He gestured to help me. 'May I?'

I let him move to stand behind me. He leant forward, brought his arms round the front of me and guided my hands further apart. A thread of energy seemed to pulse through his fingertips and shot straight to my chest; I felt it cave with my exhale, acutely aware of his arms pressed against mine and his scars just inches from my face.

He stepped back. 'Try it now.'

I took another swoop and as I brought the net down, saw a couple of butterflies fluttering frantically within. Wilf crouched down, took one of the jars and guided it into the net, carefully trapping them inside. He sat on the ground and held the jar up in front of him, scrutinising the captives. 'Red Admiral and Comma.'

I knelt beside him warily. 'How ordinary.'

'None of them are ordinary.' He passed the jar to me. 'Not really, see?'

I stared at the creatures' bright, frail wings, then imagined them in a dusty case back at the Manor and felt a heavy sense of disenchantment. Those wings could not stay brilliant forever, even pinned to a card, or caged in a case. One day the colours would perish and the wings disintegrate to powder.

'We'll let them go,' Wilf said, as if reading my thoughts. 'Unless you want to keep them.'

'You don't?'

He shook his head, his lip catching on his tooth in a charming way; I couldn't be sure if it was deliberate. 'Do you know the ancient Egyptians used to think butterflies were the souls of the dead?'

I frowned at the bright fluttering wings behind the glass. 'Like angels?'

He glanced at me with half a smile. 'I suppose so.'

'I saw the ones at the Manor. Did you catch them?'

'No, they were my mother's. She caught some here and collected the rest... I'm not sure where from. She loved their colours.' He left a short pause, long enough for a sting of unease to pass through me, remembering the grisly stories of her death, and thinking immediately of what Wilf had said about the butterflies as souls. I suppressed a shiver. Was it Mrs Whitman's ghost visiting us now? Perhaps she'd been with me that day in the water too.

Wilf took the jar back, unscrewed the lid and let the butterflies dance high up into the air. 'I never keep them. I expect you'll think I'm soft, but I don't really see the point in it anymore. If beauty still exists, then let it exist. There's not much of it around nowadays.' He gave me a self-effacing smile, then lifted his head to watch the butterflies disappear amongst the others. But I kept my eyes on his face, on the blackness of his eyelashes, the line of his brow, the ochre glow of unscarred skin.

He shifted, bent his leg and rested his elbow on his knee. He nodded towards the empty net on the ground. 'Do you want another go, or are you happy to sit for a while? It is rather hot.' He unbuttoned his collar and I tried not to stare at the further scarring there. Did it cover his whole body? His arms looked so smooth and perfect, I could only imagine the rest of him so too. I swallowed loudly, and moved slightly away from him, disoriented by his proximity. The afternoon was turning muggy, the air soupy with heat and pollen, and I could feel fresh sweat on my chest and neck.

'It really is a beautiful spot, Wilf.' I blushed as soon as I said his name, but I liked the sound of it.

Wilf tried to hide his smile too. 'Mother and I used to come here together. Years and years ago, before I even went away to school. I'm surprised I even remember it.' He gazed at the butterflies again and seemed lost for a moment, and I was touched by the intimacy of the memory, the mentions of his mother. But a shudder ran through me at the thought of those old ghost stories. I was embarrassed to think badly of her now, with her son right in front of me. Her reputation had forged my opinion of her, but what did I really know, other than she'd favoured London above Barnfield and had wanted little to do with it and its residents? She'd been Wilf's mother after all, and surely he missed her, probably more than I missed mine.

'I think about this place occasionally, in the summer, when I know they'll be crowding,' he muttered.

'It's very peaceful.'

His eyes met mine again. 'Surely we all have places like this?'

I'd once felt that way about the lake too, before the day I'd seen his mad father on the shore. The memory of him standing there made me quail and jolted me back to the sweltering present. I wondered if Wilf would mention him today, or if I'd have the courage to ask, but he was lost in his train of thought, caught up in the fairy-tale of the butterflies above us.

'I often thought about this place when we we're flying, too,' he carried on hesitantly, his voice small.

I felt the mood shift, and sensed that if I wanted to ask him about his service and scars, it was now or never. 'Are you a pilot?'

He almost laughed. 'No, I *wanted* to be a pilot. I think all boys do.'

Not Alec. He'd dreamed of being a soldier since the first mutterings of war began.

'A few friends and I joined up as reservists as soon as we got the chance, once we knew what was coming. We were all keen.' Wilf's hand went to brush his cheek, and then he ran it around the back of his neck; I sensed the feeling of his skin there beneath my fingertips and the ache in my stomach again. 'One has no interest in furthering one's career when one's friends are off dying for the country.'

He looked as if he was about to apologise, but I didn't want him to stop talking. I could feel a barrier breaking down between us and couldn't bear for it to end. 'What's it like to fly?'

'It's another world,' he answered, looking around him and sighing slowly, as if he couldn't quite believe it existed at all.

'It must be like being a bird.' I felt stupid as soon as I'd said it, and his pitying little smile didn't relieve me.

'I hope not, for the birds' sakes.'

I knew I was bright red but thankfully he wasn't looking at me. He sighed out towards the water's reflections and went on, 'You live purely in that moment. No past or future. You can't really conceive anything beyond the plane and the crew.'

'What do you do?'

He cleared his throat. 'I'm a navigator. Not very glamorous, eh?'

'Is any of it glamorous?'

He forced a crooked smile. 'Quite.' His silence then was loaded with regret, his eyes full of sadness, and I wondered what scenes were playing in his memory. I was so desperate to ask what had happened to him. 'I was lucky with the RAF. Douglas, that is, my godfather – the man you saw outside the Manor a few days ago – he pulled some strings. But I did imagine it *would* be glamorous, if you can believe it. I rather naively thought I'd be flying fighters. I thought it would be... *fun*.'

I pictured Alec's enthusiasm and could well believe it.

'But I didn't make the grade. And there are no tricks and thrills with Bomber Command.' His tone was grave and cut straight through me. 'I couldn't have been an Army man like Father, not after, well...' He coughed and looked at me cautiously, as if weighing up whether or not to trust me. 'You know he spent some time in an institution?'

Of course I knew. Everyone knew.

Wilf sighed gently and looked away. 'People who know my father imagine the same thing may happen to me, as you told me yourself the other day.'

I wished I could contradict him, but people did imagine that. It was where all conversations about him seemed to end up. I still wondered about it myself, despite my feelings for him. I had never met someone so extraordinary – so candid, yet guarded too – so unpredictable. But that didn't make him mad, did it? 'My dad fought under your father in the war,' I said carefully. 'He says he was a good man.'

'He does? That's decent of him.' He took a deep breath. 'My father *is* a good man, Gracie. He's had to cope with a lot in his life.' His eyes were dark and sorrowful. He moved his hand and placed it over mine. His palm was warm. I looked down at his fingers on mine and tried to convince myself that it wasn't extraordinary. He didn't hold my gaze for long before moving his hand away, his fingertips lingering before breaking contact entirely. Then, as if it had never happened, he said, 'My father fought for two years in the trenches. But he lost his brother at the Somme, and after that, seemed to lose his nerve too. He tried to carry on but in the end they forced him to take leave. That was what did it. He came home but still heard the guns. He couldn't sleep. He…' he hesitated, 'he raised his hand to my mother for the first time.' His voice shook. 'I was only a baby, and my mother was frightened. She didn't know what to do. In the end, the doctors decided for her.'

I thought of all the times we'd ridiculed Captain Whitman as children, calling him a lunatic and a murderer. I couldn't bring myself to look Wilf in the eye. 'I'm so sorry.'

'He never recovered. He was sectioned and spent a long time in an institution. My mother visited him, but I wasn't allowed to. My first memory of him was when he was discharged. Mother said he ought to be here, that it was more peaceful than London, more like the hospital he was used to. I was still at school, but when the holidays arrived, I came here, and met him for the first time.'

I couldn't imagine what it must have been like for the young boy, who'd lived his whole life in the shadow of a father he'd never known, to finally come face to face with him. There was pain in Wilf's eyes as he spoke, and I didn't know what I'd done to deserve such openness from him. Each word was like a blessing, a secret bestowed.

'I needn't have been frightened of him,' Wilf continued. 'He was gentle. He wasn't well – he'll never be *well* – but he was harmless enough to live at home with a nurse. So, Mother and Douglas arranged everything.' His expression clouded. 'I've never been quite sure why they did it. Guilt, I suspect.'

'What do you mean?'

'I mean, they could have just left him in the hospital. He was well looked after – it wasn't Dickensian.'

'Why would they want to leave him there?'

'So Mother could have divorced him quietly and married Douglas. It was what she really wanted.'

I stared back at him in surprise, unsure what to say.

Wilf's face softened a little. 'I don't really blame her, not anymore.'

'They were having an affair?' There'd always been rumours, so I didn't know why I felt so shocked. Perhaps I'd thought it was just part of the ghost story. Maybe it was the nonchalant way Wilf spoke about it; it didn't seem to fit with the obvious affection he felt for his parents and godfather. Or maybe it was the fact that we barely knew each other, and these secret things had nothing to do with my world.

'I don't like the word "affair". It makes it sound so sordid. They were... partners. They loved each other. I understand that now. They both cared for Father. They found a way to make it work for all of them.'

'Did your… does your father know about them?'

Wilf shook his head. 'Thankfully he knows very little about anything nowadays. But it would hurt him to learn of it. He may be… distant sometimes, but he's still there, underneath it all, and he still has his pride.'

'But she and Douglas stayed together?' I felt so awkward, prying into business that wasn't my own, but Wilf seemed unfazed by my question.

'Yes, for a while. Then…well, things can change, can't they? They hit rocky ground.'

I nodded, but I felt so foolish. Here was a man who'd seen so much, knew about people and how they behaved, lived a far greater life than mine. I felt the gap between our ages stretching us further apart. Did he see me as the child I was? What did it matter that today was my first day of adulthood? I knew nothing.

He looked concerned again. 'I've burdened you, Gracie. I shouldn't have.' He turned his face up to the sun for a moment and when he looked back at me there was an embarrassed smile on his lips. 'And didn't I promise to be a perfect gentleman?'

I smiled gingerly, wondering if he'd somehow orchestrated my being here, if he'd always known we'd meet again.

'Come, I'm getting tired of hearing my voice. It's your turn to tell me something shocking.' He was teasing me, so I laughed, but I couldn't think what to say. Everything in my life was so ordinary compared to him. 'What were your plans before the war?' he pressed.

'I'm not sure I had any plans as such. I was only just fourteen.'

His jagged smile hid any embarrassment well. 'Well, what are your mother and father's plans for you?'

I hesitated. How was he to know I had no mother? 'My father is very generous,' I said cautiously. 'He would like me to have a home of my own but I'm lucky enough not to need to work.'

'But I thought you liked your work?' he said quickly.

'Yes, yes I do. But one day I won't be needed anymore.'

He must have heard the disappointment in my voice. He nodded slowly. 'I see. And what does your mother think?'

I cleared my throat. 'My mother died when Alec and I were very young. We never knew her.' I felt my face flush, not wanting his sympathy at all, wishing we could guide our talk onto lighter topics.

But Wilf's eyes were bound with mine again. 'Gracie, I'm so sorry. What happened?'

I hesitated again, feeling almost embarrassed for him, as if he'd asked something he shouldn't have. In some ways he had. Was it normal to discuss such things with people one barely knew? But none of this was normal. 'She died in childbirth,' I answered guardedly, thinking how strange it was to say it aloud, for I'd never had to tell anyone before; everyone in Barnfield already knew. 'And the child with her.' Blood rushed to my face, carrying the threat of tears, but I forced myself to blink them away.

'I'm sorry. My mother and I were never exactly close, but...' He shook his head, as if he still found the whole idea of living without her baffling. 'You must be very close to your father.'

'Yes, I suppose I am.'

'And now you run your house for him?'

'I wouldn't put it quite like that. I'm sure he could manage without me.' I didn't believe that for a second, but didn't want Wilf to think Dad was weak. I watched him run my words through his head, digesting them.

'Would you have joined a service, do you think? If things had been different?'

I pictured Jean in her WRNS uniform and my short-lived dream of joining the WAAF. 'Perhaps. To be honest I'm rather glad to stay here.' I felt the creep of embarrassment, the remnant of a hundred teases from Alec and Cliff about how boring I was. But Wilf only raised an eyebrow and waited for me to elaborate. 'I love Barnfield, my home, my... I have no desire to leave it. I suppose that means I'm exceptionally dull.' Dull was one word for it. I wouldn't admit the alternative.

He laughed. 'Not at all. I think it's rather wonderful!'

'Oh?'

'Some people spend their whole lives searching for contentment, seeking out new people in far flung places, chasing ridiculous dreams in the hope that fulfilment lies in the next adventure, only to realise in their dying years what you have already realised. You are thankful for what you have. You love your family, and you appreciate this beautiful place.' He held his palm out to the lake and fields around us.

'I've never thought about it like that before,' I said faintly, distracted by thoughts of people travelling the world, when the furthest I'd been was Portsmouth. I still felt poorer by comparison, but appreciated his sweet words, and couldn't take my eyes off his profile as he watched the rippling water.

'And you're right, it is beautiful,' he said on the back of a sigh. 'I think I'd be happy to spend my whole life here too.' He turned back to me with a smile and I felt like he'd somehow found a crack in my chest and was filling it with liquid gold: my heart beat fast, my veins shone and buzzed with the sensation. It was so exquisite I thought I could have died right then, for no other moment could ever compare, and when he looked away again I hungered for him instantly. 'But who knows what the future holds?' He pressed his palm to his scars again and reached in his pocket for his cigarette case.

I wished I could think of something meaningful to say. I sensed unease in his short breaths. His hands shook slightly and his eyes were wide, sparkling like the lake around us. I got the feeling everything he'd just said about me – about my family and home here in Barnfield – was something he envied or yearned for. I thought of his dead mother and mad father, and the terror of sorties awaiting him, and I pitied him. Suddenly the sun seemed too warm, the scent of blooms and water sickly, the butterflies' movements almost feverish. The idyllic scene was saccharine in the face of Wilf's reality. I wished I had the words to make it better, but I couldn't make sense of any of it.

'You said you have a twin brother who's turning eighteen soon?' he asked me.

'Today, in fact.'

He grinned, then laughed, a sound so brightly melodious it instantly chased off my melancholy. 'Today? Today is your eighteenth birthday?'

I couldn't help laughing with him. 'Yes.'

He sat up a little straighter, and I could tell he was wondering if I was teasing him. 'Then...' He lit two of his expensive cigarettes and handed one to me. 'Happy birthday.' He laughed warmly again. 'I'm sure you'd rather be with your family and friends right now, wouldn't you?'

I didn't. I wanted to be right there with him; I could have stayed forever. I smoked his cigarette and felt my muscles relaxing. He watched me, and I let him, feeling bold and strangely empowered. But his next question knocked me down again.

'And what about your fiancé?'

'What? He's not my fiancé!'

'*Yet*,' Wilf said pointedly, with a hint of mockery.

I blushed again, tongue-tied, remembering what I'd told him at the Manor. The smoke felt claustrophobic; I held the cigarette away from me and let it burn. Wilf was still watching me, but now I wanted to hide away, feeling Cliff's presence between us and all the shame I should have done for being there.

'Do you love him?'

I bristled. 'You shouldn't ask me that.'

His smile had a wolfish quality about it. 'Perhaps not.' But he waited for an answer nonetheless. I wouldn't give him one. It wasn't his business, though he seemed to think it was. The very fact he'd asked me reminded me how vulnerable I was alone with him. Eventually, he drew on his cigarette slowly and turned his face away from me, as if I'd done something to offend him. When he looked back at me there seemed to be shadows behind his eyes, a cloud of darkness, but I wasn't sure if it made me want to run from him or reach out to him. 'Forgive me. I'm being impertinent.'

I threw my cigarette into the water. 'Yes, I think you are a little.' I was surprised by my confidence, and felt I had the upper hand again.

Wilf didn't seem insulted. 'You know, I've never met anyone like you, Gracie.'

I laughed. 'Ordinary?'

He smiled, then looked out onto the water. 'Far from it. You don't know what you are.'

I was so intrigued to know how he saw me. 'What am I?'

He turned back to me. 'You are… genuine. And you don't judge.'

He thought too highly of me. I had judged him just as everyone else had, and I was nervous of him and whatever it was he'd been through. He was troubling – him and his mad father – and all the secret things within him. And I was troubled too by my quickened pulse, the fear of spending one more moment with him and breaking under the pressure of it.

'You listen. You don't ask many questions…'

'I would if I could.'

He sat up straighter. 'Then what's stopping you?'

I didn't have to answer him.

He sighed. 'Gracie, all the things that used to matter don't matter anymore, don't you see that?'

I wasn't sure what he was saying.

'When I was growing up, I knew the shape of the world and how to move within it. I knew what was right and wrong. I knew who I was and who I'd be and I never thought to question any of it, however uncomfortable it made me.'

'And now you do?'

He gave me a look as if to say, *you would too, if you'd seen what I'd seen and knew what I knew*. 'The world I knew doesn't exist anymore. I'm not sure it ever did. Do you understand?' I must have looked uncertain because he went on, with passion, 'When you look at me you see my name, wealth and status and even my age, for God's sake! A great gulf of difference between us, that makes this,' he gestured to us both, 'an impossible conversation to be having. You must have asked yourself, "what am I doing here?" Haven't you?'

I nodded quickly, feeling like he or I was about to explode with nervous energy. His eyes were lively but too intense, his tone rising. He seemed more unstable than ever.

'It's refreshing, Gracie, it really is. Why shouldn't we talk to each other? Why shouldn't we…' he broke off, and I wondered what he'd been about to say. 'My God, if you had any idea! I've spent my entire life living by conventions and I've had enough of them!' He left a weighty silence trailing, full of his anger, perhaps for me, or the war, or everything. It was not an anger I knew; it was different, deeper, more painful. I didn't know what to say.

He smiled, tried to laugh. 'Ask me.'

'Ask you what?'

He gestured lazily to his face. 'How I came to look like this. I know you want to.'

I felt the prick of tears. Even with his permission I still couldn't bring myself to say it.

'It was flack.' His voice was tense but steady. 'Exploded right beside us. Shrapnel got me, and another chap, but he lost an arm and too much blood and he… he didn't make it.'

'He died?'

'Yes. He hung on for a bit, but…'

I let the words sink in slowly, trying to picture the chaotic scene.

He seemed lost in thought. 'It's the arbitrariness of it really. Why him, and not me? I've asked myself that a thousand times.' He smiled sympathetically at my glum expression, as if to try and cheer me. 'So, you see, I got off lightly. I don't even remember it. I was unconscious as soon as I got hit. The rest of the crew patched up the plane. Got it home and it lived to fight another day.' His peculiarly bright exhilaration faded suddenly, and he added wryly, 'And so did I.'

'I'm sorry.'

'You mustn't be. In a way it was a relief.' He smiled when he saw my confused expression. 'It's exhausting, living so close to death, seeing it and hearing about it every day. There are times when you just get so tired of it all. I just wish…' He stopped himself, but I sensed he wanted to say that he wished he'd died instead of his friend, as if death was some grotesque game and there was always a winner and a loser. I thought of all the nights in the shelter and the sickening tension of the raids. But to be up in the skies surrounded by fire and death? How could anyone bear it? How could it not drive one mad?

'It's so incongruous, sitting here, surrounded by all this peace and beauty, when right now there are people fighting, people imprisoned, people dying. This bloody war! It doesn't make any sense, does it?'

I shook my head dumbly, fearing the sharpness of his tone. His eyes were burdened with remorse, and for a moment I felt I could see into his mind, into a draughty fuselage on a freezing cold fateful night, air screaming, radio stuttering. I saw him bent over a map, sweating as he plotted coordinates, his face a picture of unscarred perfection. I longed to reach out and take his hand, but I was overcome by it all: his words, his eyes, his scars – so close and still so raw. I imagined his face ripped open and bloody and had to turn away.

I'd never heard anyone talk like him. Alec spoke of the war as a child describes an adventure book. Cliff's attitude to service was perfunctory. At church and in the Post Office, people either clucked over bad news or tightened their lips and said nothing. Absent boys were praised or mourned, their names mentioned in reverence. But no one ever said, 'this bloody war' – never with such depth of feeling, such naked desperation – even though we might all be thinking it a hundred times a day.

Wilf pressed his cigarette into one of the jam jar lids. 'I've spent the last few months in hospital. And now the scars have healed, I'm apparently ready to go back and do it all over again. But to tell you the truth...' He stopped himself and cleared his throat again.

I was glad he didn't go on. His words stirred up the pain within me, and all I could think of was Alec, teetering on the edge of it all; I just wanted to grab on to him and keep him safe forever. I felt feeble and beaten. Why had Wilf told me all of this? I tried to take a deep breath, but the cloying, humid air only made my head spin more. I'd had too much sun and my head was starting to ache. I couldn't listen to him anymore; the sense of enchantment had faded and now I felt like a broken branch about to fall. The blood rushed to my feet as I stood and I felt light-headed. There was a woozy sickness churning in my stomach. 'We should go.' My voice stuck as if I'd been weeping.

'I shouldn't have asked you about… about your friend. It was wrong of me. I'm sorry.'

I thanked him with a nod, for I wasn't going to excuse him.

'I hope he knows how lucky he'll be if you say yes.'

How could he say such a thing? He didn't know me at all. Was I really so beguiling? I didn't think so. I was too plain and young and ordinary to warrant such praise. I searched his face for mockery, but found only his perfectly blue eyes and torn, deathly cheek – a chaotic fusion of ugliness and beauty – I hadn't thought it possible for a man to be so beautiful. I recalled him in the shadows of the church hall, his strangeness at the Manor, his easy smile as he rowed, how he'd captivated me from the first moment I'd seen him. Could it really be possible that he felt the same way about me?

He stood and brushed a little ash from his thigh. A breeze caught his shirt again, pressing it to his chest and stomach. I bent down to help him pick up the jars, but he said, 'I'll do that.'

'It's all right, really.'

He put his hand over mine. 'Gracie, please.' He took the jars slowly and placed them at his feet. He kept hold of my hand, and I wondered for an aching moment if he'd kiss me. I realised I'd been waiting for it all afternoon. I couldn't deny it any longer. His long looks, his frank words, his gentle touch – however inappropriate, I'd encouraged them all. But it was impossible. Those conventions and barriers Wilf had so glibly disregarded still existed. We were fools to have let a couple of obscure meetings turn into this: two people facing each other beneath a cloud of butterflies, wordless, self-conscious. We had no past or future together, only this ambiguous present, which we had stumbled into and now had to somehow clamber from gracelessly.

'I shouldn't have come, Wilf,' I croaked, unable to hold back the tide of tears; with dismay I felt them rolling down my cheeks. I couldn't bear to look at him for the depth of my distress and the strength of my affection for him.

'I disagree,' he said earnestly. 'I'm glad you came. I think you're exactly where you're meant to be.'

We leant in to each other, our heads bowed, foreheads touching. My foolish tears dripped on to my feet but he didn't try to soothe me. He held my fingers and felt my pain as I felt his. He could have wept with me and I'd have thought nothing of it.

We stayed like that for a long time, until my breaths were slow and deep in time with his. My tears were spent and I'd been closing my eyes so long that the white sun dazzled me when I looked up. The butterflies still flitted around us silently. The ache in my head was gone, but it seemed to have taken my strength with it. Wilf's expression was open and understanding, eyes so deep I felt I could hide myself in them. He didn't kiss me, but I felt as if he already had; it was implied in every look and touch.

He put the jars and net back in the boat and then led me to it. He lifted me from the bank, his hands around my waist, his eyes always on mine. His shirt stuck to his skin. The scar on his neck glistened.

In blurry minutes we left the butterflies behind us. I sat beside him as he rowed me back to the bank where he'd found me, resting my head on his hard shoulder as if it belonged there. Everything we'd talked about over the last hour had been whistling like a hurricane through my head, and yet in those few silent minutes – with his oars stroking the calm water, and our breaths low and heavy – I inexplicably felt more content and peaceful than ever I could recall.

He tied the boat to the bank and helped me out. My legs felt as if I'd been in bed with flu for a week, and I placed my hand through his arm as he offered it to me. I let him walk me back through the overgrown woodland and up the wheat field to the woods, all without a word being spoken between us.

Out of the woods, with the village now in view, idyllic in the long golden shadows, we stopped and faced each other. It was time for this to end, for Wilf to return to the Manor, and then to service, and me to my ordinary existence. It was time to be rational again and forget these fanciful thoughts and feelings that had temporarily overcome us. I knew it, but I despised it even so. I hated each treacherous second that would see us parted. I'd heard people say how they wished they could freeze time, but I never understood it until then.

Wilf's eyes held a thousand words and I imagined I heard

them all. I felt his regrets and pain and desires like blood in my veins, and when he took my hand his touch was electric, so forceful and unexpected that I pulled mine away as if he was on fire. But his gentle smile coaxed me back to him until our fingers were intertwined. I yearned to kiss him; the sensation was intoxication and agony. I willed for him to seize my face in his hands and pull me closer to him. But the kiss remained on my lips, in my heart, just a glimpse of what might have been.

All he said was, 'Goodbye, Gracie. And happy birthday,' and let his hands fall.

My voice was so soft when I said goodbye that I barely heard it, but inside I was raging, thwarted and desperate.

He stepped aside, and I began walking down towards the stile, every stride uneasy, every heartbeat screaming out for him. The whole time I felt his eyes on me and willed to hear his footsteps thudding on the grass behind me. When I reached the stile I gave in and turned back, but he was gone.

I remained at the stile for a second or a minute or two. I was lost in vague thought, unsure of myself. When I turned to walk on, something – someone – caught my eye. A little further down the lane, where the road curved at the pub, watching me with cold, hard eyes, was Doris, her arms folded. For a moment our gazes locked like two animals, each waiting for the other to pounce or prowl away. Then she turned and walked quickly out of sight.

CHAPTER 9

I was so preoccupied for the rest of our birthday evening that I was hardly able to enjoy a moment of it, or indeed a morsel of Mrs B's cake. I couldn't divulge my thoughts to Alec, and even if I'd wanted to, he was in too high spirits to listen anyway. If Dad or Mrs B noticed my distraction they doubtless put it down to my concerns for Alec getting called up. If they'd asked, I would have blamed the letter from Cliff and felt all the guiltier at their sympathetic smiles.

It was a restless night. I dreamed of the lake again, its deathly fingers and indistinguishable face pulling me down. I woke with a start, choking, I was sure, my hair and nightclothes still dripping. But it was only my own sweat and fear that soaked me now. The air was close and suffocating. I sat up in bed, the nightmare still so real I felt no shame for my hammering heart. I got up and threw open my window as wide as it would go, but the blasted blackout curtain prevented any whisper of a breeze from reaching my clammy skin. And as the dream faded, my mind came alive with visions from earlier, all of Wilf's lingering looks and impassioned words. Had it really happened? In the bleary small hours, the memory of our afternoon together distorted into another golden, fantastical dream: bronzed skin and water melting into a kaleidoscope of butterflies' wings. When I thought of what he'd told me about his accident, his father, and the officer who'd stolen his mother's heart, it was too much to take in.

But it wasn't just what he'd said. I relived each touch and felt again the power of his gaze, the sweet trembling of blood in my veins. What would he have done if I'd moved to kiss him at our parting, if I'd dared to hold tighter to his hand? I wished I had. But I could never be so bold, not with him; he unhinged me. And thank God I hadn't done anything, when Doris Howard might have seen it all.

I'd thought about running over to the Howard's after supper, asking for Doris and explaining away what she saw with an innocuous excuse. But I hadn't visited Doris's since childhood, and to turn up unannounced, after sunset, would have surely seemed even more suspicious. It was obvious from the condemning glower she'd given me that she'd seen me and Wilf together and assumed the worst. It didn't seem fair that I was suffering the consequences of something I hadn't done, however much I wished I had. But I knew my thoughts, and it was too late to fool myself that our afternoon together had meant nothing. All of the afternoons and mornings and nights of my life put together seemed to pale in comparison to that golden hour or two with Wilf, but even admitting that to myself was frightening, and as the night dragged on, my anxiety grew. Wasn't he leaving on Monday? I might never see him again. The bizarre moments we'd shared might come to nothing.

By the time dawn broke, I still had no idea what I'd say when I caught Doris before church, for I'd come to the decision that that would be the best time to speak to her. My only hope was that she hadn't yet mentioned it to her mother. If the whole village suspected me of having a clandestine love affair with Wilfred Whitman, I'd never live it down. I'd have to suffer gossip for months, and there'd be no way of keeping it from Cliff, however unfounded (or at least misjudged) the rumour. And if I was to be heartbroken, as the feeling brewing inside me suggested, I would much prefer to keep it a secret.

Alec was too hungover for breakfast, and I didn't have much of an appetite, so Dad ate alone at the kitchen table while I dressed my hair in a manner in which I knew Doris would approve. I left the house earlier than needed so I could station myself near the church gate and draw her aside. I'd been there for twenty minutes, shifting from foot to foot and yawning almost constantly, when the Howards rounded the corner of the lane in their Sunday best. Doris's gay smile vanished as soon as she spotted me. I guessed from Mr and Mrs Howard's usual disinterestedness that Doris was holding on to her secret.

She followed me, without any invitation required, into the shade of the large yew in the churchyard. We faced each other again, just as we had last night. She fixed me in her stony glare and folded her arms neatly, and I guessed I would have to be the one to break the silence. 'I suppose you're wondering why Wi – why Flight Lieutenant Whitman and I were out walking together yesterday.' It felt odd to speak his name so formally now.

Doris raised a haughty eyebrow. 'I suppose Cliff would wonder that too.'

This ruffled my feathers a little, as if she knew him better than me or had some higher right to look out for him. They had never been good friends, and I knew she looked down on Cliff's bawdy jokes and rough clothes. I doubted she'd have been so high and mighty if I'd come along to all her WVS meetings and let her groom me into one of her protégés. If I'd ended up marrying a fancy pilot, like she had. But I held my composure. 'I bumped into him while I was walking in the woods.'

'I see. And because he's such a lively conversationalist you hit it off and he decided to walk you back?' Her words smarted with sarcasm and jealously. How dare a lowly post girl have a more intimate connection with the Whitmans than her? She shook her head impatiently. 'Come on, Gracie, do you take me for a fool? I know what I saw.'

'What did you see?'

Her gaze flitted to the people beginning to gather in the churchyard. She lowered her voice. 'You and Flight Lieutenant Whitman. *Together.*'

'Talking.'

She tutted. 'You were holding hands!'

How could I explain myself? I felt my cheeks flushing as I tried to think of an excuse. 'He was comforting me,' I said hurriedly.

Doris smiled dubiously. 'What?'

'I… I'd been crying.'

'Crying? With Flight Lieutenant Whitman? Why?'

'I received a letter from Cliff yesterday,' I carried on, trying not to sound too relieved, because it seemed I could actually make this sound plausible. 'I was reading it, in the woods, and I got a little teary, and that's when—'

'When you *bumped* into each other?'

'Yes. He was very kind. He was a little flustered I think, well, you can imagine, coming across a weeping woman alone in the woods.'

'Weeping?' Doris sounded unconvinced, and it was a little far-fetched even for me. 'I had no idea you were so emotional, Gracie.'

'Well, it was a difficult day. It was our birthday, you see, and I was upset about Alec getting called up.'

A glimmer of disapproval moved across Doris's lips. 'You should be proud of him.'

'Of course I am!'

'But,' she softened, 'I know how close you and Alec are. I suppose it will be a wrench when he leaves, what with Cliff gone too.'

'Yes, exactly.'

'Because you must miss Cliff awfully.'

'Of course. Of course,' I stammered. 'That's why his letter… that's why I was feeling a little wobbly yesterday, and, as I say, Flight Lieutenant Whitman was quite the gentleman and wouldn't have me walk back alone. He was rather sweet, in fact, and gave my hand a cheering little squeeze before he went, and when you saw us – you must have imagined – well, I understand what it must have looked like, which is why I wanted to clear things up straight away.'

Doris hesitated, her eyes narrowing. Eventually, she said, 'He was *rather sweet*, you say?'

I nodded, wishing I hadn't said that. It wasn't true, in any case. Wilf was an enigma, a man of many faces, but sweet was not one of them.

Doris stepped closer. 'You know, he caused quite a stir showing up at the wedding.'

I cleared my throat tensely. 'Yes, I noticed.'

'And since then, my Ron has written with some rather unsavoury information about him.'

'I'm sure half the rumours about him aren't true,' I said breezily. 'He seemed pleasant enough.'

'I'm not talking about the rumours rattling around the Post Office,' she said with a sneer. 'I'm talking about *facts*. Ron's brother – he couldn't make it to the wedding – is stationed at the same airbase as *Flight Lieutenant* Whitman, and apparently he's not very popular there at all. Most of the other officers won't even have a drink with him, let alone fly with him. They find him very disturbing. Bad luck.'

Thinking back to how he'd unnerved me, I found this easy to believe. 'Perhaps he is a little unorthodox,' I conceded.

She gave a hollow laugh. 'Unorthodox! What makes you say that? What did he say to you?'

'Nothing.'

'Nothing? He must have said *something*.'

'Nothing extraordinary.' How easily I lied! 'But I suppose there was something in his manner which could be strewn as eccentric.'

Doris frowned. 'Sweet, yet unorthodox and eccentric! Really, Gracie, you're making no sense whatsoever.' She looked back at the church momentarily and smiled and waved at someone; I guessed she was losing interest in the conversation. 'Look, Gracie, they may be a fine family, but I heartily recommend you keep your distance from Flight Lieutenant Whitman.' She held up a hand to stop me interrupting. 'I know, you merely *bumped* into him, that's all.' She paused and added, 'And I hear you bumped into him in the village a few days ago too?'

I couldn't help sighing shortly and saying, 'Doris, is any of this really your business?'

'I hope not,' she retorted. 'But I imagine it's Cliff's, and as his friend I feel I ought to look out for him while he's away.'

'Look out for him! What do you think he's in danger of?'

'Losing his fiancée.'

'I am not his fiancée.'

She rolled her eyes. 'Oh, Gracie, don't split hairs! I would hate to see you destroy your future with him for a silly fling with a rich—'

'Is that what you really think of me?' I interrupted. 'Aren't I your friend too? You seem very quick to condemn me.'

She pressed her lips together and looked briefly embarrassed. 'So you're not having an affair with him?'

'No, I'm not!'

She studied me, weighing up whether or not to believe me. 'You're telling me then, that somehow, you and Wilfred Whitman have become *friends*?' She couldn't have sounded more incredulous if she'd tried, and I had to hold back a smile.

'Not even that, Doris. Not even that.' My voice was weary now, and perhaps it betrayed some deeper emotions, for Doris frowned.

'In that case, you ought to know, Flight Lieutenant Whitman was a marked man long before his injury.' She didn't continue, waiting for me to take the bait.

I did my best to sound irritated rather than intrigued. 'What do you mean?'

'Ron's brother told him that when Wilfred was injured, half of his crew were relieved that he had to go away on medical leave, and the others were just disappointed he hadn't been killed.'

Her words gave the injury they intended, and in that second I knew I'd given myself away. I felt the blood rush to my face and I wanted to yell at her or slap that smug little grin from her lips. How dare she say such a horrible thing? What did she or Ron's blasted brother know? Spreading foul gossip just like her mother, having the audacity to call it a fact! Did she know about the crew member who'd died? I doubted it. I wished I could tell her, but I'd be playing right into her hands. As it was, she wore a look of self-satisfied triumph on her face.

'I'm quite sure Flight Lieutenant Whitman seemed very sweet yesterday, Gracie, but you ought to be careful. Imagine if someone less discreet than I had seen you together?' She smiled thinly. 'Of course, now you've explained it, I see it was all a misunderstanding, and I won't mention it again.'

It took all my strength to say, 'I'm very grateful.'

She patted my shoulder and I let her walk away. I remained

in the shadow of the great yew, seething, imagining my blood boiling and steam rising from my skin.

After a few minutes, Dad and Alec arrived, running late, and, seeing me, called me over to join them inside. We took our seats in our usual pew, and I kept my eyes lowered, frightened they'd betray my distress to anyone who looked at me. The Howards were across the aisle from us, and I felt Doris's gaze as I slunk back beside Alec. I was still smarting from her words; the desire to defend Wilf was so strong my hands trembled. But I felt exposed. Would she really keep it a secret? Wouldn't she want to spread her gossip, and worst of all, what tale would she concoct for Cliff when he next came home?

The organ ceased, and Reverend Dearling was just taking his place in the pulpit when the latch on the church door clunked loudly and some heads turn to scowl upon the latecomer. A couple of low whispers fluttered through the congregation as footsteps made their way up the central aisle, and I turned just in time to see Wilf pass our pew and offer me the minutest smile as our eyes met. In a second he'd reached the front of the church and taken his place in the Whitman's pew, although it had been empty for as long as I could remember. Doris caught my eye with a knowing look: *this is for your benefit*, it said, and despite all the confusion of the moment, I felt an auspicious tingle of joy.

The reverend began the service, and I sat and stared at the back of Wilf's head, a few pews in front of me. I was not the only one – glancing around me it seemed everyone was intrigued by the late arrival – but I doubted any of their hearts leapt as quickly as mine, or that their thoughts were drawn to imagine their arms reaching out to turn his head, to take his face in their hands and meet their lips with his. Through collect and hymn and sermon and prayer, I remained in my space, affecting a staid expression but all the while burning with passion, excitement and impatience. I would have given anything to conjure away the congregation, to be alone with him again. I studied the hairs at his nape and the scarlet scar on his neck and felt an aching need to touch them.

How had I resisted him yesterday? The pull of attraction was so much stronger today, exacerbated by a night's overthinking and regret, and the hateful things Doris had said. I lifted my head higher as we sang the last hymn. I looked over at Doris and met her gaze squarely with a perverse, defiant pride.

When the service ended the congregation seemed to hang back in the pews until Wilf got up to leave. After that, everyone rose in a clamour, and I lost sight of him in the crowd as we slowly and impatiently filed towards the door and the reverend's handshake. I began to panic that he'd leave, and this glimpse of hope had been a cruel, divine tease. But as soon as I stepped out of the porch I saw him in the lane, leaning against his shimmering Bentley, smoking. He was lingering, obviously waiting for something or somebody. Doubt shook me briefly, but then he looked up, caught my eye and smiled, and I felt such a thrill run through me, I couldn't help smiling back.

All the talk in the churchyard crowds was of Wilfred Whitman, of course. I caught fragments of conversation as I walked towards the gate, leaving Dad and Alec and Doris behind me. There was no way to speak to Wilf without attracting attention, but I *had* to speak to him. I would have to make it look like I was on my way home and anything we said was in passing. Of course Doris and Mrs B wouldn't be fooled, Dad neither probably. But I would cross those bridges when I came to them.

Wilf raised his hat when I reached him and I made a show of turning as if I'd meant to walk on. There was a sparkle of humour in his eyes as we said good morning very politely and made a few remarks about the sun. With a sinking feeling, I wondered if he'd come all this way to apologise again. Perhaps he regretted our afternoon together. But no, he flashed a glance back to the gossiping villagers and then lowered his voice slightly: 'I have something for you.'

'What is it?'

'A birthday present. But I don't think I can give it to you here.'

I smiled. 'No.'

He dropped his cigarette to the ground. 'The boathouse, then? Seven o'clock? Can you make it?'

I would find a way. 'Yes.'

He tipped his hat again. 'Until then.'

I left him with a smile and walked down the lane to our house. I hadn't heard the car start, so I glanced back when I reached the front door and saw Wilf chatting to Reverend Dearling at the church gate. The rest of the churchgoers were either making their way home or talking in the churchyard. The novelty of his presence had waned, and nobody – not even Doris – was watching me, watching him. It seemed we'd got away with it this time.

Chapter 10

Escaping to the boathouse was easy that night. Dad was used to my solitary walks, and Alec had spent most of the afternoon asleep in the garden, so neither of them batted an eyelid when I slipped away, or noticed that I hadn't yet changed out of my church dress into my usual trousers and blouse.

It was an idle summer's evening. Gnats carried the amber sunlight through the hazy air. I half expected to find Doris waiting in ambush as I left the house, but there was no one about. The warm day had brought its blanket of calm over Barnfield; a faint tune hummed from a wireless somewhere, the scent of overcooked vegetables wafted from an open window. House martins swooped and chattered above my head, and a light breeze picked up a cloud of dust from the road as I passed the sleeping Post Office and the whitewashed pub, glowing celestially in the evening light. I squinted into the sun as it clipped the spire of the church, a picture of a peaceful idyll; if it wasn't for the sandbags and Anderson shelters in people's gardens it could almost appear like we weren't at war at all.

As I leapt the stile and headed swiftly to Manor Woods, I thought about Wilf returning to service tomorrow. It was hard to imagine Barnfield without him now. Since his arrival he'd brought nothing but intrigue and excitement to my monotonous days. Every post had brought the hope of a letter for the Manor. It made my heart sink to think that after tomorrow, it would just be the old captain there again.

I'd had all day to think about what might happen tonight. Wilf had said he had a birthday present for me, and I wondered if perhaps he'd meant a kiss. I envisaged falling into his arms on the boathouse's little balcony, the evening light reflecting off the water and into his eyes. I gave into the fantasy; there was no point fighting it anymore or denying my attraction to him, especially now I was sure he felt it too.

The lake was as picturesque as my girlish daydreams when I arrived, just before seven o'clock. I made my way over to the boathouse, but it was locked and deserted, so I sat on the step by the door and waited, impatient with every second that passed. I kept a keen watch on the path to the Manor, my nerves jittering.

A quarter of an hour passed. Then another. What was keeping him? I couldn't sit still any longer. I walked over to the path and thought about following it all the way to the Manor. I remembered the gardens as I'd seen them last week, imagined traipsing up them and knocking on the French windows. But I hadn't the confidence. Perhaps he'd changed his mind. Perhaps he didn't want to see me after all. Or maybe I meant so little to him, he'd just forgotten.

I checked my watch again and decided to wait a while longer. But even as I paced a little patch by the shore, I knew he wouldn't come. I felt the excitement drain from me as I stood and watched the sun go down over the water, the island ahead of me. My nerves settled, my breathing slowed, and as dusk took over, I reluctantly began my return home.

My steps through the fields and woods were sullen and slow. What had I been thinking, losing sleep over a man I barely knew, getting carried away with romantic fantasies? I started to doubt all his meaningful words and looks yesterday. I remembered our fingers linking and my heart twisted, but I told myself I must have read too much into it.

When I got home, the lack of sleep and tumult of emotions caught up with me. I ran a six-inch bath and soaked miserably in it till the water grew cold, running the day's events through my head like a looping film reel.

I was in my bedroom, buttoning up my shirt, when I heard a knock at the front door and Dad's footsteps clomping to answer it. The light had faded and it was too late for polite calls; I wondered if it was Doris popping round to berate me further. But Dad's mumbled voice was too staid, and the front door was still open. Alec thundered up the stairs and in a moment poked his head in with his eyes shut. 'Decent?'

'Yes. Who is it?'

He opened his eyes and they were full of fire. 'Bloody Whitman!'

All hope was rekindled suddenly. I froze, my mouth open. 'Wilf?'

Alec flinched. '*Wilf?* What in God's name do you call him that for? Do you know him? What the hell's he doing here?'

'I don't know!' I whispered, panicking, and I sensed Alec relax a bit since it was blatantly obvious I'd been taken off guard. I touched my wet hair and looked around the room with my cast-off dress crumpled on the floor. There was no time to change.

Alec laughed through clenched teeth. 'Well, he's got you all in a fluster, hasn't he?'

'Don't you start,' I snapped.

'What do you mean?'

'Nothing… nothing.'

'Why has he come here, asking for you? How does he know

where you live? How does he even know who you are?'

'Maybe it's Post Office business,' I said as I gave myself one more look in the mirror.

Alec looked unconvinced. 'Why did you talk to him after church?'

I shrugged. 'Why not? Just passing the time of day.'

'With *Wilf*? Pull the other one! I saw how you looked at him at the wedding. I know when you're lying.'

'Then you'll know better than to ask too many questions, won't you?'

'All right, but I'll want an explanation later.'

'All right, I promise.'

'The truth.'

'I didn't agree to that.'

He grinned. 'Go on then, he's waiting at the door. He won't lower himself to come in.'

Wilf was just beyond the threshold, talking politely to Dad, who looked uncomfortably stiff. Wilf looked up as soon as I descended the stairs and God knows what he thought of my dishevelled appearance. Dad turned and grimaced and Wilf said, 'Ah, Gracie! I'm so sorry to barge in on you all like this.' His tone was all ease and light. He held up a brown parcel in his hand – the birthday present – and his eyes darted from me to Dad and back again. 'I just wanted to give you this.'

Dad looked down at the floor and cleared his throat. Alec was behind me, halfway down the stairs with his arms folded.

'Won't you come in?' I asked half-heartedly, knowing he wouldn't.

'Your father has already kindly offered but I don't mean to stay.'

'Well, it's rather dark,' said Dad. 'We can't stand here all night with the light on.' He gestured that I ought to join Wilf outside.

Wilf smiled gratefully. 'We won't be a moment,' he said, to Dad or me I wasn't sure.

Dad nodded and shut the door behind us, and there we were, alone on my doorstep in the last inky shreds of twilight.

Wilf's shoulders were rigid, his eyes black pools in the shadow of his hat. 'Gracie, I'm so sorry about earlier.' His voice was low and hurried. 'Father… he had a turn, and by the time I got to the boathouse it was far too late.'

Such a simple explanation. All that wasted worry and misery. 'Is your father all right?' I kept my voice low, wondering if Dad or Alec were listening from the other side of the door.

'Yes, yes, he'll be fine. I'm sorry. My God, you must have thought I'd forgotten you!'

'Or changed your mind.'

'No, not at all.'

It was a humid night but I shivered and nervously pulled my arms around me. I could smell rain in the air, a storm gathering. 'How did you know I lived here?'

'I saw you earlier on. I was spying on you.' There was mischief in his voice. He held up the little square package in his hand, wrapped in brown paper and string. 'Well here it is. Happy birthday.'

'You shouldn't have, Wilf.' I took it hesitantly, our hands touching for the briefest of moments. 'What is it?'

'Open it.'

I pulled the string and peeled away the paper. Underneath was a frame, but the light was too dim to make out what was inside it.

'Here.' He fished a lighter out of his coat pocket. He cupped his hand around the flame and held it close to the frame. Inside was a single, tiny grey butterfly. A breath of blue sheen laced its delicate rounded wings. Beneath it were the words 'Small Blue' in neat black ink. 'They're the smallest in England,' he said softly.

'It's beautiful, Wilf. Thank you.'

'You caught it,' he added, and I looked up to catch his eyes momentarily before the flame died. 'I found it when I was putting the net away yesterday. We must have missed it, and it was dead then. I'm rather fond of them, I have to say. You don't see many of them around here so they always cheer me when I spot them.'

I looked back at the frame in my hands, wishing I had light again to study it. 'Then you should keep it.' I didn't mean it. I suddenly felt that little butterfly was the most important thing in the world to me.

'No, no, you misunderstand me. It's yours.' He breathed in and out shakily.

'Thank you, Wilf.' I wished I could throw my arms around his shoulders, but once again my confidence failed me. The frustration of it was like a wound inside me.

'You could put it on your wall. Maybe it'll remind you… Maybe it'll remind you that extraordinary things come along even when we least expect it, even when we think we've seen it all. They're still there, if we look hard enough.'

I felt a lump swelling in my throat, but couldn't bring myself to turn away from his face in the gloomy half-light. I longed for him to light another flame so I could look into his eyes again, see and feel the deep spirals of blue I could only imagine in that moment. And it was only about that moment then – no uncertain future or halcyon past – it had all melted away now he was in front of me again. My common sense told me we shouldn't be there together, that he was too rich, too educated, too old, too unknown. Too complicated. He was fragile – volatile even – and I should have nothing to do with him. I was practically engaged for God's sake! But my heart had found its voice, and I felt its song in my chest, my throat. It beat in my tongue, trying to coerce my lips to release it. All common sense was futile when Wilf was so devastatingly beautiful, when all I really wanted was to reach out and touch his skin and kiss him.

'Gracie?' He stepped a little closer. I sensed the heat of his body, his gentle musky scent, his every breath. He took the frame from my hands and propped it gently against the doorstep, then rose to take my hands. He had left it too long to speak; it was as if the silence between us had choked him. He moved closer still, and a tremble of thrill shivered through me as he reached out to touch my face and run his fingers down my cheek, as if he'd done it a thousand times before. 'You're the Small Blue, Gracie. You don't know what your kindness has meant to me. You may think it's nothing, but it's not. I'll never forget it.'

I felt his chest rising and falling pressed against mine, his breath stroking my ear and hair. I knew he was going to kiss me, and the expectation of it stole all the air from my lungs. I was totally out of control, but it felt so intoxicating I didn't care. The blood trembled in my veins as I held on to him, his arms tensing beneath his jacket, the gentle contours of muscle and bone. I let my hand move across his chest, and onto his shoulders, and then ran my fingers up his neck, and the silky scar, onto his chin. The sensation made me weak, and Wilf drew himself closer. He pressed his forehead against mine, his lips so tantalisingly close I could almost taste them. And suddenly he was kissing me, and what had been acute, aching suspense dissolved instantaneously into an indecipherable blur.

The sound of the back door slamming made us both jump and ended that brief ecstasy, and when our lips parted I thought I'd die, the need for his touch was so great. I could hear Dad and Alec talking inside but I wished I could shut them out. I wasn't ready to leave this magical world that Wilf had conjured for just the two of us.

'I have to go,' he said regretfully, still holding me tight.

'I wish you didn't.'

He kissed me again.

'When will you be back?'

'I honestly don't know.'

'But you are planning on returning to Barnfield one day?'

He took my hands. 'As long as you are here, I'll wish to be nowhere else. But Gracie, you must promise me something. Whatever you hear about me, whatever people say, please just remember me as I am now, right here with you.' There was an urgency in his tone that frightened me.

'What do you mean?'

He shook his head. 'I know that a few days ago we were strangers, and in many ways we're strangers still…'

'Wilf, whatever's the matter?'

He moved away from me. 'I can't ask anything of you... I know you have your own life to lead, and I've no right to…'

'You have *every* right to,' I said, taking his shoulders again, for I could feel him slipping away from me already. I wanted to say I'd wait for him, I wanted him to ask me to. I kissed him, and held his scarred cheek with tenderness, but when he pulled away the space between us was filled with grief. I felt the pain in him again, the anguish and longing, the layers of a misunderstood man, pages of a hidden history wrought with sadness. I so wanted to understand him better. There was so much to ask and hear, yet we'd already run out of time.

'I must go.' He anxiously rubbed his scar and I ached for him. 'Your father and brother will be worried.' He moved his head, looking around at invisible faces hiding in the darkness. 'I think I've already exposed you to more than you deserve.'

'I'm not afraid of gossips,' I declared with more strength

than I felt. I thought of Doris's attack earlier and the possible ramifications. I recalled the things she'd said about Wilf and winced. 'I'm not ashamed of you, Wilf.'

I felt him smile but knew there was sorrow in it. 'I can see that. I feel it. Dear Gracie.'

I took his hands again, caressed his fingers in mine. I felt overcome with a bittersweet pain and sensed then all the tears I'd weep for him. 'Will you write?' I couldn't bear for him to leave me without hope.

He kissed my hands. 'You may regret asking me that.'

'Why would I regret it?' Did he imagine that I'd tire of him? Did he think, because of how I'd treated Cliff, I'd do the same to him?

'There may come a day when you'd rather have nothing to do with me.'

'How can you say that?'

'I will write,' he said. 'I promise.' He gestured to the frame. 'Promise me you'll keep hold of it. And remember what I said.'

'I will.' How could I forget a single word?

'I wish we'd had more time together.' He made it sound so finite, as if there was no hope for us, as if this was the end. I thought of the accident that had injured him. No wonder he feared for his life. If I'd had more faith, I'd have promised to pray for him, but it would have sounded paltry to say that now. How many dead men had been prayed into oblivion?

Dad or Alec's footsteps sounded just inside the front door. I felt the last few grains rushing through the hourglass and knew Wilf had to leave me. 'I will see you again,' I told him.

He nodded, but the dark hid his expression. 'Until then.' He tipped his hat. 'Farewell, Gracie. God bless you, and your brother too. I know you will think of him every hour he's gone. I wish him all the best.'

I couldn't bring myself to say goodbye, I knew the word would choke me. He was at the garden gate before I knew it. I watched him go with my insides screaming. How could it begin and end so suddenly? What had he meant by saying I would want nothing to do with him – had he so little faith in himself, in me? If only we'd had our evening at the boathouse, an hour or two alone. I could have asked him more, I could have held him longer, but it had all been thwarted.

I heard his engine start and saw the dull glow from half-covered headlamps a little further up the lane. The lights swung out into the road and the car turned and drove away, taking him with it.

Once inside I rested against the door and held the little frame tight to my chest. Alec was sitting at the bottom of the stairs. He looked at the tears welling in my eyes and the frame in my arms and his expression was full of irritation and confusion.

'Not now,' I told him. 'Not now.'

I slept in fits that night. The breeze picked up and began throwing rain through the open window, onto the blackout curtain and the edge of my bed. I sat up, my nightdress clinging to my skin, pushed back the curtain and fumbled groggily with the window, pulling it down so only a crack remained for air. There was no blue light of moon; heavy grey rain clouds groaned with thunder and spat lightning across the sky in shards. As another bolt cracked, the garden came alive in white light: raindrops were pounding the hard earth and fizzing on the shelter's roof; some washing I'd left out clung sodden and limp to the line, shirts flailing their arms in the wind. I saw a fox dart across the lawn and slide into the shadows of the coal shed. Across the landing, Alec snored loudly.

I pulled the curtain back in its place and fell back on the bed restlessly. When I shut my eyes, instantly Wilf was there in front of me, golden arms stretched out as he rowed, the breeze against his shirt. I didn't want to fight the image. I wanted to watch him, to study his face, to remind myself of its beauty, in case I never got to indulge in it again.

CHAPTER 11

The following morning, Alec, cross with me for not yet explaining Wilf's visit, refused to look me in the eye and moved heavily around the kitchen with sullen clunks and thuds. Dad, predictably, pretended that nothing extraordinary had happened at all.

I sipped my tea slowly but couldn't stomach anything to eat. I felt beaten, betrayed by the delightful hope that had so briefly flickered inside me. Wilf's kiss last night had felt momentous. Not in all the years of kissing Cliff had I ever felt such urgent, stirring, exquisite desire. Yet now he was gone. The sun had risen and would take him away from me today, and I feared that whatever we'd begun would come to nothing.

The early post brought a letter for the Manor, and I hurried there first on my round. I peddled furiously, thoughtless to what anyone might think of me – including Wilf – if I turned up on his doorstep, breathless and erratic. But despair enveloped me as I reached the Manor's gates, for I could sense his absence already. The turning circle was clear, the Bentley nowhere to be seen: shut away, perhaps. Would he have driven to the station? Was there anyone to drive him? I felt I had a right to know such details. I had no rational claim on him, but my heart argued otherwise.

I knocked on the door and the place seemed to echo with loneliness. The little maid answered promptly and took the letter with a nod and a frown, no doubt wondering why I hadn't just posted it through the door.

'Did Flight Lieutenant Whitman get away safely this morning?' I asked her, my voice tinged with desperation.

'Yes,' she said, wide-eyed, and nodded politely before shutting the door.

I slumped back onto my bike and dallied on the ride back to the village. The hours since our parting seemed to have stretched to a year already and my nerves were wretched. I wanted his arms around me again. The light he'd kindled inside me was already dimming, and with it all my strength. Somehow, in the space of a couple of weeks, he'd changed me, and now he was gone I wasn't sure how to *be* anymore. Even my breaths, tight and shallow, seemed to depend on him.

I made my deliveries with a vacant head and a pain in my chest like a bruise, spreading so quickly to exhaustion that by the end of the day I came straight home and fell asleep on the sofa.

Alec woke me, shaking my shoulder. I lifted my stiff neck and peered, bleary eyed, around the living room. The light was dull, the sky at the window turning the deep blue-grey of dusk. 'What time is it?' I said with a weary panic.

'Come on, up you get.' He pulled my hand to sit. 'I've made supper.'

I yawned. 'You have?'

'It's only bubble and squeak. Dad said not to wake you.'

I thanked him and said I'd lost track of time. My words were slow and lazy, as if I'd been asleep for days. I tried to stand up but Alec held my arm and sat down next to me.

'What was he doing here last night? What did he give you?'

I wished I could tell Alec the whole truth, but it seemed impossible. I knew he wouldn't understand how quickly and strangely I'd fallen under Wilf's spell; I barely believed it myself. The hollow pain inside me lingered – it showed no sign of fading yet. But Alec despised sentiment. Knowing how little he thought of Wilf, I was sure he would be angry with me and call me a fool, and I hadn't the heart to upset him or fight. I just said, 'A little farewell gift. Wilfred and I struck up a friendship while he was here.'

Alec screwed up his nose as if to question why on earth I'd want to be friends with Wilfred Whitman. I explained how my post rounds had brought us into contact but left out the details. I made it sound so innocuous, but even without his reputation, a friendship between Wilf and I would have always been remarkable.

'Is this something Cliff ought to hear about?'

I rubbed my eyes. 'Oh! Cliff is not my keeper!'

'All right, don't snap!' He hesitated a moment, then, 'Did he kiss you?'

'What? Who?'

He smiled. 'You're blushing, so I know he did.'

There was no point arguing with him.

'Did he try anything on with you?'

'No!'

'Are you going to see him again?'

Just the idea that I wouldn't made my whole body ache. I sensed my shoulders turning in, my chest caving. 'I… I don't know. I hope so.'

'You and Wilfred Whitman?' he sneered incredulously. 'You know it can't work. He's as rich as the King.'

'Hardly.'

'He might as well be, as far as we're concerned. What about

his face?'

'What about it?'

'Don't bite my head off! In case you hadn't noticed he's a bit of a gargoyle.'

'Alec!' Was I the only one who saw Wilf's beauty?

'You've decided about Cliff, then.'

I stood and stretched, walked to the mantelpiece and stared at the girl looking back at me in the mirror: eyes sunk into dark grey shadows, skin sickly and white. My hair was skewed where I'd been lying on it, the collar of my uniform all creased. 'I told Cliff exactly what I thought the minute he proposed. I told you, too, but no one seems to think I'm capable of making up my own mind about anything.'

'No one said that.'

'Then why press me? It's Cliff, for heaven's sake!'

'Exactly. You've always lived in each other's pockets.'

'But can you really imagine us getting married?'

Alec laughed at me. 'Maybe you should imagine it. Maybe you'd like it.'

'I know *you* would. You spend more time with him than anyone. You've always wanted him for a brother.'

He conceded with a knowing look. 'Not my decision though. And I'm only playing devil's advocate. I don't think you should throw him off just because you've known him all your life and he can be an arse sometimes.' A flash of anger crossed his face. 'You're not perfect either.' He stood and patted my shoulders, conciliatory now. 'I'm hungry.'

I followed him into the kitchen, wondering if Cliff would be furious with me when he got back from training. I'd wait and tell him face to face, rather than put it in a letter. Not that it should come as a surprise that my final answer was no, but he wouldn't like it when he found out about Wilf. He'd get wind of it from Doris if I didn't tell him, so I knew I had to. But what would I say? I didn't even understand what had happened with Wilf, and what might still happen. The future was as murky as the lake's depths. Even if he did write, if he did return to Barnfield, what then? I'd felt such power in his words and glances – in the boat, resting against his shoulder, and the kiss we'd shared – they'd felt truer to me than anything. But our time together seemed apart from reality; our pasts and futures had been inconsequential. If we'd had more time, we would have had to leave that fairyland eventually. Did I really imagine he'd come back for me, that he'd court me, maybe even marry me one day? Could I picture myself as Mrs Whitman, living with him and the mad old captain at the Manor? The more I thought about it, the more absurd it seemed.

I tried to silence these thoughts; they taunted me that I'd been duped, that I was just as bad as the girls who'd had their hearts broken by Cliff. I'd always laughed at their stupidity – hadn't they realised their flings wouldn't last? Maybe they hadn't thought of anything. We were at war, and the future had never been less certain. I thought of Alec's brief foray with the land girl Linda – just passing the time till his papers arrived – and I cringed with fear. Was that what Wilf had done with me? He'd only been here for two weeks. He'd met a young, impressionable girl and had a bit of fun. He didn't even live in Barnfield, yet… *as long as you are here, I'll wish to be nowhere else…*

Alec was whistling as he dished up the bubble and squeak clumsily. He went to the door to call up to Dad that supper was ready, and I took my plate and sat at the table, deflated. Alec dug into his food before I heard Dad's feet on the stairs. 'Cheer up,' he said with his mouthful. 'You never mooned over Cliff like this. I suppose you think you're in love now.' He sighed when I ignored him. 'You know, Whitman's best avoided if what I've heard is true, and for all his money, I doubt he's good enough for you anyway.'

I found a smile for him somehow: this was as sweet and generous as Alec got, and I knew he meant it as a heartfelt compliment.

'Don't give up on Cliff just yet.'

'Alec…'

'Humour me, before I leave for the bloody battlefields,' he said, laying it on thick so I couldn't interrupt. 'Cliff would forgive you a little fling, I'm sure, once you reminded him of all of his.'

Dad came in then and told Alec off for starting without him. There was no more talk of Wilf or Cliff; if Dad had heard any of it, he didn't let on.

When the meal was over, Alec kicked back in his chair and rubbed his stomach. 'Oh, I can't wait for Army rations! I can't remember the last time I had a full belly!'

Wilf had promised to write, and despite what Alec said, and my own prickling doubts, I held on to hope when the mailbags were dropped off at the Post Office every morning and afternoon. Hadn't he been the one who'd invited me into the Manor, who'd waited for me at the Post Office and after church, who'd come to my home after dark? I thought of the little butterfly beside my bed, and his words in the twilight: *extraordinary things come along even when we least expect it.* How could I doubt that he felt as I did? His wealth and rank hardly seemed to matter in the face of such feelings, and he'd already told me he was tired of conventions.

It was foolish trying to plan my future anyway. The papers reminded me daily that it could be short or non-existent, although it was hard to believe that in Barnfield. On late summer mornings, with the promise of autumn in the air, with dew-strung cobwebs draped about the hedgerows, sometimes it felt each hour would stretch for days. The milk cart clattering down the lane and the pheasants' calls in the woods spoke of slow, soft days lived in peace. But just a few miles away in Finton, the sandbags were stacked high, the newsboys yelled their ghastly headlines and ARP wardens strutted like peacocks. Uniformed men and women hurried to and from the station, and women dabbed their eyes with handkerchiefs amidst the steam clouds on the platforms.

Inevitably, the day came for the handkerchief and glistening eyes to be my own.

I hugged Alec's shoulders like a vice as he kissed the top of my head, chuckling at my tears. 'It's only training! I'll be back in a couple of months.'

I released him reluctantly. 'It won't matter until you're back for good. I'll miss you.'

'I know.'

'You have to promise to write at least twice a week.'

'All right, all right, but they'll be the dullest letters you've ever received. Now stop blubbering! You're ruining this for me.'

I kissed him and let him go, and Dad shook his hand and told him to take care of himself. That was their goodbye. I remembered what Dad had told me, about it being a grim day if he ever saw Alec in uniform. I wished I'd told Alec now, because then he seemed to be hovering for something more, a word of encouragement or gesture of pride. But Dad's face was hard and resolute, and to Alec it must have looked like indifference. The next instant the guard blew his whistle and Alec jumped up into the carriage. He grinned at me from the window. He looked like a child on Christmas morning.

Dad and I spent the bus ride home in silence. Later that evening, we solemnly sipped our soup at the kitchen table. My eyes were red from sobbing all afternoon, my throat so raw that the soup tasted blander than ever. I could think of nothing worth saying, nothing that didn't relate to Alec's departure, and since I knew Dad would squirm and change the subject if I did, I stayed quiet.

The house had never felt so empty. Alec had filled each space with noise and colour, but now the clock ticked louder, the walls and floors creaked for the lack of him. Dad and I chatted, of course, when we had the heart to. We were like an old married couple, existing gently together in a house that suddenly seemed too large for the both of us. Sometimes in the evenings, we sat by the wireless or read in the living room, and I often found myself frozen before the window in the kitchen, watching the still lane, my hands in the washing up, lost in empty thought.

It was like time was dying in Barnfield, each minute a weary last breath. I read the papers and received letters from Jean and knew the world was churning in all its horror around us, but for me, the days were long and cold. There was nothing to look forward to except the Great Hope of the war one day finishing and everything returning to normal. But thinking about that was like trying to imagine how many stars there were and what was beyond them; it made me queasy with nervousness. I didn't have a 'normal' to return to, none of us did. I didn't even know if the war *could* end – perhaps it would go on forever, until there was no one left. I'd been a child at the start of it. I was still a child. I didn't know anything beyond the inevitability of my current existence, but the idea of living like this until I died was unfathomable. There had to be a change at some point, didn't there?

Perhaps not. The village was full of spinsters and their shadows. The Misses Tarrow, who did their best with the church flowers. The aptly named Miss Fright, who taught infants at the local school. There was Miss Reed, who'd altered dresses before she'd been called up, and Miss Keane, who cleaned houses in Finton. Miss Spokes worked as a doctor's secretary and brought jam to the Post Office in the autumn. Miss Austen taught the piano and had a permanently red nose. These women had lost their husbands or chances of them in the Great War. They'd filled the spaces their children would have taken with the ephemera of quiet lives. Perhaps I was destined to end up like them, still here in forty years' time, still staring out of the window, waiting for something to move.

One day, a quaint fancy entered my imagination: 'Perhaps we should take in an evacuee?' For a few minutes I was quite excited about it. But Dad kept his eyes on his paper. 'I don't think that would be a very good idea, my dear,' he said calmly, but firmly, and I knew there was no point pressing him. I wasn't sure I had the heart for it anyway. My days were monotonous but busy enough already, as busy as I could make them. Mrs B praised my industry and joked that I'd be running the Post Office before too long. I wished I could run it. I wished I could look ahead to a time when she handed the reins to me. But, however industrious, I was only a sojourner, treading in Alfie's shoes, keeping his life warm for him. One day he'd be back and I wouldn't be needed. It was what I wanted. It *had* to be what I wanted, because to wish that Alfie wouldn't come back to his loving mother would make me wicked.

I carried on, just as the poster on the Post Office noticeboard told me to. I set my alarm clock and splashed my face and made breakfast and turned up at Mrs B's door every morning. I sorted post and peddled for miles, took down telegrams and delivered them. I issued stamps and postal orders and dog licences and listened to hours of small talk. I stayed later than needed to tidy the back room, mop the floors or balance the books. I went home and cooked dinner and tidied the house, washed out clothes, shopped in Finton on my half day and went to church on Sundays. Distractions drew my thoughts away from Alec, from Cliff. From Wilf. But in the still of the late evening, my brother's face filled my thoughts, and when I had worn all worries for him thin, it faded, and in its place, a torn lip, a flash of brilliant blue.

A few weeks passed, and still no letter from Wilf. The more I thought about our time together, the more it felt as if the whole thing had been just a daydream. I considered writing to Jean and confiding in her. It would be such a burden lifted, and also make it real somehow. If only she were here, I was sure she'd know what to say. She'd find a way to make me laugh and persuade me to go to the pictures with her. Her absence, along with Alec and Cliff's, only made me see how much I needed them. I was friendless without them. There weren't many other people our age in the village – Doris Howard was my best hope for a confidante, and even if I'd been mad enough to be tempted, her previous reaction to Wilf made me think it was best to avoid her at present.

Though I craved Jean's advice, part of me was frightened to hear it, so I held back, waiting for Wilf's promise to come to fruition and prove all my whispering doubts wrong. In the meantime, more nights than not I woke in the still, early hours, hair damp with sweat, head fuggy with the living remnant of that familiar watery prison. But now it was Alec's face that rose from the deep to pull me under, a wound on his forehead oozing blood. His wide bright eyes were lost behind murky pink clouds.

*

Towards the end of September, Mrs B received a priority telegram for the Manor: the nephew of Miss Brennan, Captain Whitman's nurse, had been wounded.

There was a chill in the air and the roads were wet from a night of rain. As I approached the Manor a car sped through a puddle and splashed me, so when I dismounted to ring the doorbell my feet were squelching in my shoes. There was no answer, so I rang again and knocked loudly, trying to push the memories of Wilf from my head: I saw him in the open doorway, a shy smile on his lips, entreating me to come inside. *I don't think a cup of tea ever hurt anyone, Grace.* Why hadn't he written? I longed for news, and if he felt just a quarter of the agony I did, wouldn't he want to hear from me too?

I was just about to give up and leave when I heard shuffling behind the door, and the lock being grappled with. The door opened a crack, and then a little further, and in the gloomy gap I saw a wan face gazing back at me. Grey eyes caught the daylight: could it really be him? His face was low; he was stooping, I assumed, although I couldn't see his body. He looked older than I'd remembered or imagined – for how much of my memory had come from dreams or conjecture? His moustache and hair were whitish grey. His skin was so pale, almost translucent, like newspaper left out in the rain, and in that moment the past few years fell away and I was thirteen again, floundering in the water with a watcher on the shore.

I don't know how long I stood there, but when I woke to the silence between us, I saw he was studying me with just as much surprise and curiosity. I kept expecting the nurse or the maid to appear, to apologise profusely and take him back into the depths of that dark, lonely place. But no one came. It was just the two of us, face to face and mute. Did he recognise me? Was that even possible? If he did, I was sure he'd be angry with me. I recalled his expression by the lake, stern yet distant. I wasn't sure he'd really seen me then. Perhaps he couldn't see me now. I didn't know the extent of his madness.

In the end, I had to speak. We couldn't stay frozen like that forever, and to ignore him or walk away seemed so rude. 'Captain Whitman?'

He didn't answer but seemed to start at the name. He looked down and a puzzled frown grew on his forehead.

'I have a telegram—'

'Your shoes are wet,' he interrupted.

Stumped and surprised by the lucidity of his tone, I followed his gaze down to my sodden feet, as if I'd only just become aware of them.

He opened the door wider and stepped forward. He was dressed in an ordinary shirt and slacks, but his feet were bare. There was an unnerving familiarity to every part of his face, as if time had swept Wilf forward thirty or forty years and now only the shell of him remained.

He kept one hand on the door. 'What have you been doing?' he asked with a queer mix of irritation and affection.

'It's been raining, sir. A car splashed me.'

'A car?'

'Yes.'

He frowned. 'You shouldn't be out and about in the wet, my dear.'

'I… I have a telegram, sir.'

It took a few seconds for him to look at me, and when he did, the confusion in his eyes turned to panic. His lip seemed to quiver, and the fingers on the door grew white.

'For Miss Brennan.'

He squinted. His lips worked at words but no sound came out. He looked utterly lost, and my heart went out to him.

'For your nurse, sir,' I said gently. 'Miss Agnes Brennan?'

'Oh! Agnes, yes…' There was relief in his voice but none in his expression. He looked beyond me and fixed his stare so intently that I was forced to turn around and see if anyone was coming down the drive. There was nothing there except the drifts of leaves in the wind.

'Would you fetch her, sir?' I continued kindly, and when he

ignored me: 'Is there a maid or someone else I can call?'

He snapped out of his reverie and met my eyes again. The suggestion of a smile graced his lips. 'No, no, my love. You have already done so much. Don't trouble yourself, come in and rest.'

I hesitated, for it was obvious he was elsewhere, with someone else. God only knew. I pitied him, and Wilf, who had to see his own father like this.

'Come on, Bixxy, don't dally,' he continued, gesturing for me to step inside. 'The warm air is getting out.'

'Sir, my name is Grace Wells. I'm from the Post Office, and I have a telegram for your nurse, Agnes Brennan.'

He smiled unsurely, then seemed to understand me. His hand fell from the door. 'Give it to me.'

'I ought to deliver it directly to Miss Brennan, sir.' In this instance I wasn't even sure the captain knew his own name, let alone his nurse's, and doubted the telegram would find its way to her. It was awkward denying his request, but I had no cause to be embarrassed, for he clearly wasn't of sound mind. I waited for him to comprehend me, then he sighed with resignation and walked away, leaving the door wide open. He shrunk into the dim hallway and disappeared into the room where Wilf had taken me, and I wondered if he was really going to fetch the nurse, or if he'd just had enough of me. I was poised to knock on the door again and call out, when I heard a little tinkling bell, and seconds later he reappeared. 'She'll be here in a minute,' he said clearly.

'Thank you.'

He nodded to the telegram in my hand. 'Not bad news, I hope?'

'I… I really can't say, sir,' I stumbled, thrown by his sudden, apparent rationality.

'I thought…' he began, then stopped himself. He cleared his

throat. 'When you mentioned a telegram, I thought perhaps it was about my son.' He held my gaze, and I knew I was dealing with a different man now.

His eccentricity and the mention of Wilf had set my pulse racing. 'No, sir.'

He smiled. 'I beg your pardon, I didn't catch your name.'

'Grace Wells, sir.'

He gave a short laugh, which startled me. 'Ah, yes, Grace! You know him, don't you? You know my Wilfred.'

My cheeks burned, with fear or pride I couldn't be sure. *My Wilfred* – the phrase was so endearing, and I was envious of its intimacy. 'Yes, sir.'

Captain Whitman nodded and said, almost to himself, 'Yes, he mentioned you.'

I wished I had the nerve to ask him what he'd said. A couple of minutes earlier I would have done, for what did a madman care for decorum? But now the old captain stood taller and seemed to all intents and purposes completely sane and proper. He was relaxed, as any man should be in his own home, and he spoke to me with an air of authority and distance appropriate to our respective stations.

Still, I was in luck. The nurse was taking her time, and the captain had a silence to fill: 'Tell me, has he written to you?'

The question cut straight to my core. If only he knew the pain it stirred. But I kept my composure. 'No, sir.'

Captain Whitman seemed to shrug, and sighed, 'No, me neither. He was never very good with letters.'

Immediately the look of confusion returned to his eyes. I wondered how often he was used to receiving letters from his son, if he could even remember reading any. My heart sank. The captain looked at me, his expression glazed, and I sensed he was in a different place again. He studied me for a moment, then opened his mouth to speak, and I braced myself. 'Have we met before, Grace?'

My pulse beat thick and hard. Had he recognised me? 'No, sir.'

'Just a minute more, I should think,' he said softly, with an apologetic smile.

I returned it, awkward and forced.

'You must forgive me,' he went on. 'They wouldn't let me see you. Forgive me.'

My smile faded. I said nothing. The nurse would appear soon, surely, and the captain was lost again.

'You must forgive me!' he repeated more fervently, his eyes wide and desperate. Behind him the dark hallway was still silent. 'I never forgot you, I swear, and I… I just couldn't…'

I was forced to respond, 'Please, there's no need to worry, sir.'

He shook his head sadly. 'Oh, no, no…' He began repeating 'no' very quietly under his breath, and I felt a little panic flicker inside me, trying to push Alec's ghost stories from my mind. What was taking the nurse so long?

'Sir,' I soothed. 'Please calm yourself. All is well.'

He looked up at me with a child's uncertainty. 'All is well?'

'Yes.'

'But I *saw* you. I saw you in the water!'

My blood froze. Was he talking to me, or someone else? The things he was saying, the name he'd called me – Bixxy – it was obvious he was only half there. But he *had* seen me in the water, hadn't he?

'Don't worry, my dear, I'm coming. I heard your call. I'm coming to save you…'

Amidst his ramblings I relaxed a little. I was sure now he didn't know me: he looked beyond me again, just as he had the first time I saw him from the lake. And his mutterings were gentle, if incoherent. He wasn't angry, he was trying to soothe me. I let him mumble on, the telegram tight in my fingers.

Suddenly there were footsteps and Miss Brennan appeared, all flusters and brusque apologies. She was a sturdy, middle-aged woman with a broad, plain face, and greying hair pulled up in a bun. She looked as though she had the strength to wrestle Captain Whitman to the ground if need be, but despite the silly tales we'd once believed, seeing him now, I couldn't imagine he was a violent sort of man. He seemed to sink a little in her presence, and his eyes kept darting around from me to the empty driveway and the dark house within.

Miss Brennan took the telegram with a grave look, stiffening when she saw it was marked 'Priority'. Mrs B usually delivered the ones that brought news of death – she was better at dealing with tears and hysterics. It had become common knowledge that Mrs B at your door with a telegram was as good as a visit from the Grim Reaper himself. Perhaps Miss Brennan knew this, because she simply slipped the telegram into her apron, then looked between me and the gibbering captain and apologised again. I told her not to worry, and turned to be on my way, but the captain called out to me as he was bustled inside – 'Grace!'

I turned at the sound of my name, and our eyes met. I couldn't be sure if he had command of his thoughts again.

'I heard your call,' he said with warmth. 'I am coming, hold on!'

Miss Brennan dismissed the remark with a shake of her head. 'Think nothing of it,' she told me, and shut the door.

Chapter 12

I could think of little but the captain as I cycled back to the village. I had finally come face to face with the legend and heard his voice, only to find the formidable lunatic was just a confused, elderly man. I tried to piece together what he'd said, but the words made no sense. The name, Bixxy, was his wife's, surely – a shorter form of Beatrice. I recalled her portrait on the mantelpiece in the Manor, and didn't imagine there was any likeness between her and me, but the captain's mind seemed unconfined by reason.

As I approached the Post Office, I shuddered at the thought of his quivering voice, imploring my forgiveness, or rather *her* forgiveness. What did he need forgiveness for? Hadn't Wilf said he'd struck her once? The poor man was obviously haunted with horrors and guilt, but I remembered what Wilf had told me of his mother's affair too. *My father is a good man, Gracie. He's had to cope with a lot in his life*. I couldn't imagine him ever being in command, leading my father into battle as a younger man. But there had been moments of clarity when he'd spoken calmly, and my nerves sang to think that Wilf had mentioned me to him. I obviously meant something to him.

I leaned my bike against the Post Office wall and felt a great weight on my shoulders as I went inside. I so wished Wilf would write, if only so I could write back. I had no address for him and I'd never asked where he was posted. I wanted him to know I was thinking of him. He had opened a space inside me that seemed to bleed with feeling, and I felt he was the only one who could understand me. He would appreciate my worries for Alec, and my loneliness now. He would know how to comfort me, just as he had in the boat on the lake. My chest burned with the memory of his strong shoulder supporting me, the bliss of his embrace.

As I hung up my coat and cap in the back room, I blinked back tears and found my feet had turned to stone. I stood alone, feeling my heart beat harder, and I admitted in that moment what I should have admitted weeks ago. I was in love with Wilfred Whitman. I think I'd loved him from the second he'd stepped onto the floor of the village hall and silenced Doris's wedding guests. I thought of his unsettling, dark eyes in the shadow of the hall, our stilted conversations at the Manor. The invisible, silent threads that had woven us together with each glance and touch. It didn't matter that I'd known him so briefly. It didn't need to make sense. He'd taken a part of me with him – a part of my soul – and I couldn't function properly without it. I didn't want it back, I wanted to be entwined with him forever. In order to live and breathe I needed to be near him.

All the time I'd been standing there in a dream, Mrs B had been serving a customer, but as the bell above the door tinkled, she called out for me to join her. I wiped my eyes and did as I was told.

She looked me up and down with concern. 'Lord, you look like a drowned rat!'

My wet trousers clung to my legs but I'd long forgotten about them. I explained about the car but was too distracted to be chatty. Mrs B pressed her palm to my forehead in a motherly way, and I felt a swell of love towards her which only brought fresh tears to my eyes.

'What's all this?' She took me into the back room and sat me down. 'What's happened?'

I tried to insist it was nothing, that I was just tired and feeling down in the dumps about Alec, but his name only made me cry more and before I knew it I was heaving great sobs, with Mrs B's arms around me. I hadn't cried much when I was younger, and when I had I usually got over it by myself or with Alec's encouragement, but today I was glad to be wrapped in Mrs B's embrace, her soothing voice in my ear. Mercifully, no customers arrived, and within a few minutes I'd got a hold of myself and Mrs B made us both a cup of weak tea with her dwindling rations.

'Did something happen at the Manor?'

I was too tired to lie, and what was the point of keeping it to myself? 'I saw the Captain,' I admitted.

'Did he frighten you?'

'No, not all. He spoke to me.'

'What did he say?' She sounded more concerned than intrigued.

'Nothing that made any sense.'

Mrs B took a sip of her tea and pressed her lips into a hard line. Then she got up and walked out into the shop, and I heard her lock the door.

'What if someone comes?' I asked when she was back with me.

'They can come back later.'

It was rare for Mrs B to shut up the Post Office, and as I was no longer crying, I guessed she had something she needed to tell me.

'Did the captain mention Wilfred at all?' she asked gently.

I held back my reply. I saw sympathy in her eyes but wasn't

sure I could trust it, thinking back to when she'd chided me about Wilf and warned me to leave him alone. What would she say if she knew I'd ignored her advice, that I'd let myself fall for him so deeply that it now felt like drowning? But perhaps she saw it in me. She pushed me to answer, and so I told her that he had spoken briefly about Wilf.

'What did he tell you?'

I tried to decipher her anxious look. 'Only that he hadn't written since he left.'

Mrs B turned away. 'And has he written to you?'

'No.' The word brimmed with heartache.

She met my gaze with pity. 'Then I ought to tell you… though I know it will do no good. I know there's something between you. I saw him at church that day.'

'Mrs B what is it?' I demanded with sick, urgent dread. 'Is it bad news?'

She saw my agony and placed her hands on my shoulders. 'Wilfred is well, Gracie. He's unhurt.'

'But he's been in another accident?'

'No, he hasn't been in an accident. He hasn't seen a minute's action since he returned.' Her words were clipped with disapproval, and she finished them with a sigh.

'I don't understand.'

'Wilfred refused service, Gracie.'

She waited for my reaction, her eyes large with disappointment, but I only blinked in dumb silence, grasping to understand the magnitude of what she'd just said, all feelings illusive.

'I thought you might have known. I thought he might have told you before he went. It was in the papers today. He was court-martialled. He's been stripped of rank.' She took my hand. 'Gracie, Wilfred is a conscientious objector.'

Now there was a term I knew. My mind darted back to Alec,

smoking as I'd hung up some washing, telling me about the 'conchie' meetings in Finton and how they were just a bunch of cowards. And then I remembered Doris telling me how unpopular Wilf was, and all the rumours that had followed him around since his return to Barnfield – mystery, madness, cowardice – could they really be true? No, I refused to believe it! He'd shown me he wasn't mad, and his injury proved he wasn't a coward. And yet, hadn't he spoken of challenging conventions? Hadn't he said – I'd never forget it – 'this bloody war' with such passion, such hatred, it had shocked me? All his words came flooding back, and with them a surge of panic, a sense of the ground being pulled from beneath me, of depths stretching down for miles. *There may come a day when you'd rather have nothing to do with me.*

'No!' I cried, though why or to whom I don't know.

'Get a hold of yourself, Gracie!' Mrs B begged. I was standing, somehow, and she pulled me down again. 'Is this really such a shock? He's a strange fellow, and all those rumours… there's no smoke without fire.'

'How can you say that? You always told me not to listen to rumours!'

'Yes, but…'

'You think he's a coward, don't you?'

'Lower your voice! Do you want the whole village to hear you?' She tutted and shook her head at me, but I was too shocked to feel ashamed.

'He's not a coward,' I muttered, to myself more than her. He'd joined up as a reservist. He'd served for four years. But a man who wouldn't fight anymore – what else could I call him, but a coward, or… The captain's grey eyes flashed in my mind.

Mrs B was watching me. 'He must have said *something* to you? I thought… You gave me the impression that you knew him.' Her words cut me open, and my chest caved suddenly as if I'd been struck. 'Oh, Gracie, what have you got yourself into?'

'Nothing,' I said weakly. 'I didn't promise him anything.'

Mrs B hesitated and brushed the hair from my face. 'But your eyes are red, and your face is pale. Your hands are shaking as if I'd just told you your own fiancé was dead!'

I refused to look at her. I couldn't admit my love for him, not when it was so new to me, and not now my head was in such turmoil. Minutes ago, he'd been the best of men, but what now? I still yearned for him. I saw his face in my mind and felt all the familiar passion. But how could I love a man who'd shirked his duty, who'd turned his back on what was right? I'd known him even less than I thought. He'd led me to believe him a hero, or at least, that is how I'd envisaged him. In truth, he'd never lied to me, but it still felt like a betrayal. He could have told me the truth on the island, or on our walk back through the woods. Had he been frightened to share it with me, in case I turned away from him in disgust? *A conscientious objector… court-martialled… stripped of rank*. How could it come to such drastic measures? He'd be shamed forever. Wherever people knew him, they'd turn their faces away. Would I too?

Now Mrs B was reading an article to me – a short excerpt in the paper – the son of a brave veteran of the Great War's fall from grace. No reference to the captain's mental decline; he was the honourable father, shamed by his son. There were few details. Flight Lieutenant W Whitman as was, who'd flown 26 sorties and escaped death with disfiguring injury, but returned from medical leave as a newly registered conscientious objector.

How long had he held such convictions? Doris alluded to them before his accident – his crew wishing him dead! – but if he was newly registered, perhaps he'd been swayed by his time in convalescence. Yet not all injured men became conscientious objectors. What set Wilf apart from them – a fervent heart or a weakened mind?

Mrs B read on that Wilf had refused both active and non-combatant duties, and consequently been declared LMF: *Lacking in Moral Fibre*. A coward. I thought of his heated words on the island and his seeming despair at the futility of war – yes, I saw it now, I heard the disdain in his tone – he had seemed then to be the most principled and passionate and honest person I'd ever met. Certainly not *lacking* in moral fibre – if anything he seemed to have too much of it. But he'd spoken so clearly and reasonably; there'd been no hint of the madness I'd seen in the old captain's eyes. Wilf wasn't crazy or shell-shocked, though he probably had a right to be. He'd made this choice rationally.

The article concluded that his case would go to tribunal, and he would probably end up doing manual labour or humanitarian work. He was out of the RAF.

A sudden fear gripped me that overrode all else. 'Will he go to prison?' I'd heard stories of conchies going to jail in the Great War, or even worse, getting shot.

Mrs B tapped the paper. 'If he accepts work, he'll be more useful down a mine than in a jail.'

'A mine? Is that where they send them?'

She scowled a little. 'I'm no authority on it,' she said briskly, 'but I have heard so, yes.'

I pictured Wilf down in the depths of the earth, his face blackened. He'd been so highly educated, I doubted he'd ever done a day's manual labour in his life. He was fit, but not strong like Cliff. He would never cope with it.

Mrs B folded up the paper. 'I wouldn't waste your tears on him now. It's what he deserves, if you ask me,' said curtly. Then, softening a little, 'I did the right thing telling you?'

'Yes,' I said with gratitude. So much better to receive a shock from her than hear it through gossips, and I would, I knew, be hearing little else for days. Once the news got out, the Post Office would be buzzing. The Howards would have a field day; I could already picture Doris's victorious, beaming smile.

To all of Barnfield the news would be scandalous but sweet, a welcome distraction, another page in the Whitman's outrageous story. Only I would feel its sting. Mrs B's reaction would prove kinder than most, I was certain, and I wouldn't blame anyone for despising Wilf. With Alec and Cliff in the Army, I should despise him too. To support him would be a betrayal of the boys' service. It would bring shame down on all of us. And how *could* I support him? How could he refuse to fight with us against such a brutal force? I knew he despaired of it, but did he think he was the only one? Did he imagine all the other men enjoyed it?

I felt like screaming with anger. I'd have given anything to keep Alec at home, out of danger, but I knew he had to go. There might not have been any glory in his service, but there was certainly honour. If no one stood up to fight, our country would be defeated. We'd be occupied just like France, in the terrible grip of Hitler's fist. To hold one's hands up and say 'no, not me', was surely cowardice and treachery, and I couldn't believe the man I'd fallen for could do it. This was war and people had to do horrible things. That was the foul nature of the beast. Even I, a paltry little post girl from Barnfield, could see that. No one wanted to do it: *this bloody war.*

My spirit raged, and in my mind I gripped Wilf's shoulders and shook him till he saw sense. But it was too late. The magic was unravelling, the scales were falling, and I feared I'd only just begun to see him for who he truly was.

CHAPTER 13

The news of Wilf's dishonourable discharge spread like a disease through the village, and within a day or so it was inescapable. Everyone who came into the Post Office or saw me on my rounds wanted to talk about it and pick apart the details. Mrs Howard – an authority on the matter, due to Doris's new brother-in-law's information – related stories of Wilf's reputation before his crash, how he'd been seen reading pacifist pamphlets, and been refused service in the airmen's pub. Others, who only knew Wilf by name and his one brief appearance at church during his leave, decided that he had untrustworthy eyes and an unhealthy air of melancholy about him. Like weeds, the tales grew taller: he'd long preached dissent in the ranks; he'd marched with pacifists; he'd really received his wounds in a pub brawl.

I did my best to shut my ears to their words. My thoughts were weary. All my memories had been blackened and blurred. I hated him for what he'd done and for letting me believe he was honourable. If I could have only known what he was from the start, I'd never have taken tea with him. I'd never have been so captivated by him. Yet I had loved him. It had just begun to bloom inside me but was now defiled, the flowers torn and trampled in the dirt. But its roots remained, stubbornly tangled and woven into my veins and flesh. I couldn't justify it. I longed to despise him entirely, but it seemed that, despite everything, some part of my affection for him refused to die.

Doris caught me on my round one morning. She ran out of the house after me, her curlers still in her hair. She was breathless by the time she'd caught up, her eyes twinkling with mirth. 'Gracie! Well, what do you think now, about that awful Wilfred Whitman? Didn't I tell you he was bad news?'

And hadn't she fawned over him at her wedding too? But 'yes' was my answer, and my voice sounded so fatigued I prayed she'd leave me be, like a wounded dog.

She seemed a little surprised and disappointed by my response. Perhaps she'd expected tears or a fight. Perhaps she thought I sympathised with him. 'Have you heard from Alec?'

'Yes. He's settled.'

'Where is he based?'

'Bedfordshire.'

'And Cliff?'

'He finishes training in a month. He'll have a few days' leave then.'

'Won't it be wonderful to see him again?'

'Yes,' I said honestly. The sooner things got back to normal the better. It might only be for a few days, but I felt having Cliff in Barnfield again would do me and the village the power of good. 'Dad's asked him to stay in Alec's room.'

Doris grinned. 'What a splendid idea!' She leaned forward a little. 'A little practice run for living under the same roof in the future?'

I hadn't the will to respond or contest her, mainly because I'd thought the same thing. I hadn't forgotten what Alec had said: *don't give up on Cliff just yet.* But I had given up on him – I'd thrown away our years together for a man I'd just met – and what good had it done me? Now I cringed when I recalled

Cliff's proposal and my hot, haughty refusal.

Doris patted my shoulder. 'I'm so glad you've seen sense, Gracie.' Her tone was so patronising but it was all I deserved. I smiled back thinly, and by the time she left me I'd agreed to attend the next WVS meeting too.

*

Wilf's letter came on a Friday: two envelopes amongst the second post, one for the captain and a thicker one for me. I'd waited so long for it, but in recent days I'd imagined it would never come, and felt some relief. Now it was here it stirred my thoughts to chaos. Part of me wished to rip it up and burn it – how dare he write to me now? But I longed for the untold side of the story, hoping foolishly it may contain some mitigating factors I'd yet to consider. I pressed it into my pocket and felt it there throughout my round, burning like a hot coal.

I posted the captain's letter through the Manor's door without ceremony, and sped off on my bike before I had a chance to catch sight of anyone who might be peering through the windows. I hadn't seen him since the day I'd delivered Miss Brennan's telegram, but I pictured him reading Wilf's letter and wondered if his heart would break. Did he already know? Would he even be able to comprehend it? He'd given half his mind for his country thirty years ago, but I doubted even a madman would be able to stomach a coward for a son.

I rode back to the village and helped Mrs B shut up shop, keeping the letter from Wilf a secret. As I prepared dinner that evening, I tried to ignore the nagging temptation to run up to my room and open it. I told myself it deserved no special urgency. Still, by bedtime I was itching to read it, and my hands shook as I tore the envelope as irreverently as possible. Despite everything, I felt a thrill at seeing my name in his handwriting.

Dear Gracie

I know you will have heard by now. I won't ask your forgiveness for what I've done, for I can guess what you must think of me and I wouldn't burden you with an impossible request. Forgive me, though, for not writing sooner and informing you of the news myself. You deserved that much from me. It's not the truth I was afraid of – I'm not ashamed of what I've done – but selfishly I wanted to have you thinking well of me for as long as possible. I've lost many things in these past few weeks, but I fear your friendship will prove to be the greatest sacrifice.

Can you bear to read on and hear my explanation? I'll trust you'll have the grace to, and write it anyway. Do you remember me telling you that my friends and I had joined up as reservists before the war? Well, we did, that is, all except one. One friend – his name is Ivan Lovekyn – did not join up. He was a pacifist, so this didn't surprise us, but we supposed in time he would 'see sense' and do his bit. I later learned that he'd refused conscription on the grounds of being a conscientious objector. By that time I'd long completed my training and was serving as a navigator with Bomber Command. The news of Ivan's refusal to enlist, and his consequent tribunal, came as a shock to some of my comrades – most found it distasteful and refused to have anything more to do with him. I, however, was intrigued by his stand and had to admit that the pacifists' cause had begun to strike a chord with me. Let me explain…

I can't go into great detail, but when the war started, our targets were military – our missions were vital in disrupting the enemy's progress. Casualties were inevitable, of course, but the greater cause was clear and, dare I say it, honourable. I had no qualms about following orders, thought of nothing but getting the job done and returning to base in one piece. I can't say I was happy about it – I'm not sure anyone is – but at least I had no wife or family to worry about like many chaps.

Things began to turn sour in early '42. Our targets moved from munitions factories to the industrial cities – in short, to civilians. I'll never forget the night I had to plot our course to Essen, with the images of Coventry and the Blitz in my mind, knowing the abject terror we were about to rain down on innocents. Yes, innocents! For do you imagine every woman and child of that godforsaken country harbour the Nazi's manic hatred in their hearts? I cannot believe it! Yet when I voiced such concerns with my friends they reproached me for siding with the enemy. I learned to keep my thoughts to myself, but as the nights wore on I found I couldn't escape the raging doubts within. I winced to hear of our 'successes' on the wireless. I hung my head in shame as the bombs dropped. I began to see myself as a murderer.

You will remember me telling you of my godfather Wing Commander Merrell. Douglas noticed my ennui – I imagine he was concerned that I was going the way of my father – and he put me on ground crew for a few months. I was happy with the arrangement, but my relief was short-lived. I couldn't shake off the sense that we'd made a wrong turn. Of course, I understood the greater cause, but it was the method I was questioning.

I began corresponding with Ivan (he drives ambulances now). He is enthusiastic to say the least, and I found his sermons on pacifism a little overzealous, but was glad of someone to confide in. Ivan himself is not against all combat, but due to his own religious upbringing, feels he cannot personally carry a weapon or be part of any operation that involves taking life. Ironically, I would have no issue taking another man's life in combat – it is the nature of war. But I draw the line at morale-crushing blanket bombing.

I spoke to Douglas, but he warned me that this kind of talk was dangerous. He forced me to accept leave, but a few days in bomb-ravaged London only seemed to compound my griefs. On my return, a fellow from my old crew – a nasty piece of work – saw me on my bed, reading a letter from Ivan, mistook it as a love-note, and whipped it from my hands. His intention was to read it aloud and embarrass me in front of the other men, but instead his face turned white and he loudly declared that 'Whitman is a conchie'. He called me many other things, besides, but I won't waste my ink on them. Despite protestation, I quickly became known as 'soft' – a pacifist, a coward, a commie… None of these were true. I have never been to a pacifist meeting in my life and don't hold sway with many of their arguments. As for a communist? The idea sickens me.

But now you are wondering how I came to register as a conscientious objector. Well, shortly after the above event, Douglas took some brief leave, and during those few days, his substitute reassigned me to ops – several logistical reasons coincided that meant an experienced navigator was required to join a sortie, and I, apparently, was their man. I didn't know the new crew well, and could tell that my poor reputation preceded me – I saw their shoulders sag on seeing me and I think they counted me as a bad omen. It seems they were right – that night our plane was hit, the wireless operator was killed, and I was injured.

I spent several weeks recovering in hospital. The time spent in that peaceful respite forced me to consider my next course of action. If I returned to service, I felt I'd be silencing my conscience. I imagined turning to drink or possibly losing my mind like Father. In the best case, I'd be killed quickly, but I would die doing something I wholly abhorred. There seemed to be no choice: I could not return to Bomber Command.

When Douglas visited me I told him of my plans to refuse service. I've never seen such disappointment in a man's eyes. He pleaded with me to reconsider. Right up until the last moment, he wrote and even visited – do you remember seeing him at the Manor that day? But I'd registered as a CO the day I left the hospital. At the court martial, they took my recent registration as a poor excuse – another example of my cowardice and lack of moral fibre. In their eyes I'd simply crumbled beneath the pressure. I was discharged. The case went to tribunal, where my voice was at least heard and understood, if not sympathised with.

And now I write to you from a dairy farm just north of Exeter. My bed is a pallet on the dirty floor of an old outbuilding. I share this dormitory with three other men – all CO's – all for completely different reasons (one of them doesn't even speak to me because of my years in active service). We have only been here for three days. The work is as you'd expect it to be – I'm sure in time I'll adjust to it and I'm glad to be useful for something. The farmer – Mr Trellis – treats us well enough, although we're not allowed to talk to his daughters and I doubt we'll be welcome in the nearby pub for a drink. But I have no cause to complain – I feel an enormous weight has been lifted from my shoulders.

Perhaps you think I don't deserve this relief. Do you too think I should have gone back and carried out my duty without question, washed my doubts away with drink and turned my heart to stone? Do you think me a coward, or weak, or touched by madness? You saw the papers too, Gracie – you saw photographs of blackened beams poking out of rubble like broken ribs from flesh. All those buildings razed and streets obliterated are awful, but it's the people beneath them we don't see. Here, we have our neat lists of dead and see their mourners… don't you think it's the same over there? I can't rejoice in their suffering, however glorious the cause. My very core detests it! I can't release bombs or plot coordinates or even file papers for such a heartless beast… If only I'd made the grade for Fighter Command, I might have died in a dogfight in my first week. At least my conscience would have been clear. As it is, I must live with the fact that I've killed more people than I can count, none of whom ever held a weapon in their hands.

This is who I am, Gracie. This is the man who held you that afternoon out on the island, the man who took a risk to kiss you… I have not changed, not really, though in your eyes I must seem like a stranger now. I'm sorry to disappoint you.

I never anticipated meeting you, but I'm so grateful I did. I felt, for those few days we knew each other, that I'd met someone who saw me and understood me, and – forgive me if I'm wrong – cared for me. Maybe I didn't tell you all my truths because I rather naively imagined you knew them anyway – I felt exposed under your gaze, like an open book. But I had intended to tell you my plans on that last night, at the boathouse. When we missed each other, it seemed it was never meant to be. There was no time. I'm not sure there ever was.

I fully understand any animosity you feel towards me – it's only right, with a brother at war, that you should hate my actions, and I would never ask you to change your mind. I don't know if I'll ever return to Barnfield, but if I do, you mustn't worry, I won't seek you out again. As it is, my father's health is deteriorating, and the estate will most likely be sold on his death.

I must sign off now. I wish so many things could have been different, but I suppose it doesn't matter now. I send you all my best wishes for a long and happy life. I won't forget the Small Blue.

Yours affectionately

Wilf

It was like I'd been playing a children's game; I'd been spun round and round and now had to find my bearings and walk, but the horizon wasn't where it was supposed to be and my mind felt strangely absent from my body. I had to read the letter through twice, and by the end of that second time I was glad I'd waited till I was alone, for I couldn't hold back my tears.

My thoughts swung like a pendulum, from outrage and unforgiveness to relief and even a glimmer of understanding. Now I knew why he'd done it, it softened the blow, but it didn't change who he was – who he'd always been, and hidden from me. But hadn't I sensed a hidden side of him? I'd glimpsed a troubling darkness in him all along and I'd loved him anyway.

My chest was seized with aching, and I read his closing lines with the deepest wrench of sorrow. He'd left no address, and the postmark only confirmed what he'd already written, that he was near Exeter somewhere. He didn't want me to write, despite his sweet words, despite the fact I'd meant something to him. Perhaps it was a blessing – I'd been saved from making a terrible decision and throwing away what I had with Cliff. I'd already run too far with fantasy. There had never been any future for me with Wilf. But I still tried to fight the thought of living apart from him forever and only thinking of him with pity and condemnation. I scoured my mind for another way, knowing there was none. To forgive him would be to betray myself and my family, not to mention Cliff – I winced to imagine Alec's reaction if he were to find out I loved such a man.

I roughly folded the letter, then clenched it in my fist till it crumpled. I wished he hadn't sent it. I wished he hadn't explained himself, or stirred up those feelings from our short time together. It would have been so much easier to hate him, to forget him, to convince myself I'd been wholly deceived, if he'd never written at all.

I woke hours later, the little lamp on my bedside table still glowing. Annoyed with myself, I turned it off and stood, aching, then peeked beyond the blackout curtains into the shapeless night sky. Something scrunched beneath my sock as I made my way back to the bed, and I stooped to pick up Wilf's letter, which had fallen to the floor in my sleep. I folded it slowly, then blindly placed it into the wooden box I kept under my bed, along with all my letters from Jean, Alec and Cliff.

Beside the box was the little frame. I pulled it out with trembling hands. It was too dark to see, but I recalled how the butterfly's blue crescents had shimmered in the flame's light. I thought of the last hazy moments the Small Blue had known before I'd unwittingly killed it. It had lain in the net without our knowing while we talked, and died as Wilf's hand brushed mine, as he worked his subtle enchantment on my soul. He had captured me that day too. Had he known it? Yes, he must have done, for *I was the Small Blue*. I wished he'd never said it. I'd thought him so romantic, but now those words seemed to carry a curse. Now I felt the pin in my chest.

CHAPTER 14

I was in Alec's room, giving it an airing and making the bed up in anticipation of Cliff's arrival. It was late September; the nights and mornings had succumbed to autumn, but the noondays still clung on to the memory of summer, with warm sepia sunlight and late ripening apples in the garden.

It was about four o'clock, and the day was cooling. It was Sunday, a week or so since Wilf's letter. I'd been for a walk after breakfast, before church. There'd been frost on the church roof and the stile, and the woods were brighter now the trees were shedding. I took myself down to the lake, back to the spot where Wilf had helped me into his boat. But the water was still and flat. The air over the island was now filled with falling leaves, drifting side to side, down and down. I couldn't help imagining them as butterflies, tumbling to rest lifeless on the water's surface.

It was odd to be in Alec's room again without him sprawled out on the bed, or yelling at me from the bathroom or downstairs. Apart from a few clothes missing from his wardrobe, everything was just as it had always been. There was a chewed pencil on his bedside table, and I opened the drawer and smiled to see his worn-out little teddy bear lying on his pristine Christening bible.

I stretched some clean sheets over the bed, smoothing them out and imagining Cliff lying there the following night. The idea warmed me with a nostalgic longing. I thought of our nights in the woods, huddled together for warmth, back when Captain Whitman was still terrifying and I didn't give two hoots about his son.

Dad's tap on the door made me jump. 'You were miles away,' he said, tentatively stepping in from the landing.

I had been – I'd been on the boat with Wilf again, reliving those moments when I'd felt so secure. The memory was grey-tinged now, the sweetness marred by pain. But I held on to it nonetheless.

'What time does Cliff's train get in tomorrow?'

'Five o'clock. Mrs B says I can leave early to meet him.'

Dad nodded. 'He'd like that.' He put his hands in his pockets and glanced around the room. 'The place doesn't feel the same without them. It'll be good to see Cliff again.'

'Yes.'

He crossed his arms, then thought better of it and put them in his pockets again. 'You mustn't take him for granted, Gracie.'

I looked away from his earnest stare. 'I know.'

He cleared his throat. 'I was disappointed to hear what happened with Flight Lieutenant – *Mr* Whitman.'

He left a long pause, and I wasn't sure what he was referring to. He would have heard all about his discharge, but I sensed he meant what had happened between *us*. I thought back to the night Wilf had knocked on the door with the frame. *Whatever you hear about me, whatever people say, please just remember me as I am now, right here with you.*

'Captain Whitman was a brave man,' Dad went on,

surprising me; the Great War and its players were subjects usually steered well clear of.

'I've met him,' I said, and Dad raised his eyebrows. 'I spoke to him once, when I delivered something to the Manor.'

'How was he?' he said with a boyish hope that twisted something inside me.

'He was… unbalanced.'

Dad's gaze fell, as if I'd just told him someone had died. He nodded softly to himself but said, 'He was a brave man.' *Unlike his son*, was what he seemed to be implying.

I didn't need any persuading that what Wilf had done was wrong. I had turned the matter over in my head for so long I was sick of it. I heard dozens of people deriding him daily, and I agreed with half of them, but it didn't stop me from aching for him still. My love for him was now a torn and battered thing, a stained old rag fit for nothing. I couldn't forgive him, but neither could I forget him. I longed for what he'd been, knowing I could never have him back now because he'd never truly existed in the first place.

I was tired of Dad's reticence. I knew he wanted to tell me that Wilf wasn't worth my time; he probably wanted to know why he'd come to the house that day, or if there was anything still between us. He was only concerned for me. 'The Whitmans are none of our business, Dad.'

He lifted his head and smiled very faintly. 'I'm pleased to hear you say that.'

I tucked in the sheet corners neatly. 'Cliff will be used to everything being ship-shape now he's finished his training.'

'I daresay. It certainly won't do Alec any harm to learn how to make his bed properly.'

I smiled but didn't look up. It was the first time Dad had mentioned his name in over a week.

'You don't mind that I insisted on Cliff staying here, do you?'

Dad asked.

'No. It's very kind of you.'

'Only, I wasn't sure if everything was all right between the two of you. I had wondered if you'd quarrelled before he left.'

I rolled out the eiderdown. 'No?'

'I know he proposed. He asked my permission.'

I stood straight again and glanced at him. His eyes were sheepish, and I felt mine were too.

'I thought, perhaps, you'd turned him down because of…' He couldn't bring himself to say Wilf's name.

I reassured him instantly. 'I didn't turn him down,' I said, feeling slightly guilty, because I had flatly refused him at first. 'He asked me to think about it.'

The look of relief that came over Dad's face was almost comical, but I saw too how much the idea of Cliff and I meant to him. Who better than a sturdy, hardworking farmer and soldier for his daughter? Who else? Certainly not an aloof coward like Wilfred Whitman, anyway.

'I'm still thinking about it,' I said guardedly. Dad looked almost puzzled so I added, 'Don't you think I'm a bit young to be getting married?'

He frowned, as if he couldn't fathom what else an eighteen-year-old girl ought to be doing. But he said, 'Whatever you think best, Gracie.' There was weariness in every word, a sense of resignation.

'I'm not sure what's best.'

'Then you must think about it further,' he said, as if I was only trying to work out the answer to a crossword puzzle.

'I will.'

He gave me another of his quiet smiles.

'I promise I won't take him for granted,' I called out as he left, and he stopped in the doorway and looked back with gratitude. I heard my words again, like an imaginary echo in the room, and pictured Cliff's face with fondness. I thought to myself, *not anymore.*

CHAPTER 15

I was looking up the opposite end of the platform for Cliff when he left the train, so the first thing I felt was a firm tap on my shoulder. When I turned he'd already dropped his bag, and he wrapped his arms around me and planted a strong kiss on my lips. We broke into smiles and I turned him around, making a show of inspecting him in his uniform. He looked taller and certainly smarter than ever. He was clean shaven and had got himself a proper haircut. It gave him an unfamiliar edge – the same old Cliff but almost imperceptibly altered – as if I were looking at his reflection in a mirror.

'Aren't you a sight for sore eyes?' he said.

'Not too sore, I hope?'

'Not at all,' he grinned. 'I can't play the sympathy card with you, can I?'

'You don't need to play any cards with me, silly.'

I couldn't help running my hand down his face, holding him to me. After so many weeks apart it felt joyful to have him back again. I hadn't realised how much I'd missed him. His broad, tanned face, his laugh, even the smell of him, felt like lost memories restored. It had been weeks since I'd felt so buoyant, and knowing he was the cause of it filled me with hope. Perhaps absence really did make the heart grow fonder, or maybe this short time apart was all I'd needed to find out I did love him after all. It had certainly been enough time to realise how foolish I could be. I pushed away thoughts of Wilf and took Cliff's arm as he slung his bag over his shoulder.

I'd thought we'd get the bus back to Barnfield straight away, but Cliff wanted to go to the pub first, so we headed out into the town. Shopkeepers were locking up and people were heading home at the end of the working day; gentleman in suits tipped their hats to my uniformed companion as we passed, and I raised my head with pride. A couple of girls at a bus stop whispered and stared at him, and he obliged them with a smile and wink, sending them into cascades of giggles.

'Hey!' I tugged on his arm playfully.

He looked at me sideways with a roguish smile. 'What?' he played. 'We're not married, Gracie. I can wink at whoever I like.'

I couldn't help chuckling with him, and kissed him again before we entered The Crown. I didn't make a habit of going into pubs – it had seemed fun and grown-up when we were a little younger, sneaking in and having too much to drink before the landlord spotted us and chucked us out. But I had no cause to do it anymore, and no one to go with anyway. It was a dingy place inside, just a few bulbs glowing around the bar and on the walls, but the air was thick with smoke. It was an overcast day anyway and the few taped panes were grimy, so by the time the light reached inside it was murky and grey, and I felt like I'd been plunged into a sink of old dishwater.

Cliff found us a table in a corner and left me there to go and get our drinks. I watched him lean against the bar and chat with the landlord; he seemed to know him. Perhaps this had been one of his regular haunts. I glanced around at the men with their pints and papers, some talking in low, rumbling tones. Apart from a sickly-looking chap at the bar, everyone was about Dad's age or older. It didn't seem like the kind of place a young lad like Cliff would frequent, but then the whole town seemed aged and slow now its young men had all been stolen away.

Cliff returned and clunked the glasses down so some beer spilled onto the table. He glanced around with an air of frustration, as if he'd been reading my mind. We talked about Alec for a while. The boys had always been so tightly bound, and I felt closer to Alec having Cliff beside me again. It was like he carried my brother's spirit in him, and I relaxed into my seat as he told me a bit about his training.

'You should have seen the place, Gracie. How the other half live! Acres of garden. Stables as big as a village. The house was like a palace.'

'Did you go inside?'

'No, they didn't let the riff raff in, only the officers. We were camped in the parklands, but it was fine.'

'And where to now?'

He tapped his nose. 'Careless talk, Frauline.'

'You have no idea, do you?'

'Of course I don't. None of us do.'

'Aren't you nervous?'

'I don't think that would help much, do you?' He took a sip of his pint and licked the foam from his lip, the picture of ease. It wasn't an act, it was just Cliff: pragmatic and self-assured. It could be infuriating sometimes, but right now it seemed brave, bearing in mind he could be anywhere by this time next week. The thought made me reach out and squeeze his arm. He looked down at my hand and raised his eyebrows with cheerful surprise. 'Don't tell me you've turned sentimental, Gracie?'

I felt my cheeks flush and narrowed my eyes at him but I couldn't hold off my smirk.

'D'you miss me then?'

'Seems so.' I couldn't believe how easy it felt to be with him again.

He smiled and took another sip. He held my gaze and I thought he might bring up our conversation after Doris's wedding; I felt braced for it. But he said, 'Anything interesting happened since I've been away?'

I updated him on all the trifling gossip: Mrs Dearling's cat having kittens; the dwindling supplies in Finton; some local children getting caught throwing stones at the phone box and receiving a public dressing down from Mrs B. He chuckled along to all of it, but I couldn't share the fun, because I knew I couldn't avoid the biggest news of all: Wilf's dismissal and disgrace. It felt now that every second was winding down to it. If I didn't tell him, he'd hear it in the village soon enough, and wonder why I hadn't.

My face burned as I recounted the article we'd read in the paper. I was certain he'd see right through me every time I mentioned Wilf's name, and I hid my hands in my lap in case they betrayed me with trembling. Cliff didn't seem to notice me though; his expression clouded as I explained what Wilfred Whitman had done; his disgust was evident even before he opened his mouth.

'Well didn't I always tell you he was a fucking coward?' He winced before he swallowed his next sip, as if the beer had turned stale.

I said nothing, only thought how much angrier he'd be if he knew I'd loved Wilf. But how could I tell him? It felt so good to be back with him again, so comfortable. I liked the flirtatious sparkle in his eye. I wanted his strong arm around me. I didn't want him to look at me with repulsion and disappointment, but I couldn't imagine him reacting in any other way, and I felt the hard nudge of shame in my back.

The news had shaken him out of his good mood. He tried

to change the subject but all his sentences felt flat. In the end he finished his pint in moody silence. We left the pub and hurried to get the bus, but we'd just missed it, so decided to start walking and catch one on the road back.

It was still light, and not too chilly, but I pulled my coat around me tightly and fiddled with the buttons as we headed out of town and fell into an easy silence. Cliff walked with his head held high, gazing out over the hedgerows to the cut fields with a faint smile on his lips. He must have missed it. I had to work tomorrow, but he'd already told me he would spend the whole day at Goffman's. He loved that farm – it ran in his blood – he was as proud of it as if it were already his own. It was one of the things I loved about him – and there were many things, I realised now. Dad was right, I had taken him for granted. He was a good man, and he could be my good man if I let him. *My Cliff.* Half the village already accepted that he was – why not make it a reality?

I cursed the war again for thrusting this decision into my lap. Why else would Cliff want a wife at eighteen? If we could just slow down a bit, I was sure I'd feel easier about it all in a year or so, and maybe by then I'd have forgotten about Wilf too, if that was possible. He was so deeply etched into me now that I didn't think I'd ever be able to go an hour without thinking about him. And I was sure Doris and Alec wouldn't forget him, even if I could. What if Cliff found out from them? Mrs B and Dad would say nothing, but Alec I couldn't be so sure about. He was fiercely loyal to Cliff, but then he also wanted him as a brother-in-law. That left Doris. It struck me then that she had kept my secret up till now. Even when the truth about Wilf came out; she'd asked me about Cliff and made me feel like a prize idiot for cheating on him, but that was all. If she hadn't said anything yet, maybe she never would. Even Doris could see that Cliff and I should be together. Maybe he never needed to find out.

Perhaps I was overthinking things. Hadn't Cliff done ten times worse with ten times more women? Except, I'd known who he was all along. He'd never pretended to be anyone different. No, Cliff had a right to know what I'd been getting up to behind his back whilst supposedly considering his proposal. He might change his mind. There were different rules for girls, after all. Boys could get away with fondling land girls, but if a girl was found with her knickers in a twist, she was trollop, like Irene Dursley. I wasn't quite a trollop, but who knows what would have happened if Wilf and I had had more time together? Even now, I couldn't recall his kisses without a surge of that strange magic that had wound us together since the day we met.

An idea fell into my head then, a way to assuage my guilt and still keep hold of my secret. I could come clean without risking losing him.

'You're quiet,' he said after we'd been walking for a while.

'Just thinking.'

He ignored me, but after a minute he said, 'What about?'

My head was fizzing with worry and thoughts and I didn't think I'd have the energy for it much longer. 'I was wondering how many girls you kissed while you were away.'

He looked askance and screwed up his nose.

'Go on. I do know you, Cliff.'

He studied me for a moment, bemused. I think he thought I was setting us up for a fight.

'I won't be cross, I promise.'

He laughed, then shrugged a shoulder. 'A couple,' he said, looking ahead as we walked on.

I nodded, doubling it in my head. I was surprised and encouraged by the little twang of jealousy I felt. I took a deep breath, too loud for Cliff to ignore. He frowned at me again. 'Why don't you ask me?' My voice shook a little.

'Hmm?'

'Ask me how many boys I kissed when you were gone.'

He grinned, but his face changed when he realised I wasn't joking. He seemed more impressed than angry. 'Go on, then. Tell me.'

'One.'

He raised his eyebrows then looked away. He took a cigarette from his pocket and lit it slowly. He said nothing for a minute or so. We had fallen into step, our boots clomping in unison. I guessed he was angry with me after all. He said, 'Is that your way of telling me you don't want to marry me?'

'No!' I hadn't meant to say it so loudly. I touched his arm so he'd look at me. His eyes were unreadable. 'I think it's the opposite.'

His lips twitched in a short smile, but he looked ahead again.

'I wanted you to know. I thought it might change your mind.'

He burst into a quick laugh. 'Did you sleep with him?'

'No! No, I didn't!'

He held up a hand. 'All right, all right, I believe you.' He threw me an amused look. 'What's his name?'

I only hesitated for a moment, but it seemed to stretch on for ages. 'William.' It seemed an easier lie than Jack or Roger or any other name.

Cliff's eyes narrowed in concentration. I couldn't tell if he was weighing up whether or not to believe me, or if he was just thinking of all the boys he knew locally called William. It was a common enough name, there must have been dozens in Finton. I sensed he was waiting for me to say more, but the lie felt so fragile, I was afraid it would fall apart if I did.

'Caught your eye, did he?'

Wilf's blue eyes darted in my memory and I wished them

away.

'So, what happened with him?'

'He wasn't who he said he was. I'd rather forget him.'

Cliff chuckled softly and took my hand. His cigarette was in his teeth. When I met his eyes again there was no animosity there. I felt a wave of relief wash through me: for his forgiveness, for the lie undetected.

He squeezed my hand then let it go. 'I don't mind, as long as you didn't fuck him.'

I flinched. 'Cliff!'

'What?' he said, all innocence. 'Oh, don't be like that! You know what I mean. A kiss doesn't mean anything, God knows. It doesn't matter.'

'What does matter to you then?'

He grinned. 'Well, fucking?'

I shoved him. 'What if I loved him?' I said hotly, despite myself. I immediately regretted it.

Cliff laughed unsurely. '*Did* you love him?'

I wavered. 'No.' It was the biggest lie of all, although I wished it was true.

He tutted and rolled his eyes. 'Then why say it?'

I crossed my arms. 'Would it have mattered then?'

He shook his head. 'Don't be stupid, Gracie. You know it would.' He sighed, finished his cigarette and flicked it away. 'This William – let me guess – wordy, was he? Won you over with poems?'

I didn't answer.

'You know I'm not one for flowery words.'

'I know.'

'I never will be.'

'I know. I'm glad.'

'You are?'

I shrugged, because I felt guilty about snapping at him, and

I was softening to him again, but I didn't want to admit I was wrong.

'Well, good. Because as it happens I do love you.'

I waited for him to laugh but he didn't. A little warmth kindled inside me, but it fizzled when I realised he wouldn't have said it if he knew the truth. 'I asked you before, at the wedding. You didn't say it then. You said you cared about me. You said we both loved Barnfield. That's not the same thing.'

His eyes lost focus for a moment and then sparked to life again with the memory. 'Maybe I didn't realise it then.' I laughed, because we were more alike than I wanted to admit, but he misunderstood me. 'You don't believe me.'

'No, it's just… I'm not sure I deserve it.'

He smiled. 'Because you had a fling with someone else?'

I shook my head. 'I've always taken you for granted, Cliff. I never really gave you a chance, because you were always there and I knew you inside out.'

'It's a good job I went away then, isn't it?' His face relaxed into a forgiving smile and he pulled me to him and kissed me. 'It's good to know you're human.'

'I don't think there was ever any doubt about that.'

'Well, no, but at least now we're as bad as each other.'

I resented the comparison, that his dozens of girls were equal to Wilf, but then I doubted he'd ever been in love with any of his, so I held my tongue.

'And now you know the grass isn't always greener, I can trust you never to do it again.' He was smiling but I sensed the threat behind the words. I thought of Wilf's butterfly and the kisses he'd given me with it.

'You didn't trust me before?' My voice was small. It didn't sound like a question. I wouldn't have blamed him if he'd said no, even now.

He threw his head back, exposing his throat. 'As far as I can throw you!'

I relaxed as he laughed. 'That's rich, coming from you! What about all your girls? Wouldn't you miss them, if we got married?'

He smiled. 'Who says I'd give them up?'

I whacked his arm but a part of me thought he might not be joking.

'Stop worrying. You'll do nicely, Gracie.'

'Oh, really?'

'And I wouldn't have to work for it anymore, if we were married.'

'I'd still make you work for it. I wouldn't want to spoil your fun.'

He cocked his head. 'That's a yes then?'

'Seems so.'

It shouldn't have been so easy, that I could change the course of my life with a few simple words. But I had the depressing sense that I probably hadn't changed a thing. Cliff and I had been as inevitable as the sunset. We couldn't have lived in Barnfield without being together; we were a part of the place and each other. I suddenly felt so powerless and tired, as if I'd crawled beneath a heavy shroud. And within my bones the lie still burned.

'We could go to the Registry Office tomorrow.'

He only sounded half serious but I blurted out, 'No! Not yet.'

He looked slightly irritated. 'Fair enough. But you can't put it off forever. We could all be dead tomorrow.'

'That's just what boys say to make girls go to bed with them.'

He broke into a wide smile. 'Is it? I don't see any beds.' He thumbed over his shoulder. 'We could do it up against a tree if you like.'

'Shut up.'

Just then we heard the growl of the bus on the road behind us, and Cliff waved it down. He helped me up as if he were a gentleman and shook hands with a few of our Barnfield neighbours who were on board. He perched on an aisle seat and got into conversation with one of them, and I leaned my head against the vibrating window as the fields spun past, imagining the look on Dad's face when I arrived home and told him the news. Just the thought of his smile was enough to reassure me that I'd done the right thing.

PART TWO

CHAPTER 16

September 1945 (two years later)

The Neal family had owned the draper's in Finton for three generations. Old Mr Neal came out of retirement when Thomas Neal's papers arrived, but Thomas ended up with a Nazi bullet in his head so the old man was still behind the counter. The top shelves were bare, the bolts of fabric few. Rationing was worse than ever, and the jars of buttons and reels of ribbon saw more action than Mr Neal's cutting table.

Mr Neal offered a short smile of recognition the day I came in from the rain to enquire about the vacant position. I'd been there many times before for material and fastenings, but no one could mistake me for a keen dressmaker, and though I'd chosen my best outfit for the occasion I was worried he'd turn me away for lack of experience. His hands trembled as he showed me round the shop and store room, explained the till and the ledgers. He was probably in his mid-sixties, but he seemed older: his skin sagged off his cheekbones like washing rung out and left to dry on the line. His lips and knuckles were chapped, the whites of his eyes tinged with yellow. The shop was meticulously clean and tidy, but his cup in the store room was stained with rings of old tea. He appeared to me like a man who'd given up on hope, who was probably just waiting for death but too polite to ask it to hurry along.

He wasn't peculiar. There were many people like him: getting up and moving around and going back to bed again. I was one of them. Perhaps that's why I liked Mr Neal instantly and asked for the job, and it's probably why he took pity on me and agreed, despite the fact I knew next to nothing about bias bindings and needle widths.

That was in June, a few weeks after Cliff came home and we were married.

Cliff and Alfie Bainbridge were demobbed around the same time, and I'd watched Mrs B excitedly prepare for her son's return with a strange numbness where my heart should have been. I'd long since resigned myself to losing my job at the Post Office. In fact, I'd been anticipating it for so long that it was a strange kind of relief when I hung up my uniform for the last time and wheeled my bicycle the short distance home. I'd been running those rounds for nearly four years. I'd once dreamed I'd never have to leave, but now it was over, because the war was over, and Alfie had survived, and my fiancé was coming home to me. All reasons to be cheerful, even if my smiles were forced.

Cliff and I were married the first Saturday after he got back. We'd talked about it during his odd leave days over the past two years. He didn't want to return to his room in the farmhouse alone. It made much more sense for him to come and live with us until Goffman retired, so Dad and I swapped rooms and beds.

Late on my wedding night, unable to sleep, I stared up at the ceiling, at the crack that had always been there, a wavy line that looked like a face. It had watched as my mother died and my father wept for her. And it watched me then as my new husband dozed beside me, his mouth just open, his face flushed.

After a couple of weeks, I realised I'd have to find another job or I'd go mad. For years I'd ploughed my energy into the Post Office; without it, the house – cleaner than ever – closed in around me. I even started to volunteer more with the WVS, but it wasn't enough, and Doris's friends looked down on me, their conversation always condescending and insipid.

It was on my way home from a WVS meeting that I saw Mr Neal's advertisement in his window, and that night I spoke to Cliff about it. He'd had a bath before supper, and his hair was scruffy and smelled of soap. Rain purred against the window pane; we left the curtains undrawn now we were allowed to, and the cloud-dulled moonlight cast his naked body in a blue haze. We'd made love every night since he got back. Cliff hated calling it making love. He said it sounded sentimental and I was inclined to agree, but I couldn't bring myself to call it what he did; it made us sound like animals. His appetite was ferocious, as I'd expected it would be. It didn't bother me. I liked it. I was glad to have him back again, and every time I thought about it I wanted to grab him tight and lose myself in him.

I rested my hand on his chest as it rose and fell, and traced the path of chocolate-brown hair to his navel. The Army had made him leaner, but he was as strong as ever and still looked older than his years, especially now he'd stopped shaving again. Everyone told me how lucky I was; he was such a handsome man. It was true – he always had been – but I couldn't see the man without seeing the boy first, without the memories that bound our pasts together, more sacred now than ever. I wondered if that's how he saw me.

He twitched, turned his head and seemed to smile, but sighed deeply again, beginning to snore slightly as I pressed myself against his warm side. 'Cliff?'

He grunted, so I shook his shoulder.

'I'm sleeping,' he murmured.

'Wake up.'

'Go to sleep.'

'I will. I need to ask you something.'

He screwed up his face and yawned. 'In the morning.'

'Not in front of Dad.'

He opened an eye. 'You're not pregnant are you?'

I laughed.

He stretched and propped himself up on his elbow. 'What?'

'How would you feel if I got another job? There's a vacancy at the draper's in Finton.' I saw the irritation and reticence in his sleepy eyes. 'It wouldn't be forever. I could just stay until the farm's ready.'

He fell back on his pillow. 'Haven't you got enough to do here all day? And with Doris's la-de-da ladies?'

'I only go to those meetings to get out of the house. You know I hate being cooped up in here all day.' I tugged on his arm. 'Come on, Cliff, what harm can it do?'

'You'd be exhausted.'

'I know I can manage it – I did it for years at the Post Office.'

'You didn't have a husband then.'

'You'd still have your clothes washed, and floor scrubbed and food on the table each night… And me in your bed, if that's what you're worried about.'

He smiled and rolled on top of me. 'What'll you do if I say no?'

'I'll whine and nag you until you change your mind. And I'll make you sleep on the floor.'

'Fine!' He kissed me. 'All right then, do what you like. But if it gets too much you'll have to stop it, no arguments.'

'All right,' I said with relief.

He kissed me again, stronger, and moved his hand up my side to my breast. Then he stopped, and sighed. 'You know it won't change anything, Grace.'

I hesitated. 'It will.'

'It won't bring him back.'

'It might bring *me* back.'

He frowned and looked like he might say something else, but decided against it and moved his hand down to my thigh.

*

The previous Christmas, 1944, Alec had been in Barnfield on leave for a few days. He hadn't quite made it for Christmas Day, but it hadn't mattered because having him back home – healthy and smiling, with the tree up and the cards hanging over the mantelpiece – had felt like a benediction.

He'd been in Africa for over a year, and then India, and hadn't had home leave in all that time, so when he arrived at the station I almost didn't recognise him. His skin was a dark, raw pink – another man might have tanned, but not my fair brother. His hair was flaming, bright orange streaked with sun, his eyebrows bleached blonde. He was a little taller, and his face had lost some of its soft youth, but it was still the same old Alec I saw in his eyes and smile.

For forty-eight hours I doted on him. I took leave from the Post Office to sit with him on the sofa as the bitter winds howled outside. I made him tea and shortbread with all our saved butter and sugar, sandwiches with my bacon rations, a crumble with the best of that autumn's apples. I waited till he was in bed to clean the house; I didn't want to spend a minute away from him. I wanted to soak him up – his scent and laughter and energy – store as much of him within me as I could, as if enough of his memory would make him real once he left me again. In the grey-white whirl of midwinter, he was like a burst of dry heat, with his sunburned lips and desert stories. Even Dad stayed to listen to his heroic tales of checking for booby traps in sandy trenches, or firing at Japanese troops through sheets of monsoon rain. His enthusiasm only wavered for a few seconds, when he lowered his head and spoke of the lads who hadn't come back with him.

When he was worn out, he asked what I'd been doing, but Barnfield was so damp and slow and meaningless compared to him. He asked after Cliff too, and demanded that I read him all of his letters, even if I had to leave out the indecent bits.

'I knew things would work out between you two eventually,' he said as he helped me wash up the night before he left. 'I bet you're glad you didn't run away with Wilfred Whitman now.'

I flushed scarlet. I hadn't heard that name for months. He was a blight on Barnfield's consciousness, but the scandal had lost its novelty and now only the stink of shame remained. Tenants grumbled when it was time to pay their rents, wishing they didn't have to fill a coward's pockets. I'd burned his letter not long after Cliff and I got engaged, feeling uneasy about having it, and I'd hidden the frame in the back of my wardrobe, more because I didn't know how to get rid of it without suspicion than because I wanted to keep it.

When Alec mentioned Wilf again then, I recalled our moments together in a brief, blurry second. They had seemed dreamlike even at the time, but since then they'd grown positively otherworldly. I remembered our afternoon on the island like a faded photograph; I'd made such an effort to forget him that I couldn't clearly recall his face now. I knew his eyes had been the richest blue I'd ever seen, but I couldn't picture them. I knew I'd loved him with a pain like bleeding. The whole affair felt like a story I'd once known by heart but now struggled to recollect. Or perhaps I was just too afraid to.

'I can't believe you liked him,' Alec pressed jovially, nudging me so I slopped dishwater on my sleeves.

'We've all done stupid things,' I said, trying to ignore the twist of shame I felt.

'Good job I was there to save you,' he said, and carried on chuckling, but my mind spun back to when Cliff had said the very same thing on the shore of the lake, all those years ago when he pulled me from the water. The memory sparked a flash of rage inside me: anger for being so thoughtless. Anger for being helpless. Would I always require Cliff or Alec to rescue me from stupid situations?

Alec dried his hands on a tea towel and stretched. He leant back on his elbows and watched as I drained the sink and wiped it down. 'Isn't it strange to think you've been here – all that time I've been away – you've just been here, at this sink, every night.' His tone was kind, his expression relaxed. He hadn't meant anything by it. It was just an observation, but it made me feel smaller and more insignificant than ever. He smiled gently when he saw my shoulders fall, then brushed my arm. 'Don't frown! It makes me glad.'

'Why?'

'Because when I'm stuck out in God knows where, sweating like a pig or freezing my balls off, I can think of you at this sink and remember why I'm doing it.'

'What about King and Country?' I teased. 'What about bringing Hitler's head back on a stick?'

His thin smile showed the glamour had long worn off. I thought of the men he'd fought alongside, buried in foreign soils. 'It's just good to know you're here, Gracie.'

I wished I'd embraced him then. He would have tutted and told me to pull myself together, but I should have done it anyway.

He left the following day. The bus was late so we were

running onto the platform as the guard blew his whistle. We'd said our farewells at home but I clung on to him for a few more seconds and breathed in the scent of his neck and uniform, smoothing down his beautiful hair, so vibrant against the drab of the station.

He glanced nervously over his shoulder at the train. 'I can't miss it!' He pecked my cheek.

I let him go. I must have called out a goodbye or something when he opened the window and poked his head out, but I can't remember. I remember his face – wide and smiling – and the steam as the engine chuffed away, his head merging into it until only his hair was visible, like a smear of blood on a misted mirror.

On January 1st 1945, the telegraph machine clicked to life, and Mrs B shrieked, so I knew someone had died. My first thought was for Alfie. I wasn't afraid for Alec – he was still in England.

Mrs B started sobbing. I knew then it *had* to be Alfie. She hadn't cried for any of the other dead men. I placed a trembling hand on her shoulder, shocked at her tears and violent, shuddering cries. I guided her to embrace me, but when she did she pressed my head to her neck and rubbed my back. She told me, 'shh, shh', but I wasn't the one crying. I pulled back and searched her anguished face for answers, and somehow, through her uneven breaths, I heard the words, 'Alec, Alec… oh my dear boy, Alec!'

CHAPTER 17

I caught the early bus into Finton with Dad each morning. We always sat in the same seat, second from the front on the left. I wondered if it was where Alec had sat on his journeys to work. I was so worried that Dad would shatter my illusion and say 'Oh, no, we used to sit over there', that I never dared ask him about it. I let my hand rest on the seat in front as we rode along, imagining Alec had done the same. Dad's shoulder bounced against mine with the sway of each bend.

We hadn't had to wait long for the funeral, and it was a blessing, we were told, that we had a body to bury. A comfort, apparently, that we knew how he'd died, that it had been quick, that he hadn't been frightened in the end.

Perhaps it was a blessing. Perhaps, if he'd joined his regiment as planned, he might have lived for another month or so, but died a terrible bloody death. But there was no honest comfort in that thought, or the grim reality. He hadn't died a hero – not in the way he would have wanted – not in the way Thomas Neal supposedly had. But it wouldn't have made any difference. Mr Neal's hollowed out life only showed me that looking for any comfort in death was senseless. What remained were all those years behind, all the thousands of memories knitted together, climaxing in nothingness. All the years ahead with their myriad possibilities, suddenly cut off.

At the bus stop in town, Dad and I parted ways with a kiss on the cheek. He'd aged more in the last few months than I'd ever noticed in the whole of my life: his face had thinned so his skin looked softer; he'd lost even more hair and his moustache was fully grey now. It frightened me to imagine him becoming an old man. I wondered how he'd live when Cliff and I moved out, if he'd shut the door after work and never mutter a word to anyone until nine o'clock the following morning. When I suggested to Cliff that Dad should come with us to the farm, he looked askance and said, 'Don't you think he'll be glad to finally have some peace and quiet? He'll always be welcome, of course, but I'd have thought he'd be glad to see the back of us.'

Mr Neal always had a cup of tea ready for me when I arrived, and we usually remarked on the weather and the newspaper headlines before he retreated to the store room to start on alterations. He kept a cane back there but never brought it into the shop, always appearing sprightly with customers and wilting as soon as they left. Most of the time he left me to it, but I had to call him in whenever customers had questions I couldn't answer. He gave me a little exasperated look when I did, but I think he liked it really, otherwise he would have fallen into a stupor and spent all day in silence.

Doris usually popped in after her WVS meetings, and sometimes with Mrs Howard if they'd been out to the tea room. Doris lived in Finton now, but Ron was still in the Army, having had 'a very good war', and he spent little time at home.

'How are you enjoying married life, Gracie?' Doris asked me one day while she perused tweeds. I told her it suited me, and she nodded approvingly. It did suit me to have another person around our kitchen table again, even if it wasn't the one it should have been. It suited me to have Cliff's warm body in bed beside me and know he was back where he belonged. If any shred of the halcyon days remained – if there was any hope for future joys – I was certain it lived on in Cliff. We shared a past, so would share a future too.

When he was demobbed, the first place he'd asked to go was to Alec's grave. He dropped his haversack by a puddle at the gate and I pointed to the far corner of the graveyard, where the new stone steamed in the sunshine. I waited there and watched him trudge past his parents' graves with heavy strides. He stopped with his back to me and pulled the hat from his head with an exhausted arm. His shoulders slumped forward, and I turned back towards home when they started to shake. It was the only time I'd ever known him to cry.

Half an hour later he tapped on our door and opened it without knocking. In the hallway he held me in a hard embrace and said nothing. I pressed my face into his chest and felt his pulse in my forehead. I was so tired of everything, and just then I felt I could let go of all my grief and worries and he'd fix me, somehow. The relief of his return was tangible, as if I'd been folded as tight as a sheet for six years, and now I was being flung out and aired in the breeze.

'I dare say your little house must feel very cramped with the three of you there,' Doris went on, snapping me back to the present. 'You must be looking forward to Mr Goffman's retirement.'

'Yes, next year…' I said absentmindedly, thinking of our 'little' house with Alec's empty bedroom and how Doris could have no idea how hollow it felt without him. If I stuffed the place with a hundred men, his absence would still make an echo.

'The farmhouse will be a far better place to start a family.' Doris nudged me with a dimpled smile. Alec had always liked her dimples.

'Well, one thing at a time.'

'You can't plan these things, Gracie,' she said airily, pointing to another bolt on the shelf. I slid it out for her and wondered if I'd imagined an unpleasant edge to her tone. She'd been married for years now but had probably spent fewer nights with Ron than I had with Cliff. And the rate Cliff was going, we were bound to hear the patter of tiny feet sooner rather than later. The thought stirred nothing inside me. I generally found babies loud and irritating, so I felt I should be more anxious about it if anything, but there was an inevitability to the prospect that seemed to fit with the general pattern of my life. I hadn't the energy to fight it, and I'd got into the habit of not thinking too far ahead anyway.

*

I hurried into the Post Office on a Saturday morning in mid-October, half blown in by the wind. Alfie was at the counter, his shirtsleeves rolled halfway up his arms, a broad grin beneath his moustache. He was a solid, slightly portly man, about ten years my senior, but he'd always seemed older to me. His cheeks told the tale of a bad bout of childhood pox, but his eyes were kind and lively like Mrs B's. He made a joke about the wind blowing my letter away if I wasn't careful and I smiled along dutifully, trying to fight off the awkward sense that one of us didn't belong here, and hating the fact it was me.

Even after all these months, it was hard to ignore the press of the usual routines. Just the smell of the polished shelves and fusty mailbags was enough to make me want to lift the counter, pop on my cap and start sorting. It was like an itch I couldn't reach to scratch. Alfie had never been anything other than kind to me, but I still felt like my years here didn't count anymore. Now he was back it was business as usual. But this had been my world – my salvation – for nearly four years, and I wondered if I'd ever be able to buy stamps without a lump in my throat.

Mrs B heard my voice and opened the door that joined the Post Office to her home. 'Gracie!' I was enveloped in her arms before I could say a word. 'Won't you stay for tea?'

'I'm off to the farm. Cliff forgot his lunch this morning.' I held up the brown bag in my hand.

She laughed and checked the clock. 'Still time for tea.' She ushered me through the little passage to her warm kitchen and clunked the kettle on the stove. I'd been there a hundred times before. It was as dark and low as the Post Office, and smelled of wood smoke and boiled fruit. Mrs B's grumpy tabby cat – Sir – was in his usual spot on the windowsill, gazing at condensation-clouded panes.

'I've been making quince jelly.' She gestured to the pots on the table with a flourish. They were topped with threadbare scraps of old fabric and tied with twine. 'Take one before you go, and another for Goffman.'

'Of course, thank you.' My mouth watered at the thought of some on scones – but grey bread would have to do. It would still be good.

'Alec used to love it,' she said without any trace of misery. I didn't know how she managed it. I nodded and said nothing, but my appetite had gone.

The kettle began to whistle.

'How's Mr Neal? I do miss you around here, you know.'

'I miss it too. Mr Neal's not one for conversation.'

'Suits you to a tee, then,' she chuckled. 'The amount of time I caught you daydreaming!' She poured the tea. 'Cliff doesn't mind you working?'

'He indulges me. It's not the same as being here though.'

Mrs B sat down beside me, cradling her tea. 'You always

liked doing the rounds, didn't you?'

'The best part. Being stuck in the draper's all day's almost as bad as being stuck at home.'

She gave me a long look. 'Alfie wants to take on a post boy. I'm too old for it and I think he thinks it's beneath him.' Her eyes glimmered. 'I don't suppose you'd be interested?'

'Really?' I couldn't hide my excitement. To be back at the Post Office again would be wonderful. It would be like reclaiming a part of myself I'd thought lost forever.

'You'll have to ask Cliff, of course.'

My enthusiasm faltered. 'Ah, yes...'

'You don't think he'd be keen on it?'

I placed my tea cup on the table. 'He was hardly enamoured when I started with Mr Neal.'

'I thought you said he didn't mind.'

I sighed. 'I don't think he does, really. But he made it very clear it was only temporary, until the farm's his. And then…' I wasn't sure what happened then. Then I'd be a farmer's wife, with a big – mostly dilapidated – farmhouse to run, and workers and crops to help manage.

'Planning on getting out in the fields, are you?'

'I wouldn't mind it.'

'You don't have the arms for it, dear. Those land girls were built like oxen!' She chuckled. I smiled, thinking of Alec's Linda, who'd moved on and ended up marrying a chap she'd met in Finton, someone from the electricity board who'd fought his war with wires. My mind jumped to Wilf then, and how different things might have been if he'd been in a reserved occupation, if he'd never been made to drop bombs, if his face had never been ripped open and he'd never ended up being called a coward. How different might it have been, too, if I'd been the one expected to sit in his place in the fuselage rather than ride my bicycle through Barnfield's peaceful lanes. I willed the thought away, for it brought a shadow of guilt so strong I couldn't bear to face it. I pressed my nail into my wrist until it was gone.

'You could always come back here temporarily,' Mrs B went on. 'It would save us training up some lad.' She leaned forward and lowered her voice. 'Between you and me, Alfie's a bit rusty. He could do with someone else about the place who knows what they're doing. Someone other than his dear old mother.'

'Mrs B, you really mean it, don't you?'

'Now there's a smile I haven't seen for a while!' She patted my hand. 'Of course I mean it.' She nodded to my tea. 'Don't let it get cold.'

I sipped dutifully. 'I'll have to ask Cliff, and then of course, there's poor Mr Neal…'

'Poor Mr Neal would find someone else who enjoys trimmings and pleats far more than you do.'

I nodded decisively. 'You're right.'

Mrs B patted my shoulder. 'Right then, off you go and see what that gorgeous husband of yours says.'

By the time I reached Manor Farm, the wind had whipped my hair into a bird's nest, and I grappled to tie a scarf around it as Mrs Goffman thanked me for bringing the quince jelly. 'That's good of Edna. I'll bring her some of my bramble and apple in a few days, you tell her.' She brushed the wisps of grey hair from her tanned brow, only for them to fall right back again. She must have been in her sixties, but she was as healthy as any forty-year-old, save for a few lost teeth and a missing finger from her left hand, which I'd heard was from carving knife (it had always secretly made me smile, for it meant the three blind mice had got their own back that time).

'Cliff's out with the tractor, dear. In the wide field. You needn't have brought him lunch, I could have fixed him something.'

'I wouldn't want you stretching your rations, Mrs Goffman.'

'We don't do too badly on the farm. You'll see.' She looked me up and down with a smile. 'You'll get some meat on those bones once you're mistress of this house.'

I reddened. I hated to think I was turfing her out of her home.

She just grinned good-naturedly and said, 'Want me to get Goffman to take it down for him?'

'No, thank you. I need to speak to Cliff about something anyway.'

'Ha! Love's Young Dream! Give it a year and you'll be kicking him out of the door every morning.' She chuckled so hard she made herself cough.

I said goodbye and headed out through the farmyard, following the muddy track to the 'wide field', which was in fact the field that stretched down from Manor Woods to the lake. I guessed Cliff wouldn't be as thrilled as me about the Post Office job, but hoped the prospect of me being in the village rather than Finton all day would be more palatable. Plus, we'd save money on the bus fare.

When I spotted the tractor, he was riding with his back to me. The shuddering engine and rushing wind meant he'd never hear my cry, so I stood and watched as he pulled the plough through the earth, drawing up folds of thick mud, turning the ground into a brown ocean of choppy clay waves. The air above him swarmed with spinning leaves and shrieking birds, looping and wavering in the wind before diving down to fight over worms.

The trees around the lake were awash with colour – vibrant reds and golds, burnt orange – all the shades of Alec's hair, as if they remembered and missed him. But they were only announcing their winter slumbers with a final joyous cry: a glorious, blazing, raging death of a season. Where the lake was visible, I saw their reflections like colours spilled from a paint box, and felt if I cupped my hands in the water, it would stain my fingers amber and crimson.

The clouds raced along, breaking every now and then so Cliff and the field were luminous in dazzling sunlight, only to fade moments later. At the bottom of the hill, Cliff turned the tractor and after a minute or so looked up to see me waving at him. He raised an arm and turned off the engine.

'If I can't get that started again, it's your fault,' he said when I reached him, and gave me a kiss. His face was cold, but his sleeves were rolled up and he smelled of sweat and soil. I gave him his lunch and he leaned against the big wheel to eat it, surveying his work. There was still about three quarters of the field to go. He told me they'd be sowing next year's crop in a week or so. All the fields would be planted; they couldn't afford to let any go fallow, however much the ground needed it.

He took a bite of his apple. 'I better get back to it. No time for a quickie today if that's what you're after.' He winked and clicked his teeth as if I were a horse.

'Next time you forget your lunch, you'll go hungry.' He pretended to tremble with fear so I kicked his muddy boot. 'I wanted to ask you something. Mrs B wants me back at the Post Office.'

'And?'

I didn't think I'd need to spell it out. 'I'd like to go back.'

He chewed his apple, waiting to finish, so I knew he was thinking, because nothing would usually stop him from speaking with his mouth full. I was growing impatient when he finally said, 'You haven't been at the draper's for long.'

'I know, but Mrs B says—'

'Mrs B says!' he echoed, spitting bits of apple. 'Mrs B wants an easy life! She wants to retire and can't be arsed to train anyone new.'

'Cliff!' I cried with indignation.

'Well, it's true and you know it.'

'So what? Mr Neal would find someone else quickly.'

'You can't mess him around like that. He's an old man. What happens when you change your mind about the Post Office next month?'

'I won't change my mind.'

'Why not?'

'Because I loved it there! I only left because I had to, and now there's a chance…'

'We all miss the war, Gracie,' he said wearily, and I didn't know what to say to that, because I didn't miss the war a jot, it had ruined everything. I missed my *job*, and as he watched me silently I realised he must be missing the Army, or he'd never have said it. Still, it seemed a funny way of putting it.

He scratched his chin and raised his shoulders as if to sigh, but said, 'You can't change what's happened.'

He didn't need to tell me that. But perhaps this was something I could change. 'I don't want to look a gift horse in the mouth.'

He squinted at me, as if I were a child throwing a tantrum. 'This is not a gift horse, Grace. Things are different now. Your job is only temporary anyway. I'd much rather you gave it up altogether.'

'Oh, would you? What about the money?'

He lifted his chin proudly. 'I can provide for you. You know that.'

'Doesn't it matter what I want?'

'You don't know what you want!' he laughed. 'That's why you keep changing your mind.'

I heard my breath, sharp and shallow, as if I'd been running. 'What do you mean? I don't keep changing my mind.'

He finished off his apple, ate the core and brooded while the wind and the birds filled our silence. I wondered what he'd do if I slapped him. I imagined he'd trap me in a hard embrace and laugh at me, which oddly made me want to do it even more.

Finally, I huffed and crossed my arms and told him, 'You're not making any sense.'

He forced a loud guffaw, turned his back on me and took a piss on the ground.

'Charming,' I mumbled.

'Oh, you never expected me to be charming, did you?' He shook himself off and turned back to me with folded arms, mirroring me. 'Don't worry, there's no one around.' He flicked his eyes over to the lake. 'Not even the old madman today.'

My eyes narrowed. I wasn't going to rise to his teasing. Alec had been right, he could be such an arse sometimes. I hated Cliff in these moments: once again he was the infuriating twelve-year old who'd taunted me about getting breasts and not being able to adjust my blouses properly. In the old days I would have stormed off or hit him and ignored him for a while, but I couldn't do that now he was my husband. I had to stick it out and argue with him, even if he was maddening.

He took a step forward. 'You ever been back in the water?'

I shrugged and balled up the paper bag in my hands. 'Of course I have. That was years ago.' I thought about his hands on my waist and the relief I'd felt, and stiffened.

Cliff leaned towards me and softened his voice: 'Didn't you think he'd be taller? I always imagined he'd be tall.' He smirked at my questioning expression.

Slowly, it began to dawn on me what he was saying. Nevertheless, I fought the notion of it for a second, trying to make sense of its implications, finding no sense at all. 'You *saw* him?'

He chuckled so deeply it made the hairs on my neck and arms prickle. 'Of course I bloody saw him! I'm not blind!'

I slapped his arm in a flash of anger and he grabbed my wrists, still laughing. 'Clifford Archer, I could kill you!' I was all heat and rage and humiliation. 'You should have said! Why didn't you say? You made me think I'd seen a ghost!'

He pressed his fingers into my skin, pulled my wrists down and forced me closer. 'It was much more fun that way.' He smirked flirtatiously and tried to kiss me, but I turned my face from him so he petulantly let me go. 'I'd seen him before, you know,' he said nonchalantly as he leapt back on the tractor. 'And since. Wandering around near the boathouse in his pyjamas, the old looney.'

'You never said a word.'

'You don't have to tell everybody everything. It's not the law. You know that, don't you?'

I thought of my encounter with the captain on the Manor's doorstep, the butterfly hidden in my wardrobe, and stayed silent.

'Come on, Gracie, cheer up.'

'Did you tell Alec?'

'What?'

'Did you tell Alec you saw the captain that day?'

Cliff shrugged.

'What does that mean?'

'Can't remember. Does it matter?'

'Yes!' I snapped, though I couldn't say why. I'd hated seeing that sceptical look in Alec's eyes when I was pulled from the lake, hearing his little snigger. 'I just… I wanted him to believe me. I didn't want him to think I was making it up…'

Cliff shook his head slowly. 'It's not important now. And I'm sure he believed you. He could always tell when you were lying.'

I let myself smile at him.

'As can I,' he added, once the kindness had left his eyes. 'I can always tell when you're lying too.'

He turned the key and the tractor shook into life before I could say anything else. He gave me a little salute and lurched off, leaving me standing there in the mud, with the lake and its ghosts behind me. The wind snatched the screwed-up paper bag from my hands; trees shivered like pebbles beneath waves.

I pulled my arms around myself and began my trudge back to the village, wondering if I'd imagined the threat in Cliff's tone. What had he meant by it? Was it just another taunt? I was sure I had no reason to feel so ruffled by it. I was just angry with him and miserable because he'd turned his nose up at the Post Office idea, but I'd try him again when he was in a better mood. I had nothing to worry about, and certainly no reason to feel guilty. After all, the only lie I'd ever told him was so small, and so irrelevant now, it didn't really matter at all.

I tried to speak to Cliff about the job again that night, but he answered with a grunt, and said he was tired. The next evening he went to the pub after work, so I asked Dad what he thought, but he only told me that it was something I needed to discuss with my husband. Cliff was drunk when he got in, and not in the mood for anything beyond stumbling to the outhouse and passing out on the bed, fully clothed.

At breakfast, he squinted, red-eyed, at his porridge, and later that day, while I chewed on my sandwich during my lunch break, I let go of the matter, realising I'd already lost. Cliff wouldn't change his mind. I wouldn't go back to the Post Office. I'd work at Mr Neal's until the farm was handed over or I fell pregnant. That was my future. The Post Office was my past. I thought about saying yes to Mrs B anyway and to hell with the consequences, but I knew what would happen: when Cliff found out he'd put a stop to it anyway. We'd argue, and I'd end up resenting him more than I realised I already did.

Chapter 18

One day in December, about a week before Christmas, I said goodbye to Dad at the bus stop and trotted along as fast as I could in my heeled shoes, rubbing my gloved hands together and blinking back tears from the bitterly cold air. My coat was threadbare, I'd patched it up so many times over the years that it really belonged on a scarecrow. It wasn't the best coat for a draper's girl, and Mr Neal had advised me to hide my face in public when wearing it, in case anyone recognised me and saw it as a poor reflection of our wares. I'd promised to buy a new one as soon as I had enough coupons.

I reached the shop and cried out as I nearly slammed my head against the door; I'd run to push it open but it was stuck fast. I gave it a kick, thinking the cold had stiffened it, but a rattle of the handle revealed it was locked. I rapped on the window impatiently, hopping to keep warm, and peered in when there was no reply; the glass was freezing against my forehead, and it misted immediately, so I had to wipe it and hold my breath. The shop was dark inside, Mr Neal nowhere to be seen. I banged on the door again a few times and called through the letterbox, but the only response I got was a few disapproving looks from passers-by.

It was so unusual that I stood there for a minute feeling completely lost. Then I remembered that Mr Neal kept a spare key with a jeweller friend of his a few doors down. I found the jewellers sparkling and open for business, virtually tropical in comparison to the street outside. Mr Eakley insisted on accompanying me back to Mr Neal's with the key; at first I'd assured him that it was unnecessary, but the penny dropped when I caught the anxious shade of his expression. I'd just thought Mr Neal must have overslept. It was clear Mr Eakley suspected something more serious, and I suddenly felt a wave of nausea in my stomach.

Mr Eakley locked up behind him and led me back to the drapers with sharp, neat strides. The door was open in an instant, and he called for Mr Neal as he flicked the light switch and popped his head into the store room. 'You stay here, dear. I'll go upstairs.'

I nodded and waited in the stillness as he ascended the little staircase to the flat above. I heard his footsteps creak through the ceiling, and my heart beat heavily. Mr Eakley knocked on a door and called for Mr Neal again. I heard a door click and more footsteps, then silence.

Within a minute, Mr Eakley descended with a funereal gait, his face grave. 'I'm terribly sorry, dear, but Mr Neal has passed away. It seems to have happened peacefully in his sleep… I say, do you need a chair?'

I didn't go to Mr Neal's funeral. Mrs B felt I was likely to weep all the way through, and she was probably right. It made little sense, because although I was sad he was gone, Mr Neal had been old and finished with life. I hadn't cried at all at Alec's funeral. In fact, I'd watched the sniffing mourners in the pews with a mixture of irritation and envy. I was quite sure that's how Mr Neal's sister, his only relative, would have looked at me.

I laid flowers on his grave the Sunday after the funeral, while Cliff stood behind me and blew air into his cupped hands. He took me to the tea room afterwards, and I tried to muster a smile or two over my carrot cake. The waitress spent all her time grinning at Cliff when she cleared our plates and cups, and cast a quick, wary glance at me before she left us. I found a mirror in my handbag and saw my face was sallow and swollen from grief; my eyes were ill-defined and small, my lips the shade of dying roses.

'Is there anything you need to collect from the shop? Anything you left there?'

I shook my head. The shop was going to be taken over by a young man and his wife – they would run it together and didn't need me anymore. The day before Mr Neal's death had ended up being my last day of work; it had been entirely unremarkable and I could barely recall a moment of it.

'It's for the best,' Cliff said matter-of-factly. 'All that toing and froing – it's worn you out. You'll be far better off at home, taking things a bit more gently.'

I didn't want gentleness. I wanted distraction. 'I need to keep busy.'

'There's plenty to do.'

'But not… The house is not… It's too…' I sighed in frustration. 'It's Alec. He's everywhere, in everything. I don't want to forget him – of course not – but sometimes I just don't have the strength…'

'I know you miss him,' Cliff interrupted. 'You're not the only one.'

I tried to meet his eyes but he wouldn't look at me. He bit his lip and played with his fork. I felt a stab of guilt. Alec had been my brother by blood, but he'd been the closest thing Cliff had ever had to one. 'I'm sorry. I forget sometimes that you loved him too.'

He cleared his throat, colouring from embarrassment.

'Well, it's good to know we can talk about him and remember him together.' I reached out to take his hand but he drew his away.

'I'd rather not,' he said brusquely, and finished his tea with a slurp before clunking the cup into the saucer.

*

The Post Office position had long since been taken up by a boy in the village, so I had no other choice than to accept a return to the quiet life of home. Surprisingly, I found it quite pleasant at first. I enjoyed the stillness of the house with Cliff and Dad at work, and found I had more time to run my errands and even take daily strolls again. The winter landscape was pale and unassuming; I watched the birds in the skeletal trees and trod the rock-hard ground, crunching on frosty leaves that glistened like jewels when the sun stretched through the branches.

Doris invited me to tea at her Finton townhouse and I sat and listened to her talk about the possibility of moving with Ron, who was very likely to be stationed overseas soon. Their house was at least a hundred years old, but smelt of new carpets and fresh paint, things that seemed to belong to another era. It felt offensively incongruous, when just minutes before I'd been queuing at the butchers for meat that turned out to be non-existent. It wasn't as if I didn't have the rations, but there was less to go around now than during the war. Now we were no longer fighting, people had let their brave faces slide into grim, hard frowns, and the streets were full of disgruntled mumbling. But somehow, Doris's eyes and hair still shone. Her clothes were neat and bright. Her living room windows opened onto a manicured walled garden with fruit trees and an ornamental fountain that showered water in symmetrical arcs, and we gazed out on it as we nibbled on tiny cakes that were so pretentiously sweet they made my eyes water.

I called in on Mrs B a few times a week. I stopped to have conversations with anyone I saw, even the Smythe sisters, to whom I'd once given a wide berth when doing my rounds. One day I got chatting to Reverend Dearling and ended up volunteering to clean the church every Friday. The ladies who did the flowers talked to me while I swept the aisles and polished the candlesticks; they always gave me a flower for Alec's grave before I left.

On Saturdays I walked to the farm with Cliff early in the morning, because Dad liked an extra hour in bed and I sometimes worried I wouldn't get up if I didn't have anything to get up for. I joked about it with Cliff but he just nudged me and said, 'What are you talking about? You always need to get up to make me breakfast.'

Most weeks were the same, which didn't bother me as much as I used to think it would. At least, not until everything changed.

CHAPTER 19

One Sunday in mid-January, the sun rose pale and slow over the garden, trapped in white. Icicles hung from the tiles above our bedroom window. The world glistened, enticing me out. After breakfast I pulled on my hat and gloves and left Cliff trying to thaw the cistern and Dad in front of the fire, telling them I'd meet them at church later. I buttoned up my new navy coat; it was the smartest thing I owned and I knew Mr Neal would have heartily approved of it.

The stile was frosted silver and I climbed it warily but managed not to slip. The snowy field up to Manor Woods was untrodden, and I strode on with lungs full of blissfully icy air, feeling like the only person truly awake and alive on earth. It was a delightful and selfish solitude; the morning was perfect but I didn't want to share it with anyone. It was only when walking that I came close to the carefree optimism of childhood, and somehow managed to shrug off the shadow of grief that otherwise cloaked my days from waking till sleeping.

My boots scrunched the snow, and my toes were numb by the time I reached the woods. I cast a wistful glance at our old camping spot. The trees ticked and dripped in the sun; I sensed their slow, quiet spirits rousing. Somewhere in their memories lived a red-headed sprite, a fair little tomboy, and a boy whose heart beat with the pulse of the earth.

When I emerged onto the brow of the wide field, I saw the frosted lake, stark and white through the scratched lines of bare branches. The wind rose to bite my cheeks, and I thought of the fire at home and my church dress hung up in our bedroom. But the scene drew me into it. The lake's shimmering crystals beckoned me closer, like the flirtatious glint of buried treasure; I could almost hear its sleeping pulse resonating through the ground.

I reached the trees and battled through the knotted undergrowth, finding the remnant of a path untrodden for months. Finally, I was at the edge of the lake, my breath conjuring frozen clouds in front of me. The morning sun streamed through the bare trees and painted the ice lemon and lavender. No birds moved. There was perfect silence, save for my breathlessness, for I'd almost run down the field and could feel a chilled pain in my chest.

I gazed at the expanse in front of me. Sleeping now, but I knew, beneath the ice, the still black water lay waiting. My past was littered with memories of this place, but all of them were tainted with sadness now. I couldn't recall the summer days swimming without seeing Alec ducking and splashing, or the day the waters had seemed to turn against me. And then that long afternoon with Wilf, the one I'd tried to blot out. I shook with a sudden, violent shiver, and wondered why I'd come here to spoil the morning's serenity.

I wasn't surprised to see the small grey figure on the far shore by the boathouse. He was exactly where my mind had left him, and it made sense that my memory would find him here again. The old man dressed in a loose, white shift which moved like spirits in the icy breeze. I watched and waited for him to fade. It felt like minutes, but it must have only been a few seconds before I realised the phantom was real. I couldn't blink him away.

Instinctively I looked around me, as if there was someone else who'd be able to help him. To help me. But we were alone. I didn't want to speak to him again, but I couldn't leave him like that. He wasn't wearing any shoes. He could freeze to death.

I followed the overgrown path round to meet him, wondering where his nurse had got to and how he could be allowed to stray so far unnoticed. He was in an old-fashioned nightshirt, and didn't look up as I approached. 'Hello there? Captain Whitman?' My hot breath whirled in the bitter, crisp air.

The captain turned his head and saw me for the first time. He was shivering. He fixed his pale eyes on me and his lips fell open. 'Bixxy?' His voice was croaky, unused to speaking.

Her name again.

'No, sir. It's Grace... Wells,' I said, because he wouldn't have known who Grace Archer was. But I saw from his blank expression he didn't know Grace Wells either. 'I think you ought to go home, sir.' I unbuttoned my coat and draped it over him. The cold immediately got under my skin and made me stiffen; I doubted he could even feel my touch. I kept my arm on his shoulder and felt only bone beneath the coat. I couldn't trust him to get home safely alone. I would have to take him. The path to the Manor was nearby. I tried to coax him to walk. 'Sir? If you could just come with me…'

'I don't remember.' His gaze fluttered like a butterfly, from the ground to the ice and finally to me. 'I don't remember what happened here.' I felt my stomach knot as he pressed his white hands to his face. 'Can you tell me, Grace?'

My name startled me. It sharpened him. I still didn't know which side of him I was talking to – the mad or sane one – but he seemed to have lost some of his fragility. He held my gaze like an ordinary man, a man who'd lived and worked an ordinary life, whose mind had never been lost within the years of war and the walls of an asylum.

'I came to find you,' he said.

I knew he didn't mean me, even if he had said my name. He was talking to his dead wife, just as he had been when I'd delivered that telegram a couple of years ago.

'I heard you.'

'Sir, you really need to get warm…'

'You shouldn't be here, my dear, it's dangerous.'

'It's cold, sir. You're cold.'

'Yes, yes…very cold'

'Come with me, please.'

'You must hold on,' he pleaded. 'Hold on! I'm coming!'

I wished I knew what to say to alleviate his troubles, but he wasn't making any sense. 'It's all right, sir,' was all I could manage, but he looked disappointed. Then his eyes glazed, lost once more in the shadows of his mind.

I tried to guide him to the path again but his feet were rooted to the ground; for a frail old lunatic, he was surprisingly strong. I was starting to despair, when a faint sound came through the stillness around us, a name being called from further up the path. A ghostly voice, as if I'd imagined it. Perhaps this whole thing was a dream, and I'd wake up next to Cliff any moment and there'd be rain beyond our window.

When I heard the voice again, I thought for a split second that it was the nurse coming to rescue us, before realising… 'That's Wilf!' I said it without thinking, without feeling for a second.

The captain snapped to attention and looked to the path. He turned back to me with beseeching eyes, as if pleading for me to stay. But my head was throbbing with panic, my feet itching to run. I could hear Wilf clearly now – that voice so warm and painfully familiar – calling for his father and getting louder by the second. Any moment he'd appear and I knew I was too far from the path home to escape without him seeing me. I'd have to stay and see him. I'd have to talk to him, and I wasn't ready for it at all.

'I'm sorry,' Captain Whitman whispered, though not to me, I was sure. He was gazing at the lake again, the weight of grief on his face. 'I'm sorry! I'm sorry!' he carried on, and began to cry.

I placed my hands on his shoulders, trying to calm him, but it was no use, and Wilf's voice was so close now. I flicked my head and stepped back just in time to see him emerge from the trees. He was running, but slowed as soon as he saw us. His surprise was clear, and he held my gaze for just a second before turning his focus on his father.

'Father, thank God!' He seemed to hesitate before placing his hand on the captain's back, on my coat. 'Come on, you'll freeze!' The old man was still muttering to himself. 'It's all right, Father.' Then Wilf looked at me, and asked without emotion, 'How long have you been with him?'

I swallowed to find my voice. 'Just a few minutes.'

'We need to get him inside.'

I nodded. It was not a suggestion. I was going back to the Manor too.

Wilf's attention was on his father. 'Take his arm.'

Captain Whitman grasped my hand with icy thin fingers as I moved next to him. His muttering dissolved into shivers as he allowed Wilf and me to lead him.

'That's it, Father,' Wilf continued patiently. 'That's it. Not far to go now. Let's get you home. The fire's roaring. Not far…' He kept talking, but I was mute, my head empty except for the pounding of my heart.

We made slow progress through the trees. I winced at the sight of Captain Whitman's bare feet treading over the frosted thorns and twigs. His toes were stained with blood.

We began the path through the field. 'There! We can see the house now, Father,' Wilf cried, and I looked up to see the Manor's roof, smoke snaking from its chimneys.

In minutes we reached the garden gate. Wilf was still speaking gentle encouragements to his father. His voice was soporific; the old man's hold on my hand was loosening, his eyes looked drained. As we made our way up the garden, his legs seemed to falter and his eyes closed. Wilf shared an anxious look with me – the first time he'd acknowledged me since leaving the lakeside. Pressure built behind my eyes; I felt I had too much blood in me. How long had he been back? *Why* was he back? I'd convinced myself I'd never see him again, but now he was next to me and I didn't know how to act. I'd blocked out so much of our short past and lived so many lonely and painful days since then. I'd started a new life, or rather continued along the path I'd been set on from the beginning. I had thrown away the dream of him, because it had become a nightmare.

'Come on, Father.' His voice was firm now. 'Nearly there.'

Grief and guilt turned in my chest. The last time I'd seen him I'd been in love with him, even if I hadn't realised it. But now I didn't know him at all.

A woman's voice broke my reverie. 'Oh, not again!' It was Miss Brennan, running out of the French windows with a blanket. She acknowledged me with a confused little frown before wriggling my coat off the captain and holding it out to me like a soiled rag, arm waving impatiently. She and Wilf wrapped his father in the blanket and she rubbed his arms briskly.

'Can you run him a bath?' Wilf asked as they bustled him

over the icy terrace into the house.

I stood on the edge of the frosty grass with my coat in my hands, sweltering despite the cold. I was filled with shame, for my concern for the old man had disappeared. All I could see was the blueness of Wilf's eyes, how the scars on his lip and cheek had faded. I couldn't take my eyes off them – off him – and his bizarre beauty despite them. An angel's face with the devil's fingerprints. How had I survived so long apart from him?

When they'd gone, I started back down the garden in a daze. Then there were the faintest footsteps, and I turned to see him on the terrace, looking at me like I'd just appeared in front of him, surprised and curious, his lips slightly apart, his shoulders rising with every short breath. 'Come inside, Gracie.' My name on his lips seemed to shatter the silence we'd carried between us since the lake.

'I can't…'

'No, you've had a shock,' he said with the same gentle authority he had used with his father. 'Wait by the fire. I'll be with you shortly.'

CHAPTER 20

I stepped through the French windows and shut them behind me. A fire crackled and the room heaved with warmth. It looked just as it had the last time I'd been there. I was alone, but could hear anxious footsteps on the stairs and through the ceiling. The clunk of hidden pipes and Miss Brennan's muffled voice. I perched on the sofa nearest the fire and felt my cheeks and fingers begin to thaw. My chilblains burned. I looked around for somewhere to put my coat but decided to keep it in my lap. I wouldn't stay long. I'd felt obliged to come in but I couldn't think why now. I should have made an excuse and left. Cliff and Dad would be expecting me back. I would leave as soon as Wilf came down.

A log shifted in the grate. I clasped my hands and waited, running the bizarre events of the last half hour through my head, from the moment I'd seen the captain on the shore, to now, sitting in the Manor and waiting for Wilf to reappear. I couldn't believe he was back. I hadn't given much thought to where he'd been since the war ended; I'd resisted that temptation with devout dedication. Crucially, he hadn't been *here*, and I'd rather naively expected he might never come back. But here he was. Was he staying, or just visiting? Either way, I shouldn't be just sitting there, waiting for him. It didn't feel right. The look he'd given me told me he hadn't forgotten any of what had happened two and a half years ago. My eyes flicked to the butterflies in their cases. *You're the Small Blue, Gracie.*

I grasped my coat. I had to go. I hurried to the French windows.

'You're leaving?'

I froze, trapped, just inches from my escape. Wilf was in the doorway, his shirtsleeves rolled up. I felt the breath catch in my throat.

'Won't you stay for a cup of tea?'

'I need to get back for church.'

He glanced at the grandfather clock in the corner of the room. 'You've plenty of time. Please, sit down.'

I looked back to the sofa reluctantly, searching for excuses, but couldn't seem to find a single word from the millions spiralling around my brain. I didn't have to be polite; it didn't matter if I offended him. I never had to see him again.

'It's the least I can do to say thank you.'

I let my shoulders fall with the surrender. 'All right.'

He seemed to smile. 'Let me take your coat. I won't be a moment.' He disappeared again.

I trudged back to the sofa. When he returned, he sat opposite and we said nothing for a few moments. I sensed his gaze on me, and words waiting to be spoken – niceties, apologies, regrets. I didn't want to hear them. I wanted to tell him I was leaving, with enough confidence that he'd let me go. But he had me pinned to the spot, and I couldn't even look him in the eye.

'It's good to see you again.' He sounded unsure of himself.

'I didn't know you were back.'

'I arrived yesterday.'

I took a breath and it came out louder than I wished.

'I've been living in London. I'm renting some rooms while I decide what to do about the house.'

I guessed he meant his other house, not this one. It wasn't my business to ask. I was trying to think what to say. What came out was unplanned: 'I'm married.'

His lip twitched. 'I know.'

'How do you know?' My tone was too accusing; it betrayed me.

'Bridges keeps me informed.'

I nodded. Bridges – the estate manager who counted our rents each quarter.

'I hear your husband will take over the farm when Mr Goffman retires in the autumn.'

'Yes.'

'Well, congratulations.' He sounded like he meant it. There was no bitterness in his manner. It should have reassured me but instead I felt unbalanced. I wanted him to seem annoyed or jealous. I wanted him to care. 'Are you still at the Post Office?'

'No.'

'But you're well?'

'Yes, thank you.' I flicked my gaze back to him. He was resting his forearms on his knees, managing to look at ease and uncomfortable at the same time. 'And you?'

He nodded. The silence that followed was charged with unspoken questions. He stood abruptly. 'I think I hear the kettle boiling. Excuse me.'

I exhaled slowly once he'd gone. I didn't know how I'd manage to sit through tea with him. It was like my first visit all over again. I glanced at the clock. They'd start ringing the bells soon.

Unannounced, Miss Brennan bustled into the room. 'I've put him to bed. He was worn out…' She stopped dead and scowled at me. 'Oh, you're still here! Where's Mr Whitman?'

It had been a while since I'd heard Wilf referred to as Mr Whitman. It had always been Flight Lieutenant, and then, after his fall from grace, just Wilfred Whitman or derogatory nicknames, spoken with disdain. Miss Brennan waited for my answer with impatience. 'He's fetching tea.'

'Right.' She eyed me suspiciously, then nodded in a grateful sort of way and left. I heard voices in the distance.

Wilf reappeared and set down the tea tray. He poured me a cup, then sat, running his hand over the back of his neck. I remembered the feel of his short hair there, how my fingertips had brushed it when he kissed me.

'Agnes likes to take charge somewhat,' he said fondly. 'She looks after Father.'

I nodded. I wasn't going to tell him I'd met her before. I wondered if she'd mention it later.

We sipped our tea.

'And how are your father and brother?'

I'd assumed if he knew about my marriage then he'd know about Alec too. I gripped my tea cup and tightened the knot inside me that held my emotions together. 'My father is well, thank you. My brother… was killed just over a year ago now.'

He covered his mouth with his hand. 'Oh God, no… I'm so sorry.'

He looked genuinely devastated, and something else too: ashamed. I realised he assumed Alec had been killed in combat. He must have thought I hated him all the more for it. I could have told him the truth, but I kept quiet.

'Please give my condolences to your father,' he said.

I gave him a worn-out smile. I wouldn't be telling anyone about this.

He got up to add another log to the fire and a spray of amber sparks burst and flew up the chimney. He lingered by the mantelpiece, where Mrs Whitman's photograph watched on. There was a hint of panic in his movements, in the arching of his shoulders and his hand nervously touching his face. I sensed he wanted to say something. He didn't look back at me. Eventually he cleared his throat. 'Thank you for helping me with Father today.'

'I was out walking. It was nothing.'

'Many people would have run a mile as soon as they saw him.'

'Will he be all right?'

'He's a little shaken, but he'll be fine.' He eyed me knowingly. 'This isn't the first time. He tends to wander.'

I remembered what Cliff had told me. 'He seemed to think I was someone else.' I glanced at Mrs Whitman's film star face. 'He called me Bixxy.'

A darkness crept into Wilf's eyes. 'That's what he used to call Mother.'

'I'd wondered that. But I don't look anything like her.'

'He didn't really see you.' He sat down again and pulled his silver cigarette case from his pocket. He had that look that he'd carried with him when we first met – an uncomfortable reticence. I knew now what he'd been hiding then. I wondered what secrets he was still keeping.

I took the cigarette he offered me and the taste of it sent me back to our afternoon on the island. I hardly smoked at all now – Cliff's ones made me feel sick – and so the effect was all the more intoxicating.

'Gracie, have you met my father before?'

'Why do you ask that?' I sounded ridiculously guilty, and Wilf's eyes widened. He almost laughed. 'Yes, I spoke to him once. I was delivering a telegram. It was a couple of years ago now.'

Wilf nodded slowly but his eyes lacked satisfaction. He was trying to make sense of something.

'There was one other time too,' I admitted hesitantly. I didn't want to mention that day at the lake but something told me it might be important. I felt my cheeks flushing. 'I saw him once when I was swimming.'

'When?' There was more concern in his tone than I felt the statement had warranted.

'Years ago. Before the war.'

'Where was he?'

'Almost exactly where I found him today, near the boathouse.'

'And you were in the water?'

I nodded, unsettled by his insistent questions. 'I'd got into a bit of trouble, actually.'

'What do you mean?'

'It was silly. Cramp or headache or something. I'd had too much sun.' I tried to laugh it off but Wilf looked deadly serious.

'Were you on your own?'

'No, the boys were with me, but they were further off.'

'What happened?'

'Nothing. I spluttered and struggled a bit. Then Cliff noticed and came to help me.' I felt the cold prickling along my arms and down my neck again. I wished Wilf would just leave it alone.

'And Father?'

I shrugged. 'He was gone when I got out of the water.'

'Did he say anything to you?'

'Not a word.'

He sighed and held his chin in his hands. I couldn't understand why he seemed so put out by it. I looked at the clock again and stood. 'I ought to go.'

He nodded and went to get my coat without saying anything. When he came back he held it out for me and I slipped my arms inside. I faced him again, and my heart seemed to stop for a moment. Ever since I'd found out the truth, I'd cursed myself for falling for him. But now I saw how easily it had happened, being next to him again, catching the splintered shades of blue in his eyes, the waxy smoothness of his scars. I remembered the night he came to our house, how he touched my cheek in the twilit gloom. I felt the spell being cast all over again, and looked away, willing to break it.

'Well then, goodbye.'

I grabbed the door handle and stepped out into the crisp morning. The peel of bells sang out across the fields. I felt compelled to glance back at him as I walked away, but I fought the urge, clenching my fists in my pockets and biting the inside of my cheek so hard that there was blood on my tongue by the time I reached the gate.

CHAPTER 21

I hurried into church just in time for the service. Dad and Cliff – washed and stiff in his suit – were already seated, and I had to squeeze past Mrs B and Alfie to get to them.

'Where have you been?' Cliff hissed as the organ blasted out the first hymn. He frowned at my trousers and boots. I hadn't had time to change.

I spent all service thinking about what I'd say to him, but in the end I didn't see what was wrong with the truth. All I'd done was help an old man and had half a cup of tea. Wilf hadn't said anything improper. There was no use pretending I'd slipped or something, and having to feign an injury.

I told Cliff once we were home and I was battling to get the stove lit. Dad was in and out of the garden, bringing in more firewood.

'You had tea with Wilfred Whitman?' Cliff scoffed.

'Just a sip. He offered; he was ever so grateful.'

He paused and watched me with a severe look, as if I'd said something completely different, something repulsive. 'You make him sound like a gentleman.'

'Well, I couldn't very well say no.' My voice was higher than it should have been.

'Why not? I would have. You wouldn't catch me within a mile of his place.'

'This is his place too, don't forget. And half the village.'

'Are you defending him?'

'What? No, why would I—'

'That man is a fucking disgrace!'

'Keep your voice down!' I whispered, and shut the kitchen door as he leant his hands on the table. 'I don't know what you're getting so het up about. It wasn't my fault, and I was only trying to help. The captain was out there all on his own.'

He tutted gruffly. 'You should have just left him.'

'To freeze to death?'

'He'd have found his way back, or the coward would have found him.' I winced at that word. 'You told me yourself he was looking for him.'

I muttered, 'Yes, well, I know that *now*,' feeling suddenly unable to meet his steely gaze.

He stood and ran his fingers through his hair, sighing as if I exhausted him. 'Next time, leave him.'

'Next time? I'm not planning—'

'Gracie, I've lost count of the times I've seen that old nutter milling about near the boathouse. Chances are you'll see him again, so just leave him alone, all right?'

It hit me then that even though he'd seen the old captain lost and confused on innumerable occasions, he'd never once thought to help him. I felt a queasy sensation in my stomach.

'Better still, stay away from the lake altogether.'

'What?'

'It always seems to land you in trouble.'

I couldn't sleep that night, tossing and turning with Cliff snoring beside me. In the end the mattress felt like it was made of rocks and I had to get up and go down to the kitchen for a glass of water. The kitchen was cold but there was still a hint of warmth in the stove; I leant against it and watched the still, snowy scene outside, glowing a soft blue in the moonlight.

I didn't know if Cliff had been serious about me staying away from the lake. I'd never been able to read him well, but since turning down the Post Office job we seemed to have locked ourselves away from each other. Mrs B just laughed when I mentioned concerns about it; she said the honeymoon was over. She was probably right, but I couldn't shake the feeling that it was something deeper. Cliff went to the pub more often now and came back later. He didn't press me to sleep with him every night, and when he did, he seemed rougher than before. He didn't always have breakfast with us – he said it made sense to get to the farm early and eat with the Goffmans, and I agreed. But it worried me that I didn't miss him at our table; I loved those mornings with just Dad and me. It felt like the old days. It felt like Alec was still with us, upstairs, asleep in his bed.

*

The snow was starting to thaw by the middle of the week. Errands that had been put off owing to the ice became possible, and the village shuffled back to life. I'd already had two visitors knocking by Wednesday lunchtime, so it didn't surprise me when I heard another tap at the door. I had my hair tied up in a scarf and had worked up a sweat scrubbing the kitchen floor; my housecoat was splattered with water. I was ready to laugh off my appearance with whoever was on the doorstep, but my smile evaporated and words failed me when I opened the door and saw Wilf.

He was wrapped up in his coat and scarf. I had no idea why he'd come, but seeing the lane empty behind him, and thinking blessedly that he may not have been spotted yet, I did the only thing that seemed rational: I took hold of his lapels, quickly dragged him over the threshold and slammed the door. Suddenly we were facing each other in the cramped hallway, his face a picture of surprise and confusion.

I tried to take a step back, but I hit the wall. There was barely a foot between us. I caught the scent of his familiar aftershave, tried not to look in his eyes. 'Mr Whitman...'

He shook his head vigorously. 'Good God, Gracie, don't call me that!'

'What are you doing here?'

He took off his hat. 'I came to see you.' He glanced towards the living room and stairs. 'I expected you'd be alone.'

'I am alone,' I admitted warily. 'But what if someone sees you? My husband will have a fit.'

'I'm sorry.' He was pinching his hat, turning the brim. 'I… There's something I wish to talk to you about. Actually, there are several things I wish to talk to you about.'

'Wilf, you shouldn't be here.'

'I understand you don't want to see me, and that you're married now, but there are some things you ought to know. Some things about the past…'

'Your past has nothing to do with me.'

The words were so cutting I could see the wound in his eyes. He didn't break my stare, just looked at me as if he'd noticed something new, as if studying my face for the first time. 'I'm not so sure about that, Gracie.'

'Wilf, what happened between us was so long ago now. It was a mistake—'

'Was it? I'm sorry you think so.'

'I'm sorry,' I panicked. 'That's not what I meant.' The heat was rising beneath my collar. 'Only that…' The memory of our kiss played in my mind and on my lips again. I took a steadying breath. 'So much has changed. And I *am* married, Wilf.'

'I understand that.'

'Then you ought to go. You shouldn't have come.'

'I don't mean to try and explain myself. I've already done that. I sent you a letter, did you receive it?'

'Yes, I did.' It was ashes now but I still remembered it. *I fear your friendship will prove to be the greatest sacrifice.* The memory brought a great hollow ache to my chest, and its intensity took my breath away. With alarm I realised I was on the verge of tears, and worse, of giving in to him again. I remembered the lake and the butterflies, the way he'd touched my cheek before kissing me. I thought how easy it would be to kiss him again now, where no one would see, how I could run my fingers down his scar, and trace the line of his collarbone… 'Please leave.'

He nodded once and looked down at his feet. 'Very well.' He replaced his hat. 'I return to London in a week. If you change your mind, I'll be at the Manor every day until then. Goodbye, Gracie.'

'Goodbye.'

He stepped towards the door and I opened it a crack, checking to see if the coast was clear. His coat brushed my hand, and I fought the urge to hold on to him, to grab him back and pull him to me. To taste those lips again and feel his weight against me. To breathe in his scent. It was only a second before I opened the door wider, but it felt like an eternity resisting him, balancing on the precipice of my desire. He left swiftly, without looking back. In a few seconds he'd disappeared up the lane, and I exhaled loudly, my heart pummelling my ribs.

I felt dirty with shame, but not for the reason I should have done. I should have been mortified for being attracted to him still, for wanting him when I was a married woman. And I did want him, more than ever, more than anyone. But I knew I'd really been ashamed to be seen with him, and I hated myself for that above all. It stayed with me long after he'd gone. And later, in my cold bed, I fought fruitlessly to remove his face from my thoughts, and the memory of his broken lips against mine.

CHAPTER 22

The following day, in the Post Office, Mrs B popped her head in when she heard my voice, hooked my arm and bustled me through to her sitting room. Her beady eyes were anxious and stern. 'I ought to warn you. Wilfred Whitman's back at the Manor.'

It would be tiresome to explain that I already knew, so I feigned surprise, but Mrs B looked suspicious.

'Did you know he was returning?'

'No, why would I?'

'You know why, Gracie Wells.'

'Archer.'

She raised her eyebrows. 'Indeed.'

'Yes. *Indeed.*'

She tutted and sat me down. 'Enough cheek. If I remember correctly, you and he were caught up in something a couple of summers ago.'

'You're imagining things.'

'I didn't imagine him here waiting for you, did I? Or that he came to your house at night and stood outside with you alone – yes, your father told me – don't look at me like that; he was worried about you. And don't pretend you weren't heartbroken when Wilfred left and you found out what he was. I saw you every day and I knew it wasn't Cliff you were pining over.'

'It was a silly crush. And it doesn't matter now, does it?'

'I should hope not.' She watched me for a few seconds and I wondered if she could see my fear: even as I'd said the words I'd felt them shatter inside me. It hadn't been a crush – I'd loved him. I'd thought I'd forgotten him because I burned his letter and numbed my heartache with willpower. I'd put him out of my thoughts for so long, replaced him with Cliff and duty and Alec, and never missed his memory when it finally left me. But it was only because my head had been elsewhere. Alec's death had taken over everything. I hadn't imagined the smoke of grief would ever clear – I wasn't sure I wanted it to – but it seemed, in the ruins of my heart, Wilf's memory endured.

'Well, hopefully he'll keep himself to himself as always and won't stay long.'

'He could stay for fifty years and it wouldn't make a difference.' I'd meant it to sound light-hearted but it came out bitter. It was true. It wouldn't make a difference. It wouldn't change the facts.

'Don't tempt fate, Gracie. That man carries trouble with him. The sooner he's gone, the better.'

I wished for Wilf to go. It would be so much easier to get on with things if he was far away. Out of sight, out of mind, although I sensed the adage would prove false in this case. It set me on edge to know he was just a mile from my home. It was like a cloying heat, slowing me down, pulling at all my thoughts. It made me clumsy and irritable, made me forget the salt in our pie and bite Cliff's head off when he complained about it. It brought out a side of me that I hated, yet Cliff seemed to find it funny. He teased me for my mistakes and I went about the house with a sour face and short, brusque sighs.

I went to Alec's grave and stood in the drizzle for half an hour, reminding myself of how much he'd disliked Wilf and how happy he'd been when Cliff and I got engaged. I recalled Dad and Mrs B's smiles on my wedding day, how wary they were of the Whitmans. It was madness to let Wilf occupy my thoughts again now. If Alec were around he'd tell me to snap out of it. I thought back to how I'd made a fool out of myself with Wilf that summer, and I agreed. *Snap out of it, Gracie.*

But my mounting panic was getting harder to ignore. Wilf had told me on Wednesday that he'd be leaving in a week. After church on Sunday I was filled with such disappointment that I realised I'd been hoping to see him. I hadn't envisaged it at all, or planned to say a word to him, but it felt like a great injustice that he hadn't been there.

On Tuesday morning we woke to rain, and Cliff spent breakfast telling me how lucky I was not to have to go out in it, painting a cosy picture of domestic happiness, no doubt imagining me curled up by the fire with a book, thinking of him. When I was alone, I stared at the pile of dirty laundry and the dripping washing line in the garden and prayed for a lamp and three wishes, so I could be rid of the rain, and the washing and the infinite stretch of tedium ahead of me.

By lunchtime the house was decorated with makeshift lines, and clothes wrung within an inch of their lives were drooping down like miserable ghosts, while the fire and stove blazed. I opened the windows to clear the condensation, and waved at the Smythe sisters in the lane, arm in arm and making the most of a break in the weather. I was too hot and fed up to spend another moment inside, so I decided to jump on my bicycle and go for a quick ride.

I hastily fixed my hair in the steamy mirror by the front door;

the humidity had all but ruined it, and my cheeks were puce and glistening, but I looked presentable enough. I glanced at the sky as I wiped down my seat. It was ominously grey and I guessed I'd be caught in another downpour before I made it home. No matter: a few more clothes draped in front of the fireguard would make little difference.

I told myself afterwards, because I'd made no effort in my appearance, and thought of nothing but the fresh air and the need to be away from the house for a while, that it was a complete accident that I ended up at the Manor. I simply started pedalling and followed the lane, lost in thoughts of nothing, and before I knew it I'd reached the gateposts and slowed to a stop.

I hadn't ridden down the driveway since my days at the Post Office, but as I reached the turning circle it felt like only yesterday. The house hadn't changed, although it looked sadder without the summer sunlight glimmering in its panes. I knocked on the door and wondered what I'd say. My heart wasn't thundering, my palms weren't sweaty. Above all else I felt weariness, and a little relief, as if I'd just found my way home after a long and gruelling journey.

Wilf opened the door with a book in his hand. He was wearing reading glasses and his hair was endearingly scruffy; it made me hide a little smile as he cried, 'Gracie!' His surprise was evident but he seemed happy to see me. 'I hoped you'd come.'

'I didn't think I would until this moment.'

'Well, I'm glad. Come in.'

Once more I crossed the threshold and stood in the grand hallway as he hung up my coat. I let Cliff into my thoughts for a second and then shut out the doubts that warned me I shouldn't be there.

'You missed the rain,' he said as I followed him into the living room where a fire glowed. 'Tea?'

I shook my head and he looked a little thrown. He gestured

to the sofa, where I'd sat just over a week ago. In the absence of tea, and obviously needing something to occupy his hands, he offered me a cigarette and I leant forward for him to light it. My fingers brushed his hand as he held out his lighter. It was the briefest contact, but it awoke me to him, and my surroundings, as if I'd left our house just moments ago, blinked and found myself here.

He held his cigarette by his thigh, hesitating as if deciding whether to sit or walk away. The sun somehow broke through the cloud and filled the room suddenly; it caught the edge of his hair and framed him in an angelic light. He looked like an apparition. Perhaps he wasn't really there. Perhaps neither of us were. I felt the rush of my subconscious, the tingle of life in my veins, and I braced myself for the sudden spin of cold reality: the disappointment and darkness of my bedroom and my husband sleeping beside me.

As quickly as it had come, the bright sunbeam vanished, but Wilf was still there, as real and vital as the blood in my veins. He sat opposite me and I tried not to think of how beautiful he was, or why my skin felt feverish and cold, despite the fire.

'You'll have to excuse the state of the place. We haven't had a maid since Daphne was called up and left us.'

I remembered the slight girl who'd served me tea on my first visit. It was a relief to know there was one less person who'd know I was here. Cliff's face flashed in my mind again and I drew on my cigarette as if the smoke would cover my guilt. I glanced around the room and it did seem shabbier than before. There were lines of dust around the sofa feet, and mud trodden into the carpet by the French windows.

Wilf followed my gaze. 'Not much point getting someone new now.'

I gave him a questioning look. I didn't want to seem too curious or eager.

'I've decided to sell.'

A quiver of panic. 'Sell? Everything?' I could only think of the farm and the land and the myriad Whitman-owned properties in the village, not least our own.

Wilf understood my concern. 'You needn't worry. I'll see to it that no one is disturbed. But this house is eating money and…well, my present circumstances don't really lend themselves to major renovations. And I've no reason to keep it. It's too big for just me and Father.'

There was no mention of a possible Mrs Whitman to grace the rooms in the future, of a family to fill the nursery. But the idea hovered in the silence, and I wondered if he was thinking of it too. He was still a young man, and wealthy; he had principles, albeit controversial ones, but not everyone would share Barnfield's view of him. It would still be possible for him to marry if that's what he wanted, to find someone to bear his name and children and be the object of his devotion. But whoever she was, he wouldn't be bringing the future Mrs Whitman here. I'd only ever be able to imagine her – more beautiful and talented than she probably was – and the two of them living in eternal happiness far away. The vision would torment me forever. My mind raged against it now. I felt the clench of jealousy in my stomach. Why should I care? Why should I feel such betrayal, when I'd known for a long time that woman wouldn't be me? Even if things had been different, I don't think it ever could have been. His was another world; I'd glimpse it through the window of those few summer days, but the door had always been locked to me.

I had to think of something to say. 'You'll return to your house in Kensington?'

His mouth twitched and I thought he must be pleased that I'd remembered it. 'Sadly not. It's beyond repair, I'm afraid. But I've found a place in Hampstead, which will suit us well enough.'

'So, you won't be coming back to Barnfield?' My voice sounded wretched but I couldn't hide it. The thought of never seeing him again made my insides lurch like seasickness.

As long as you are here, I'll wish to be nowhere else.

He looked down at his fingers. 'No.'

I held my breath and focused on the fire with wide eyes, willing the tears to stay back.

'I'm making arrangements so Father can come and live with me,' he went on. 'And Agnes will join us.' He glanced to the ceiling and I guessed she and the old captain were cloistered away upstairs.

'How is he?'

'He's as well as can be expected. His little excursion last week didn't seem to do too much damage. But overall he's deteriorating.' He tapped the ashtray next to him and exhaled slowly so the smoke wound around him.

'I'm sorry.'

He smiled appreciatively. 'It's Father I wanted to speak to you about. That's why I came to see you the other day. I know it was untoward of me, but I didn't know if I'd see you again, and I thought you deserved an explanation.'

'I don't understand,' I stammered, trying not to focus on the fact that this could be the last time I saw him. All my nerves pulsed with energy and fear; they seemed to warn me that it was wrong, that we oughtn't part. I tried to ignore the sensation.

He pinched his lips in thought. 'The other day, when you told me how you'd seen Father a few years ago, when you got into trouble swimming… I could tell you were trying to make light of it, but I saw how it had affected you.'

I looked down in embarrassment.

'The thing is, your story struck a chord with me. It's one I've heard before.'

'What do you mean?'

He stubbed out his cigarette and walked over to the mantelpiece. 'Do you know how my mother died, Gracie?'

I hesitated. 'I heard it was pneumonia.'

He nodded. 'And did you hear anything else?'

I glanced at her picture, remembering all the stories I'd once believed. 'There used to be a silly rumour, but it was just children making things up.'

'Go on.'

I was too embarrassed to look at him. I heard Alec's voice in my memory. 'They used to say she was murdered.' I couldn't bring myself to add that his father had been the supposed culprit.

'Hmm.' Wilf sounded more disappointed than shocked. 'Well, it *was* pneumonia, although she very nearly drowned.'

'Drowned?' The word burst out thoughtlessly.

He came back to the sofa and rested his wrists on his knees. 'I was at school at the time. I heard it all from Mother on her sick bed. She'd been swimming in the lake one day. She was a strong swimmer, but for some reason she struggled and before she knew it, she was in real trouble.'

My heart began to race as I remembered the water in my throat and the sense of doom as it closed in around me. I didn't want to imagine what would have happened if Cliff hadn't saved me, although my nightmares had played out that ghastly end time and time again. I imagined Bixxy Whitman as I had been, flailing and spluttering, but I couldn't recall the event now without that devilish dream creeping in, and the clawing hands and grey face beneath the water seemed just as real as Cliff's rescuing embrace. 'How did she get out?'

'She made it to the shore somehow, but she was unconscious when…' He cleared his throat. 'Gracie. My father was there too. He saw it happen.'

I felt the blood drain from my face in an instant.

'He *watched* it happen,' Wilf clarified, in a tight, flat voice that seemed to hide a hundred different emotions.

It couldn't possibly be true, could it? It was too similar, too bizarre a coincidence. I shut my eyes briefly and I was back in the water, with the old captain watching on. 'He didn't help her?' I asked, but I knew the answer.

Wilf's expression seemed apologetic, disappointed. 'Did he help you?'

I shook my head. 'No wonder he calls me by your mother's name,' I said, trying to make sense of it all. 'He must remember seeing me there.'

'I expect he does, although I can't say how he adds all of it up in his mind. He probably thought you were a vision. He gets them a lot. He would have told Agnes about seeing you that day and she'd have thought nothing of it – just another fantasy. He deeply regrets not helping her, you see, but…'

'He remembers it clearly?'

'He remembers nothing clearly. He knows she was in trouble, and that he didn't help her. She died a couple of weeks later.'

I felt an ache of sympathy for the old man. 'But surely you can't blame him? I don't blame him for not helping me. He's confused, and… no one can expect him to act rationally.'

'No, I never blamed him, not really. It was a horrible accident. Father probably didn't understand what was happening and I know for a fact he's nervous of water – many of his men drowned in the mud in Flanders. If he'd gone in he'd probably have been in more danger than she. But I can't help wondering if Mother would have survived had she got out of the water sooner.' He rubbed his scars and his fingers touched his glasses; he took them off quickly and put them on the little table near him. 'I'm not even sure he could have helped her. The fact he did nothing to help you seems to confirm it. But it disturbs him, and as I said, he has dreams, and for a long time…' He stopped and took a deep breath. 'For a long time he talked about seeing "a girl" in the water, and I, well I thought he meant Mother, of course, but since I've come back this time, he's been saying it was *you*. He uses your name – 'Grace in the water'. I couldn't understand it until you explained what had happened. It was a bit of a relief, because, I have to say, I found it rather disconcerting to hear him talk about you like that, and how he could hear you crying and needed to get to you.'

'Yes, he said something similar to me.'

'He did?'

'Once, when I delivered a telegram. He must remember it. He must have got me muddled up with your mother in his head.' I felt I ought to apologise for disrupting the old man's mind even further.

But Wilf held out his hands with a smile. 'Well, there you have it. Mystery solved.'

I couldn't share his satisfaction. It didn't explain why Mrs Whitman and I, both strong swimmers, had inexplicably got into trouble in the first place, and though the captain was known to wander, it was still quite a coincidence that he'd witnessed both incidents. There was something not right about it. A shiver rose up my back. I thought of Mrs Whitman struggling in the lake, and the old captain watching her just as he'd watched me. *Many of his men drowned in the mud in Flanders…* I pictured hands reaching out, sinking down; had Dad seen them too? Then the old captain's glazed, childlike eyes blinked in my memory. How could he be expected to play the hero, when he was barely there at all, just the shadow of a once brave man? No, he wasn't to blame. It was just an accident. But an accident that had nearly happened twice.

'I felt you ought to know the whole story, that it would explain Father's behaviour a little better, and perhaps put you more at ease.' Wilf sounded unsure of himself, as if he'd noticed it had done the exact opposite. But he misread my concern: 'I expect you ought to be getting back.'

I had no reason to stay. I'd heard what he wanted to tell me, although it didn't seem enough. I had so many questions for him, but all of them belonged to another time, long since passed. Nevertheless, the thought of leaving now and never seeing him again sent me into a panic, so I gabbled, 'What will you do?'

He arched his eyebrow. There was a hint of humour in eyes.

'I mean, when the Manor's sold. How will you live?'

He smiled. 'The estate takes more money than it gives, Gracie. It's a burden, not a blessing, especially now… Well, it's not the ideal place for me. And when it's gone I will continue to manage our investments, just as I always have.' He lowered his voice a little to say: 'Thankfully there are still some people who'll do business with me.'

He must have known what Barnfield thought of him. I doubted it surprised him, but I didn't want him to think I was like them: I might have been once, for a few months, and pretended to be so for a few months longer. I knew their feelings – that he'd shirked his duty and run away from danger – but I'd heard his explanation too, and even the newspapers wanted to sweep Bomber Command's misdeeds under the carpet now. No one mentioned those razed German cities anymore – Dresden, Berlin, Cologne – we didn't talk about anything. I hadn't let myself think about it long enough to realise it until that moment, but as Wilf rose to stand I knew, without a doubt, that he was no coward, and it had been wrong of me to distrust him. It was I who'd hidden out the war in the safety of Barnfield, after all. I was the one who'd happily taken the excuses of my sex and my circumstances and made a shelter out of them.

'You needn't be embarrassed,' he said gently. 'With my face *and* reputation ruined, it's little wonder I've become something of a social pariah.' He walked to the French windows and gazed out onto the dreary garden. 'And I wouldn't blame you if you hated me too.' His voice was low and uncertain. He kept his back to me.

There was a long pause and I thought of all the things I'd felt for him, from the beginning until now. There was so much I could have said, but in the end, I only managed: 'I don't hate you.'

'Even now you know who I am – that I worked out the rest of my war on a farm, while others gave their lives for their country, like your brother?'

The question took me by surprise, and I wavered for a moment, but I had to release him from his assumptions. My words came out quick and loud: 'Alec was knocked down by a car in the blackout.'

Wilf turned, his face all confusion and pity.

'He was on leave. It was… it was just an accident.' My voice trembled, and for a horrible moment I thought I was going to laugh. It happened sometimes at inappropriate moments. It made me feel frightened and lightheaded and possibly a little mad. I was just trying to make sense of it, and realising I couldn't, and never would. It was all so arbitrary. All those months we'd grown together in my mother's womb, the dull days in the classroom, the summers and winters and birthdays. It had all amounted to nothing. His life had ended in an instant and all that was left were our memories, to slowly fade until we too were all dead. It was the bleak reality, and it wasn't worth talking about, because everyone else knew it too.

Wilf took a few steps towards me, as if he meant to console me with an embrace, but he stopped and checked himself and hovered awkwardly with his hands by his side. 'I'm sorry.'

'Yes, everyone says that. It's all you can say, really. But sometimes I think they mean they're sorry he was killed like that, that he died for nothing.' Cliff had said as much one evening, when he'd come home from the pub drunk and ended up weeping for Alec. My heart had gone out to him. We'd held each other close in our bed, and I'd felt for a few minutes that he wholly understood my grief. But in the end, he just clenched his fist and punched the pillow and grimaced and said: 'If I'd been there, I would have grabbed him, I know I would. It's such a bloody stupid way to go! Such a bloody waste!' I wondered if he'd have wept as much if Alec had died a hero.

'There's no sense in death,' said Wilf solemnly. 'My first couple of weeks in Bomber Command taught me that.'

I remembered what he'd told me about his accident, how one of his crew had been killed. He must have known countless others, not to mention all the bombing raids he'd been involved with. 26 sorties. He'd been surrounded by death. He was no coward. 'I understand why you did what you did,' I muttered. 'At least, I think I do. I thought it was wrong when I found out, but maybe it would have been madness to continue with it.'

Wilf sat on the edge of my sofa. 'Thousands did. Perhaps they had far more courage than me.'

'Or far less.' He held me in his gaze for an agonising moment. He was only an arm's length away and it was all I could do not to reach out and touch him. I felt a surge of desire, a remnant of the fire he'd lit in me two years ago. 'You gave no address,' I said, almost a whisper. 'I was angry with you, but I would have written back. I would—'

'I know.' His fleeting smile was framed with remorse. 'I

didn't want you to.'

My chest ached; the pain choked me, and I had to look away from him.

'I was angry too, Gracie, with myself more than anyone. I didn't want to hear from you. I couldn't have borne it. I didn't want to read your accusations – they would have all been justified.'

'I would have accused you, yes,' I admitted. But I would have forgiven him too, eventually. 'I only wished you'd told me the truth and not hidden it.'

'Would you have joined me that afternoon, if I had? Would you have accepted my gift and—' He stopped himself, and in the silence I thought of his kiss and knew he was doing the same. I heard him swallow, and sat motionless as he moved closer and placed his hand over mine. His touch burned with magic; it brought me to life again, as if I'd been dead in the years without him. But he quickly withdrew it, and I felt the wrench of it as if his flesh had been torn from mine. 'You had a right to be angry,' he said. 'I shouldn't have misled you.'

'You must have known I wouldn't be angry forever.'

He nodded. 'I feared it.'

'Feared what? My forgiveness?'

He seemed to be struggling to explain, his eyes were burdened with regret. He absentmindedly ran his hand across his scars again but I reached out in frustration and pulled it away from his face. 'Don't! You don't have to cover them!'

He looked startled. 'They're ugly.'

I shook my head. 'No.' I reached for his face and ran my fingers across his broken cheek. His eyes glistened. He lifted his hand and held it over mine, then turned his face to kiss it, and I leant forward so our foreheads touched, just as we'd done on the island years ago. It felt a lifetime away now. I'd been on the brink of being his then, but I'd stepped back from the edge. I'd loved him without understanding it, without really believing it, and certainly never declaring it. I'd loved him fearfully and run from it at the first opportunity. I'd wilfully forgotten him, and spent the last two years hiding from him in a safer life. But now he'd found me again and my refuge, I realised, was actually my prison.

'I'm sorry, Gracie. I *was* a coward. I abandoned you.'

'I know why you did it. There was no real future for you with someone like me.'

'No!' He gripped my hand tighter. 'Do you really imagine that I'm so shallow? That's not why I did it at all! You already had a future, a better one! You were always meant to be with Cliff.'

I drew back.

'He was the one you grew up with and made plans with. I couldn't take that away from you – for what – a life of gossip and shame? You were so young, so… You didn't deserve that. *I* deserve it, but you don't. I was only an interruption. If you hadn't stumbled across me at the Fielding's wedding, would you be sitting beside me now?'

I let go of him and walked to the mantelpiece despite feeling too warm already. I tried to control my voice. 'An interruption? You don't truly believe that?'

'I know it,' he said sadly. 'Because you *did* marry him, didn't you?' It sounded like an accusation.

'Yes, I did, but…' I clasped my fist in frustration. I was suddenly so angry, I didn't know what to say. I wished I could grab that damned frame on the mantelpiece and hurl it across the room, watch its glass shatter. It was like the rug had been pulled from beneath me, like discovering a new room in the house I'd lived in and known forever. 'You should have given me a choice!' I cried, barely able to suppress my resentment. 'Why do you think I married him, Wilf?'

He hesitated, perhaps unsure if I really wanted an answer. I didn't need one, but I was too furious to put him at ease. 'For the reasons I've already said.'

'Did you think I loved him?'

'That's none of my business.'

'Not now, perhaps, but it was then.'

His look was wretched; it held me till my eyes brimmed with tears. 'I would never have expected you to turn your life upside down for me, for the sake of…' I could see how he struggled with it too: the notion that a handful of chance meetings could mean so much.

'I did care about him,' I said, more measuredly. 'I do. I suppose I thought it would be foolish to throw him off for someone I'd just met.'

'Well, it seems you made a wise decision then. Everything's as it should be.'

'Is it?'

He ran his fingers through his hair in exasperation. 'Aren't you happy with him?'

'Nobody's happy!'

His eyes grew large and insistent. 'But he's good to you, isn't he?'

I nodded begrudgingly, thinking of the meals spent in laughter, the nights nestled against Cliff's warm side. I wasn't completely heartless; I had loved him. I'd loved him for being natural and dependable, for the way he brought me back to Alec and the girl I always thought I'd been. I recalled how we used to walk together beneath the trees, making fun of each other, listening to the buzzards shrieking above. When had we stopped doing that – when Mr Neal passed away, or when we married, or when Alec died? I thought of Cliff's face when I told him about the Post Office job, the way he'd laughed and goaded me about Captain Whitman. I heard his voice clearly in my mind: *I can always tell when you're lying.*

'He has a bright future, hasn't he?' Wilf pressed on, with mounting desperation, clutching at straws, as if he too was only just beginning to realise the gravity of our foolish choices.

'Yes, yes, he does. And I know I didn't have to marry him. I chose to, because – you're right – we had made plans, and all the people I value most in the world convinced me that we should. But don't imagine for a second that I'd have done it if I'd thought… if I'd really believed there was *any* hope of a future with you!'

The fire snapped in the stillness that followed and the rain began again, scattering the panes with silver, like shooting stars streaked across a grey night. My head and heart thrummed. I heard the words I'd just spoken repeat over and over, and felt the weight of regret pressing me down. I couldn't look at him in case it brought on the sobs I felt rising inside me. I left the fire and went to the French windows as he had done. The rain had descended on the garden in a cloud of drizzle. The gate was just visible in the mist but the field and lake and everything beyond were obscured, as if the rain had drawn a circle around us and hidden us from the rest of the world. I wished it was reality.

Wilf sighed sharply as if to calm himself. 'He knows your family and is loved by them, and he fits this place. He fits you. I don't fit… I don't belong anywhere, Gracie.'

'Well it doesn't matter now anyway,' I snapped bitterly, my breath clouding the glass. I hated how childish I sounded, and worse still how I felt: trapped and devastated and enraged at my own stupidity. I sensed Wilf behind me, watching me. I felt a ribbon tighten in my chest, tugging me back to him. I resisted, but the force only increased, and I imagined if I ripped my blouse I'd look down and see blood blooming beneath my skin.

His voice cut into the thick silence: 'After my discharge, I was in a very dark place. I buried myself in work. I wanted to forget myself, and I thought it best that you forgot me too. I was convinced I could only have brought you shame.'

'Not only shame,' I said firmly. He would have brought me love too, I knew it, and it would have been enough.

I heard him stand and move towards me. I could have turned and stopped him. I could have walked out and left, but I hungered for his arms around me again. Cliff didn't matter then – nothing else did. We were cocooned in the grey mist, safe in our make-believe world. When I left, the spell would unravel, I'd return home and be Cliff's wife again. But I couldn't bring myself to part from Wilf just yet.

His arms encircled my waist, and I leant back against him, entwining my fingers with his, as if we'd always stood and watched the rain together like this, the heat of our bodies combining. His touch was tender; he held me like treasure. I imagined a lifetime of being held by him and felt another stab in my heart. My eyes stung with tears, and I pressed them shut, thinking of the years we'd already wasted, and the decades still to follow.

A memory fizzled inside me: VE Day; it spilled out of me in trembling breaths. 'When the war ended, we had a party. Someone found a gramophone and put it outside the pub, and we danced in the road for hours.' Wilf's hands closed around me, and I pictured the scene in my mind: the flags in the windows, the children running up and down the lane. Everyone turned out for it. Everyone danced, even Dad with Mrs B, and the old folks with their sticks. Even me, with my heavy, grieving heart. 'There was a young lad – he's only sixteen now – he whirled me round and round. I couldn't stop laughing. Mrs B tapped me on the shoulder and said it wouldn't be long before I was dancing with Cliff, but… I only thought of you. I wondered where you were, and if you were dancing too. If I could have danced with anyone that night, it would have been you, Wilf.'

He kissed my hair, my neck, pulling me tighter until the heat of him overpowered me, and I turned and cradled his face in my hands. All this time without him I'd been like a ghost, moving through the spaces of my life without ever truly touching them. It was like I'd died with Alec. But it had started long before Alec left us. I'd come to life the day I first set eyes on Wilf, and it was his absence that had dulled me into a shadow. Now, as I gave in to him, I felt the stutter of life inside me again, eternity in my veins.

Why had I been so blind before? I should have trusted the mystery that brought us together, but instead I'd thrashed and railed against it and clung on to Cliff out of fear. I'd convinced myself my feelings for Wilf meant nothing. But I'd been lying – to myself, to everyone. I had to surrender to the painful truth: that I was Wilf's, and always had been, and even though my life would be spent apart from him, I'd love him for every minute of it.

The force of regret drew the strength out of me, and for a second I couldn't breathe. The feel of his lips on mine was such excruciating joy, and with each kiss it cut deeper. I pressed my hands through his hair and down his neck. We pulled each other tighter, but it wasn't enough. I could never have enough of him.

Before I knew it, my hands were at his collar, and he'd wrenched my blouse from my trousers. Miraculously, the guilt disappeared. It was right that his fingers pressed the skin of my waist, and my lips traced the smooth scars along his shoulders. There was no thought of stopping as he began to shake off his shirt. His body was firm and lean, the scars ended just below his chest. I squirmed out of my blouse and fell against him as he grappled with my brassiere, and the feel of his skin against my stomach burned a fire from my neck to my toes.

The creak of the ceiling made us freeze, our eyes caught in fear as our lips still touched. We heard brisk footsteps across the floor above, the sound of a door opening, and suddenly my skin turned cold and we drew back from one another. In the sliver of a second we stared at each other with desperate frustration, but there was no time to speak. I could hear the squeaking stairs, and I grabbed my blouse as Wilf buttoned up his shirt, covering the scars and his heavenly body.

I was dressed just in time, before the living room door swung open and in bustled Miss Brennan, full of purpose and distraction. She stopped dead when she saw me, and God knows what she thought of me, breathless and dishevelled. Wilf was running his hands through his hair, his face was flushed and gleaming.

'Oh, I beg your pardon!' Miss Brennan said hurriedly.

Wilf cleared his throat. 'Oh, that's quite all right Agnes. Miss… Mrs Archer…' he began, but then hesitated too long, so my name floated in the silence like a cruel condemnation.

'I was just leaving,' I mumbled, and nodded to Wilf as I headed to the door. The look of desperation on his face was almost more than I could bear, but I felt the nurse's eyes on me and my gnawing guilt roused itself again. I had to get out.

I hurried past Miss Brennan and snatched my coat from the hallway. Outside, the rain hit me like the spray of a fountain, but I grabbed my bicycle and started pedalling with as much energy as I could find in the wreck of my senses.

I somehow made it home, only to collapse in exhaustion and tears as soon as I shut the front door. I lay there in the hallway like a pathetic wretch, sobbing and shivering in my wet clothes, my head pounding with visions of Wilf: his electric eyes and extraordinary skin. I felt his tender embrace again and moaned with visceral longing, for all that couldn't be. Just a couple of hours beforehand, I'd been here, thinking I could go on without him. Might I still be able to manage it? Once the farm was ours, and I was busy again, I'd have work to take my mind off him. I'd learn to forget him like I had before. It was the only way, I knew. I'd made my choice long ago and there was no undoing it now.

And yet.

What if I couldn't forget? How long would I be able to live the lie before it crippled me? My head reeled with regret, the blood thronged inside me, more fiercely than it had done for years. I'd been in a stupor for so long, but Wilf had jolted me awake again; the world was clearer, but more painful. I wasn't sure I could bear it. I thought of the moment at the lake when he'd come running for his father and we'd seen each other. What if I hadn't stopped to help the old man? What if he'd come and gone and left forever? Cliff and I might have got away with it. I might have been able to live the rest of my life as a ghost, fooling myself.

Everyone had always said Cliff and I were meant to be together, and even I'd been convinced of it after a while. It had been easy and made sense, and after Alec died, Cliff made me feel like perhaps everything hadn't changed after all. But it had. If Alec had come home, then it could have worked, but without him – even if Wilf was out of the picture – the threads that tied us together before had all frayed. Cliff hadn't lured me with false promises; my marriage, my life, were just as I'd expected them to be. We had some things in common, but the greatest was that we both loved my brother more than each other. We'd always known it. It was never a problem when Alec was alive, but he was the one who'd made us work. Now, with just the two of us, we were off balance.

But it was too late. We were locked together. Our marriage would limp on as a dark and broken thing. Already we'd begun to tire of each other, picking at each other's faults. Even the good things about him were tainted with my stupidity and the fact he wasn't Wilf. I would forever look at Cliff with disappointment and bitterness. Our marriage was rotten at heart, and it wasn't Cliff's fault, it was mine. I'd always judged Mrs Whitman for loving another man while her husband lived, however damaged he was. The captain fought bravely and she betrayed him. How much worse was my betrayal! I'd married a decent man, who'd fought too and come home with his mind intact. He'd come home to *me*, and I had no excuse for not loving him. But I couldn't make my heart understand it. I wanted Wilf – even now, when it was more impossible than ever – still I wanted only him.

I scrambled to the kitchen, ran the tap and splashed my face with water. The cold shocked away my tears. I clung to the sink, bent over and trembling, and forced my breathing to slow. Stars whisked in my vision; I shut my eyes but they persisted. I slumped into a chair and buried my head in my arms on the table.

For a long time I was silent and my thoughts were still. Then, with the chime of the clock, I lifted my groggy head and wiped the stray tears from my eyes. There was still washing everywhere, so I went to the living room, stoked the fire, and threw everything that was dry into the ironing basket. I moved the clothes from the kitchen in front of the fire, then stood and watched the flames until my eyes felt gritty. I caught my reflection in the mirror: my hair was still damp, tangled in places; tiny, tired eyes stared back at me from a puffy face, pale lips gaping.

I dragged my aching body to the stairs, climbing them slowly and carefully. My feet felt weak. I imagined stumbling, falling backwards and hitting my head. I pictured my blood on the hallway carpet, and it made me feel calm and soft.

CHAPTER 23

By the time Cliff got in, I'd made myself look presentable somehow, although I had no memory of washing and dressing. My rain-sodden clothes were hanging by the stove, I supposed I must have put them there. The kitchen was filled with the scent of cooking – a pot on the stove stewing meat and onions – I must have done that too.

I sat at the table. Cliff talked and clattered with the kettle and cups, but I couldn't take in a word he was saying. My head was turning with Mrs Whitman's name, and the memory of the lake in my lungs, how I'd coughed and spluttered in vain to be rid of it. I could feel it now – the ominous threat of the darkness beneath my flailing legs, the sense it would go on forever, the lake's hands pulling me down. Had she felt them too? Was that why we'd both floundered so irrationally? It felt like I was missing something, an obvious reason why we might share such a strange connection. I thought of Captain Whitman watching me, and watching her, doing nothing, then raving about it for years afterwards. What might have happened if Cliff hadn't saved me? I could be dead, just like her, another ghost to haunt the waters.

I remembered the handsome airman who I'd seen at the Manor years ago – the man she'd loved – the man who'd loved her so dearly that he'd looked out for her son and tried to steer him away from disgrace. I recalled the captain's trembling apologies when he'd thought I was her, and her beautiful son, scarred and humiliated and adored by a girl who could never be his. It was all so pitiful, so much love thwarted and hope quashed. It dragged my spirits so low I thought my heart would stop, and again I felt the lure of oblivion inside me, the dark, endless depths. If I kept my eyes shut, I might never wake up.

I looked up at Cliff when he shook my shoulder.

'Well?' he said. He rolled his eyes. 'Haven't you been listening?'

'Sorry.' My voice was feeble. I touched my head where it ached at the temples.

'What's got into you?' he said with impatience, and sat down opposite me with his tea. He gave me a jaded look and tapped his fingers on the table top. 'You need to snap out of this. This…' he grasped the air for the word, 'this constant misery.'

'I'm just tired.'

'Why? What have you been doing?' His tone was accusing but I thought nothing of it. I shrugged, and gestured to the stove and the washing, these drab domestic things that summed up my existence.

'If you can't cope with this, how will you manage when we have the farm?'

'I'll manage… It's just…'

'What?' he pressed.

I was so very weary of him, of everything. I didn't have the strength to explain.

'You behave like you're the only person who's ever lost someone,' he said cuttingly, and I closed my eyes and saw Alec. I guessed Cliff thought all my sorrow was rooted in Alec. He was right in a way, and I was ashamed of letting my grief get to me. But I had *let* it. I'd welcomed it, I'd willingly fallen into a waking slumber, and only now Wilf was back did I really understand why. I thought of him alone at the Manor, the firelight playing on his face, and my soul cried out to him. If I hadn't hidden in grief for so long, I might have seen my mistakes sooner and found the courage to admit I'd been wrong. I might have never married Cliff at all. But it had all come too late. I wiped the tears as they dropped from my cheeks.

Cliff sighed irritably. 'I've had enough of this.' He stood and walked over to me, patted my shoulder and then kept his hand there. 'It's time you grew up.'

I looked up at him quickly, ready to protest, but his eyes were dark and reproachful. Anger flared in my veins. Was he really condemning me for missing my brother? As if reading my mind, his lip curled to a sneer, and the air in the room seemed to tighten around us. I sensed then that he wasn't talking about Alec anymore.

'You've been very stupid,' he said with calm menace. 'Did you think I wouldn't find out?' He stared at me with a mixture of self-satisfaction and revulsion, and I fought the realisation as it dawned on me: he knew.

In shock, I grappled to marshal my thoughts, but the confusion and questions and even relief all quailed in the wake of my mounting fear. Had he seen us? Had someone told him? My chest trembled and I wriggled to be free of him, but he pressed his hand down harder and I felt like an insect trapped beneath a rock. 'I don't understand,' I said weakly, thinking it was the right thing to say, what an innocent person would say. 'I don't know what you're talking about…'

The slap was quick and powerful. The next thing I knew I was cowed, clutching my shaking hands to my mouth. There was blood on my tongue, and my face felt like it would burst with pain. As soon as I could, I scrambled to stand and run, but

Cliff wasn't poised to retaliate. He was leaning against the sink, casually sipping his tea and watching me with an unreadable expression.

I wanted to shout at him but I had no voice. I gazed at him, breathless, unable to stand straight. I couldn't believe he'd struck me. In all the years I'd known him – our whole lives – he'd never violently lost his temper with me. I'd always felt it brewing, always known what he was capable of, but never believed he'd raise a hand to me.

'You left me with no choice,' he said flatly.

Still dumbstruck, I could only stare back in shock and anger and fear.

'I'm not stupid, Gracie! I heard what people said about you and Whitman when I came back, how you were seen together in the village. Did you imagine they wouldn't tell me?'

'There was nothing to tell—'

'Don't lie to me!' he bellowed, and I jumped and shook and despised myself for it. I'd always hated the thought of him thinking I was weak – even as children I'd wished to prove myself to him, always climbing higher in the tree, or swimming further, until he overtook me with his brawn and confidence. I'd thought it was for Alec's sake, to show him I was just as good as Cliff, that I was better. I'd so wanted Alec to love me the most. But now I trembled in Cliff's steely glare. I saw his fist clenching again and braced myself as the blood in my veins grew colder. Was this the real reason I'd hated him seeing my weakness? Had I been afraid of him all this time?

'I know he was the one you were with when I was training.' He laughed suddenly. 'It wasn't hard to work it out once I'd heard the rumours. It made me sick to think about it. I never understood why you'd wanted *him*, of all people, but I honestly, truly didn't hold it against you.' His eyes demanded me to believe him, but they were full of fire too. 'But I wondered why you'd lied to me about him. I guessed you were ashamed. I understood that. But last week, when you were late for church and came back smelling of his cigarettes, then I knew why.'

'Cliff, I didn't even know he was back. You have to believe me!'

'Why? Why does that matter? Are you going to pretend you haven't seen him since? I know you have. I smelt it as soon as I came in the door – your coat reeks of him. You must think I'm stupid.'

'I don't! I—'

'I won't bother asking if you're fucking him now. You probably were back then too.'

'No, you're wrong! I… I've only seen him a couple of times, and only then because of his father. I'm not having an affair with him,' I insisted, but thought of our kiss earlier and turned away. 'It's not what you imagine. We've made no plans…'

'Plans!' he barked, and laughed angrily. 'What plans could you make? You are my wife. The only plan Wilfred Whitman could have would be to make you his whore!'

I winced at his words. I wanted to yell at him for being so cruel, for not letting me explain. But what could I say? I had betrayed him. I loved another. Perhaps I wanted him to hate me. Perhaps I wanted the bleeding lip too, for with every heartbeat the pain pounded and numbed my thoughts, and I knew he wouldn't have done it if he loved me. I searched his callous stare and saw no regret in his eyes. There was disgust, certainly, and wounded pride, but he wasn't hurt.

'Alec would be ashamed of you,' he spat, turning his nose up at me.

'Yes, he would,' I admitted, thinking of the things he'd said against Wilf in the past, and the endless praise he'd heaped upon Cliff. I'd held Alec and his opinions on a pedestal all my life, never wanting to believe it when he made mistakes, always turning a blind eye to his faults. Now he was dead it was even easier to sugar-coat all he'd ever done and said. But he'd been human, and just as foolish as me. 'I can't live to please him anymore,' I said, lisping because of my lip.

'No, you should live to please *me*, your husband!' Cliff snapped, sounding more like the boy I'd fought with as a child, and even with his violence and spiteful words I felt a wave of pity for him. Had I been stronger than him, I might have reached out and held him.

'I'm not having an affair, Cliff,' I repeated, desperate to placate him. I wished I could tell him I loved him, but I knew how insincere it would sound. 'Nothing's changed. I am still your wife. And Wilf's leaving tomorrow, for good, so we'll never see him again.' The last words were choked with tears; I couldn't hide the pain of my broken heart.

'No, you won't see him again! I never even want to hear that bastard's name. You know how I hate him. Is that why you chose him, to spite me?'

'Of course not. I never meant to do anything…'

'Then you are weak, Gracie.'

I hung my head in shame. When I looked at him again, he bit his lower lip and glowered at me, saying, 'You'll be sorry, Gracie. You'll be sorry.' I sensed from his cold stare that it was more than violence he threatened me with now. Perhaps that would come too; in fact, as soon as I thought it I knew it would be so. But even the fear of that paled in the face of my true punishment: a lifetime of sorrow and regret. I felt the echo of his words again: *What plans could you make? You are my wife.*

He walked slowly towards me and my every muscle tensed in anticipation of another blow. He placed his hands on my face and lifted it, until I reluctantly met his gaze. He smiled faintly, as if the fear in my eyes pleased him. I took a breath, short and shallow, and felt his pulse through his fingers pressing on my cheeks.

Just then the front door opened and Dad called out a cheerful hello. The air around us lightened suddenly, and I felt Cliff's grip relax a little. He kept his eyes on mine, ignoring the blood that ran down my chin. 'Go and clean yourself up. I don't want to speak about this ever again,' he said quietly, then released my face, and walked swiftly out of the room. I heard him gruffly tell Dad he was going to the pub, and the front door clicked shut.

My breath came out in a mad, shuddering rush, and I slumped down to my knees in exhaustion. There was a long silence, as if Dad was holding his breath and putting off coming into the kitchen for as long as possible. Had he read the look in Cliff's eyes? Could he guess what awaited him? I thought about running up to the bathroom to wash, but even without the blood I wouldn't be able to hide the swelling. I heard the shuffle of shoes being removed, the faint brush of fabric as Dad hung up his coat next to mine. Could he smell Wilf's cigarettes too? Would he hate me once he knew what I'd done?

He stopped in the kitchen doorway and I didn't turn to look at him. I was still hunched forward. There was blood on the tiles. I wondered if he'd say anything at all. Perhaps he'd ignore it, just as he ignored everything else he didn't want to face: Alec, Mum's death, the wars that had shaped and ruined his life in turn.

His hands on my shoulders made me flinch, although his touch was gentle. I let him guide me up and sit me at the table. He crouched down so our faces were level, and when I dared to look at him, his eyes brimmed with sorrow and compassion.

'Oh, Gracie,' he said, wiping my eyes with his fingers. 'What has he done?' He frowned at my lip, then grimaced with anguish, before finding a handkerchief in his pocket and passing it to me.

I dabbed my lip delicately. The bleeding had almost stopped. 'He's angry with me. He has a right to be.'

Dad held my gaze and I begged with my eyes that he wouldn't ask me to explain. I couldn't bear to see his disappointment. But he shook his head sadly, as if I'd told him everything, as if he'd always known that my heart belonged to Wilfred Whitman and I'd married a man who would grow to despise me.

'You must tell me what you want to do,' he said earnestly.

'What can I do?' I wasn't expecting an answer. I wasn't the first wife to argue with her husband and end up with bruises.

'If you're frightened of him, then…' His eyes roamed the room for a solution. I knew he wouldn't find one.

'I'm not frightened of him.' I wanted to reassure him, but I didn't sound very convincing.

'You don't have to stay with him,' Dad said with tight lips.

'Yes, I do!' What was he suggesting? Some couples might dare to separate or divorce, but not in Barnfield. It was inconceivable. What life could I hope to have apart from Cliff? Where would we go where the other was not? We were both bound to this place. We could not hide from each other. Our paths would forever cross; it would be unbearable.

Dad's eyes glimmered with tears. He looked beaten. It wasn't just seeing me like this, it was more: he'd been let down. He'd always thought so highly of Cliff. He'd invited him into our family and respected him, perhaps even more than he'd respected Alec. But now the scales had fallen.

'Cliff is just upset,' I said with resignation.

'He shouldn't beat you.'

'No, but I shouldn't…' I didn't want to continue, but Dad deserved my honesty. 'I love someone else, Dad. What man wouldn't be angry to learn that?'

Dad hesitated, his eyes wide with misery and pity. He had nothing to say to me.

'If I left Cliff,' I said, stiffening with the words, for they carried so many hopes and fears, 'then I would be shamed for it. No matter what Cliff's done, people don't look kindly on women who betray their husbands. Look at Mrs Whitman.'

He frowned. 'Mrs Whitman?'

'Listen to how the village slates her for her affair, even though she's long dead. Even though her own son forgives her.'

'He does?'

I nodded, guilty that I'd had to keep so much from him. He knew nothing of the hours Wilf and I had spent together, and yet our intimacy had led me here, and it was no longer just the two of us in our magical cloud. Now Cliff and Dad couldn't escape the consequences.

Dad hauled himself to stand, wincing at the stiffness in his knees. He stretched and paced the kitchen, then stopped by the window to gaze out into the moonlit lane. When he spoke, his voice was so quiet I almost missed it: 'I never knew Beatrice Whitman, but I did know Wing Commander Merrell.'

'What?'

'Well, I fought alongside him. Many of us did.' He took a deep breath and kept his back turned to me. I wondered if he'd be able to go on, since even mentioning the war was usually enough to choke him. 'I spent nearly two years with him, in… in France and Belgium,' he carried on in a measured tone. 'After Captain Whitman was discharged on medical grounds, Captain Merrell – as he was then – was my senior, of course, but we spoke on a few occasions. Sometimes…' his voice trailed into silence, and for a few suspended seconds he was lost in his memories. 'Sometimes men are just men, regardless of who you are or where you're from. When you really need someone to chat with, the nearest fellow will do.'

'And you… *chatted* with … Captain Merrell?'

He nodded, and turned reluctantly. His face was pale and he fixed his eyes on the living room door. 'He used to tell me about his sweetheart. He used to tell me about Beatrice.' He looked at me and half smiled. There was a wistfulness in his voice that didn't belong to the words.

'Didn't you think that was a bit strange, bearing in mind she was married to Captain Whitman?'

'Yes, I was a little surprised. But I pitied them. They were in love, and I knew what that was like.' He smiled briefly and I knew he was thinking of my mother; there was such rare devotion in his eyes that it made me uneasy. He suddenly seemed like a stranger to me. 'They met just before she was married to Captain Whitman. The men had been to university together, I think. Merrell fell in love with her instantly, but kept his feelings to himself. She and Captain Whitman were happy, and he was a close and loyal friend to him.'

'But they were together during the war? Wilf told me…' Dad's expression clouded as I said Wilf's name, and I felt my face flush. I strained to remember what Wilf had told me. 'I'd always thought their affair began afterwards.'

Dad shook his head. 'War has a way of sharpening things, as you know. After Captain Whitman was… taken ill, their friendship deepened and changed. Beatrice had lost a brother, too, I think. They were desperate times. Merrell spoke of their guilt, but also their joy, and it's hard to let that go when there's not much around.'

Hadn't Wilf told me something similar once? That beauty must be preserved when there was so little of it to be found? We'd been looking at the butterflies. We'd been looking at each other.

'He told me he felt they'd been destined for each other,' Dad went on, 'though I don't doubt they planned to end it if Captain

Whitman recovered. He was a good man, and kind. Neither of them wanted to hurt him.'

I pictured the fragile Captain. 'But he didn't recover.'

'No, sadly not.'

'Do you think they were wrong to go on with it?'

'Who am I to say? It may not have been right, but would it have been better to end it, and both of them to live in misery?' He sat down at the table next to me. 'I saw Merrell a couple of times after the war. He came to visit whenever the family were staying here. I saw him out walking with the boy – with Wilfred. He must have been about ten. I caught Merrell's eye, and he smiled, but that was all. I didn't approach them. I didn't dare to. The war was over then and, well… I had no wish to speak of it again, and didn't imagine we could hide all those years in small talk. It seemed right to leave them be. There was something almost sacred about them, walking side by side like that. They looked almost like father and son.'

'He is Wilf's godfather.' Dad raised his eyebrows in a way that made me ask, 'You don't think he could be Wilf's father, do you?'

'No. I did once, but not now. The resemblance between Captain Whitman and Wilfred is irrefutable. Plus…' He stopped himself and looked down sheepishly.

'You think their characters are similar too?'

'I don't know.'

'Captain Whitman seems troubled, certainly, and distant… confused, as if he were only half there. But Wilf is different,' I insisted. 'His thoughts and words are clear, and what he did… It was brave, Dad. Don't you see? I don't think I could have done it. I *know* I couldn't.' I sobbed suddenly at the thought of Alec and Cliff and Jean and the millions whose war had seen so much more action than the inside of a postbag. Hadn't Wilf told me once I was wise, to have found contentment in the place and people I knew? But I hadn't been wise, I'd been scared. Too scared to leave my father alone, to travel anywhere without my brother, to sacrifice familiarity for true duty. 'It was courage, Dad, what Wilf did. It was courage, not cowardice.'

'I've never called him a coward. I wouldn't call any young man who fights a coward.'

'Then you understand why he did it.'

'I didn't say that, Gracie. I don't know him, but you seem to.'

'Yes, I do. I know him.' *And I love him.*

'Has he asked you to leave Cliff?'

'No! No, and I don't think he ever would. Even if he did, I couldn't…' I could pretend that it was right to stay to honour my marriage, that I'd made my bed and now I must lie in it, but the truth was, Cliff meant nothing at all really. The realisation was brutal. I did have a choice, a choice between two men, but my husband wasn't one of them. Dad had already lost his son, and his wife and baby daughter. How much more grief could he bear? 'I couldn't bring such shame on you, and I couldn't leave you.'

'No, and I wouldn't want you to, but neither would I…' He shook his head in frustration, and for a few moments said nothing. Then, 'You know, Captain Merrell and Mrs Whitman were happy. People talked, yes. They still do, and always will, but the people who mattered forgave them. They saw the value in their love – even Wilfred, you say, who of all people had a right to hate them for it.'

'What are you saying? That I should leave Cliff?' There was so much hope in the question, but Dad only frowned. My throat went dry. 'Wilf is leaving tomorrow. He plans to sell everything and move on.'

'Well, that would be a blessing for you and Cliff.'

'Yes, it would.'

Dad tentatively placed his hand on my shoulder. 'Perhaps you should try and forget Wilfred.'

I nodded. I knew that's what I ought to do, but I hated to imagine I'd never see him again, and never get a chance to say goodbye. I didn't want him to think this was what I wanted. I needed him to know how much it pained me. 'I have to see him…' I said feverishly, suddenly standing.

Dad reared back, concern written across his face. I must have looked mad: my manic eyes swollen from crying, my lip oozing blood. 'Surely that's a dangerous idea?'

'But I have to!'

He started. 'Not now?'

'Yes!' I said it as I realised it. He'd be gone tomorrow. I'd let him go before, and if I was to do it again, at least this time he'd know how I really felt. I darted to the hall and scrambled to put my coat on.

'But it's dark!' Dad protested, following behind me.

I couldn't look at him as I fumbled with my buttons. 'The moon is bright, and I know the way.' I heard the tremor in my voice, tasted the blood in my mouth.

'I won't have you cycling about in the dark,' he said with greater force. Neither of us trusted the roads at night after what had happened to Alec.

I hesitated. He would not stop me. 'I'd rather walk anyway. It's quicker.'

'Please, Gracie – your face!' He grabbed me by the shoulders and made me look at him. His eyes were wide with fear. I hated seeing him like this. I wanted to soothe him but I couldn't, not this time. He must have read the resolve in my stare. 'You need to clean yourself up, to rest,' he said, but his tone was defeated. 'You've had a shock. Wait until the morning.'

'He might be gone then!'

'Then let him go!'

I would not let him go.

'What if Cliff comes home? What do I tell him, that I let you run off into the night after another man?' Dad was shouting now and it shocked me. I'd never seen him so undone. He was terrified for me, and for himself – of losing me. I felt a surge of sickness, thinking of all those nights hiding from bombs without him, and his insistence that I'd never join a service. He'd managed to keep me from harm up until now, but it wasn't the war that threatened us anymore. It wasn't even the arbitrary threat of cars in the blackout. It was my own husband.

'Say I was upset,' I thought aloud, 'and that I went over to Mrs B's. He'll be drunk. He'll believe it.' I hoped I was right. I hoped he wouldn't come back, that he'd drink himself stupid and wake up in a ditch.

Dad looked pained and overcome.

'Please, Dad. I'm not… I'm not *running off* with anyone.' I opened the door, and forced a smile to say, 'Look, the rain's cleared!' as if he were a child. 'And I need some air. I know my way.' I kissed his forehead, but when I pulled away there was blood smeared on his skin. I wiped it away with trembling fingers. 'I'll be back in a couple of hours.'

CHAPTER 24

I left the house in a trance, buttoning my coat against the cool, damp air, with Dad's words weaving through thoughts of Wilf and Cliff and Beatrice Whitman. I felt like I'd been awake for days. My limbs were aching and heavy, and the sensible part of me screamed to stop, listen to Dad, go home and rest. But my gut fought the idea. I had to see Wilf.

I hastened my steps as I pictured his face, and the thought of never seeing him again grew new grief within me: the augur of loss; a visceral knowledge that my path now led to greater sorrow. But it was one I was compelled to take.

There was a streetlamp by the phone box, and its light shimmered on the wet lane as I clomped past in my boots. I wasn't dressed elegantly, but the mud would have destroyed my good shoes, and what use was elegance now? I pressed my hand to my tender lip and winced. I thought of my swollen eyes and wondered if Wilf would even recognise me. But I wasn't out to impress him. The thought made me feel a little safer. I wasn't going to flirt with him, or kiss him, or make promises I couldn't keep. I was going to say goodbye. Fresh tears blurred my vision, and I stifled a swelling sob.

The church and graveyard loomed out of the darkness to my right; I couldn't make out the shape of Alec's stone, but I felt him watching me. I felt him beside me, within me, saying 'I told you so', shaking his head despairingly but then smiling and taking my hand. I passed the pub and wondered how long it would be before Cliff came home. He was furious, so would probably stay there till he was kicked out. The windows were glowing but all steamed up; I knew he couldn't see me but I hurried on nevertheless.

What do you make of him now, Alec? I asked the spirit. *Did you think him capable of this?* But I received no answer, and could no longer feel his presence. The wind rustled the yew in the churchyard, and my heart caught in my throat, for I was alone.

I jumped the slimy stile and started the trudge towards Manor Woods. The moon was waning, but bright enough; some clouds skirted across it every few moments, dimming its light, but my steps were sure. I thought I heard the bang of the pub door behind me in the distance and I jumped like a startled animal, stopping for a moment to look back. The village dozed in the night, a few lights shining. The pub was bright in the midst of it, but I saw no sign of anyone. Something uneasy pulled inside me, and I wavered for a moment, but found my courage with the next breath and carried on into the woods.

I couldn't stop thinking of Beatrice, how the more I found out about her, the more I seemed to understand her. I'd once raised eyebrows at her rumoured promiscuity. How could a woman betray her husband like that? Hadn't she vowed to love him in sickness and in health? Yet she'd given herself to another man, recklessly discarded her duty for passion. That's what I'd thought, before I met Wilf, before Alec died, before I rashly married my husband. Now I saw Bixxy Whitman's story for what it really was: a tragedy, a broken mess of a life. I saw a woman gasping for breath as dark waters pulled her under – all those years trying to keep her head above the water.

I left the woods, breaking out into the wide field, with the lake winking in the shifting moonlight. I stopped – I couldn't help myself – it was as if the ground was clinging on to me, begging me to go no further. The lake was so silent and beautiful behind the dormant winter trees, but I felt its eyes on me. I felt its soft fingers creeping through the cold night, coaxing me on. My stomach churned with the memory of sinking under the water, and Wilf's voice came back to me: *she very nearly drowned.* A voice from my imagination seemed to whisper, *and so did you.*

I shivered, and cursed myself for being fanciful. I was too tired, and my heart was breaking for Wilf all over again. 'I didn't drown,' I said forcefully.

You didn't drown because Cliff saved you.

I checked over my shoulder again, spiked by guilt, but the dark woods behind me were silent. Still I hesitated. What if he hadn't saved me? I'd run it through my head so many times I'd worn it out. Would I have died? Would I have married him? What was the point in thinking about it? He *had* saved me, and I had married him. I hadn't drowned, and neither had Beatrice.

But I got her in the end, the voice seemed to say, and I felt a new fear tightening my chest.

My heart raced. It wasn't too late to turn back, but the lights of the Manor glowed in the distance, so I pressed on.

At some point I started running. Maybe because I'd decided not to turn back, or perhaps my guilt quickened me as I drew closer to the silver glimmer of the moonlit water. God knows, but suddenly I couldn't stop. All I could hear was my breath and the pounding of feet on hard, ploughed ground, my chest shaking with each heavy thud. The air had turned bitter – there was ice and wood smoke in it – but I was clammy with sweat. My skin burned with panic. I kept thinking Cliff was following me, but knew I was just being stupid, and I wasn't going to stop again to prove it.

When I reached the woods around the lake, the ground was a dark blur; I snagged my feet on wiry brambles and stumbled. My lungs heaved. There were cracks and rustles in the hidden undergrowth but my pulse beat louder than them all. Through the trees, the silent water gleamed.

Something was there, I could feel it in the pit of my stomach. It terrified me, but I wasn't shocked; I'd known it long before I'd heard its menacing whisper or dreamed its nightmares. I'd known ever since that day I cheated death, when the water was warmer and my legs were stronger and my ears were filled with the eerie tinkling of bubbles. Limbs reaching out to grasp at nothing. I shut my eyes and saw the mottled light of the surface again, my arms through the murky water, floating like reeds. I felt it pulling the life from me. Perhaps the ghost stories were true. Perhaps the waters were haunted, but not by Mrs Whitman, for it had nearly taken her too. What then? What dark force inhabited these waters? It had nearly killed me, and drawn me into the Whitman's story time and time again. And now I was back here. What did it have in store for me next? Fear shook up from inside and I willed it to disappear. It was a kind of madness. Silly, childish thoughts! But suddenly there were tears in my eyes, and my path was just black shapes and the taunt of the water.

The next moment I was falling, screaming. My cry echoed out over the lake, so chilling it winded me. I bent, almost retching for breath, my hands digging into the dirt and thorns. I scrambled to my feet, but the fall had taken all my energy. I tasted blood again, but I didn't care. The ghost was at my back. It was too late to turn around now.

I limped on, despising my weakness. My head whirled with

memories. The old captain on the shore. Bixxy Whitman trapped in her frame. Cliff's stubbly jaw, his strong hand gripping my waist, then slapping my mouth. Wilf's scars in the golden evening sun. And Alec, his wild grin, his mischievous laugh. I could almost hear it in the night air. My whole body shook with pangs of fresh grief. I saw his face again in my mind and reached out to him with my will, calling him back to me from wherever he'd gone. Just for a second, I imagined the relief of falling into each other's arms again, but it was too much.

I tried to steady my breath. I had to keep going now. I'd let my imagination take over again. I was just being paranoid. My breathing slowed, though sobs still shook me. But whimpering wouldn't bring him back, or take me forward. I heaved myself on like a wounded animal, one foot in front of the other.

Some twigs snapped behind me and I froze. There *was* something there. Something real. A body moved in the darkness, coming closer. I'd been found. But I couldn't place the noise – where had it come from? I was caught between relief and terror. Could it be Wilf? Was I being rescued, or had Cliff been following me after all?

CHAPTER 25

I waited helplessly as the steps approached. I was poised to run, but had no idea where to, when suddenly I saw a smouldering yellow light: the boathouse's windows glowing. In an instant my brain caught up and I realised the person was coming from that direction. Just as quickly, I heard Wilf's voice calling out with concern, 'Hello there?'

My shoulders sagged with relief. 'Wilf!'

He was almost upon me and in a matter of seconds we'd found each other. We clung on to each other's arms in the dim light and he laughed and said, 'What are you doing here?' But his joy vanished quickly as I held on to him, my breaths ragged and uneven, still sniffling and trembling like a woman deranged.

I couldn't say a word. I'd worked myself into a frenzy with visions of Alec and Bixxy Whitman. I was shivering with cold, but my face burned hot where Cliff's wound stung. I still felt his presence at my heels, and the threat of the silver water. I wanted nothing more than to be away from it. I gladly fell into Wilf's embrace and let him walk me out of the trees, on to the shore where I'd first seen Captain Whitman, and where, just last week, my love for Wilf had been resurrected so violently.

He held my chin up. 'My God, you're hurt! You've scratches all over your face and your lip is bleeding.'

I thought of my fall into the brambles, Cliff's sudden flare of temper.

Wilf rubbed my shoulders briskly. 'You're cold, and shocked. Here—' He took my arm and led me towards the boathouse.

The little door was ajar. The wooden steps that led up to it were rickety and slippery, but Wilf steadied me. Once inside, he shut the door and bustled me over to a wicker chair beside a small stove; some embers glowed inside it and filled the room with warmth. There was an oil lamp burning on a table, and another chair nearby. The floor was bare and damp and through the cracks in the boards I could hear the gentle slosh of water below. A draught spun above us, where long oars rested on wooden rafters and years of dusty spider's webs. The walls were empty, except for a few shelves and an old map in a frame. There was another oar leaning in the corner, broken, some fishing rods and nets, and various crates stacked near the closed French windows. Through the grubby glass the lake shone, watching us, as Wilf found a musty blanket to wrap around my shoulders.

He knelt before me and clasped both my hands. He rubbed my fingers like Mrs B had done when I was little and gone out without my gloves. 'Here…' He passed me a bottle, and I smelled the whisky. I took a sip and it warmed me instantly. I thought of the bottle of brandy we'd kept in our Anderson, how we'd drunk it dry eventually and never had enough money to buy another.

I don't know how long it was before Wilf spoke. It felt like I'd been dozing, but his words brought me back to life, to the little warm room, to the pain in my lip and head. 'Gracie, what are you doing out here all alone?'

'I came to see you.' My voice was hoarse and slow. I lifted my hand to my lip and winced.

Wilf sighed and frowned, then fumbled in his pocket for a handkerchief. He doused a little whisky onto it, saying, 'Sorry, I haven't any water.' I let him dab my lip and closed my eyes as it burned. 'What happened here?'

'I fell. In the woods.'

'That might explain the scratches, but you didn't get this from brambles.'

I turned my gaze away in shame, and he didn't pursue it. I was grateful, and devastated, because the explanation was so plain.

He cleaned up the rest of my face, and the cuts on my hands, then put the bottle down somewhere and pulled the other chair over so he could sit in front of me without blocking my heat. The wind bothered the flue, filling the room with its quiet roar. Then it fell away, and there was nothing except our slow breaths and the creaks of the roof.

'I had to see you before you left,' I said. 'I know it's stupid… Dad warned me…'

'Your father knows you're here?'

I nodded.

His eyes filled with fresh concern. 'He'll be worried about you. I must drive you home.'

I grabbed his hand. 'No!' My grip was urgent and I couldn't seem to loosen it. 'No, not yet, please.'

His shoulders fell a little. He looked down at our hands and then to my lip again. 'And Cliff… does he know you're here?'

'No.' My mouth was too dry suddenly and I struggled to swallow. 'He knows… That is, he suspects…'

Wilf nodded slowly, then pulled his hand away and stood. 'I'm sorry, Gracie. I've put you in a God-awful situation and now look what's happened. I should have left you well alone!'

'No, I'm glad,' I said faintly, and waited for him to look at me again. The soft light was kind to his face, catching the glint of his sapphire eyes, turning his skin to gold. 'I'm glad you didn't leave me alone.'

He smiled and came back to me, kneeling again. He took my hands and kissed them with reverence, his eyes closed in pain. 'I wish I'd had the courage, that day we took the boat out, to tell you the truth.'

'I don't blame you for it. Not anymore. You knew I'd react badly and… If you'd told me, I would have run away and we'd have lost those moments together.' They hadn't been long enough, but they'd meant everything to me.

Wilf shook his head. 'What I mean is, I wish I'd had the courage to tell you I loved you.' His eyes were laden with remorse; I couldn't bear to look at him, for in them I saw my own broken soul.

I clutched his hands tighter. My body shook and we sunk into one another's embrace. We held each other so tightly I almost couldn't breathe, but it wasn't close enough. I loved him too – I said it aloud. I wished I'd known it then as I did now.

'I would have told you,' he said, 'if I'd met you here like I said I would. But in the end, outside your house, with your father and brother…' I felt the sinews in his arms tighten, his whole body tense with the fury of his own regret. 'I shouldn't have left you. I'm sorry.'

I pulled free to take his face in my hands. His eyes were full of tears, his face a wretched image of despair. 'I shouldn't have believed it would be so easy to stop loving you. That was my mistake. Because it turns out it's impossible.' I kissed him – what else could I do? He made my veins run with stars; without him I was nothing but clay.

But Wilf was stronger. He drew back, let his arms fall and our passion crumble. His eyes spoke of tenderness but his jaw was firm, his posture as resolute as his gentleman's will. I slunk back in the chair, desperate in defeat. I looked around the cosy room, imagining it in summer with the setting sun streaming through the windows, the twinkling lake like a view lifted from the pages of a romantic novel. I remembered the evening I'd sat and waited, feeling the hope of seeing him slip away, along with the possibility of *us*. I pictured it now as it could have been: Wilf emerging from the woods on the Manor path, meeting him with a tentative embrace. He would have taken my hand and unlocked the boathouse, flung open the windows so we could step out onto the balcony. Leaning on the balustrade, we would have talked and watched the sun sink to melt the water gold and pink. He would have taken my hands again and kissed me. He would have told me he loved me, and hearing him say those words would have given me permission to echo them. I would have realised then and there what he meant to me, and held on to him in the dying light. I wouldn't have let him go.

I looked around the boathouse now. There were more blankets hanging off a ladder in one of the gloomy corners. They looked ragged and mouldy, but, two years ago, they might have seemed soft and inviting. We might have spread them on the floor and laid down together. I could have loved him completely, given myself to him in the way I wished I could. But it was Cliff who'd claimed that prize. It was Cliff I'd waited for in the end.

I closed my eyes. The blanket dragged heavy on my shoulders. I felt the fire had warmed me through, my blood pulsed slow and hard. My lip throbbed. I sensed the pull of time, and thought of Dad at home worrying, how it was cruel to keep him waiting.

When I looked up Wilf was still sitting in front of me, watching me.

'I have to say goodbye,' I whispered.

He nodded gravely. 'I'll take you away from here,' he said

quietly and seriously. 'If you want, if you let me… I'll take you away from him.'

My voice caught in my throat. 'And I'd go. I'd leave my home, I'd leave everything, everyone, but…' I shook my head slowly.

'Cliff?' he said with disdain.

'You know I don't love him.'

'I only wanted you to be happy, Gracie, but now I see you're not, and I can't stand it.'

'It is my own fault.'

'No! You don't deserve this.' He gestured to my lip. 'I'm loathe to send you back to him!'

'You don't send me. I am choosing to stay with him.'

'Why? When he beats you, and I *love* you?'

A fresh pain cut my heart; I didn't think it was possible. 'Please, Wilf, don't make this harder than it is. You know I love you, but what are you suggesting, that I divorce him?'

'Is it such an impossible thought?'

'I can't… I have no grounds to…'

'Then give him a reason!' He held my face and kissed me.

I pulled away. 'And what, run away with you? You know I'd ruin myself for you, and I'd do it a thousand times, but I can't do it to Dad. He's lost everyone. I can't leave him all alone with my shame. It would destroy him.' I twisted the handkerchief in my hands. 'I love him, Wilf. I don't want to part from him.'

'I'd never ask you to do that.'

'But we couldn't stay here! Don't you see? I might be able to give up my life to be with you, but I can't ask him to do the same. His home is here – his job, his world – and there is no life for *us* in Barnfield, you must see that.'

He heaved himself to his feet with a weariness that I

recognised, the kind that couldn't be healed with long nights of sleep. 'Yes, I see.' He took my hand and helped me to stand, and reluctantly I pulled the blanket from my shoulders and put it on the chair. Without it, I felt the night's chill scratching at my bones again; the fire had faded to a feeble smudge of red. He pulled me into his embrace, and I rested my head against his chest, listening to the sound of his heartbeat, breathing in the scent of him.

'You will never wholly leave me, Wilf.'

'Nor you I.'

He kissed the top of my head, then stepped away and ran his hand along his scars in his absentminded way; the thought of never seeing him do that again brought another stab of sorrow to my chest. I knew we'd run out of time, but I couldn't bring myself to say my final goodbye.

'What time are you leaving tomorrow?'

'I'll go back up to London after breakfast, and Father will join me in a few weeks, I hope.' He gave me an apologetic look, then gestured to the bottle he'd put down by the stove. 'I came down here tonight to say goodbye to it all, I suppose.' He flicked his eyes in the direction of the Manor. 'And I needed a little peace. Father is very disturbed tonight. I haven't told him anything but I think he can sense it.'

'He may be easier, when he's away from here.'

Wilf gave me a knowing look. 'I wonder if you're right, although he never cared for the city much.' He cleared his throat. 'I'm sure I'll be back once or twice to see Bridges and sign papers, but I don't plan to stay again.' He smiled faintly and moved his arm as if he'd touch me again. 'I think it's best, don't you? I'm not sure I could bear it, being back here, being close to you but not being able to see you or hold you…'

'No, you're right.' A gust of wind howled through the cracks in the boathouse and I pulled my arms around me and glanced towards the door. I felt tears running down my cheeks, knowing there was nothing left to do but leave. 'I must go.'

He nodded curtly. 'I'll drive you.'

'No.' I thought of Cliff's face when he'd warned me never to see or speak of Wilf again. 'We mustn't be seen together.'

'Then I'll walk you to the village. I won't let you go out into the night alone.'

I thought of my scratched face, the terror that had seized me on my way to the lake, and I nodded in surrender and relief. With Wilf beside me I wouldn't be afraid. I imagined our journey home together, silent and painful. Two years ago, he'd walked me back from the lake on a summer's afternoon in much the same way. We'd said goodbye then, not realising what we meant to each other, not believing love could take hold so quickly. Now our feet would follow the same path, but I guessed words would fail me again. What could I hope to say with a heart so broken? I would hold on to him nonetheless. I'd savour every moment with him.

He opened the door to the swelling roar of the wind. All around us the trees shook and creaked. The clouds had gathered in and the moon was hidden. The night was grim, and I was glad of Wilf's arm as he grabbed the lamp and we left the warmth of the boathouse behind us.

The black water shifted in the gloom, ripples catching the lamplight as we began on our way. It was too dark to make out the banks or the island or the far trees; it felt like they'd disappeared, and the lake had spread out for miles, across the fields and the village, all the way to bustling Finton and the other towns beyond. In my fevered state, I sensed it all around me – a giant, endless sea, biding its time, waiting for me to tire and falter so it could bring me into its depths again.

I leant into Wilf and held tighter to his arm, but it brought me little comfort. I still felt we were being watched. I turned my face away from the water and tried to peer ahead: the lamp lit the ground a few feet ahead of us. The muddy shore was slippery and strewn with twigs and branches. A light rain had blown in and the lamplight turned the droplets to flecks of bronze in the grimy air.

We were almost at the trees, and I thought I caught a shape – dark and bulky – gliding amongst the grey, blurry trunks. It seemed like a trick of the light on my tired eyes, but my heartbeat picked up again and I squinted into the drizzle. All of a sudden Wilf stopped, for whatever it was, he'd seen it too.

Then the shadow formed limbs. A charcoal figure emerged. Broad shoulders, ruddy skin, and a face that turned my blood to ice.

'Well, well, look who we have here!' Cliff taunted as he stepped into our path.

I felt Wilf's arm stiffen and held on to him even tighter. Cliff wore a menacing smile and stood with his hand on his hips. I could smell his breath from a few feet away. I was repelled by him, ashamed of him, and sickeningly afraid. He forced a surly laugh and held out his arms as if to embrace or congratulate us.

'You followed me,' I said stupidly.

'Of course I bloody followed you,' he spat.

'I say!' Wilf cried, pulling me to him protectively.

'Oh, pipe down! This isn't any of your business, Whitman. I'm here to get my wife.' He lurched forward to grab my arm, but I shied away and Wilf moved to stand between us. Cliff's arm darted out and suddenly there was a grunt and a thump of flesh on bone as Wilf fell to the ground.

I swiftly crouched and turned him over. The lamp was lying in the mud, lighting his face from beneath; he was clutching his nose and his blood looked slick and black, covering his face and hands. I could feel it, warm and sticky on my fingers. 'Look what you did!' I screamed at Cliff, who was standing over us. I helped Wilf to sit. 'Are you all right? Oh God, there's blood everywhere!'

'I'm fine,' he managed to say. He lowered his voice: 'Gracie, you're not safe here. Forget everything – just go up to the house, now!'

'Not without you.'

He held me in a warning look for a second and squeezed my hand. 'Don't wait,' he whispered, then raised his voice so Cliff would hear: 'I'm all right. I think he's broken my nose.'

'And I'll do a lot worse if you try and stop me again,' Cliff shouted with impatience. He stepped forward and shoved my shoulder. 'Leave him. Get up, we're going.'

'No!'

'Oh, enough! Come on…'

'You're drunk, Cliff. Go home.'

'And leave you two to it?'

'Go to the house,' Wilf mumbled.

'He needs help…' I said as I tried to get him to stand, but his head hung down groggily and it looked like he was about to pass out.

'*You* need help!' Cliff cried with a vicious laugh. 'What the hell's wrong with you? You must be mad too if you'd rather have him than me!'

'Listen to the words coming out of your mouth, Cliff! Look at the blood on his face and mine! Do you really wonder why I don't want you?' I could hardly believe I'd had the gall to say it; my voice juddered with anger and fear. But he only laughed at my newfound confidence. He wheezed and coughed and sniggered as he kicked Wilf's leg and swore at him to get up. 'Stop it!'

Cliff kicked Wilf harder, until he cried out.

'Leave him alone!'

Wilf was upright now, rocking on his feet as if he was about to keel over. I put my arm around him to take his weight, but Cliff pushed me away.

'Get off him!' I cried, as they began to scrap, but it was only seconds before he'd knocked Wilf down again. The sight of him lying there in the mud stoked the fire inside me and I leapt towards Cliff, pounding his chest with my fists. But it made no difference; his body was too bulky and solid. I screamed at him in frustration and fury, and swung at him, clipping his cheek so hard that my knuckles burst with agony. He staggered back for a moment, suddenly silent, then regained his footing and looked at me with fierce eyes. There was blood on his cheek, but I didn't know if it was his or Wilf's or mine. He jutted out his jaw and sneered slightly, and all my righteous anger morphed back to fear and panic. I stumbled back, but like an animal he pounced to seize my shoulders and shook me so hard I thought my neck would break. There was a ringing in my ears and when he finally stopped, the thwack across my face was almost a relief – another bright flash of pain. Suddenly, cold, slimy mud was in my mouth.

I lift my head in a daze. Everything hurt. I wasn't sure where I was, but my fingers sunk into the mud as I pushed myself up. Behind me I heard grunting, and turned just in time to see Cliff's arm around Wilf's neck. Cliff's mouth was caught in a vile grimace, his neck muscles bulging taut. He squeezed hard as Wilf scrambled helplessly to release himself, his face stained with blood, his eyes gleaming with terror.

I screamed at Cliff: no words, just noises borne from the depth of my horror. Somehow I managed to stand, and through the clanging in my head I reached them and clawed at Cliff's face. Wilf crumpled to the ground, and Cliff kicked him hard in the side, then spat on him.

I lost sight of Cliff then, and all my senses were filled with Wilf. I was on the ground with him, in the mud. He seemed lifeless. I shook him gently but he would not wake. I felt through the filth to his cold skin and lifted his eyelids, but his eyes were rolled back. His nose was still streaming blood – it was everywhere – and his eyebrow was split open too. I begged him to wake. I shook him, harder, angrier, and screamed until my voice was hoarse and my mouth was filled with my own tears.

Then hands wrenched me from him, hands I'd known to rescue me once.

Cliff dragged me to stand. 'Shut up!' he yelled, as he tried to pull me on, but I strained away from him. 'For God's sake, Gracie, don't make me hit you again. I swear…'

'We have to get him help!' I shrieked, returning to Wilf. 'He's hurt! Oh, God, I don't even know if he's breathing!'

'Good.'

'How could you?' I cried. Cliff said nothing, just folded his arms and grinned. Had he always been like this? Had the war changed him? Had I?

I turned back to Wilf and tried to lift him, but he was too heavy and I was too weak. I threw myself against him and wept.

'Get up, Gracie.'

'No!' I bent and spoke into Wilf's still body, pleading with him to wake up.

'*Get up!*'

Suddenly my back exploded with pain and I lurched forward. The moment after was suffocating: I gasped with no air, gaped to cry, but nothing came. Then my breath came back to me. My eyes blinked into the cold rain and tiny specks of silver flew in my vision. I wheezed, and yelped, and felt the burn where Cliff's boot had struck me. I rolled over, my bruised back up against Wilf, my head spinning as I struggled to focus. Cliff's knotted brow swung into view and I felt him drag me in the mud. I saw his face but he didn't look at me; he was muttering something, but I couldn't hear what.

I tried to stand but I was dizzy and Cliff's vice grip was round one of my ankles. I kicked at him feebly. 'What are you doing?' I wasn't sure it was my voice, it didn't sound right.

'You're a slut,' I heard him say, and I was shaking my head when he dropped my leg. I could hear him talking but only made out some of the words: '…always been good to you… your father, and Alec… did you think that I'd…. was stupid, Gracie… what's the matter with you?' He grabbed my shoulders and sat me up. My head throbbed. He was crouched in front of me, eyes level. 'What's the matter with you?'

'I think I'm going to be sick.'

He tutted. 'That's just the blow,' he said dismissively.

I remembered Wilf and tried to turn back to him but Cliff held my head so I'd look only at him. I started to whimper again. A voice in my head was whispering: *He's dead. Wilf's dead.*

Cliff slapped my cheek as if to rouse me, but I was bleeding already and it stung all the same. 'Do you think I'm an idiot?' he said. 'You won't make a fool out of me, Gracie. Didn't I make that clear earlier?'

'You're drunk. You're not thinking straight…'

'I'm not that drunk.'

'Please Cliff… we need to get help. You've hurt him!'

'I don't care! Stop whinging!' He started muttering to himself again. 'First moment you get, you go running back to him, well…' He shook his head.

'I didn't…' I tried to protest, but my mouth was full of wool. 'I just came to say goodbye…'

'You're a slut.'

'No… we didn't… no…'

'What's wrong with you? Why would you want him – a coward – a fucking *moron*, and look at him!' He clenched my chin and turned my head towards Wilf, still and silent in the mud. 'A moron, and a *cripple* too!'

I managed to wriggle out of his grip. 'I love him,' I said defiantly, and the look of disgust in Cliff's eyes thrilled as much as terrified me. 'He is no coward. He never was! I was the coward, Cliff! I should have stood up for him then. I should have done something, anything, but all I did was hide – in you, in Alec, in Dad…'

'What are you talking about?' he yelled, flicking his face towards Wilf on the ground. 'You're as mad as him.'

Wilf was still slumped there like a bag of dropped coal. 'Look what you've done to him!' I cried, coughing as my lungs threatened to give up on me. 'If you've… if you've killed him, I will never forgive you.'

He glanced at Wilf and I saw his hard expression falter, as if he'd only just realised he'd seriously hurt him.

My voice had broken again into sobs. I willed for the strength to pull myself up. 'How could you?'

'He was fucking my wife!' Cliff yelled, drawing out each word, his breath rank and hot. 'What'd you expect me to do?'

'You're wrong! Believe it if you want, but you're wrong, and I won't go back with you.' I would have done, even just an hour before, but not now. It was finally time to find my own courage.

'You will. I'm your husband.'

'You are not the man I married. You're mad!'

He laughed sarcastically. 'Ha! You'd like that, I bet!'

'I hate you.'

He knocked my ear again, a cat playing with its prey. 'Shut up.'

'I do. I hate you!'

He bared his teeth and dug his fingers into my neck so I choked. 'I said shut up!' he screamed again. His voice was raw and deafening. 'Damn you!' He threw my head down, and when I lifted it again he was standing, pacing the ground beside me, his face in his hands. He unleashed a maddened roar of anguish into the darkness, and stared back at Wilf, then me, then Wilf again, until his face creased into a grimace and he pounded his head with his fist. 'Damn you!' he bellowed again.

Suddenly I heard a frail cry from behind me. I twisted in the mud, and cried out in desperate joy when I saw Wilf was stirring. His eyes were still shut but his mouth opened a little and twitched.

I started to crawl to him, calling his name, my voice shrill. But just as he was within my reach, Cliff kicked my arm away and I watched, screaming, as my husband bent down to savagely deliver his final blow: he threw his fist into Wilf's head and I heard a crack of teeth or bone. The life that had glimmered disappeared again, and fresh blood ran amidst the mud on Wilf's lips.

I was still shouting, possessed by fury and despair. I didn't even think as Cliff pulled my arms and rolled me back. I expected another blow to silence me, but all I could feel was pressure on my legs. I looked up and he was kneeling over me. He was staring down and looking through me: his eyes were glazed like a dead man's. His mouth was shut. His jaw twitched. He was pulling down his braces.

I realised too late what was happening. I gasped as I tried to stand, but I was too feeble, and the mud too slippery. He had me pinned with his weight. 'Get off!'

'I'm going to teach you a lesson!' He slapped me – twice, maybe three times – it dazed me, and he turned me over so my face was flat in the mud. I felt him clawing at my back, round my waist. He grabbed to undo my trousers, but I found some animal strength from somewhere and kicked at him. I must have got him where it hurt, because just then his grip loosened, and in a second I'd somehow managed to get myself up and started running, or moving, at least. But I didn't know which way was which. I had to get to the Manor, to call for help. I had to get away from Cliff. It was too dark and the rain was coming down hard; my hair was plastered all over my face. I moved my feet anyway, but suddenly they plunged into water and I spun around, disorientated and petrified, for I'd walked straight into the lake.

The water was freezing, lapping at my calves. I began to wade back but it was no use, for he was already there. His punch threw me backwards. I had no time to take a breath before my world was all water. The howling of the wind and my own ragged breaths turned to soft metallic, bubbling echoes. I was numb in an instant, cocooned, halfway between reality and another world. I could taste the lake in my mouth again. What would have happened if Cliff hadn't saved me that day? Surely I was about to find out, for he would not save me now.

In a jerk, my head reared out the water, back into the hell of the storm, with the rain lashing and Cliff still bearing down on me. I struggled, but he pulled me into the shallows, dropping me so the water lapped round my ears and grit sliced into the back of my head. In an instant he was on me, crushing me. I writhed as much as I could but I was barely moving. I felt his rough hands at my waist again, then heard a sound: a low, guttural wail – like a vixen, or a woman in labour – and it was only a second later that I realised it was me, and I was crying, for he'd ripped my trousers from my body.

I wished I could see Wilf or call out to him. Was he dead now? Had Cliff meant to kill him? Did he mean to kill me? I saw Dad's face in my mind and prayed that I'd live; I couldn't leave him all alone. I screamed and raged to survive.

Cliff pressed his hand over my face to silence me, and rolled my head into the water. I felt his other hand jabbing, scratching to prise my thighs apart, and though I squeezed and tried with all my being to fight him, it was no use. My eyes were full of grime. I opened my mouth to breathe, but only water surged into me. I convulsed, desperate to cough it away, but Cliff's weight held my head down as he forced himself into me.

I couldn't fight him anymore. There was water in my lungs and I could feel the life draining from me: my head no longer ached and my bones felt light. My eyes were open, but there was nothing but black. I closed them again, suddenly desperate for rest.

Hadn't the lake been after me for years? It had tried to steal me as a girl, and haunted me ever since. It had come to me through dreams, over and over and over again. Its shadows and reflections had seeped through my skin to touch the beating heart beneath. But now my heart was slowing, and there was no one to rescue me, for my love lay unmoving in the mud, and my once hero had become my tormenter. I wouldn't escape this time.

Suddenly the lake's low warning whisper became an acute shout: Cliff should never have saved me then. It was always my destiny to die in these black waters, and now he would atone for his disruption.

My last thought, my last feeling, though I'd long since left my body, was gratitude. I was strangely grateful to this brutal man hell bent on destroying me, for he'd given me the chance to live once. He'd give me the chance to meet the man I'd love for all eternity, beyond death.

PART THREE

CHAPTER 26

There was a moment in the Manor. A bright lamp and a fire surging. Someone talking. But that was it.

The first real thing I remember was the smell: chemical, sharp, cold. A world of grey and white. Footsteps and whispers and the faceless nurse who told me not to try and sit.

The next moment – or maybe it was hours later – Dad was holding my hand. His face was at an angle; his chin looked too large and he kept lifting his glasses and dabbing a handkerchief to his eyes. I didn't realise he was crying, or notice, then, how remarkable that was, because I'd never seen his tears before. I didn't realise where I was, or who I was, or that I'd been there for a day. I hadn't yet been told about Wilf or Cliff, or my broken bones and stitched wounds.

When I tried to move I winced and cried out, and a nurse – Dad had gone, and it was dark again – came in and gave me an injection. When I woke, a doctor was there, and he listed my injuries in a perfunctory tone: six broken ribs, a broken wrist, concussion, multiple stitches. The morning sun bounced off his bald head. I called him Humpty Dumpty, and he scowled at the nurse and told her to reduce my morphine.

'What happened?' I croaked, when Dad arrived to sit with

me again.

'You were attacked.'

The memory was hazy and incomplete, but real enough to bring fear scuttling back into my breaths. I remembered my screams as Cliff had forced my legs apart. I saw his evil stare and lurched with nausea, shivering and gasping at the pain in my side. It was like a knife had been lodged there. 'Where is he?' I panicked.

'Try not to move,' Dad said soothingly. 'Your ribs are broken.'

I nodded, my eyes tight shut in pain.

'You're safe now. Cliff is in custody. They won't let him out.'

'He killed him,' I whimpered, trying not to cry, for each breath was torture, but the memory of Wilf lying bleeding in the mud brought its own agony. It had crept back to me in my intoxicated state, then vanished just as quickly. I'd seen his face in hallucinogenic nightmares, but hadn't had the courage or wherewithal to ask the nurses about him. Now Dad was here, I squeezed his hand and held myself as stiff as possible as the tears and snot streamed down my face.

'He's not dead, Gracie!' His tone was too forced, unnaturally bright and comforting. He was lying, trying to appease me. He hadn't seen him there, after all: his lifeless body on the ground, the blood pooling in the mud. He hadn't heard the crack of his bones.

'Please tell me the truth,' I begged in a whisper.

'It is the truth.' Dad's face was animated, his eyes earnest but wary too. 'He's not dead.'

'But…' I remembered how heavy and cold he'd been when I tried to move him.

'He's badly injured.'

'He's here?' Intuitively I tried to sit again, but it

automatically made me shout out.

Dad smoothed my shoulder. 'You must keep still.'

'Where is he?'

'He's upstairs.'

'I want to see him.'

'You're not going anywhere for a while.'

'Have you seen him? You have to tell him…' My head was all hope and energy but my body was dull and broken. 'Tell him I'm sorry. Tell him…'

'Gracie, I can't tell him anything. He's unconscious.'

My joy and relief left as suddenly as they'd come. 'What's the matter with him?'

Dad couldn't look me in the eyes. 'He took quite a beating. He has several broken bones, but internal injuries too. And his head…'

'What is it? Won't he recover?'

Dad stroked my hand and sighed. 'They don't know. His skull is fractured. If he wakes up, they'll have a better idea.' He let me cry for a while – that word 'if' hanging in between us – then made me sip some water. 'This isn't good for you. You need to focus on getting better.'

'But I love him,' I cried pathetically, replaying our last moments in the boathouse. How long had Cliff been lying in wait? If I'd stayed at home, Wilf would have been safe. But how could I have stayed away? How could I have stayed with Cliff?

Dad was saying something about visiting hours being nearly over.

'No, don't go!'

'I have to, but I'll be back tomorrow.'

'How long must I stay here?'

'Until you're well enough to come home. Mrs B will help look after you, but it'll be at least a few weeks I expect.'

'However will we afford it?'

He gave me a sad little smile and said, 'Never you mind about that.'

Mrs B explained further when she came to visit a day or so later: 'You mustn't worry about the expense. The Whitmans are paying for all of it.'

I thought I'd misheard. 'What? On whose authority?'

'The captain's, of course.'

'But…' I struggled to gather my thoughts. 'But, he's…' I could only picture his frail face, the childlike fear in his eyes. Was I remembering correctly? 'Is he allowed to do that? Does he even understand what it means?'

Mrs B leaned forward and lowered her voice, even though I was in a room on my own, a room that would undoubtedly be costing the captain a fortune. 'He evidently understands a lot more than you or I or anyone else gave him credit for.'

I thought of his feverish ramblings when I first met him, and on the lake shore. I couldn't help feeling I was taking advantage. 'He knows that Wilf's here?'

She nodded gravely.

'Oh, poor man!'

'Gracie, I thought your father had told you…' She hesitated, pinching her lips in concern.

'What?' I grew impatient when she stayed quiet. 'Told me what?'

'How you got here. How… who came to your aid.'

I frowned, trying to remember, but only drew a blank. There was a great dark gap in my memory, and I wondered why I hadn't thought of it before.

'Your father went out to look for you when you didn't come home. He was worried, because of the storm and… well…' Her face coloured, and we shared a look of contempt for my despicable husband.

'Dad saved me?' I imagined him stumbling through the woods and the mud in panic, hearing my cries in the distance. Oh, poor Dad, what a sight to be met with! But thank God for him!

'No, when your father arrived, he was already there.'

'Who?'

'Captain Whitman.'

I jolted and my hand went to my side. 'Captain… *What?* Captain Whitman was there?'

'He was more than just there. He'd managed to get Cliff off you and had wrestled him to the ground.'

I blinked and waited for my head to clear. Certainly the nurse had given me too much morphine again, either that or the concussion was playing tricks on me. 'But Captain Whitman is a feeble old man…' I remembered his trembling fingers in my hand. 'And Cliff is a brute. There's no way…'

Mrs B raised her eyebrows as if she was bemused as I was. 'I don't dispute it. But ask your father, he'll tell you what he saw. I'm sorry, I thought he would have already. Perhaps I shouldn't have said anything, but there it is. He arrived at the lake and found the two of them brawling.'

'Cliff and Captain Whitman?' I said incredulously.

'Stranger things have happened. You do hear of people summoning unnatural strength in extreme situations.'

'But, what happened? He can't have kept it up for long. One blow from Cliff would have finished him.'

'Indeed. Your father arrived just in time. He saw you and Mr Whitman on the ground – dead to the world – and the old man and Cliff writhing about in the mud. I daresay he knew enough of Cliff by then to understand what he was capable of, and he didn't hesitate to punch his lights out.'

Dad knocked Cliff out! Dad, who I'd never known to lift a

finger against anyone! I could barely entertain the idea – it played like a broken film reel in my head.

Mrs B read my thoughts. 'I know, I didn't know he had it in him. But then…' She breathed a long sigh and fixed her gaze on something out of the window for a moment before rousing herself again. 'Well, we think we know people, don't we?' She shook her head, perhaps still thinking of Dad and Captain Whitman, or maybe Cliff, as I was.

'What happened after Dad knocked Cliff out?'

'It's a funny thing. The captain was *his* captain again. He knew what was going on, and he gave clear orders and kept a steady head. But he called your father Sergeant Wells. It was like the clock had been turned back thirty years.'

That I could believe. 'Yes… when I met him before, there were moments when he almost seemed reasonable, but never quite complete.'

'He told your father to carry you up to the Manor and send for help.'

'And Captain Whitman stayed? What happened when Cliff woke up?'

Mrs B smirked. 'When your father had got you to the Manor and raised the alarm, he left you with the nurse before going back for Wilfred. By the time he returned, Captain Whitman had bound Cliff's wrists and ankles with his braces! And it's a good job too, for he was coming to by then, and thrashing about like a wild thing.'

My lip curled just to think of it. 'What did they do with him?'

'Left him to it,' said Mrs B matter-of-factly. 'The constables went down to get him in the end. Your father and Captain Whitman carried Wilf back up to the Manor…' She stopped because my hands had gone to my mouth and there were fresh tears on my cheeks. The thought of the old man carrying his son, when just days before it had been Wilf helping him up the same path to safety, was too much for my frayed nerves.

'They must have thought he was dead,' I murmured. 'I thought he was dead.'

Mrs B's expression was sombre. 'I believe they did.'

I took her handkerchief with thanks. When I calmed down again I told her, 'This whole business was my fault.'

'How d'you work that one out?'

'I should never have married Cliff. I should have had the guts to—'

'We none of us knew what he was.'

Didn't we? I had a niggling feeling I'd known all along.

'There's only one person to blame for what happened.'

I shuddered to think of Cliff in a police cell. I didn't want to remember his face, it seemed a waste of thoughts. Dad had told me there was no option for bail – he would be convicted, there was no doubt. I didn't have to see him again, but a policeman would come and interview me soon, and Dad would testify in court when the time came. Cliff would go to prison, and if anything happened to Wilf… Well, I couldn't bear to think about that.

I drew my mind away from such morbid thoughts and pictured Wilf lying motionless somewhere within the hospital walls. I wished I had the strength to go to him. I would sit with him, hold his hand, kiss him, however beaten and bruised he was. I would tell him I loved him and will him back to me.

Mrs B watched me cry. My husband was a monster and my love for Wilf was no longer a secret. I was ashamed to think I'd ever hidden it at all. I'd known him to be good and decent from the first moment I saw him; I'd been stirred to stand up for him and love him even before I knew him. And I *did* know him. It didn't matter that we'd only spent a handful of hours together over the past few years. I'd spent half my life with Cliff and thought I knew him – I'd chosen him over Wilf because of it –

and look at the havoc that decision had wrought.

When Mrs B left, I drifted in and out of sleep, recalling all the things she'd told me, marvelling at Dad and Captain Whitman's heroism. How was such strength possible in one so frail and broken? But hadn't the lake stolen my strength once, and Bixxy Whitman's? If it could inexplicably take strength away, maybe it could give it also. The thoughts swam through my morphine dreams, shapes and shadows in a watery expanse of green and grey. I couldn't hold on to any of them.

The captain was back at the Manor now with his nurse; he hadn't been to the hospital as far as Mrs B was aware. I wondered if he'd slipped back into himself, if he even knew his son lay half-dead in a hospital bed. I was on the edge of sleep once again when I heard his words echo in my memory, and their clarity brought me back to reality with a cold shock.

Don't worry, my dear, I'm coming. I heard your call. I'm coming to save you.

CHAPTER 27

Captain Whitman's words and warnings snaked through my consciousness for days as I lay in my bed, listening to the muted sounds of the hospital beyond the door. We'd assumed he'd mistaken me for Mrs Whitman and his ramblings were just a manifestation of the guilt he felt for not coming to her aid. But what if they were more than that? What if he'd known exactly what he was saying to me and why? Could he have foreseen what would happen? A couple of weeks before I would have dismissed it as ridiculous, but after all that had happened, and my own sense of foreboding the night Cliff attacked us, now I wasn't so sure. Hadn't the captain proved himself to have sense and reason, when he took charge at the lake, and bore all my medical expenses on his shoulders?

There was no one with whom I could share my thoughts. Dad and Mrs B visited regularly, and Jean wrote, but if I told them I thought Captain Whitman had predicted my accident, they'd have worried for my sanity. Only Wilf would have heard me without prejudice, and only the old captain himself could answer my questions. But Captain Whitman was back at the Manor, and his beautiful son still hadn't regained consciousness.

The window in my room overlooked a road. I could hear

traffic and see the tops of buildings on the other side of the street. I gazed out at the tiles and chimneys, longing for trees and green and open space. Occasionally a pigeon would settle on a gutter, or birds too far away to identify would scatter across the cloudy sky. When it rained, my little view melted into dreary shapes on the glass, and I felt like I would suffocate beneath my tight sheets with only the books Dad brought me for company. He visited every day without fail, bringing newspapers and shreds of gossip from Mrs B that served to distract from the monotony of my recovery. The only news I really cared for was regarding Wilf, but each day the answer was the same: no change.

I felt the thread of time had been snipped the moment I'd lost consciousness in the lake: everything beyond – the new reality I found myself living in – seemed like a fragile fantasy. I thought of our home, and Mrs B at the Post Office, and everything going on in Barnfield and Finton as usual, but I didn't feel part of it anymore. My mind and breaths and hopes were all inside the man who lay sleeping just a few walls and doors away from me.

When the doctor told me I was ready to stand, I had visions of running to Wilf's bedside to see him, but my legs were as slack as yarn, and my ribs burned so fiercely that a few tottering steps with crutches were all I could manage before exhaustion defeated me.

I opened my eyes one morning to see the nurse coming in with a breakfast tray. She was called Collis. She was young and had pale auburn hair tucked under her cap which reminded me of Alec's when he'd come home on leave. She liked to chat and, unlike the moody ward sister, didn't look down her nose at me when she came to change my dressings. The nurses had doubtless heard what had happened; they knew the man I kept asking after wasn't my husband; they knew the police had come to visit me. Despite what Cliff had done to me and Wilf, the ward sister obviously felt we'd had it coming, and had me down as a harlot. But Nurse Collis had a sweet manner, and called me Gracie even though she wasn't supposed to, for she saw how I flinched whenever the doctor called me Mrs Archer.

She asked how I was feeling and helped me to the commode and back before tidying me up and settling the tray on my lap. She did it all with a fizzing kind of impatience that made me wonder if she was in a bad mood, but then she clasped her hands restlessly and gave me a wide, expectant grin. 'I have some very good news for you. Mr Whitman is awake.'

I must have cried out or turned deathly pale, because she leaned forward suddenly and rested a concerned hand on my shoulder.

'Are you sure?'

She laughed. 'Yes, quite sure.'

'And, is he…? How is he?' I had no faith in the hope I felt – I didn't want to run away with it – but Nurse Collis was still smiling. She told me he was speaking. He knew his name, his address.

'Unsurprisingly, his memory is hazy in places but he seems to remember some of what… happened.' She looked away in embarrassment, then told me to eat my breakfast.

But I had too many questions. 'What about his injuries? Are they permanent? Will he recover?'

Nurse Collis was reluctant to give definite answers. 'We'll know more in a couple of days.'

'But… I need to see him. Can I see him?'

She gave me a dubious look. 'I don't think so. He's not up to visitors and you have some getting better to do yourself. I hope I did the right thing telling you – you shouldn't get over excited, it won't help. Strictly speaking I shouldn't have said anything, because you're not his next of kin, but you ask after him so much, and seem so very fond of him.'

'Oh yes! You did the right thing. Thank you. I am very fond of him!' I laughed delightedly, as if my love for him could be condensed into mere fondness. If he hadn't woken, I felt sure I would have been trapped in this numb limbo forever. But just knowing he was awake thrilled me. I could feel the light returning to the dark places inside me.

She left me to my breakfast but I was too overcome to eat. When she returned, I asked for a pen and paper, and, feeling like I would burst, jotted down a few hurried lines for Wilf. Nurse Collis promised to give it to him when she felt he was well enough to read it. I didn't like to think how long that might be, and the next two days seemed interminable. Dad was permitted to wheel me around the hospital garden in a chair when he visited, but the bracing fresh air and sight of grass did little to distract me from my impatience. I begged Dad to take me to Wilf's bedside but he was as adamant as Nurse Collis that no visitors were allowed. I began to wonder if they were keeping something from me, and my thoughts turned to paranoia and dread. Nurse Collis tutted and said she regretted telling me, but one afternoon, a few days after I'd written the letter, she walked in with a folded piece of paper in her hand.

I was standing by the window. I was getting stronger and able to walk without crutches for short distances. A book was laid open on the chair in the corner; I'd lost focus and gone to watch the shoppers and workers and businesspeople hurrying about in the rain on the street below.

She held up the paper. 'We are not a postal service,' she said with a raised eyebrow, and handed it over. I hesitated to open it, suddenly shy, but she told me not to be too bashful. 'He dictated it to me, after all, so there's nothing too scandalous.' She flashed a smile and added, 'You can't make a habit of this. And don't let Sister find out, or she'll have my guts for garters!'

The light was fading so I turned on the lamp and unfurled the little note, just a few lines in Nurse Collis's unfamiliar, hurried hand:

Dearest Gracie,

I pray for your quick recovery, and the day I'll see you again. All my thoughts are with you, and my love.

Your Wilf.

*

Finally, I was allowed to visit him. Nurse Collis wheeled me through the wards and corridors to his room, then knocked gently on the door. I'd never felt so nervous. My head was a siren drone of rushing blood and fear. I knotted my fingers tightly in my lap and pushed back the panic within me, holding my breath. I thought of the first time I'd seen him, across the village hall at Doris's wedding. I'd been prepared for horror then, too, but I'd glimpsed something unexpected instead: a beauty deep and terrifying. From the moment I first laid eyes on Wilf I seemed to sense the danger he carried, and as we crossed the threshold of his room, I searched my heart for it again – that foreboding – but it was gone.

I viewed him first without emotion. I'd seen other sick men and women in the hospital, and here was another, lying down, with sheets neatly tucked over his body, his arms free, limp and bandaged. It could have been any man's body, and there was nothing shocking in its weakness and inertia, but his head – his face – made my stomach quail, my gaze faltering as our eyes met.

They were his arrestingly blue eyes, but the skin around them was purple and inflamed. His whole face was taut and swollen, with clouds of green and grey bruises, and singed lines of stitches above his eyes and around his broken nose. He was unshaven, and in the stubble I saw lines of scabs and new scars. His burnt skin looked blurred and strange with the swelling, but the line across his cheek and neck were unmistakable. His forehead was bandaged all around, and his hair spiked above it, dark and ragged; I wanted to reach out and smooth it. I wanted to take him in my arms and heal him somehow, but my hands went to my mouth, and all I could say was 'Wilf, Wilf…' his name like a prayer on my trembling lips.

'Gracie.' His voice was unchanged, if a little slow. He lifted his fingers with effort, and I noticed the cast on his arm and the blood, dried beneath his nails. I was frightened to touch him, but Nurse Collis nodded at my entreating expression, so I reached for his hand and wrapped my fingers over his. I held his gaze and saw the tears well in his eyes as they fell down my cheeks. I'd thought I'd have too much to say to him – so many apologies and so much love to profess – but the words seemed useless now I was beside him again.

Nurse Collis checked the jug of water beside Wilf's bed and announced that she had to go and refill it. She told me she'd be back in five minutes, and shut the door behind her, leaving us alone for the first time since the moment we'd left the boathouse in the storm. I'd felt so desperate then, so hopeless and defeated. I'd loved him so dearly, but I hadn't seen how there could ever be a way for us to be together. I hadn't imagined the fate that lurked in the woods for us.

'I'm so sorry, Wilf,' I stuttered, overwhelmed with the shock and joy of seeing him. It was like a wound, tearing down my chest and bleeding out around me. I felt the ebb and flow of my breaths, as if my spirit was leaving and returning to me with each sob, forever caught in the veil between life and death.

Wilf hushed me soothingly. 'You have nothing to apologise for.' His words were laboured. His chest rasped. 'I wish I could have protected you.' His eyes rested on my own bruises, and fell to the arms of my wheelchair.

'This is nothing, Wilf. I will heal.' I squeezed his fingers gently. 'As will you.'

His eyes shut briefly. 'I did all I could, but your husband is a stronger man than I.'

'Don't call him that.' My tone was suddenly fierce, my face hot. I steadied myself before I went on: 'He's a brute, and you're the stronger man by far. I only wish I'd seen it sooner.'

He seemed to smile. 'I wish that too. And I wish I'd told you I loved you when I first knew it.' He moved his fingers over mine, and I thought of the island and the butterflies, how my heart had leapt with them, how I'd known then I would never love a better man than him. 'But then, you would have thought me mad, wouldn't you?'

I shook my head, though he might have been right. 'If I'd been honest – if I'd been brave – I would have told you I loved you too.' My ribs burned as I leant forward and kissed his hand, but I ignored the pain. I could feel Nurse Collis's footsteps coming closer, sense them even though I couldn't hear them yet.

'When will you be discharged?' he asked.

'Soon, they say.'

'Good. I shall miss knowing you are so close to me, but I'd rather you were being looked after at home.'

I smiled at the thought of Mrs B and her promises to stay with me night and day if I wanted. 'I admit I'm looking forward to it, but I can't fault the nurses here. I have so much to thank them for, and your father… Do you know of all he's done for me?'

Wilf gave a slight nod.

'You must thank him for me, and I will as soon as I'm able.'

'I shall, but I haven't seen him yet.'

'He hasn't visited you?'

'He's not keen on hospitals,' he said dryly, and I felt a little embarrassed.

'But you know what he did for us, how he saved us both?'

He paused, blinking a few times, tightening his fingers round mine. 'Yes, I do. Your father told me.'

I waited for him to explain, but he stayed silent. 'Dad came to visit you? When?'

'A few days ago. I asked the nurses to catch him after he'd seen you. He thought I knew, but he told me everything.'

I was speechless again, feeling oddly hot at the thought of Dad having seen Wilf before me and not even mentioning it. All those times I'd asked after him…

Wilf read my expression and said, 'Please, don't blame him for saying nothing to you, I asked him not to.'

'Why?'

'Because I wanted to tell you… to *ask* you myself.'

He watched and smiled as the penny dropped, as my face lit with smiles.

'You're asking me to be your wife,' I said slowly, as if I didn't really believe it.

'Yes.'

I looked down at my hands, at the faded impression in my finger where my wedding ring had been. A few weeks ago, the idea of a life without Cliff had seemed impossible, a future with Wilf just a dream. And now here he was, asking me to be his wife. I couldn't take it in. Was it even possible? I was still married to Cliff, not that I'd let that stop me. If there was a way to end our marriage now, I'd take it, regardless of what anyone said. There was no future for us anymore, not in Barnfield, not anywhere.

Wilf's gaze had saddened. Perhaps he took my hesitation as indecision, or worse.

'What did Dad say?' I asked.

'He consented. Gladly, I think. He said he only wants you to be happy.'

I felt like laughing. Happy! I couldn't remember the last time I'd felt happy – not without the tinges of despair and sorrow that had shrouded the wartime years and all the months since. Happiness belonged in my memories, in the tranquil hours with Alec before the war, forever golden, and purer in retrospect that they'd probably ever been in reality.

'I should have waited,' Wilf said.

I shook my head. 'No. No more waiting.'

His voice quickened: 'Do you think you could ever make your home with me?'

'In Hampstead?' was all I could manage, as if the question hadn't thrilled me, as if there was any doubt I'd refuse him.

He laughed – it was strained and short but lovely, and it made me forget the pain in my sides and months of recovery ahead of us. 'If you wish, but I was thinking, how would you feel about living at the Manor, after what's happened?'

I pictured the house and the lake and it all seemed like a dream from long ago. I thought of the oars pulling through the water, the reflection of the setting summer sun, and then the frost in winter. Captain Whitman shivering on the shore. My arms and legs failing, the water closing over me: Mrs Whitman and I, falling foul to the lake's malevolent trap. Cliff's hands saving me, then holding me under to die. It was hard not to wince and shiver at the thought of it. I didn't know how I could face it again, let alone live there. But wasn't there also some colour in my memories? Hadn't the lake once been the sanctuary of hot summer afternoons, the scene of countless hours spent with Alec? And it had witnessed me fall in love with the man who lay beside me now, beaten and broken for my sake.

'We'd be close to your father,' Wilf was saying. 'And I shall need someone to help me manage the place—'

'You want me to manage the estate with you?'

He smiled. 'Gracie, I want to share my whole life with you. I've known for a long time that I'd never be as happy without you as I could be…' He stopped himself and took a shaky breath. 'It would be more than I could ever deserve to have you as my wife, and I don't know if it's possible, if you want to—'

'I do!' I interrupted. 'Of course I do!'

He laughed. 'I'd kiss you if I could move!'

I stood and bent to kiss him, but my ribs protested and I cried out just as Nurse Collis opened the door. 'Mrs – Gracie!' she exclaimed, clunking down the full jug and helping me back into my chair.

'Is she all right?' Wilf said with concern.

'I'm fine.'

'What on earth were you doing?' she fussed, throwing stern looks at both of us, but we both laughed, and eventually she couldn't hide her smile.

I told Nurse Collis about the proposal on the way back to my room. Later, when her shift was over, she crept in with a bottle of sherry and two glasses, which we sipped surreptitiously, and she made me promise to invite her to the wedding.

CHAPTER 28

It was April when Wilf was finally well enough to leave hospital. I'd been home for weeks, almost fully recovered from my own injuries. My wounds had all healed, although I had a scar above my eyebrow now. It was a deep crimson, but I knew it would fade in time, as Wilf's had, and Mrs B said she'd take me into Finton to get some powder to cover it if I wanted. My ribs still felt tender and stiff, and I had little stamina for walking, but Cliff's attack had left me wary of it anyway. It was what I hated the most, that he'd robbed me of the bliss I'd always found in the landscape. I prayed in time it would fade too, like the scar, and that one day I'd hear the call of the fields again and go to them without hesitation or fear.

Cliff was convicted for his brutal assaults and would be incarcerated for nine years. Dad had already employed a solicitor to facilitate the divorce. He asked me if I wanted to go and visit Cliff in prison, and I spent a restless night pondering it, wondering at the expression on his face when I saw him, what I'd say to him. I pictured him apologetic and contrite, begging my forgiveness. I couldn't imagine it for long. It was easier to see him smiling, snarling in the same way he had on the night of the attack, before letting his rage loose on us. The memory always lit an angry flame inside me. I winced when I thought of the blood on Wilf's face, mingling with mud in the darkness.

I told Dad I wouldn't go and see Cliff, not now, not ever. I didn't want to see his regret, or indeed his cruel remorselessness; I sensed the latter would be more likely. I didn't want further torment, but most of all, I didn't want the possibility of forgiving him. For despite the viciousness of his attacks, his actions – however wicked – had released me from him. It put me in mind of the butterflies Wilf and I had caught in a jar and then let go, except, instead of just lifting the lid, Cliff had shattered the glass and nearly destroyed everything. Perhaps I would thank him for it one day, but I resisted the urge to do so now. His future after prison was unknown, but it would never be in Barnfield. He had no family or friends left. When he got out, if he had any sense, he'd disappear to another part of the country and we'd never hear from him again. But if he had no sense, if he dared to return, if only for a day, he'd see how little he was missed. He'd see the world that was once his going on without him, and he'd find no welcome here.

Wilf said we'd find another tenant for the farm when Goffman retired, and one day the village would discover something new to gossip about. I'd be able to go to church again without children pointing and ladies whispering when they thought my eyes were diverted. I couldn't blame them for talking. Not much happened in Barnfield. Cliff's attack and our divorce would have been enough to shake tongues for years, even if I hadn't then announced my engagement to the local outcast. I'd be forever connected with that family of tragic secrets. I'd be the new Mrs Whitman, trailing my own dubious rumours in my wake wherever I went. But I didn't mind. Wilf and I were alive, finally together. The locals might still call him a coward and a madman, but I knew differently. I was proud to wear his mother's engagement ring. I was proud the day we left the registry office as man and wife later that summer.

*

The wedding was a small affair, much like my first, but the joy I felt this time was incomparable. I'd married Cliff in a stupor of grief, but I took Wilf's name with my eyes and heart wide open, knowing without a doubt that our friendship would weather all future storms. Nancy Collis came, as promised, as did Doris, who wished us warm congratulations, all disapproving thoughts forgotten now she was better linked with the most prominent family in the village. Jean sent a telegram, being unable to travel due to the imminent arrival of her first baby. Douglas Merrell cast his smooth, handsome smile over the proceedings, and arranged cars to take us all back to the Manor for celebratory drinks. The new maid had glasses laid out on trays on the terrace for us when we arrived, and the small party toasted our health as the sun softened the garden with warmth.

Dad and Captain Whitman sat side by side in comfortable silence, watching the spark of gnats in the sunlight over the vegetable patch. Occasionally the old captain would remark on a bird, or thank the maid who refilled his drink. I caught a smile in his eye as he watched Merrell and Nancy chatting; she touched his arm as she laughed and the space between them narrowed as he lit her cigarette.

After Miss Brennan took the captain inside, Mrs B kissed me goodbye with tears that only quelled when I reminded her that we'd be round in the week for dinner with her and Dad. Merrell made sure everyone was chauffeured home, and offered to give Nancy a lift himself since he was conveniently heading in the right direction. Before he left, he took my hand and kissed it. 'What an honour it is to finally call you Mrs Whitman,' he said with sparkling eyes.

'Oh, come, Douglas, you must call her Gracie,' said Wilf,

whose arm was round my shoulder.

Merrell looked to me for assurance.

'I insist. And come and visit us again soon.' I had learned enough in the last few months to understand just how valued this man was, by Wilf and the captain alike, despite the twists of his history with Beatrice. Wilf believed his father to be ignorant of it, but there were times when I was sure he knew. There was so much more to the captain than met the eye – as many quick remarks and moments of clarity as there were exhausted and nonsensical ramblings. I'd watched how the two men had said farewell: Merrell taking the captain's hand, the hesitation before their warm embrace. Would the old man hold him like that if he knew how his wife had loved him? Or was it gratitude I saw in the captain's eyes as Merrell shook Wilf's hand, and congratulated him with the pride of a father?

There was so much I'd never know about Captain Whitman. Sometimes we talked – often benignly – and a glimmer of light would surge into his words suddenly. He'd mention Wilf, or Bixxy, and his eyes would widen like a child's. He'd tell me about his garden and the books he'd once read. His memory could be remarkable, but it was scarred: great chunks of years scored away or twisted out of shape. He talked about the hospital and the nurse's footsteps, and sometimes he'd make me laugh by scolding the formidable Miss Brennan behind her back. But there were periods of silence too, when his eyes seemed dead and unfocused. There were fits of disturbed rage. He had vivid dreams; Wilf had prepared me for the screams I could expect at night. I imagined waking to hear his cries or the slam of the door as he went wandering. Would I find him at the lake again? Would he return, night after night, still searching for me or Bixxy in the water?

Wilf said the captain was doing better. Since the night of the attack he hadn't been found wandering; he wasn't as restless. He didn't rant to Miss Brennan about the girl in the water anymore. It was as if his heroic rescue had released him too. Wilf said it must have eased the guilt he'd held on to since Bixxy's death.

But I had another idea.

'What if he knew?' I'd asked Wilf one Sunday on our walk back from church. 'I know it sounds ridiculous, but I can't help thinking he knew exactly what he was saying to me… he was warning me, and he was reassuring me. He knew he would come and save me.'

Wilf did his best to hide his misgivings, but his tone was wary when he said, 'You think my father's some kind of clairvoyant?'

'I don't know. It sounds mad saying it aloud.'

Wilf grinned. 'Well then, perhaps there's something to it. If you're going to be a Whitman, you ought to be a little mad. At least, that's what I've heard.'

He kissed me then, and we didn't talk about it anymore. I sensed if I tried to pick it apart I'd never get to the bottom of it. What mattered was the man beside me and the life in our veins. We'd so nearly lost everything, but for some reason we'd had it restored to us. Perhaps there was no reason at all. I thought of Alec, and all the thousands who'd never come back from the war, the nameless boys who'd perished, the bullet or shrapnel or car just an inch too close. Hadn't it nearly been Wilf? Couldn't it have been me, like Bixxy, with the lake in my lungs? And what of Mum and baby Annie – at what point had their fate been sealed? But the questions would go on forever; I'd never find the answers I sought.

*

On our wedding day, when the guests were gone, Wilf and I took a walk down to the lake. I'd been back many times since the accident and the place no longer filled me with trepidation. I could gaze beyond the spot when Cliff had thrown me to the ground, and see the island in the water beyond. I could hear Alec's shouts as I beat him to it, panting and laughing in the cool water, his red hair dripping. I could stand on the boathouse balcony and watch the ripples in the rushes, hear the water sloshing against the boat below me, and think only of its peace and beauty.

The lake was silent now. It no longer whispered to me or haunted my dreams. I'd slept soundly since my first night back in my old bed, in my old room. Dad and Mrs B had made the changes while I was in hospital, removing all traces of Cliff from the house, so when I got back it was like he'd never been there. For weeks I'd pottered about the house and village, taking the bus to the hospital a couple of times a week, and then, once Wilf was home and the weather improved, rediscovering the routes I hadn't walked for months. First Mrs B accompanied me, but eventually I had the strength and courage to go alone. The paths were unchanged, scattered only with the signs of the seasons, so familiar it was hard to imagine the primroses and bluebells would soon give way to the shade of the summer leaves, and one day the frosted leaves would crunch beneath my winter boots again.

I'd spent most of my days at the Manor since Wilf's return, and in recent weeks we'd begun the process of opening up the house again, unlocking doors that had been shut for years and lifting greying dust sheets to reveal the treasures or trash beneath. I was now familiar with the books, and I'd met with Bridges to discuss the tenants. We'd employed a couple of part-time maids, a cook and a new gardener (all from Barnfield, on my insistence), and the place seemed to be coming to life again. Wilf was teaching me to drive, trying not to wince when I ground the gears of the Bentley up and down the driveway. Whenever I returned to the turning circle, I'd look up at the house and think how cheerful it seemed now. It was no longer shrouded in secrecy, falling into disrepair; the rooms had been aired, the kitchen was busy. Miss Brennan and the maids hurried around the corridors, and the scrubbed windows let sunlight pour through onto polished furniture and clean carpets.

More often than not, I'd find the captain in his chair reading the paper or dozing, and Wilf at his bureau or in the office above the old stables. He had only spent a handful of days away from Barnfield since his discharge, seeing to his affairs in London – a world of investments and committees I was only just beginning to learn about. The house he'd arranged in Hampstead was no longer needed. We would have a flat, he told me, for our visits there in the future, but the Manor was his home now. And now it was mine too.

We reached the boathouse as the sun touched the treetops at the far end of the lake, and shadows scarred the water. Wilf unlocked the door and I laughed when I saw inside: the dusty little interior had been transformed into a bohemian den of rugs, drapes and cushions. Around the unlit stove stood candles awaiting flames. The French windows were already open, and the room held the memory of the day's heat in its hidden corners. An upturned crate on the little balcony served as a makeshift table: a bottle peeked out from a dripping ice bucket, and two champagne flutes caught the buttery evening light.

We toasted our marriage, and I leaned into Wilf's chest as the sun melted orange and lavender over the water.

'We don't have to stay here,' he said, glancing to the pillows and blankets on the floor. He wore the frown that always accompanied the memory of that fateful night.

I took his hand. The room was delightful, the setting idyllic. We would make better memories here. We'd destroy the legacy Cliff's cruelty had left. 'It's perfect.'

He kissed my cheek, then told me, 'Wait there, I have something to show you.' He slipped back into the boathouse with a secretive smile, emerging again with something held behind his back. 'Close your eyes.'

I heard him step forward and felt his warmth in front of me. I didn't care for gifts, it was him I wanted. I'd waited so long to hold him without interruption, to get to know the scars that marked his body as well as those on his face. I'd waited since that night I'd stood by him in the shadows of the church hall, and felt a dark magic enchanting me. I'd kissed him so many times, but it was never enough, and now we were alone together the need for him burned stronger than ever. I shifted my feet impatiently. 'Can I open my eyes now?'

He was holding a jar, covered in pierced newspaper, tied with string. I gasped when I saw what was inside, and all of a sudden I was back with him outside our front door, yearning for a glimpse of his eyes in the darkness.

'A Small Blue!'

This time the wings shivered with life. The little butterfly flitted about the jar, beating the glass. I thought of the one in the frame; I'd put it on my wall the day I returned from hospital and woken to its fragile beauty every morning since. I thought of the moment Wilf had given it to me, and the kiss that had followed. Alec waiting for me on the stairs.

I took the jar and untied the string, letting the paper fall to our feet. With the air on its wings the butterfly stopped, its antennae twitching. For a couple of seconds I studied its feathered grey-blue wings, before it leapt up and gracefully swept free. My heart lightened. I watched it dart about in the air just above our heads, zigzagging up and up, smaller and smaller still, until I couldn't make it out at all.

AFTERWORD

Gracie's story grew from a single picture in my imagination: a couple facing each other in the shadows of a church hall on a sultry summer's evening, wordless yet captivated. Who were these people, how did they know each other, and what did the future have in store for them? From there, Gracie and Wilf's love story was born. The Small Blue is an unapologetically romantic novel, but I hope too that it sheds light on a time and place in history. The paradox of women's 'quiet' lives on the rural home front during an era of such worldwide upheaval has always fascinated me. Gracie's story shows how war touched all aspects of civilian life.

If you are interested in learning more about any of the historical aspects of this book, I recommend visiting The Imperial War Museum in London, if you can. I could not have written this novel without the invaluable research I gathered there on my visits.

This book has been a long time in the making, so I want to thank everyone who listened to me talk about it over the years, and the family and friends who gave your time to read it (in its various stages) and give feedback. Special thanks go to Liz Ward, for your excellent editing skills and much needed words of encouragement.

ABOUT THE AUTHOR

Hannah Shelbourne has been writing short stories and novels since she was fourteen. She trained at the University for the Creative Arts (Farnham) and worked as an illustrator and youth worker in her twenties. In her thirties, Hannah achieved her BA (Hons) in History with the Open University, developing her research and writing skills alongside raising her young children.

The Small Blue is Hannah's debut published novel.

Printed in Dunstable, United Kingdom

79925090R00190